Sign up for our newsletter to hear
about new and upcoming releases.

www.ylva-publishing.com

Other books in
The Midnight Coffee Series

Long-Distance Coffee
Coffee and Conclusions

The Midnight Coffee Series Part Two

Coffee and Conclusions

Emma Sterner-Radley

Chapter 1

At the Airport

Isabella hadn't been this busy since the height of her career. The past six weeks had flown by in a flurry of conversations with her parents, arranging a place to live in Philadelphia, and the tricky task of planning Richard's part in Alberto's life when they were no longer living under the same roof.

A new companionship had blossomed between them. Accepting they weren't meant to be a couple—and the honesty between them that came with that acceptance—made their relationship much more comfortable.

Richard had helped Isabella find the least disruptive and most financially sensible way to transport her few prized belongings and Alberto's baby things up to Philadelphia. Then he'd put their house up for sale and moved in with Shay and Joshua again.

While most of their things were making their way slowly up the country, Isabella, Alberto, and her biggest suitcase were on their way to the airport. They would stay with Isabella's parents for two nights—until the moving company Isabella's mother had hired delivered their belongings to their rented apartment.

Grudgingly, Isabella had to admit that, for all her mother's faults, Judith had been a godsend when it came to planning the move. Granted, she was undoubtedly driven by selfish reasons—wanting her daughter and grandson back with her was one of them. Saying "I told you so" regarding Isabella's failed relationship with "the hippie-Florida-hobo" was another.

Nevertheless, she'd made the process a lot faster by shouting at people and throwing money at every problem that arose.

Sipping an airport macchiato, Isabella looked at the sleeping Alberto in the harness strapped to her chest. He seemed utterly content and clueless that they were embarking on a trip that would change everything. Isabella smiled at his little sleeping face, and she ignored the pang of guilt that hit. Again.

She should be using the time to write. Her book had been left to collect dust through the last few weeks of planning. Between caring for Alberto, the plans for future living and travel arrangements, discussions with Richard, and, of course, chatting to Erin, her writing had been put on the back burner.

The little wireless keyboard she'd bought was to make writing on the iPad less mind numbing. She opened the tablet's writing app to her latest chapter and read with knitted brows, not sure where she had been going with the last paragraph. She sighed and closed the app. Writing could wait until things settled down.

A smile spread across her face. Behind her apps was a picture of Alberto banging a toy on the ground and grinning widely. Erin had explained how to use a picture for the lock screen and wallpaper. Erin. Wonderful, sweet, helpful Erin. Thinking about her favorite New Yorker had quickly become second nature. She didn't feel guilty in the slightest, as she daydreamed about Erin teaching techie things in person.

During their chats, Erin would make silly jokes or send pictures of cute dogs she wanted to get, but they also had serious conversations about relationships and their everyday lives. Isabella knew most of Erin's regular clients by name, and infuriatingly, she also knew the girl Erin lost her virginity to at eighteen was called AJ. That was new. Isabella had never experienced jealousy like that before.

More frequent video chats were a luxury that had allowed Isabella to see a lot more of Erin. Yet it still wasn't nearly enough. Isabella desperately wanted to be closer to her. She wondered what Erin smelled like, how it would feel to be in the presence of her amazing smile and perfect body.

Isabella bit her lip. She shouldn't think about Erin's body; she'd already lost too much of the rare commodity that was sleep, and she felt acutely guilty. Objectifying women was something she hated in men. Now she was doing it, although she comforted herself with the fact that she respected and cared for Erin more than she drooled over her. But those damned muscles were her downfall.

When Erin had demonstrated shadowboxing, wrapping her hands, taking her stance away from her laptop, and boxing the hell out of the air in front of her, Isabella's skin had goose-pimpled at the sight of the ripples in the slender muscles of Erin's arms and chest.

Isabella had a weakness for muscles. Not extreme bodybuilders, just cut muscles and a body that looked like it could pounce into action at any second. She'd always loved the visual poetry of muscles moving under a man's skin.

But she hadn't realized that she could be attracted to this sort of build on a woman. Perhaps even more so. A thin waist and chiseled abs, the contrast of soft breasts and sharply defined pecs above them, it was... alluring, to say the least.

In Erin, she'd found the beauty and elegance of a woman, combined with the strength and power she normally associated with a man. All the things she admired could exist in one person, and that person had come crashing into her life with long eyelashes and sexy, toned arms. Like one of the Amazons in *Wonder Woman*.

She continued to ignore the airport bustle and let her mind obsess about Erin. Isabella remembered a conversation they'd had during a video chat, on a rainy afternoon last week.

"You know what I find strange about being attracted to you?" she asked.

Erin put her coffee down and looked worried for a moment. "Um... no?"

"That I look at you and see all your amazing qualities and can't decide if I want to be like you or be with you."

With a chuckle, Erin brought her mug up toward the laptop camera to toast Isabella. "Yep, welcome to the woman-loving-woman community. That's, like, the first thing that a lot of women feel when they come across a woman they find attractive. And for the record, I refuse to let you be anything like me. That would ruin everything awesome that you are. So just be with me. Uh, I mean, you know, someday. If I'm lucky."

The panicked tone in Erin's voice filled Isabella with affection.

She'd been so respectful since the breakup. After the revelation that they were both attracted to each other and that Isabella was breaking up with Richard, Erin had backed off and tried desperately not to flirt. She'd stayed friendly, and while they spoke openly about their attraction, neither of them had taken it any further.

Her respectful behavior was endearing, and it made Isabella feel safe and much appreciated. However, she also felt appreciated when Erin would falter and stare at her body. Or come out with a comment that was too close to a double entendre to be purely platonic.

She'd be apologetic, and Isabella—for a moment or two—would find herself wishing Erin would stop being so respectful and just flirt her brains out. There had been a lot more flirting recently. Right after the breakup, Isabella had given herself kudos for being good at keeping things platonic. Sadly, it hadn't lasted.

At the end of the day, they were both adults and knew what was at stake. First, Isabella had to get her life in order and make a new, safe home for her and Alberto. Then she could think about making Erin blush.

She couldn't wait to talk to Erin, even if it was just to say hi and tell her that they were boarding in twenty minutes. There was no point using Skype, Twitter, or even the e-mail address Erin had given her. Erin would be busy with clients, and they'd planned to text each other after six, when Erin would be free and at home, eating a bucketful of lean calories.

Isabella retrieved her phone. A quick text message couldn't hurt.

In the airport. Alberto's sleeping, I can't focus on writing, and my macchiato tastes like iron. Unless you are busy, this would be an excellent time for my court jester to entertain me.

Isabella put the phone down and took another sip of her disappointing beverage. A moment later, it beeped.

Hey there, Martinez. Is that your way of saying "dance, monkey, dance?" I don't get paid to entertain you, you know. In fact, I'm not getting paid at all right now, because my client just cancelled. Wanna talk?

A ball of joy exploded in her belly. How could talking to someone make her this excited? With quick fingers she dialed, grinning when Erin answered immediately.

"Hey, Ms. Writer! Sorry your day sucks."

Her grin broadened at the sound of Erin's voice. "Well, some might say it just got better, now that I can while away some time with you," she said quietly.

She was trying not to wake Alberto, who might wake from hearing her voice amplified in his position tied to her chest.

"Charmer. I like that better than being ordered to entertain you. So, almost on your way to your new life in Philly. You pumped?"

The question confused Isabella for a moment. She wondered if Erin was wondering if she had pumped out milk for Alberto, but then she realized that Erin was asking if she was excited. She worried that motherhood had erased everything else from her once-so-sharp brain.

"I suppose so, yes. It's strange going back. I feel a little like I'm returning to a chapter of my life that's over and done with. Then I remember I'm going there with Alberto, and it all feels new and thrilling again."

"Yeah, and it means you won't be as bothered by loads of cheerful sunshine, huh?" Erin asked in a teasing tone.

"Precisely. The Philadelphia weather suits me much better. Hopefully, I'll see fewer men who think that a warm day is an excuse to walk around topless. Or worse, topless but wearing camouflage shorts, socks, and flip-flops," Isabella said with disdain.

"All right, Fashion Police, chill. I'm sure most Floridians had better taste than that."

"Oh, that was the damned tourists."

Erin chuckled, and Isabella was startled at how the sound of it made her feel safe. *Strange.*

"So, you got a good seat on the plane?"

"Aisle seat. I usually prefer the window seat, but I have to be able to walk around with Alberto if he needs comforting."

"Well, at least you'll be closer to the stewardesses, so you'll get your coffee quicker." Erin pointed out.

Isabella's mouth curled into a wicked smile. "Oh, I thought you meant that it was good that I was closer to the stewardesses, so I could check them out."

"Whoa! Isabella, you can't go from 'I would be open to dating a woman if I was ever attracted to one' to objectifying women in short-skirted uniforms in, like, six weeks."

Isabella pitched her voice a little deeper, as she always did when she wanted to make Erin blush. "Can't I? Who's going to stop me? You?"

At Erin's little laugh, Isabella closed her eyes, willing Erin to take this further. There were so many replies to that comment which would be seductive, or at least suggestive. Isabella knew she shouldn't be hoping for that, not right now. But it was so very tempting.

Erin cleared her throat. To Isabella's simultaneous disappointment and relief, it was a serious, sobering throat clearing.

"So, are you sure about staying with your parents? I know you want to move back to Philadelphia because it feels like home, but staying with your parents? After all your mother's abuse?"

Isabella felt herself tense up to full rigidity. *Why would she bring that up when I'm in an airport?*

"I wouldn't call it abuse. She never physically hurt me," Isabella said quietly, increasingly aware of the people around her.

"There is more than one kind of abuse, Isabella."

"I'm fine staying with them for a couple of days. I've missed Daddy, and I can handle my mother."

"Okay, if you are comfortable staying there, then great. I was just thinking about it last night when I couldn't sleep. I know it's ridiculous, but I just laid there, staring at the damn ceiling and worrying about you."

"Thank you for your concern. Really. Can we please change the topic?"

"Yeah, of course. Sorry. I didn't mean to upset you. Anyway, um, I checked the weather this morning, and most of the country seems to have okay conditions, so there shouldn't be much turbulence."

Isabella's tense body relaxed. Erin had actually taken time out of her morning routine to check the weather for the whole country to make sure that she and Alberto wouldn't be buffeted around by bad weather somewhere on their flight.

"Thank you for checking. I really appreciate that. I'm not used to that kind of consideration."

"Hey, I gotta look after my…new friend. And the stressed-out lil' man. Turbulence might give him an ulcer."

"Erin, he's not that bad. That does remind me, though. I'll need to find him a new doctor when I get settled."

"Yeah. Um, what else are you going to do when you get settled?"

"Hmm. Are you asking me if I'm hoping to get a visit from a certain New Yorker?"

Erin started stuttering, and Isabella cut her off right away.

"Please don't freak out, Erin. I do want to meet you face-to-face soon, yes. Obviously not right away, as I have two days with my family and then I have to decorate my new home. But when the dust settles, I would be very happy to meet you."

"Yes!" Erin shouted into her phone.

Isabella held the phone away from her ear and watched Alberto squeeze his eyes shut and fidget a little at the noise.

A couple walking past stared at her. She ignored them; she'd made Erin and herself happy. Their stares were unimportant compared to that.

"Sounds like you want to see me too, *preciosa*."

"Hell, yeah. Even if it's just as friends, I'd love to meet you and maybe even get a hug or something. If you're a hugger, that is."

"I will be when I meet you. As I say, just give me a little time before we set a date," Isabella reiterated.

"Of course, as much time as you need. Just let me know a little bit in advance, so I can warn my clients and refer them to someone else while I'm away."

Isabella carefully watched Alberto as he fidgeted again then relaxed and resettled. She took more care to be quiet when she replied. "Isn't that a tad risky? What if they decide to stay with your competitors when you come back?"

"Nah, once you've had Erin Black, you won't settle for any less."

A snigger that was pure naughtiness escaped Isabella. "Oh, I bet."

"Hey! Mind out of the gutter."

"Why? I'm a single woman reclaiming her sexuality."

"Reclaiming it? What does that mean? Did someone steal it?"

"You know what I mean. I haven't been in the right headspace to think of anything amorous whatsoever. That's obviously changed now, but I'm not discussing this in an airport. Speaking of which, I should probably start making my way over to the gate. My flight was just called."

"Yeah, you should get going. Hey, do me a favor?"

Isabella stood and pushed her chair in under the table. "Of course. What?"

"Text me when you've landed so I know everything's okay?"

Suddenly, the day was a whole lot better than Isabella had given it credit for. "I will. Thank you for looking out for me and the little prince."

"Um, yeah, well, you're really precious, y'know?" Erin replied, sounding embarrassed.

"So are you, Erin. I'll text you as soon as we land."

"Cool. Have a safe flight."

"I'll try. Speak soon."

Isabella realized with amusement that they both sounded so reluctant to hang up. She kissed Alberto's sleeping head and wondered if Erin was smiling stupidly and feeling her heart beat faster. Just like she was.

Chapter 2

Change Is Hard and Distance Is Worse

ERIN WAS FINALLY HOME FROM work and listening to the radio as she prepared her dinner. She whistled along to the music, thinking about things that might make the distance between her and Isabella feel smaller.

It was odd; the distance hadn't preyed on her mind when Isabella was in Florida. But now that she was closer and there were fewer hurdles to overcome, Erin felt the distance between them like a constant ache.

Erika had been helpful, sharing sisterly advice and brainstorms. She'd mentioned watching TV shows simultaneously so that they could discuss them over Skype and playing games online together. Neither of those ideas seemed very fitting. She certainly couldn't imagine Isabella playing online games.

The song stopped, and the radio DJ came on. That's when it hit her. *Music! We could talk about music and share our faves.*

She washed her hands and grabbed her phone from her back pocket.

Hey you! When you land and have time to message me, remind me to ask you about your favorite music. I hope your flight was good. Xoxo

A smile was on her face as she went back to preparing her salad and steak. Her mind continuously fixed on Isabella and what kind of music she might like.

It was almost 7 p.m. Erin was sitting on her bed, watching some ridiculous game show on TV. Her phone buzzed and startled her.

"Christ," she muttered, as she retrieved her phone and looked at the text message.

Hello. I'm not your external memory bank, you know. ;-) But by all means: remember to ask me about music. The flight was fine. Alberto did have a screaming fit halfway through and caused some angry looks, but I was expecting that. We're in a taxi on the way to my parents' house now.

Erin looked at the winking emoji in the text with pride. Isabella had always refused to use emojis. She'd bent the rules to ensure that Erin knew she was kidding. Isabella, with her sharp edges and sarcastic comments, was trying hard not to offend. And that said a lot.

Hm. Discussing music via text might be complicated.

Okay. Can I call you? It'll make your taxi ride go faster.

The answer came back quickly.

Sure. Any excuse to talk to you, preciosa.

Erin bit her lip around a smile as she called.

"Hello. Well, hello again, I suppose," Isabella answered.

"Yeah, hi again. Anyway, let's get to the important stuff! I can't believe we have been talking for months and never discussed music. What do you like?"

Isabella laughed. "You're so impatient when you have something you want to discuss."

"Oh, yeah, I guess. Sorry."

"No, no, don't apologize. It's sweet. It shows passion and focus. Hmm, what sort of music do I particularly enjoy? I have quite a few Billie Holiday and Nina Simone CDs. Some classical albums and a few contemporary compilations I've picked up on road trips. To be honest, I've not really listened to much music since Alberto was born."

"Wow, okay, that's gotta change. Why don't you make me a playlist of your favorite songs, and I'll do the same? It'll be something we can do for each other from a distance. I mean, other than just talk."

They were both quiet for a few moments. Over the phone, Erin could hear the muffled sounds of traffic and the *tick-tick* of the taxi driver's indicator.

"Is the distance bothering you, Erin?"

Erin grinned up at the ceiling. "Ah, man, am I that transparent? Never mind, it doesn't matter. What matters is that music is important, and it's a good way to get to know each other. Do you wanna try the playlist idea?"

"Well, I'm certain I would, if you could just explain to your favorite technophobe which program or platform we would use to make them. I'd burn you a CD of songs like I used to for friends in the old days, but this tablet doesn't seem to have any place to insert one..."

It was impossible for Erin not to love how clueless Isabella was about this stuff. "Tell you what. I was thinking of sending you a little package when you got settled in your new place. A bit like the packages you've sent me. I'll find my old USB stick, fill it with music I like, and put it in the box I post to you. Then you just plug it into your PC and press *play*. Sound good?"

"On one condition, that you are not sitting there pitying me for not getting all this techy stuff," Isabella said tersely.

"Nah, the only thing I'm pitying you for is having a BlackBerry."

"Oh, shut up," Isabella grumbled.

Erin laughed. "I'm sorry. Can you *ever* forgive me?"

"I'll think about it," Isabella said playfully. "Anyway, we're about to pull up at my parents' house now. Obviously, we shouldn't video chat or call each other while I'm there, not without my eagle-eyed and equally eagle-*eared* mother asking a million questions. But you can still text me, and we can text chat on Skype."

Even though Isabella obviously couldn't see her, Erin nodded. "Sure, it's only two days, right?"

"Yes. In two days, I'll have my own place, and we can talk as much as we like, well, as long as we don't wake Alberto."

"I can wait. It's not like it's that great to see you or anything. You're kinda hideous."

Isabella scoffed. "Hideous, am I?"

"Yep, terrible face-wise, as they say on *Parks and Rec*." A wide smile tugged at Erin's cheeks.

"Oh, hang on. I know that reference, I used to watch reruns while I fed Alberto in the afternoon."

"Busted. You act all serious, like all you do is adult stuff, caring for a baby, cleaning a house, writing a book, but you were watching TV at some point. You *are* human after all."

"Yes, dear, you caught me. I'm a terrible person. Can I go now? I believe the taxi driver wants payment." Isabella's tone dripped with sarcasm.

Erin's cheeks ached from grinning so much. "Yeah, all right. Try not to scare him or her off with your terrible face."

"Thank you for the advice. I'll text you later."

"Yep, let me know how seeing your mom again works out."

"I will. Bye for now."

When Isabella hung up, Erin sat down at her table. After some searching, she found a pen and started a list on the back of an envelope from an insurance company wanting her business.

The playlist ended up mainly classic rock with female leads, and Erin realized she was aging herself. She chuckled and let a few newer bands like *Ex Hex* and *The Pretty Reckless* join the likes of *Siouxsie and the Banshees* and *The Runaways*.

Pleased with her choices, she sat back, chewing the pen as she wondered where she'd put the damn USB stick. She made a mental note to check the drawers in her bedside table.

A deeply uncomfortable feeling niggled at her, and slowly she realized what it was. She missed Isabella. She squeezed her eyes closed. *How can I miss someone I've never met?*

It seemed meeting someone face-to-face wasn't necessary to miss a person so much that it felt like someone had punched you in the heart.

Chapter 3

Arriving at the Martinez Residence

AFTER ADJUSTING ALBERTO IN THE baby harness, Isabella put her hand on the brass handle, but the grand, white door opened first.

"*Mija!*" Alberto Sr. exclaimed.

He pulled Isabella, and the harness-attached baby, into his arms for a bear hug.

"Daddy! Careful, you're squashing Alberto," Isabella said with a happy laugh.

Alberto Sr. immediately backed off, making way for Isabella to walk into the spacious hallway. *Has it always been this big?*

The hallway might look different to her now. But so did her father. He'd lost more of his thick, salt-and-pepper hair since she'd last seen him, leaving his head more bald than covered. His face was wrinkled, but his sparkling smile made him look twenty-five again. God, she'd missed him. She was still such a daddy's girl, and she leaned in to kiss him tenderly on the cheek.

"I've missed you, Daddy. ¿Cómo estás?"

He beamed at her. "I was good, but now that you are here, I'm excellent. How are you, *mija*? And how is my little namesake?"

Alberto Sr. put his big hand on his grandson's head and managed to wake little Alberto, who gave an annoyed little squeak that sounded more like a seal than a baby. Both Isabella and her father laughed.

"He's fine. As you can hear, a little grumpy, but otherwise fine."

"Your flight arrived safely and on time?"

A voice answered from the staircase. "Clearly, otherwise she wouldn't be here, Alberto."

Isabella counted to ten in her head before turning to her mother. "Don't snap at Daddy. Come down here and say hello politely."

"Oh my, look at that," Judith said tersely. "Barely through the front door and already giving orders in someone else's home." Her face cracked into a sneaky smile, and she added, "That's my girl."

Isabella shook her head, forcing down a smile at her mother's approval.

While she hated her mother, the child inside still needed to impress her. And, yes, sometimes she even wanted her mother's company. A strange quirk she could never quite accept—nor forgive herself for.

Isabella knew that trauma from her mother's own childhood made her so cold and unkind. They'd even spoken of it after Isabella had moved out.

Her mother loved her and wanted the best for her. Of that, Isabella was convinced. It was simply Judith's own issues that warped her love and made it controlling in the extreme. Understanding the past didn't make her mother's actions forgivable. Far from it. But sometimes it was enough to make Isabella able to be around her. At least for short intervals. Like two days. Maximum.

Judith walked gracefully down the stairs, all purpose and class and beauty. Her shiny, brown, shoulder-length hair was perfectly coiffured. Her milk-white skin might have started to wrinkle, but Isabella knew her mother used only the best potions and makeup to keep herself looking youthful. Isabella's own vanity hoped she would look as good when she got to Judith's age.

Judith kissed the air in the vicinity of Isabella's cheek. When she bent down to kiss her grandson on the head, she left a trace of dark lipstick on the skin under his hair.

Isabella could see her father looking over her shoulder and waving to the baby. She smiled and loosened the harness to lift Alberto free. She held Alberto Jr. out to her father.

"Would you mind holding him, Daddy? Having him in the harness has done a number on my shoulders and back."

For a moment, Alberto Sr. looked frightened. Then he beamed again, reaching out to grab his grandson. He held him like he was made of glass before cradling him close to his chest.

It was only the second time Alberto Sr. had held him, and just like the last time, it took a while to get used to such an important job. Isabella prayed her son wouldn't start crying and terrify his grandfather, but Alberto snuggled into his granddad's mohair sweater and gurgled happily. Alberto Sr. puffed out his chest.

"Oh, look at the old fool, he looks like he struck gold," Judith sniped.

"They both look happy to me. You're just jealous because he got to hold Alberto first," Isabella replied.

Her mother threw her a scornful look, which Isabella ignored. Instead, she focused on removing the harness and hanging it up with her coat before retrieving the luggage the taxi driver had carried to the doorstep. She rolled the overfilled suitcase inside, and Judith helped pull it farther into the hallway so they could close the door.

Alberto Sr. was busy whispering in Spanish to his grandson, and Isabella was happy to let him get on with it, keeping Mother's sharp tongue away from the two happy Albertos.

A little after nine, Isabella had finally dispensed with the pleasantries and the late dinner to escape to the guestroom. While feeding Alberto, she gathered her iPad from her rucksack and connected to her parents' Wi-Fi, before opening the Skype app and looking for Erin. To Isabella's joy and relief, Erin was online.

She typed out a message with her free hand and grimaced at how slow she was.

IsabellaMartinez1: So, guess who has done serious damage to her back and shoulders carrying around a baby in a harness for half the day?

BlackVelvetBitches: Judge Judy? Miss Piggy? Hillary Clinton?

Isabella rolled her eyes and went to answer just as Alberto let go and stopped eating. She looked down at him and saw that he was drifting to sleep. She started to rock him as much as she could with one arm.

IsabellaMartinez1: Very funny.

BlackVelvetBitches: I know, right? I'm hilarious!

IsabellaMartinez1: I wouldn't go that far, Erin. If I did, you'd start with those silly jokes off the radio again. Anyway, can we get back to my aching muscles?

BlackVelvetBitches: Sure! I'll run you a hot bath and then give you a full body massage.

What Isabella felt at that comment was anything but pure.

IsabellaMartinez1: I'll remember that offer for when we meet. Especially the full-body massage, I'm thinking nicely scented massage oil and sensual music?

She could imagine the look on Erin's face as she read those words. She wished she could see Erin's face.

BlackVelvetBitches: Dammit! I hate it when you make me blush like this.

IsabellaMartinez1: Really? I love it. Those high cheekbones of yours look amazing in that warm shade of pink.

BlackVelvetBitches: They do not. Shush. :-(Anyway, we shouldn't be talking like this. We're just friends, remember?

Alberto was getting heavy on her arm, and she put the sleeping baby in the crib her mother had bought for their visit.

IsabellaMartinez1: I know. I'm sorry. I just can't help myself. You're being so respectful. I shouldn't test you by tempting you.

BlackVelvetBitches: That's right! You could make it up to me, tho.

IsabellaMartinez1: Really? How?

BlackVelvetBitches: Video call me. I'll mute my mic so no one will hear me. We'll just type, but I'll be able to look at you. I just want to see you, you know? Just to make sure you didn't lose any limbs on your travels today.

Isabella glanced around the empty room as though she was about to do something naughty. It struck her that this room had once, for all of two years, been hers. It had been redecorated since, but still, these walls had heard her sneak calls on the house phone to whatever bad boy she'd been crushing on.

Now, here she was, feeling the same thrill at letting a crush see her on camera as they spoke. She'd swapped Philadelphia's teenaged bad boys, with strong arms and leather jackets, for...well, a woman in New York with strong arms and a leather jacket.

IsabellaMartinez1: Yes. As long as you come on camera too.

BlackVelvetBitches: As long as I...COME on camera?

BlackVelvetBitches: Whoa there, sailor. ;-)

IsabellaMartinez1: Erin! Behave.

BlackVelvetBitches: Sorry, sorry! Dammit, I was doing so well.

Isabella experienced that light-headed, buzzed feeling she got after a couple glasses of champagne. Erin was so damn intoxicating.

IsabellaMartinez1: Yes, well, I quite like it when you can't help yourself.

BlackVelvetBitches: Ditto. Okay, I'm gonna video call you with my mic muted now. You ready?

Isabella turned the volume down, just in case the muted microphone thing didn't take. Technology couldn't be trusted.

IsabellaMartinez1: Absolutely. Call me.

Her screen resolved into the gorgeous view of Erin Black in a thin, tight, gray hoodie. It looked soft, and it fit her like a second skin.

Erin was beaming, and that extraordinary smile hit Isabella like a ton of bricks. She was overwhelmed by the wish to hug Erin, to hold her tight and bury her face in the blonde hair that hung loose and straight. She swallowed and forced herself to calm down.

IsabellaMartinez1: My, don't you look cozy in that sweater.

Isabella saw Erin look down at her top and give a shy, lopsided smile before typing her reply.

BlackVelvetBitches: I'm glad you like it. I've had this hoodie for ages and was thinking about throwing it away, actually.

IsabellaMartinez1: While it's not my style, I'd like to request you keep it. You look very...huggable.

Erin grinned widely and held out her arms as if to hug her laptop. Isabella felt her breath catch. God, she wanted that hug.

BlackVelvetBitches: Hey, don't look so sad. We'll meet up soon, and I'll hug you so tight you'll wish that we were in different cities again!

Isabella looked right at the camera, seeking eye contact.

IsabellaMartinez1: I doubt you could ever make me wish that. I don't doubt your strength to hug the breath out of me, though.

Erin shrugged, looking humble.

BlackVelvetBitches: I'd say that I'm pretty strong. But mostly I'm just a helluva lot invested in the idea of hugging you.

Isabella sat up and cleared her throat.

IsabellaMartinez1: All right, that's too much sappiness for me. Let's either talk about your day or go back to being borderline inappropriate. Better yet, let's combine the two, and you can tell me about working out today, preferably in hot, sweaty detail.

BlackVelvetBitches: Hey, has anyone ever told you that sometimes your smile looks REALLY wicked? It's killer sexy. ;-)

Isabella sighed pointedly.

IsabellaMartinez1: I had an ex-boyfriend who said I often looked "evil."

BlackVelvetBitches: Yeah, well, no offense, but that's dumb. It's not an evil look as much as, I don't know, wolfish? Wicked? I don't have an exact word for it, but I really love it. It makes me feel like you could eat me whole, and I'd end up thanking you for it.

With a suggestive smirk and a raised eyebrow, Isabella looked into the camera.

IsabellaMartinez1: I might be new to girl-on-girl relationships, but should you really talk about me eating you if you plan to keep this platonic?

Erin looked down. Was she hiding a smile? Then she started typing, a frown forming.

BlackVelvetBitches: Okay, first of all, don't call it girl-on-girl. That makes me think of lesbian porn for straight guys and creeps me out. Pick "woman-loving-woman" or "sapphic" or "queer" or whatever else you're happy with. Secondly, you're the one leading me astray, damned temptress!

Isabella read the message and winked, trying to make it as seductive as she could.

IsabellaMartinez1: Guilty as charged.

BlackVelvetBitches: Yeah, well, behave until we decide we're ready to start dating each other. If we ever are, I mean. No pressure. But if we do, then you can be as bad as you want, I'm very good at punishing bad girls. ;-)

Isabella laughed at Erin's grinning face on the screen.

IsabellaMartinez1: Oh, I bet. We'll see what you dare to try when we are face-to-face. I can be quite scary.

BlackVelvetBitches: Scarily flawless, yeah.

IsabellaMartinez1: Flatterer! So, how was your day?

Erin read the message and shrugged noncommittally.

BlackVelvetBitches: Pretty dull and normal, really. Like I told you, I had a cancellation and got to talk to this annoying but pretty chick instead.

IsabellaMartinez1: Pretty AND scarily flawless? I thought I was "terrible face-wise?"

BlackVelvetBitches: Well, yeah. But I've gotta to be nice to you, since you bought me coffee, that awesome book about women in comics, and this thing.

Erin pulled up the sleeve of her hoodie to show her wrist with the FitWatch 9000.

IsabellaMartinez1: It looks good on you.

Isabella was going to add that she assumed everything would look good on Erin, but she was interrupted by the door being opened without any warning. From the doorway, Judith looked at her and then at the iPad in her lap.

"Isabella? Sorry, I wanted to ask if you and Alberto had everything you needed in here. Am I interrupting something?"

"Oh! Of course not, Mother."

She pushed the lock button on her iPad, turning the screen black in an instant. She was almost certain it was in vain, and her mother had seen Erin on the screen.

Why was she feeling so guilty and caught in the act?

Chapter 4

Music, Sex, and Making Yourself Laugh

ERIN LOOKED AT THE SKYPE window and realized that the screen had gone dark, though the chat window was still open. She'd seen Isabella look away from the camera, then her olive skin had turned strangely pale and the screen had gone black.

Chewing at her lip, she wondered if one of Isabella's parents had come into the room. If so, she was extremely happy they hadn't fallen into doing something dirty.

Leaving the chat window open in case Isabella returned, she decided to distract herself. She looked down at the list of music she planned to put on that USB stick. She'd already checked that she had all the music stored on her laptop; she just needed to find the damn stick. She remembered her earlier idea about the drawers of her bedside table and went to have a look.

The top drawer had her sleeping pills, some aspirin, a couple of membership cards for places she didn't go to anymore, and a bunch of receipts from God knows when and what. In the next drawer a book about poker tricks she'd never gotten around to reading was crammed in with an old protein bar wrapper and some fitness magazines.

When she opened the bottom drawer, her rabbit vibrator and a blue dildo with its strap-on harness and a bottle of lube stared back at her. She laughed at the sight of her poor, innocent USB stick tangled up in the strap of the harness. *How the hell did it end up there?* Shaking her head, she picked up the toys and the stick, setting off a cloud of dust.

"Eww. That's it, Black. You need to use this stuff more and give your fingers a rest," she muttered to herself. She threw the USB stick on the bed and went to wash the toys. Thoroughly.

Once they were cleaned and the battery in the rabbit checked, Erin dusted the drawer and put them away again, all the while offering a prayer to the sex gods that she'd get a chance to use them with someone again. The image of Isabella popped into her head. Just thinking about her and a strap-on in the same room made Erin's heart pound dangerously.

She chased the thoughts away, having indulged the naughtiness far too long. *Just friends, remember?*

She sat down and started to put music onto the freshly dusted memory stick. She got to "Cherry Bomb" by *The Runaways* before a message popped up in the Skype window.

> **IsabellaMartinez1:** Well, that was mortifying.

> **BlackVelvetBitches:** What happened?

> **IsabellaMartinez:** Sorry about disappearing. My mother came in to talk, and I'm quite sure she glimpsed you on my screen before I cleared it and went to talk to her.

> **BlackVelvetBitches:** Okay, with the risk of sounding clueless... does that matter? I mean, it wasn't like I was topless or anything.

> **IsabellaMartinez:** I know. It's just that I haven't mentioned to them that there might be someone in my life. And certainly not that this person happens to be a woman.

Erin blew out a breath and bit her lip as she typed.

> **BlackVelvetBitches:** Right. Well, it makes sense that you haven't told them about someone new on the horizon. I mean, that can wait until later. But, um, do you think they'll have a problem with me being a woman?

> **IsabellaMartinez:** Daddy won't. He might be a little surprised, but when that wears off, he won't care. He's generally open-minded. As long as I'm happy, he'll be happy. Mother might cause

trouble, though. She usually does when something happens that she didn't orchestrate. If for nothing else, then because you are not rich or powerful. She might use your gender as a reason when (not if) she tries to push me away from you.

BlackVelvetBitches: Okay, well, I guess we'll cross that bridge if and when we get to it. Should we keep our chats secret until then?

IsabellaMartinez: If it's okay with you, that might be best. My relationship with my parents, well, with my mother, is complicated, as you know. I try to make it as smooth as I can, where I can. I should just tell them that you are a friend, but she usually sees right through me. I'm afraid that if I talk about you, she'll see what I really feel.

Erin's heart skipped a beat at those words, and she sat up straighter in her chair.

BlackVelvetBitches: Okay. So, what exactly is it you feel for me? Have you figured that out yet? Or is it too early for me to ask you that? Tell me to shut up, and I will.

The reply took a while to appear on her screen, and Erin had time to start freaking out.

IsabellaMartinez: It's a little early, yes.

BlackVelvetBitches: Shit. I'm sorry, Isabella. I promised I wouldn't pressure you. So sorry.

IsabellaMartinez: No, it's quite all right. You have a right to know, and I'd be anxious for answers in your position too. Just know that I don't want to string you along. I'm just not quite ready for any commitment yet. And we have both said that we are too old and wise to just hurry into relationships, right?

After a weary sigh, Erin decided to be honest.

BlackVelvetBitches: Yeah. But honestly, I'm starting to realize that something about you makes me a helluva lot less wise and grown up. :-D I just want to tattoo your name on my ass and spend every night making out with you.

IsabellaMartinez: That sounds strangely tempting. I'm sure that firm little behind of yours would look great with my name on it.

BlackVelvetBitches: Are you saying you have checked out my ass?

IsabellaMartinez: Don't make a big deal out of this, and please excuse me if it's offensive, but I've checked out every bit of you that I could.

Erin's cheeks grew hot, and her toes curled.

BlackVelvetBitches: Okay. So, what's the verdict? Like what you see or do you want to throw me back into the ocean and keep fishing?

IsabellaMartinez: The only thing I want to throw you in, Miss Black, is my bed.

A noise halfway between a squeak and a yelp left Erin.

BlackVelvetBitches: Awesome! Say the word, and I'm there. I mean, hypothetically. You know, when you're ready. If you ever are.

IsabellaMartinez: Preciosa, do stop rambling. I know what you meant. We'll see what happens. Being with a woman, and being with someone after Richard, is all very new to me. I need to take it slow. Just don't doubt that I find you insanely attractive and I definitely want to take you to bed. You're the first woman I've ever felt that for. Well, not counting celebrities.

BlackVelvetBitches: Oooooh! Tell me what female celebrities you've wanted to bang!

IsabellaMartinez: Bang? Wow, that was crude.

Erin wasn't sure if Isabella really minded the word or if she was just messing with her. Either way she grimaced.

BlackVelvetBitches: Fine, fine. What celebrities you wanted to seduce? Spill!

IsabellaMartinez: All right. Calm down, dear. Hmm, let me think. Scarlett Johansson, Helen Mirren, Ming-Na Wen, Emily Blunt. Oh, and I had a period where I watched anything Angela Bassett played in. I told the man I was dating at that point that I was a big fan of her acting, which was true, but that wasn't the main reason. She just makes me weak in the knees. But I was never sure if those were just girl crushes, a lot of straight women seem to have those on celebrities.

BlackVelvetBitches: True, but it sounds like yours ran pretty deep.

IsabellaMartinez: I suppose they did. I probably shouldn't admit this, but I once found myself thinking about Angela Bassett during sex with the guy I was dating. It was only for a second, before I got my mind under control again.

The confession provoked a gasp. Then Erin laughed. The little pen symbol on her screen appeared. Isabella was clearly adding more to her story.

IsabellaMartinez: I shouldn't have told you that. Please ignore that I said that! Why do you make me so damn honest?

A mischievous thought popped into Erin's head. She bit her lip, as she decided to roll with it and play a little game with Isabella.

BlackVelvetBitches: Hmm. What will I get if I promise not to tease you about that?

There was a moment's pause before Isabella posted her reply.

IsabellaMartinez: (I'm going to regret this, aren't I?) Name your price.

BlackVelvetBitches: Tell me what you fantasized about her.

IsabellaMartinez: At that moment? Nothing, really. Just the way she looks, moves, talks.

BlackVelvetBitches: Okay, um, have you ever had a fantasy about having sex with a woman?

There was another pause.

IsabellaMartinez: Yes.

Erin looked at that simple little word. Her skin burned, and she fidgeted in her chair. She swallowed and typed quickly.

BlackVelvetBitches: Tell me about it, and I won't mention the Angela Bassett incident ever again.

IsabellaMartinez: Erin, this is embarrassing.

Should she push it? Well, Isabella was old enough to say stop if she wanted to.

BlackVelvetBitches: Please? If you do it, I'll tell you something slightly embarrassing that happened to me while you were away talking to your mom.

IsabellaMartinez: Fine. But don't make me regret this, Miss Black!

BlackVelvetBitches: I won't. Just tell me, and remember, you don't have to be too graphic if you're not comfortable.

IsabellaMartinez: Well, it's nothing too exotic. I suppose I have fantasized about using my mouth and my fingers to probe what a woman feels like inside. I've thought about that while touching myself. It's so soft and warm, isn't it? I'd like to feel what another

woman feels like inside. Oh, and maybe I've fantasized once or
twice about a woman tying me up. And that's all I'm saying!

Erin swallowed again, but her mouth was dry. She shifted uncomfortably
on the chair. Other parts weren't quite so dry after those confessions. She
closed her eyes and took a deep breath. Her mind filled with painfully
tempting images. Distractedly, she saw a new message pop up in the chat.

IsabellaMartinez: Erin? You're not laughing at me, are you?

Shaking her head to clear it from the feverish thoughts and images,
Erin quickly leaned forward to reply.

BlackVelvetBitches: No! God, no! Of course not! Sorry for
disappearing for a bit. I was just a bit blown away by the mental
images coming from what you said. You're so fucking hot, and
the thought of you and those things...kinda, short-circuited my
brain.

IsabellaMartinez: Well, you asked, preciosa.

Erin could imagine the smug look Isabella was probably wearing. Good.
That was better than the worried one she'd probably been wearing earlier.

IsabellaMartinez: Anyway, your turn. Tell me about what
happened earlier.

BlackVelvetBitches: Well, it's not as embarrassing as talking
about fantasies, I suppose, but it's a start. Guess what happened.
:)

IsabellaMartinez: I couldn't possibly guess.

Erin imagined Isabella's perfectly shaped eyebrow quirking as she had
typed that.

BlackVelvetBitches: I went to look for a USB stick to put some
of my favorite music on it for you. It took me a while to find,
which is weird, coz I have a small apartment and not much stuff.
You'll never guess where I found it...

IsabellaMartinez: Skip the guessing games and just tell me, Erin.

Erin smiled. She could almost hear the snarky, impatient tone of Isabella's deep voice.

BlackVelvetBitches: Yeah, okay. It was in a drawer with my toys, all tangled up in a harness! :D

There was a pause before Isabella responded, long enough for Erin to wonder if she'd gone to see to Alberto. Or if something in her statement had been offensive.

IsabellaMartinez: All right, I give up. I'll have to ask and risk you laughing at me. My child-centered brain probably has a different connotation for toys and harness than yours. I was thinking building blocks and a baby harness. But I'm assuming you are talking about something a little more sexual?

BlackVelvetBitches: Lol. Yes, I meant sex toys and a harness for a strap-on. ;-) I'm telling you, the USB stick was just hanging out with the big girl toys in that drawer. I have no idea how it got there. It doesn't even have dirty pics on it. Funny as hell!

IsabellaMartinez: Possibly not as hilarious as you think, preciosa. Nevertheless, I'm glad you found it. I look forward to receiving the music.

Erin chuckled as she looked at the USB stick, which was now pushed into her laptop in the dimly lit apartment. She should probably curb her tendency to talk and laugh to herself if she was, possibly, going to start dating again soon. But for now, she was going to enjoy how much she amused herself. And wonder how the hell the USB had gotten into that drawer.

Chapter 5

Unfiltered

ISABELLA SHOOK HER HEAD AT Erin and her bad sense of humor. The jokes were lousy, and the way she amused herself with little things was ridiculous. Yet, it was also extremely endearing, and Isabella envied her. Erin, despite her sad backstory, found fun and passion in anything, while Isabella struggled to see the silver lining, to just relax and have fun. Erin's outlook was just another of the many reasons Isabella was so drawn to her. It wasn't just her charm and her strength; there seemed to be pure sunshine streaming out of Erin.

She had been kicked around and probably learned many hard lessons as an orphan, but she still got childishly excited over cute dogs and bear claw pastries. Isabella felt very protective of that.

To ensure that spirit never changed, she'd do anything to keep Erin as enthusiastic and passionate as she seemed in those moments. Not just because she wanted to be close to Erin and warm herself in that sunshine, but because Erin deserved those moments of excitement and joy.

Her *preciosa*. Erin was rare, marvelous, and undeniably precious.

She heard footsteps outside, and her head shot up to look at the closed door. Was Mother going to burst in again?

When they'd spoken earlier, Isabella made sure to be very short with her mother to show her that knocking was expected. But her heart had been racing with fear. What if Mother asked about the woman on the screen?

Could she keep how much Erin meant to her away from her mother's sharp eyes? Should she even bother trying?

In the end, her mother had just asked if Isabella saw the towels she'd laid out for her, checked that Isabella knew her father prepared breakfast at 7:15 a.m, and told Isabella to ask if she needed anything else. Isabella thanked her, and they spoke a little about Alberto Sr.'s steadfast breakfast habits, before Judith excused herself to go downstairs.

The footfalls dissipated, and Isabella sighed with relief. It was ridiculous. She wasn't doing anything wrong. Not only was she single and a grown adult, she was a mother and a modern woman. She could do whatever she wanted and take responsibility for her actions. Despite that, she was terrified that her parents would see her flushed skin from telling Erin about her fantasies and hearing about Erin's sex toy drawer. It had made her feel warm and tingly in a way she hadn't felt since before Alberto was born.

There hadn't been anything sexual in her life since about four months into her pregnancy. No wonder she was burning up with embarrassment and lust just from talking about sex. The thrill of talking to someone who made no secret of wanting to do very sexy things to her didn't help either. Isabella shivered, and her nipples tightened inside her bra.

Suddenly, she remembered she was supposed to be talking to Erin but had gotten lost in her own thoughts. She looked down at the screen.

> **BlackVelvetBitches:** Hey, Martinez. You still there? I didn't scare you away with my weird sense of humor, did I? Or, you know, talking about sex toys? I don't have a lot of them or anything really kinky, if you were worried about that. Just two little things. No sex swings or whips in my little drawer. :-D

Isabella's shoulders relaxed as soon as she was talking to Erin again. She sunk back into her seat.

> **IsabellaMartinez:** Oh, well, that's disappointing. But I suppose it is hard to hang a sex swing inside a drawer. Sorry I disappeared for a while. Lost in thought.

BlackVelvetBitches: They weren't sexy thoughts, were they? (Just tell me to shut up if you want to stop talking about this stuff and go back to being platonic.)

IsabellaMartinez: We probably should stop talking about this soon. But we have another few minutes, I think—a treat for your long work day and my grueling day of travel.

BlackVelvetBitches: Glad to hear it. :-) Penny for your thoughts, then. (Just say if you need to go to bed, though. Traveling always tuckers me out.)

She was tired. Bone tired from traveling and seeing her parents again. Tired enough to let her guard down again and allow herself the dangerous relief of telling Erin exactly what was on her mind.

IsabellaMartinez: Honestly, I was thinking about my lack of love life since around the middle of my pregnancy.

BlackVelvetBitches: Whoa, really? Well, join the club. My sex toys were all dusty, and I can't remember the last time I had fingers in my panties that weren't my own.

IsabellaMartinez: Ah, well you're leagues ahead of me. Not even my own fingers have snuck in there.

BlackVelvetBitches: WHAT? You haven't even played with yourself since you were pregnant? :-O

Isabella gave a little hum of annoyance at Erin's incredulous response.

IsabellaMartinez: No, Erin. When you have small children and you're numbly going through the motions of an unhappy relationship, your libido tends to be nonexistent.

The seconds ticked by, and there was no response from Erin. Isabella huffed. For the hundredth time, she asked herself why this woman made her spill her secrets like this. Why did Erin have to be so disarming?

31

BlackVelvetBitches: Sorry. I was just trying to find something to say that was understanding and not raunchy. My brain just seems to be giving me filth here.

Isabella smiled, relieved at Erin's reaction and that she seemed to be just as forthcoming as she made Isabella. It was odd to be this honest and open, but somehow freeing as well.

IsabellaMartinez: Feel free to be filthy, just not judgmental. I don't always have a voracious appetite for sex, and this has been a period of my life where my interest has been zero.

BlackVelvetBitches: Hey, I'd never judge you. Is it okay if I ask if you still feel kinda, um, asexual or nonsexual or whatever?

IsabellaMartinez: Wouldn't the suggestive comments I've blurted out prove that's not the case?

BlackVelvetBitches: That was kinda why I asked. I wanted to make sure that the sexy banter wasn't just for my sake. I'd still be interested in you, even if you weren't into sex.

IsabellaMartinez: Oh, preciosa, no. That's very considerate of you, but I've wanted to jump you since the second I saw your back muscles when you did that yoga stretch.

BlackVelvetBitches: AWESOME. Well, if nothing ever happens between us, I'll always know that you at least liked me and wanted to...you know, do me. And that is one hell of a compliment. :-D

Isabella found it impossible not to smile.

IsabellaMartinez: Funny, that's exactly what I think every time I see you blush and try not to look at my cleavage.

BlackVelvetBitches: Ah. Right, that's me busted, then. Speaking of that, um, wanna come on camera again, or don't you want to risk it?

IsabellaMartinez: Erin, I'll be brutally honest. If I come on camera now, while we are talking so intimately and I feel like a frisky teenager in my old room...I think I might end up asking you to show me those back muscles again.

BlackVelvetBitches: Hey, 'nuff about my back. My abs will be jealous. ;-)

Isabella was almost ashamed at how thrilled this conversation made her. She'd spent far too much time wondering about Erin's abs. Why did she have this pathetic weakness for sculpted muscles?

IsabellaMartinez: Am I to assume that you have a six-pack, Miss Black?

BlackVelvetBitches: Well, if you're not pretty fit in my line of work, people start wondering if you're a good trainer. My body is kinda my resume and advertising board, all rolled into one. It shows what results I can get.

Isabella drew in a quick breath. Images of Erin's resume/advertising board without any clothes on swam across her mind. Her self-control was pathetic tonight, and she could only blame it on being tired. Maybe.

Looking out the window, Isabella thought hard to find something to seamlessly change the topic. Instead her wicked mind and typing fingers betrayed her.

IsabellaMartinez: It's getting late, and I'm tired. So more chatting (be it text or video) is probably a bad idea. However, why don't you send me a picture of your stomach when we've said good-bye? I'll have a look and let you know if I might want to hire you as a trainer in the future.

BlackVelvetBitches: Honestly, I'd be more interested to know if you'd like to eat ice cream off it one day. ;-)

A certain small, but important, part of Isabella's body tightened, joining her nipples.

33

IsabellaMartinez: Deal. In fact, I'll go get ready for bed and check on Alberto. When I come back to my iPad, I expect to see a picture waiting to be downloaded. In return, before I go to sleep, I'll let you know whether or not I'd be willing to eat dessert off those abs of yours. Although, I suspect I already know the answer to that.

BlackVelvetBitches: You're on! Take your time with your evening cleaning routine, and I'll get working on that pic.

Isabella felt elated and giddy and berated herself for being so childish. It was just a picture of someone's stomach. But she knew it was more than that. It was Erin's stomach and Erin entrusting her with a naked picture of a part of her body.

That telltale tightening increased, and the pull in her lower stomach kept it company. For the first time in a very long time, she was aroused. And boy, had she missed that sensation.

Chapter 6

Discomfort and Questions

ERIN WAS FRANTICALLY DOING AB exercises on the floor. She did have a visible six-pack; it was the reason she suffered through a low-fat diet most days. But it was late, and between the bad lighting in her apartment and the fact that the human stomach tended to be more bloated at night, she worried her abs wouldn't pop the way she wanted.

From their chats over the last few weeks, she'd gathered that Isabella liked muscles. This was her chance to prove she could give Isabella what she wanted on that front.

So she was doing crunches and Russian twists like crazy to make her abs look extra chiseled in the pic. When she'd done enough to feel her heart race and her abs buzz from use, she got up and pulled her hoodie off. She switched on all the lights and stood in front of her laptop, just in the right spot for her stomach to be in front of the camera. As she was about to click the timer on the laptop's camera software. She thought better of it and took a step back, and included the bottom of her bra-clad breasts in the picture. Couldn't hurt, right?

She reached forward, clicked the timer, and then stood back, abs tensed. The camera clicked, and Erin dove back into her chair, located the file, checked it was okay, and pressed *send*.

As she put her hoodie back on, she tried to relax while awaiting the verdict. She put coffee on and listened nervously for Skype's indicative ping. She hoped Isabella would be impressed and would let that show in her reply. She knew Isabella would be interested no matter what her abs looked like, but dammit, she wanted to blow Isabella's designer socks off!

The coffee machine had almost finished before Isabella's message came in. Erin threw herself toward the laptop and read the message before she had even sat down.

> **IsabellaMartinez:** Oh...my...God! What is wrong with you, woman? I get myself all cleaned up for bed, and you risk making me soak my clean pajamas with that sort of porn. How inconsiderate!

Erin laughed and punched the air. It was an even better reaction than she'd dared hope for.

> **BlackVelvetBitches:** I'm not sure if you mean that I made you sweaty or if it was just the crotch getting wet? I'm hoping both. Careful with your parents' sheets, Martinez. ;-) So I guess my abs passed muster?

> **IsabellaMartinez:** Erin, I can't imagine a part of you that I wouldn't be absolutely crazy about. But, yes, that stomach looks incredibly...delicious. I just wish that the camera zoomed out a little more, so I could see what was in that bra of yours.

Erin chewed her lower lip. This was escalating quickly, and her control was slipping. She took a deep breath. Isabella was a responsible adult. If she wanted to put a stop to this game and bring them back to neutral ground, she was more than capable of saying so. If she wanted to. Was this a sign that Isabella was feeling ready for something romantic earlier than expected?

Erin closed her eyes tightly, trying to figure out the right thing to do. All she wanted was to go further, to achieve more intimacy, and attract this fascinating woman by any means she could. *Go big or go home, right?*

> **BlackVelvetBitches:** I could always send you another picture. Or maybe even call you on mute again? Maybe give you a personal show of what's in the bra?

The reply took a while to come. Time enough for Erin feel an uncomfortable churning in her stomach. Her mind seemed to take pleasure in using the milliseconds to torture her with questions. Had she overstepped? Had she rushed Isabella? Or was it the other way around? What if Isabella replied that she wanted a nude show with touching involved? Was she ready for that? Could she even do that without feeling self-conscious and silly?

IsabellaMartinez: My precious Erin, that's such an amazing offer, and a big part of me wants to say yes, but considering that I am under my parents' roof and that we're supposed to take this slow, it's probably not a good idea. Please don't think I don't want (desperately) to see all of you, I'm just trying to curb my inner wolf and keep from eating you whole before either of us is ready.

Erin ran her hand through her hair and sighed.

BlackVelvetBitches: You're right. Sorry, I went too far.

IsabellaMartinez: Please don't apologize, preciosa. I'm the one who should be sorry. You're being so good at giving me space and not taking advantage of the situation, and I cruelly return the favor by flirting mercilessly with you. I'm sorry if it seems like I blow hot and cold. I suppose I just came to my senses there. Although, I hasten to add that half of my resolve comes from being in my parents' house and not wanting to end up orgasming with them one room away. So I can't really pat myself on the back for sticking to my decision to not get too involved.

BlackVelvetBitches: It's not your fault. I'm more than happy to play along. You're just so freaking hot.

IsabellaMartinez: And you're not? Look at those abs! I know I'm going to be looking at them, over and over, until I wear out my iPad screen.

Erin smiled, suddenly feeling as shy as if she had never shown her stomach to anyone before. It was unnerving how Isabella made her feel like every sensation was new.

BlackVelvetBitches: Thanks. Now stop making me embarrassed. :-P By the way, do you have your address for your new place? I want to send that package to you, but I haven't got the money to send it express right now, so it'll probably arrive at the new place when you do. Or later, even.

IsabellaMartinez: Of course. One moment while I go look for the address. I can't recall the zip code right now. I'll be back in a second.

BlackVelvetBitches: I'll be here. :-) In fact, I'll go get the coffee I brewed (and totally forgot about) while you look for the address.

When Erin came back with her mug of hot coffee, the message with Isabella's new address in Philly was waiting for her.

BlackVelvetBitches: Thanks. I'll finish up the package and send it tomorrow.

IsabellaMartinez: That sounds good. Oh damn, Alberto is waking up, and he sounds like it's bad. This might take a while. I'll say good night to you now. Speak tomorrow?

BlackVelvetBitches: Abso-freakin-lutely. Go get the poor kid. 'Night, 'night, beautiful. :-*

There was no reply, and Erin assumed that Isabella had thrown the tablet aside to focus on taking care of Alberto and not ruin too much of her parents' sleep.

Erin blew on her scalding hot coffee, as she crossed the room to the package she was sending to Isabella. She'd seen the book in a shop window on the way back from work, *Dog Breeds for Those with Children*. Inside, Erin had written a jokey note about Isabella getting the dog Erin wasn't allowed and then letting her come play with it.

There was also a chart of illustrated back stretches she'd printed out from a physical fitness forum she was a member of. She wasn't sure if Isabella would need it anymore, as she'd probably be sleeping in a real bed now, but it couldn't hurt.

The finishing touch was a little metal sign with a vintage print.

Coffee—because you can sleep when you're dead.

Erin had bought it in a garage sale, years ago, and had hung it wherever she'd lived since. It might not be Isabella's taste in decorations and might not make it onto the walls of Isabella's Philadelphia apartment, but Erin was sure it would at least make her smile. And that was worth the two dollars she'd spent on it back in the day.

She went back to her laptop and looked at the files on the USB stick. She was happy with her music selection, but there was still room for more. She considered including another picture of her abs as a surprise. Maybe even a picture of what was above her abs. Would that be inappropriate, considering their discussion tonight?

Yes, Isabella had backpedaled somewhat, but she'd also admitted she would've said yes to more pictures, maybe even a video, had she not been at her parents' house. And she would be in the privacy and comfort of her own home when she got this package.

Unsure of what to do, Erin sat down and sent a text to her flirting expert: Riley.

> Hey, I need your help. You know roughly where I'm up to with Isabella, right? I'm thinking about sending her a pic of my chest, wearing only my bra. She liked a pic of my abs earlier, so it should be okay to send a naughtier picture too, right?

She was driving herself crazy, fretting about taking things too far too fast, so she put on some warm clothes and decided to take a brisk walk. She wasn't a huge fan of walking alone late at night in her neighborhood. While it wasn't rough, it sure as hell wasn't without predators either. She knew she could hit and outrun most guys, but she also knew that some guys had weapons. Or friends. Or both. But it wasn't all that late, and she knew where it was well lit and usually safe to walk.

She took a gulp of her cooled coffee, put on her beat-up vintage Dragon Adidas, and headed for the fresh April evening air.

Twenty minutes into the walk, she heard from Riley.

> No, Erin, you dumbass, that's not okay. Listen, babe, my homie, my man, my dude…you can't send her a pic of yourself in a bra. What are you, 17?

Take the fucking bra off, snap a pic of the girls, and show the woman what she's getting if she boards the Erin Black Express to Sexytown! DO IIIIIT!

Erin snorted and headed for home. She'd ignore Riley's over-the-top suggestion but take her enthusiasm and go with her own instincts.

When she got home, she stripped down to her bra and jeans, stood in front of the laptop again, and set the timer to take a close-up, her breasts safely tucked away in her white bra. She prepped the picture, stuck it on the USB and named it, open_in_private. She removed the USB stick, put the cap on, and added it to the box. She taped up the package before she had time to change her mind.

She considered another cup of coffee but decided against it. She needed some sleep, but that niggling discomfort was there as soon as she contemplated it. The idea of going to bed, of closing her eyes, even of falling asleep made her feel…uneasy. Just like it always did.

She took a deep breath and tried to ignore the tension that crept into her shoulders. Poker. That would have to be Plan B. She went over to the laptop and sighed in defeat.

Chapter 7

A New Day, A New Town

ISABELLA WOKE UP TO A fidgeting Alberto. He'd woken up so many times last night that she'd decided to let him sleep in the bed, nestled in her arms.

Long gone were the days when she couldn't sleep next to him for fear that she'd roll over and flatten him. Somewhere in the parental brain was a built-in function which distinguished where he was and made her sleep very still. It wasn't necessarily restful sleep, but it was still more sleep than she achieved by constantly getting out of bed to get him from his crib. He slept better too, seeming to draw comfort from her warmth and familiar scent.

His little hand had reached out and bumped into her cheekbone a little too hard for her to sleep through. She groaned and opened her eyes. It was strange seeing the small but luxurious guestroom and not her former Florida home. The muffled noises filtered into her consciousness, sounds of pigeons outside the window and what she assumed was her father making breakfast in the kitchen.

Alberto Martinez Sr. was a big believer in breakfast and would experiment with new foods. His efforts were usually wasted on his wife, who believed breakfast consisted of an espresso. Dark roasted and served black. And, at a push, a piece of fruit.

Isabella smiled at the baby who was just opening his eyes and beginning to whine.

"Good morning, *cariño*. Want to see what your grandfather's making? Let's feed you and get you into a fresh diaper, then we'll go see what yummy madness he's cooking up."

He sneezed, and she looked at him.

"Bless you, and I'll take that as a yes." Isabella sat up with him and unbuttoned her pajama shirt.

Isabella descended the staircase with a freshly changed and fed Alberto in her arms. She was comfy in her robe, pajamas, and slippers, while Alberto was equally warm and cozy in his Winnie the Pooh fleece onesie. It was important to her that they were both comfortable in the house that tended to be anything but *cozy*.

She assumed most people would react in some way to the opulence of the marble and dark wood throughout this house. *Does it only feel cold and ostentatious to me?* She and her parents had moved into the house when she was a teenager, and her mother had staff to keep it in a state of perfection. It never looked or felt like *home* to Isabella.

Alberto Sr. had put his foot down when it came to getting a chef. He wanted to do the cooking, and Judith had reluctantly indulged him. Isabella suspected that it was mainly to keep him out of her hair.

Isabella's paternal grandfather had been one of the biggest landowners in Isabela, Puerto Rico. He sold all his land to move to America and invest his fortune in business ventures on land and at sea. He'd done well and passed on the investments and the tricks of that trade to Alberto. As a dutiful son, Alberto had learned from his father and built on the family fortune, investing in the stock market. But his heart had always been cooking, which had eventually inspired Isabella to get into the catering business. He had been proud of her and had always taken an interest. But, unlike Isabella, he was more interested in the dishes than the business decisions behind the scenes. Isabella was sure that in a parallel universe her father had rebelled and run off to be a chef.

Crockery clinked in the kitchen, and a startled Alberto cooed in Isabella's arms. Her father looked through the door and saw them coming.

"*Mija!* 'Beto! I didn't know what you would want for breakfast, so I am ready to cook up a few different things. Eggs any way you like them, some bacon, maybe a Spanish omelet? There's three kinds of bread, two sorts of cheese, some cuts of meat, and some vegetables laid out over there, if you'd prefer."

"My, what a feast." Isabella gave him a warm smile. "I'm not that hungry, though. I think I'll just have some bread and cheese."

Alberto Sr. looked more than a little deflated, and the spatula he had been holding drooped in his hand.

Isabella's heart gave an all-too-familiar twinge, and she kept smiling at him as she amended her breakfast order. "Actually, a poached egg does sound lovely. Would you mind making me one?"

"Of course not. Poached eggs for the both of us, then. Judith says they are better for my health than omelets, anyway."

"In a sense, she's right, Daddy. You need to keep an eye on your cholesterol and fat intake. However, I think cutting down on the churros that you wolf down with your friends every Sunday would help more."

"How do you know we still eat churros at Santiago's house on Sundays?"

She kissed her father on the cheek before answering him. "Because you never change, and I know you sneak in your treats when Mother isn't around."

Alberto Jr. wriggled in her arms, kicking his little foot out and softly thumping his grandfather on the arm. Alberto Sr. pretended to be mortally wounded and made a big show of rubbing his arm and croaking out accusations in Spanish.

Isabella laughed at his antics. "Save it, Daddy. You can play with him when he is big enough to understand your silliness."

"Everyone's a critic." Alberto Sr. brandished his spatula at her.

Judith walked in with a half-empty cup of espresso in one hand. "Ah, you're awake, dear. Good. How is my darling little grandson?"

"He's been fed, changed, and he just kicked his granddad," Isabella replied.

She grabbed Alberto's little fist and kissed it. "I see. Well, having had enough nutrients to start the day and a chance to kick the old fool is how I like to start the day too."

"Mother!" Isabella exclaimed angrily at the same time as Alberto Sr. muttered, "Judith."

Judith held up her hands. "It was a joke. No need for a fuss. You both know I would never stoop so low as to use physical violence, especially not toward the only person who puts up with my bad moods."

Isabella schooled her facial features, knowing full well that her mother admitting to her bad moods and acknowledging that Alberto put up with them, was as close to an apology and show of affection as they were ever going to get.

After putting her cup down on the table, Judith held out her hands toward baby Alberto. "May I hold him for a while?"

"Of course." Isabella disentangled Alberto's hands from her robe.

Judith picked him up and held him close, smiling proudly at him, as if he had just won the Nobel Prize and thanked her in his speech.

"Well, little Alberto. How do you like Philadelphia so far?" Judith asked him seriously.

Alberto Jr. said nothing but reached out to grab for his grandmother's perfectly styled hair. Judith pulled him away snappily and the movement startled him, making him hiccup and spit up some milk.

"Oh no," Isabella said in a gasp.

She grabbed him and headed to the kitchen counter to get some paper towels. Her father beat her to it and gave her a sheet before handing another to his wife.

Isabella wiped Alberto's mouth and chin before turning to see what the damage was to her mother's burgundy Chanel suit.

Judith held up her hand to signal she was fine, as she wiped at a small stain on her shoulder, but her whole body was tense with barely controlled anger. The image made Isabella still. She'd been eight years old when she'd spilled juice on one of her mother's lightly colored dresses. Judith had screamed at her, refused to give her any food for the rest of the day, and called her things so vicious they still hurt Isabella to this day.

That memory was vivid, as she watched her mother wipe at the stain. The perfect mask of makeup and calm features almost hid Judith's simmering rage, but Isabella could recognize the unmistakable shade of it underneath.

Alberto Jr. cried in her arms, and Isabella rocked him as she recognized what she'd done. As scared as she'd been of her mother's reaction, her first instinct had been to take care of her son. The fear gripping her stomach settled to discomfort, as she straightened her back and stood a little taller.

She wasn't a frightened child anymore; she was a mother. And she was already doing a better job than her own mother had. The moment felt like a victory in a fight she hadn't known she was in.

Her voice was strong, her face unapologetic, as Isabella looked at her mother and said, "Sorry about that. I fed him just before I came down, and you frightened him."

To Isabella's happy surprise, her father replied, "I'm sure we all understand. Little 'Beto is a baby. They throw up. Even you did that. You ruined a pair of my suede shoes once."

"And I remember thanking you for it, Isabella. Those shoes were hideous," Judith muttered, as she threw away the paper towel and then shrugged out of her suit jacket.

What little discomfort that was left in Isabella's stomach dissipated. Her mother no longer dared to have a fit of fury, and her father had almost stood up for her and her son. Almost. And she'd overcome her own fear by pure instinct. It seemed both she and her parents were evolving.

She kissed Alberto's head and felt him calm. He was quiet now, gumming on the collar of her robe. Judith folded up the jacket, looking at it disdainfully.

"I'll pay for the dry cleaning, Mother."

"No need. I've been planning on replacing this suit anyway. The skirt doesn't quite fit right. Like with your father's shoes, the baby spit was probably a sign that the garment needed to go," Judith said and retrieved her espresso. She didn't ask for Alberto back and Isabella didn't press the point. She wanted to hold him close anyway.

Alberto Sr. gasped. "Oh, the eggs! I forgot to set the timer. Do you think they're done, *mija*?"

"I don't know. It doesn't matter if they're not perfect," Isabella soothed him.

He looked at the eggs in the pan as if they might explode if they were not done. He hummed and scratched the bald part of his head. "I'll give them another minute or two, I think," he mumbled.

Judith rolled her eyes at Isabella, who promptly ignored her.

"Alberto is fidgeting. He seems warm, probably because I'm quite warm in this thick robe. I think I'll go get his baby bouncer so he can sit with us but not in my arms."

Judith walked past her. "Allow me. You entertain the baby, and I'll be back with the bouncer."

Isabella's brow furrowed, but she saw no reason to argue. "Um, all right. Thank you. It's folded up and currently on top of my suitcase, I think."

"I'm sure I'll find it, dear," Judith said, as she headed up the stairs.

Isabella sat down with Alberto Jr. and watched her father run the eggs under cold water and then scoop them up, humming an old Chubby Checker song under his breath. It calmed Isabella, and they shared a smile.

A couple of minutes later, Judith returned with the baby bouncer, unfolded it, and put it on the floor next to Isabella. As she did, she spoke without taking her eyes off her task.

"I saw your little machine up there. What are they called? A tablet?"

Isabella froze. "My iPad?"

"Yes, that's the one. You seem very fond of it."

"I am. I find it useful for a number of things," Isabella said.

Task completed, Judith stood up. "I see. Like keeping in touch with your friends?"

"That's one example, yes."

"And perhaps suitors? I mean, you are single now," Judith said casually.

"Just barely, but yes, I am single. And no, I'm not 'entertaining suitors' on my iPad. I'm just talking to people I enjoy speaking to."

Isabella felt a little unease at saying that. While she wasn't officially dating Erin, they were certainly more than friends. However, she hadn't said that she spoke only to friends, she said she spent time talking to people she enjoyed. Erin certainly fit into that category.

That was the power of words. Choose your wording carefully, and you could get away with most things. She'd been taught that by the ruthless, but clever, Rupert Claremont, the cofounder of her mother's law firm. He'd helped Isabella cover up her theft of a piece of cake when she was six.

Mr. Claremont had instructed that, when she was accused, she was to tell her mother that she had certainly not stolen a piece of cake. He showed Isabella that she could say that in all honesty, because she hadn't eaten it yet and could therefore return it, guaranteeing that she hadn't "stolen" the cake but merely borrowed it. So, when she promised that she hadn't stolen it, she hadn't lied to her mother, she had just chosen her words carefully.

Whatever Erin was to Isabella, she was certainly someone Isabella liked to talk to. In fact, right after her son, Erin was currently Isabella's favorite person. She just wouldn't be telling her mother that.

Judith gave her a searching look before replying, "I see. Well, if you do enter into a new relationship, remember you don't have to hide it from me and your father, dear. We want you to be happy."

He wants me to be happy. You want to know exactly what I'm doing and if I'm doing it with someone you deem suitable.

"Of course I'll let you know if I start a new relationship, Mother."

Judith nodded before wandering off, drinking the last of her espresso, and Isabella added bread and cheese to her plate.

Chapter 8

Parents and Children

ERIN TRIED FOR A CALMING breath and repeated the same point she'd been making to her client for the last twenty minutes.

"No, Lemmy. You can't just keep doing ten minutes of weight lifting twice a week. Your body's gotten used to that now, so you won't lose any more weight unless you change your routine. You paid me to teach you about cardio, and that's what I'm trying to do. I'm afraid you have to vary your exercise and work harder if you want to keep shedding the weight."

The short man ran his hand over his beard and scowled at her. "Huh. That's shitty and annoying, but fine. What about that machine over there? Can I check out ladies on Tinder while I'm on that one? And, you know, go slow on it so it won't be so hard?"

As if the gods were intervening to keep Erin from showing her frustration, her phone beeped to say she had a text. She'd always made a habit of keeping her phone on silent and normally stowed it in her locker when she was working. These days, she found herself keeping it with her in case Isabella made contact.

However, the sound was only on, because she'd forgotten about it. She seemed extra forgetful at work these days. She just didn't know if it was her insomnia catching up with her or the fact that she couldn't stop thinking about Isabella.

Normally, she would've apologized for the disruption and ignored her phone, but she was so close to snapping at the lethargic Lemmy and his disinterest, she took the excuse to calm herself down.

"I'm so sorry, Lemmy, but this is really important. Why don't you try that machine over there? It's a cross-trainer, and the instructions are on the panel. I'll be over in a sec to see how you are getting on, okay?"

He looked skeptically at the machine. "Yeah, all right. Then I want to go get a Gatorade."

"Sure. I'll be right with you." Erin swallowed down the comment about the sugar contents in most sports drinks and the fact that most people didn't need them. Especially if they didn't even work up a sweat.

He lumbered off, and Erin got her phone out of the pocket of her peach hoodie. The text was, as she had hoped, from Isabella.

Hello. I know you're working, I just thought I'd send you a text for when you are on a break. Do you want to chat today? Me and Alberto are free all day. Or we can be, if we manage to shake Mother's prying eyes. Xx

She smiled to herself, unable to stop, as she read the text again. Someone tall accidentally bumped into her shoulder. It turned out to be Chris Nash, the gym's owner.

He was sweaty from pumping iron, but she forgave him since he was smiling at her as if she were a hundred-dollar bill he just found on the street. She liked Chris, despite his clumsiness. He had good taste in comics, was a proud feminist, and was a social justice warrior. And his sense of humor was just as bad as hers.

"Hey there, Er. I haven't seen you for a few days. You look in a good mood. Actually, you look all googly-eyed. Texting a girl?"

She bumped him back, aware that her shoulder only hit his bicep.

"You shouldn't call me Er. I keep telling you and Riley that it sounds weird. But yeah, actually. Or, well, she's texting me. She's a woman, though, definitely not a girl. She's a couple of years older than me, and a real grown-up. She's got a kid and everything!"

"Ah, be careful there. Get together with her, and you'll be an instant parent. I mean, I love kids, but dating women who already have them means you get thrown in the deep end. You don't get to prep and see if you're ready. The kid's just there, and you make an impression on it."

Erin frowned. "Make an impression on it?"

He scratched his short-cropped hair pensively. "You know, you'll be shaping what kind of a person the kid turns out to be, whether you're ready for that responsibility or not. I've dated a few women with kids, but I think twice about it now. The last time I tried, it broke my heart twice: first because the relationship ended, and second because the little toddler was devastated. Everything gets harder, more complicated, when kids are involved."

Erin shrugged. "She's worth it."

But fear reared its ugly head. What would it be like if she started really dating Isabella? She knew nothing about babies. She never thought she'd have kids. Little Alberto was cute and all, but he was…like something from a different planet. Her mind took it further, as her pulse picked up. Alberto was all squidgy and fragile now, but when he got older, he'd be shaped by her and her actions toward him. Just like Chris said. Her breathing got uneven just from thinking about the implications.

Worry painted all over Chris's kind features. "Hey. Sorry if I freaked you out. I mean, I'm sure it'll be okay. If you really like her, and she likes you, then you'll figure it out. I was just babbling away without thinking. As per."

Erin swallowed hard but tried to mask it and give Chris a calm, cheerful smile. "It's fine. I'm glad you got me thinking about this. Don't worry, you haven't talked me out of it or anything. I'm a grown-up. I can make my own decisions."

Despite her assurances, she felt less than confident about her own decision making. Her pulse wasn't slowing, and she kept wondering what the hell she was doing. She was flirting with someone's mom. What if they did start up a relationship?

Someone called out to Chris, and Erin dazedly felt him squeeze her shoulder with a calloused hand before he walked away. She stood there, biting her lip and trying to calm down.

"Erin? I don't get how that machine works. I went on it, and one of those big sticks hit me in the head."

Startled out of her reverie, Erin came face-to-face with Lemmy. "What? Oh, right. Yeah, that's the handles. You'll want to hold on to those. Come with me, and I'll give you the demonstration I should've given you earlier."

Trying to ignore the Alberto-themed panic that had taken root in her chest, she walked over to the cross-trainer with Lemmy in tow.

It was early evening. Erin was home and had eaten in front of the laptop while chatting to Isabella. They'd covered Isabella's failed attempts to get any work done on her book and Alberto throwing up on his grandmother at breakfast.

Once Erin had cleared up, she gave Isabella her full attention. She'd decided not to mention her worries about Alberto. There was no point until she knew if they were actually dating or not.

She'd let Isabella heal and decide whether or not she was ready for a new relationship before bringing up the topic—if she didn't panic and end up burying her head in the sand about the whole thing, of course.

A new message from Isabella popped up on her screen.

> **IsabellaMartinez:** Oh, by the way, Mother voiced an interest in my love life today. I'm not sure, but I think she might have gauged more than I hoped from catching us talking last night. Probably my reaction tipped her off.

> **BlackVelvetBitches:** Really? What did she say?

> **IsabellaMartinez:** Nothing definitive. Just asked me about my iPad and if I used it for dating. And added that she and Daddy would be fine with me dating again.

Erin chuckled and brushed her hair away from her face.

> **BlackVelvetBitches:** Lol. That's generous of her!

> **IsabellaMartinez:** Oh, yes, she tends to give the impression of being a magnanimous ruler. With her words, at least. The sentiment behind them is usually different though. I suspect she just wanted to snoop and find out if I am seeing someone who is "more suitable" than she felt Richard was.

> **BlackVelvetBitches:** Ooookay. Wow. So what is "more suitable" in her world?

IsabellaMartinez: Someone successful. Preferably rich, but definitely ambitious and hardworking. She probably still dreams of me marrying one of the lawyers she works with.

BlackVelvetBitches: Your mom's a lawyer?

IsabellaMartinez: One of the most highly rated lawyers in Philadelphia, yes. She's the Martinez in "Martinez & Claremont—Attorneys at Law." But let's not talk about her. I just wanted to let you know that she asked the question and I dodged it. As you know, Mother can be...difficult.

From everything Isabella had told her about Judith Martinez, the term "difficult" was being polite. Very polite.

BlackVelvetBitches: Yeah, difficult and then some. :-(

IsabellaMartinez: Scared off yet?

BlackVelvetBitches: By her? Nope.

Some rich, lawyer shark didn't scare her. What frightened her was a sweet, little baby she could drop or give nightmares or generally just screw up for life.

IsabellaMartinez: Good. Then let's talk about something nicer. Let's talk about you. Did you get any sleep last night?

Erin sighed and decided to be honest.

BlackVelvetBitches: Nope. Well, a few hours, but that's about it.

IsabellaMartinez: I know we've talked about this before, but I have to ask, do you think it's time to go back to a doctor for your insomnia? Perhaps find someone who isn't a complete quack and will actually help you, instead of just giving you medication and sending you home?

Wincing, Erin read the message twice. If anyone else but Isabella had asked, she would've changed the subject or made a deflecting joke. Somehow, that seemed wrong when it came to Isabella.

Their surprising honesty with each other had been a trademark of their relationship from the start. They both had characteristics challenged by the honesty they shared: her own tendency to run away from problems, and Isabella's reluctance to be open and vulnerable. She shouldn't back down from that now. Especially not when she was already avoiding the Alberto discussion.

BlackVelvetBitches: Yeah. Probably. I'm scared of it, though.

IsabellaMartinez: Frightened of doctors?

BlackVelvetBitches: Nah, not doctors...psychiatrists. Someone with my past tends to have issues, and I don't like to admit that I might have 'em. I'm the type who just lives with my hang-ups and keeps moving forward. Stopping to analyze my screwed-up brain scares me.

IsabellaMartinez: I don't think you are screwed up, Erin. I don't think you have as much to fear from this as you think. But I understand and respect that you're uncomfortable. Does this mean that you think your sleeplessness has to do with what you call your "issues?"

Erin ran her hand through her hair and felt a lump forming in her throat.

BlackVelvetBitches: Yeah.

IsabellaMartinez: Want to talk to me about it? You don't have to, of course. I can change the topic, if you like?

She really didn't want to talk about this. Tears welled in her eyes, and her breathing became shallow. She cleared her throat and tried to relax her shoulders.

BlackVelvetBitches: No, I'll try to answer. It started when I was a kid, but then it went away when I grew up and got my first home and some steady friends. A while ago, it came back.

IsabellaMartinez: Thank you for telling me. Well, that raises two questions in my mind. 1. What happened to trigger the insomnia when you were a child? 2. Why did it suddenly come back?

The tears fell, and Erin sniffed loudly, looking around for a tissue. She couldn't help feeling embarrassed for crying at something so stupid.

BlackVelvetBitches: Look, I'm crying now, and I really don't want to do this. Not like this. Not right now. Is that okay?

IsabellaMartinez: Of course, preciosa. I'm sorry. Just...think about those questions. Maybe one day soon, perhaps when we are face-to-face, we can talk about it a little more? Perhaps be casual about it and talk about it in little increments? Or maybe you prefer to talk to a therapist about it after all. Either way, don't bury it again, now that it has come to the surface. Just let it stay in the back of your mind until you are ready to deal with it. Could you do that for me, Erin?

Erin hugged her arms around herself and stared at Isabella's words. Time ticked by as she tried to sort out her turmoil of emotions and figure out what to say. After a while, she loosened the grip and freed her arms to type.

BlackVelvetBitches: Yeah. Okay. I won't bury it, and we can talk about it again sometime. Just not now. I need to calm down. I don't want to cry. I'm not very good at stopping once I start.

IsabellaMartinez: I understand completely. I'm so sorry, preciosa. I wish I was there to give you a hug.

Despite her sniffles, Erin felt herself smile, just a little.

BlackVelvetBitches: You'd do that? Hug me?

IsabellaMartinez: Of course. Talking about this is obviously difficult for you, and there is something big buried here. Something big enough to have you go through life sleep deprived instead of dealing with it. I wish I could help you. I wish I could comfort you.

BlackVelvetBitches: Maybe you can soon. Well, at least the comfort part, and that's what I want most. You're going to your new place tomorrow, right? After that, we can start thinking about meeting up one day soon?

IsabellaMartinez: Certainly. I still want to wait a little so that I can get Alberto settled and have a working home. Give me a day or two, and then I could have a visit from a certain New Yorker. We can meet up somewhere in town or at my apartment. As long as you don't mind the moving-in mess.

Erin went to blow her nose and let the idea of meeting Isabella lessen her anxiety, just a little. Feeling a smidge lighter, she typed her reply.

BlackVelvetBitches: Are you kidding? I love mess. ;-)

IsabellaMartinez: Don't say that until you've seen the mess that can be created by vast amounts of baby paraphernalia cluttering up a room.

Her improving mood slipped back into anxiety. Alberto. She'd meet Alberto then. That cute little kid who…terrified her. There were so many ways she could screw that one up. Erin took a deep breath and willed herself not to freak out. Not now. She changed the topic.

BlackVelvetBitches: Speaking of the lil' man and the two of you living alone, are you worried about being a single mom?

IsabellaMartinez: Of course I am. I'm worried about being a parent in general. It's a huge undertaking, and sometimes I worry I'm in over my head. But then, when you've gone through the ordeal of climbing the corporate ladder as a woman and as a Latina, you learn you can fight a hell of a lot harder than you

55

thought. If I could survive growing up with my mother, getting into an Ivy League university, and becoming the CEO of a successful catering company, I can raise a child on my own too.

She sat forward to read the words again with more focus. Erin felt her eyebrows raise.

BlackVelvetBitches: You know, I never thought of that. Good point. If you don't mind me asking, did you face any, like, discrimination? You know, for being a woman or for being Latina?

It took a while before the reply came in, and Erin wondered if she had put her foot in it. Maybe it was insensitive to ask. Or maybe Isabella was disgusted at how her white privilege hadn't made her consider what Isabella might have gone through.

Soon, a long message popped up, and Erin realized, with relief, that it had taken a while to type.

IsabellaMartinez: Oh, yes. I can think of a few examples right off the bat. I had a college lecturer who always assumed I and a Korean woman named Sun-Mi wouldn't have any meaningful input in discussions. Later, when I'd worked my way up through the business, there were several people at work who met me and assumed I was a chef in one of the catering franchises, not the CEO of the whole company. Then there's everyday ridiculous things, like people expecting my company to only provide Latin food because of my heritage. Or employees suggesting they be the face of a marketing campaign, because people would trust a white, male face more than mine. I had to fight to get to the top, and I had to fight to stay there. Sometimes, I had to fight dirty. That's what I meant that night, when I said I've done things I'm not proud of to achieve my goals.

There was a pause, and then another message came in, saving Erin from figuring out how to respond.

IsabellaMartinez: Anyway, raising Alberto will probably be my biggest challenge. But after a whole pregnancy of doubting myself, I decided that I simply have to give it all I have and pray it will be enough. Being on my own hasn't changed that. Richard was never a big part of Alberto's life anyway. I was always more or less raising him on my own. And as I'm financially stable and don't need to go back to work for quite a few years, I'm not in deep waters yet.

BlackVelvetBitches: I'm sure you'll do great. You're smart, dedicated, and from what I've seen so far, you have a lot of love to give. You're clearly over the moon about the kid. :-)

IsabellaMartinez: I'm sure most mothers would be. But, yes, he means the world to me, and there's nothing I won't do to ensure he grows up safe and happy. I've come to realize that means letting other people into his life. Right now, he's sleeping in my father's arms while Daddy watches a baseball game on TV. I've been trying not to go down there and check on him, but I must admit I'm struggling.

Erin smiled at the thought of Isabella fighting her super-strength maternal instinct by being on a different floor of the house than Alberto. She was proud of Isabella for making it this long.

BlackVelvetBitches: Aw. Well, you've done nicely so far. I think you can allow yourself to go down there and be the mother hen. Your dad might want your help but not be able to call you coz it would wake the kid.

IsabellaMartinez: Oh. I hadn't thought of that. I should go down there immediately, just to make sure. Shall I text you when we've arrived in our apartment tomorrow?

BlackVelvetBitches: Yep. Sounds good. :-) Enjoy the rest of the evening with your parents and the kid, and I'll wait to hear from you tomorrow. Maybe I can call you when I leave work?

IsabellaMartinez: I'd like that. Good night, preciosa.

BlackVelvetBitches: Good night, Isabella. xo

Erin sat back and contemplated the obstacles Isabella had overcome. Clearly, being born with a silver spoon in your mouth didn't always mean you got an easy life. Even if Isabella had to make choices she wasn't proud of, Erin was. Proud and impressed, and mightily pissed at how unfair the world could be.

Her mind wandered to her sleeplessness and her fears about dating a mother. She squeezed her eyes shut and managed to ignore both issues, only to start fretting about that picture she'd included on the USB. Tomorrow, Isabella would be in her new home and find the package.

Well, it was something different to worry about, but at least it was something she could deal with. Unlike her two other problems.

Chapter 9

Moving In

THE FIRST-FLOOR APARTMENT LOOKED SPARSE but bright and cozy in the afternoon light, and Isabella looked around appreciatively. Her parents had driven them over, and together they had eaten store-bought *tuna Niçoise* before taking the grand tour. The tour was short, as the apartment consisted of an open plan kitchen, dining, and living room, a bathroom, a small nursery, and a slightly larger bedroom.

Since most of her capital was tied up until the Florida property sold, she'd been forced to choose a smaller place than she wanted. Nevertheless, for the moment, she was happy enough with a smaller home.

Despite its petite size, both her parents were pleased. Her father liked the safe neighborhood and her mother the Victorian details; apparently they made the renovated apartment look grander and more expensive than it was.

Isabella looked down at the baby bouncer next to her and watched her son examining his hands. Alberto seemed completely unaffected by his surroundings. As long as he had his mother, a full belly, and a clean diaper, he was fine.

"*Cariño*, I think we'll be happy here. Well, for a while, at least. You'll soon outgrow your nursery, so we'll move somewhere bigger. But, for now, welcome to our new home, Alberto."

He cooed at the sound of her voice, then went back to investigating his fingers.

Isabella glanced around again. The movers had put all the furniture into the correct rooms, but nothing was where she wanted it. She'd have to start that project this evening.

Her gaze fell on the box that was delivered while they were having lunch.

It was most annoying that her mother had been the one to open the door and take in the package. She'd pointed out that it was posted from New York and asked Isabella who she knew there. "A friend, clearly sending a moving-in present," Isabella replied. When Judith suggested she open it right away to see what was inside, Isabella feigned hunger and distracted her parents with lunch. However, she'd seen her mother cast long glances at the box on her way out to the car, when they left ten minutes ago.

She checked Alberto was still happy, then located and opened a box of cutlery. Not finding any scissors, she picked up a knife and cut open the tape. Chuckling at the metal sign inside the box, she decided to find a fitting place to hang it, preferably somewhere her mother wouldn't notice. The book made her laugh too, and the back stretches looked interesting. Then she found the USB stick and remembered that Erin had sent her some of her favorite music.

Luckily, the movers had placed her computer in its box on top of the desk, which was haphazardly stuck in the furthermost corner of the living room. Isabella unpacked the computer and plugged it in. While it booted, she hummed a tuneless lullaby to entertain Alberto.

When the computer was finally ready, Isabella connected to the Wi-Fi her mother had made sure was up and running before Isabella was even on the flight to Philadelphia. She plugged in the USB stick and waited for the computer to do what it needed to.

"We're going to put this in and listen to some of the music Erin likes," Isabella told Alberto. "You remember Erin, don't you? I know you haven't seen her in a while, but we'll video chat with her tonight. That will remind you of what she looks like."

He glanced in her general direction and then went back to gumming his little stuffed toy. Isabella smiled at him. She was only talking to him to help him get a feel for the sounds of language, but it amused her how many of her recent conversations with him were about Erin.

Isabella opened the document folder. There were quite a few folders with different band names. There was also a JPEG named *open_in_private*. Isabella frowned and clicked open the top of a familiar set of chiseled abs and the full view of a pair of petite breasts covered by a white bra.

She smiled from ear to ear.

The picture Erin had taken of herself was oddly sweet—and definitely sexy. Biting her lip, Isabella picked up her phone and sent Erin a text.

> *Me and Alberto are alone in the apartment now, and I just opened your package. I want to thank you for everything in it, but most of all, I want to talk about a certain picture. Bad girl! (Thank you so very much.) Want to video chat tonight? Alberto says he's forgotten what you look like. Xx*

It didn't take long before Erin replied.

> *Hey, beautiful. Welcome home. :-) I'm so glad you liked it. I had to get expert advice on if it was a bad idea, and, well, my advisor thought I should have been totally topless. So I'm not as much of a bad girl as I could have been. ;-) Tell Alberto I look like the Cookie Monster. Gotta get back to work before my client kills himself with a kettlebell. I'll text you when I leave work. xo*

Isabella smiled at her phone. She couldn't even imagine how she would've reacted to a naked Erin in that picture. Suddenly, she wondered if she could get Alberto to sleep during the video chat. She wanted to see those breasts completely exposed. And all hers to stare at.

No. This was ridiculous. How was she supposed to stay single if she kept wanting Erin to strip for her? But, then, sexy chats didn't have to mean romance, right? It could just be casual, no-strings-attached sex?

She looked up at the ceiling and sighed in frustration. *Maybe not between me and Erin. I really don't know. Why is nothing ever easy*

Alberto fidgeted in his bouncer, whining in that way that always led to crying. Isabella hurried over to pick him up and rub his tummy.

It was a little past six when Isabella's phone rang, startling her. She'd been so busy moving her desk and listening to the music Erin sent her that she'd lost track of time.

She hurried over and saw Erin's name on the display. She answered with a quick, breathless, "Hello, stranger."

"Hey there, Ms. Writer. You doing okay in the new place?"

Isabella could hear the sound of traffic in the background, and Erin sounded slightly out of breath, so she assumed Erin was power walking home.

"I'm fine, yes. A bit stressed, as the movers have placed furniture and boxes erratically, but I suppose I should be happy everything's all in the correct rooms. How are you? How was work today?"

"Work was the same as always. The nice clients were fun; the annoying ones were pains in the ass. I'm doing good, better than good, now that I can talk to you. I missed the sound of your voice while you were at your parents'."

Happiness spread through Isabella's chest like heat. "Me too. Text chats are all well and good, but they lack the personal touch."

"Yeah, and I don't get the porn qualities of your voice."

She rolled her eyes. "Would you stop going on about my voice? It's low and annoyingly masculine. Nothing to rave about."

"What? What are you talking about, woman? Yeah, it's deep, but it's perfectly female, sensual, and, like...I don't know...frickin' dessert!"

Despite herself, Isabella felt her cheeks blush at the compliment. "Fine, *preciosa*. Let's drop the subject. I'm assuming you are almost home? Will you call me on video chat when you get in?"

"I will after I've eaten. I'm making a masala frittata with avocado salsa, which takes a while, but I'll try to hurry. Don't forget to eat something yourself. I know you feed the kid but sometimes forget filling your own little belly."

"Yes, yes. I have some leftover salad from lunch. I'll have that," Isabella said dismissively.

"Only salad? Fine, if that'll make you feel full. What about coffee? Do you have coffee? Do I need to get Starbucks to do an emergency delivery?"

Isabella rolled her eyes again. "Calm down. I have coffee, and I've gotten the coffeemaker out and plugged in. I'll be ready for my evening cup, don't worry."

"Oh, thank God!"

"You know, you really are exceedingly silly," she said with a chuckle.

"Yeah, and you love it."

Isabella closed her eyes, marveling at how true that was. "I do…I'm growing somewhat addicted to it, actually. But don't let that go to your head. Call me when you're ready."

"Will do, boss," Erin said cheerfully.

"Be careful in traffic."

"Careful in traffic? Isabella, I'm not ten, for Pete's sake. Talk soon, babe." With that, Erin had hung up.

Isabella looked at her phone with a bemused smile. "Did she just call me babe?" she murmured. From the floor, she heard Alberto coo happily. She laughed and looked over at him. "She just called me babe, Alberto. I used to roll my eyes when your father called me that. And every man before him. Why does it make me so happy when she does it? Your mother's ridiculous."

She picked him up and kissed his head before heading to the kitchen. "Right, let's get some salad and coffee going."

An hour later, Isabella was sitting by her desk with her app open and Alberto snoozing in his baby bouncer by her feet.

In a few minutes, she'd be talking to Erin, and that made her struggle to catch her breath. Something had changed—a slight but significant shift. Was it the pictures of Erin's body or her own reaction when her mother caught her talking to Erin? She simply couldn't tell. The butterflies in her stomach were impossible to ignore, as was the feeling that their relationship was moving slowly, but surely, into something more physical.

She closed her eyes and accepted reality. She wanted Erin. Not just because of her body, the way she would want attractive actresses on TV, but for every little thing Erin was and did. She wanted to make love to her because of the way Erin enthused about things, how she talked to herself, and how she stood up for people. She wanted to be close to Erin physically, because somehow she'd crept into her mind and taken over most of her waking thoughts. She wanted to touch her, kiss her, and make her feel so unbelievably good.

Denial served no point. She could resist, of course. It was still too early for them to start something serious. But she could admit—to herself—she wanted Erin. All of her. From that sweet smile to her considerate actions to those damn sexy abs.

The call signal sounded, and Isabella's face erupted into a smile she was sure was downright dirty. Erin had amazing timing.

When she answered Erin's greeting, her voice was even lower than usual. The timbre she used to seduce. But for the first time in her life, she didn't do so consciously. Accepting her desire for Erin had led her to it.

Erin, staring back at her in a wrinkled, lilac button-down shirt with snap fasteners, clearly noticed the tone of voice too, because her cheerful smile faded. She stared unblinkingly at Isabella. There was a certain deer-in-headlights look to Erin Black at that moment.

It was clear she couldn't speak, so Isabella took charge. "I'm sorry, my precious beauty. Did I startle you?"

Erin licked her lips before replying. "Uh, no. You just, uh, sound really…uh, sexy. And your cheeks are kinda flushed. What's going on? Are you okay?"

"Yes. I'm fine. I was just thinking about that picture you sent me."

It was very gratifying to see Erin blush. At least now she wasn't the only one who looked flushed.

"So, um, it wasn't too much, then?" Erin asked bashfully.

"No, I told you earlier, I liked it. Very much. Yes, it goes against our plan to keep our chats platonic, but if we're honest, we've crossed that line quite a bit already."

"Well, a toe or two over the line can't hurt, can it? It's just a little flirting."

Isabella tilted her head slightly to the side, trying to read Erin's expression.

"It was already a given that we were attracted to each other. We've already admitted that. We've just decided to wait to act on those…feelings. But that word has been occupying my thoughts all afternoon. *Feelings*. That word can mean a lot of different things."

Erin tucked her long hair behind her ear. Her brows knitted. "I'm not sure I'm getting this."

Isabella took a moment to choose her words. "I mean I'm attracted to you in two ways—emotionally and physically. The fact that I can't easily separate the two tells me that what I feel for you is not just friendly admiration or lust, but something deeper, Erin. Much deeper."

"What are you saying?" Erin asked, eyes widening.

The thumbnail image of Isabella showed a heavy-lidded eyes in a face wrought with lust. She was smiling as if she planned to devour Erin at any second. A pang of embarrassment hit her, and she quickly looked away from the little screen, focusing instead on Erin's beautiful face.

"You know what I'm saying, *preciosa*. Please, don't make me spell out what I feel for you. When that's out in the open, it's hard to stay even remotely platonic. Anyway, my point was that I wonder if we could be bold and try to separate those two sets of feelings for a while. Perhaps focus on the lust part for now?"

Erin picked up a mug, undoubtedly filled with coffee, and slowly took a sip. "You're asking if we can be an online version of 'friends with benefits' until you're ready for a relationship?"

Why did Erin have to be so direct and literal all the time? Isabella closed her eyes and rubbed at her forehead. "Yes, if we're being simplistic, I suppose that's what I'm asking. Do you think we can send sexy pictures and flirt like this without actually making a serious commitment? Can we just…have fun?"

A grin overtook Erin's face. She put the mug down with a loud thwack. "*Hell*, yeah."

Isabella laughed so loud she almost woke Alberto. "You sure you don't want to think about that for a while?" she teased.

She was rewarded with Erin looking down shyly and then back up with a huge, dimpled, mischievous smile. That dazzling smile that Isabella was certain would be the death of her. A moment later, Erin ripped that lilac shirt open.

Isabella gasped as the snaps popped away and showed the pale skin underneath the light-gray bra that looked slightly padded. She was shamelessly staring. What she could see of Erin's breasts looked so soft and enticing that she had to groan.

"Oh no," she breathed. "Erin. I think I'm a…breast man."

Erin laughed. "I thought you said the other day that you liked my long legs. Are you now saying that you're more of a breast man than a leg man?"

"I'd rather not be any man at all. Anyway. Hm. Could you put those away again, so we can continue this conversation eye to eye?"

"Nah, you'll either have to stare at them or force yourself to look away. I like you ogling me. I can pan the camera down a bit so you see more of my abs, though. But the way I'm sitting isn't very flattering for my six-pack, and you wouldn't be able to see my face."

Inside her head, Isabella cursed herself back into a controlled state. "No, I want to see your face, obviously. You could perhaps take your shirt all the way off, though. That way I could see your arms and shoulders as well."

"God, I am so glad not to be the one who's drooling for once." Erin laughed again and took her shirt off with an infectious grin.

Isabella groaned in shame. "Flex your arms for me?" she asked weakly.

Erin obeyed, and Isabella tried to just casually look at the elegant movement and the expansion and contraction of Erin's biceps and deltoids. She was failing and knew she probably looked like a lovestruck teenage girl. Still, Erin didn't seem to mind, nor did it seem to go to her head.

"I'm so glad you like my body. I hope you'll like the rest of it," she simply said.

"Oh, I'm certain I will. Look at that delicious definition." Isabella actually whined.

Erin stopped flexing and relaxed back in her chair. She licked her lips nervously again, but she was smiling, and there was still a hint of pink on her cheeks.

"I can't help but notice that I'm the one showing skin here," Erin said, not unkindly.

"Yes, and I'm the one making flirtatious innuendos. You flirt with your body, I flirt with my words."

"Well, that makes sense, considering you're a writer. But you know… it seems a shame not to let your body play as well. I've seen you stretch, remember? Your body looks gorgeous and fit, despite you saying you never work out."

"I have a small appetite and was lucky not to gain much baby weight during my pregnancy. Despite eating a frightening amount of apple yogurt, I hasten to add. Neither did Mother when she carried me. Good genes, I suppose."

She was proud of the fact that she was looking into Erin's eyes now and not focusing on the way Erin's blonde tresses rested against her sculpted shoulders and elegant collarbones.

"Got stretch marks?" Erin asked casually. "I have some on my inner thighs."

Isabella blinked rapidly. There was an openness about how women discussed their bodies, even when discussing what society would consider bodily flaws. But this was coupled with clear erotic intent, and that was new to her.

"Oh, well, yes. Some on my lower abdomen, actually. You don't mind that?"

"Of course not. It's natural, and tiger stripes can be kinda sexy. To me, they're like your body's own version of tattoos or scarification. It makes a body look less like a blank canvas and more…real. Plus, they're excellent for gathering up chocolate sauce when poured over a naked body," Erin said with waggling eyebrows.

Isabella actually giggled. "Please don't do that with your eyebrows. You look silly," she said.

In a surprisingly coy gesture, Erin bit her lip. "But cute?"

Isabella hummed appreciatively. "Oh God, yes. Far too cute for your own good, young lady!"

"Hey, I'm not that much younger than you. How old are you, anyway? Are you going to tell me this time?"

"Fine. I'm 36," Isabella replied.

As a treat for daring to say the dreaded age out loud, she allowed herself another glance of Erin's physique, pausing at the pale mounds peeking out of the bra.

"Well, there you go. I'm turning thirty-one this year, so there's only five years between us."

Isabella opened her mouth to reply but was cut off.

"Wow," Erin said. "I like the fact that you're not even pretending not to stare at them anymore."

That wasn't fair. Isabella moved her gaze up and glared at her. "You've made it very clear that you want me to look."

"Oh, I do. It's just that I'm finding it hard to talk, because you're turning me on."

"Just imagine how I feel, having to look at that much irresistible skin," Isabella grumbled.

"So, I think we can decide that you're into women, then?"

Isabella nodded. "I think I'll change my status in my head from bi-curious to bisexual, yes."

"Or pansexual."

"As in Peter Pan, or cooking pans?" Isabella queried.

She saw Erin's chest move as she laughed and felt herself grow warmer. "I don't think it comes from either. Riley identifies as pansexual. She told me that bisexual people are attracted to someone of any gender, while pansexuals are attracted to people without caring what they define themselves as. Like, they don't see gender, I guess? Riley's dated people who were transgender and intersex. And the last person she went out with was gender-fluid."

"I see. Wow. That's a lot of new information."

"Yep. It can be really confusing before you get used to it. All those things that people throughout history felt they were but couldn't put their finger on—they have names now. It's a big relief for a lot of people who can finally find others like them and a word that describes them," Erin said.

"Right. Well, I don't know what I am, then," Isabella said with a frustrated sigh. She'd always thought she was quite politically correct and in the know, but she was quickly learning that she was rather clueless.

Erin moved closer to the camera. "Hey, babe, don't worry about it. All that matters to me is that you like me. You don't need a label if you don't want one, and you certainly don't need to figure it all out right now."

Out of the blue, Alberto burst out crying. Isabella pushed her chair back and retrieved the still half-asleep baby from the bouncer. She hushed him and rocked him.

After a moment, she heard, "What's the matter, little guy?" from her screen and looked up to see Erin buttoning up her shirt and looking worriedly at Alberto's scrunched-up face.

It was strangely touching and reassuring that Erin had immediately put her shirt back on when Alberto came into view, even if he was too small to see breasts as anything but food containers. The concern on Erin's face at Alberto's ceaseless crying touched Isabella too. It struck her that Erin truly cared about his wellbeing.

"I think his stomach hurts. I'm just going to do a tummy rubbing exercise that the doctor showed me," Isabella said.

She put Alberto on her lap, on his back, and began to make circles on his belly. From the corner of her eye, she could see that Erin had leaned in closer to her screen to see what she was doing. Her chest flooded with warmth. It was clearly true that the way to every mother's heart was through their children.

Erin worrying about Alberto didn't completely shut out Isabella's lust, but for the moment, it was overshadowed by the clear realization that Erin wouldn't just be good for her; she'd be good for Alberto too.

"Erin. This doesn't seem to be working. He's too riled up. I need to take him in the other room and calm him, maybe feed him. Could you wait for me? Hopefully I won't be long—fifteen, maybe twenty minutes."

"Of course. Go help the lil' man. I'll be here when you come back," Erin said just loud enough to be heard over Alberto's heartbreaking wails.

Isabella gave Erin the most affectionate smile she could, then walked into Alberto's nursery with the screaming baby held tight to her chest.

Chapter 10

Three Times Unbuttoned

It turned out to be exactly seventeen minutes before Isabella returned. Erin felt every one tick by so slowly, it might as well have been an hour.

She'd calmed down from their conversation. Truth be told, the sexual tension had started to wane the second Isabella went into mom mode and Erin could hear Alberto's sad little cries. His wails had made her feel helpless, and she had started to panic. What the hell would she do if he were to cry like that when she was with him? Would Isabella always be in the room? What if she went to the bathroom and Alberto started wailing? What would Erin be able to do?

Erin sipped a second mug of coffee, this one freshly made, and looked out the window. It was dark now, but she marveled at how long the daylight had lasted. Winter was coming to an end. She hoped that Isabella and Alberto would visit and see the beauty of New York in Spring.

When Isabella finally came back, her voice was subdued and tired. "Hello there. Sorry about that."

"Don't apologize. Is he okay?"

"Yes. He just needed a quick feed and to calm down. He's sleeping in his crib now. I left the door ajar, so I'll hear if he wakes up. That's the joy of this apartment. It's so much easier to listen out for him than it was back in that big house."

Erin wasn't quite sure what to say, so she merely nodded and looked at Isabella. She was as beautiful when she was solemn as when she'd been playful earlier. Like a work of art, Erin mused, amazed at how weak Isabella's beauty made her feel.

"God, you're pretty," she whimpered before she could stop herself.

Isabella looked up quickly. A flattered smile blossomed and slowly grew.

Erin kept staring, unable to look away. Her gaze lowered to the skin of Isabella's elegant neck, down to her shoulders, and then to her cleavage. It suddenly struck Erin that she could see more now than she could before.

Isabella was now wearing a button-down shirt too. Isabella's was classy, fitted, and white with normal buttons, ones that were undone down to her white bra. Erin could see a clasp at the front and olive-skinned breasts tucked away.

She felt bad for staring. Considering Isabella had come back all serious and no longer flirty, she'd clearly just forgotten to button her shirt up properly. This wasn't something Erin should sexualize. But these were Isabella's breasts, and she was seeing more of them than ever before. Obviously, her body hadn't received the memo that this was bad timing to be getting turned on.

"Um, you, um, haven't done your shirt up all the way," she said eventually.

Isabella stared down at her front and gave a tired chuckle. "Ah. Turns out I wasn't the only one seeing some chest tonight, then. But, in the case of my chest, it was a lot less sexy than yours."

"What? Less sexy? I can't think of a single thing that's sexier than you," Erin said.

That provoked an eye roll. Isabella began to button up. "My shirt's undone because I was breastfeeding, and I'm too tired to dress myself properly these days. Not particularly seductive."

"Why don't you let me be the judge of that? And considering what you just did to my crotch, I think the verdict's in: you're frickin' hot, Isabella."

Her hands stilled, Isabella looked up at the camera, slowly and deliberately. Her tiredness and solemnity were suddenly replaced with something…else.

"What exactly did I do to your crotch, Miss Black?"

There it was. The seduction voice. *Man, just that's enough to make me catch on goddamn fire.*

"Well, um, you know. Certain bits of it are getting wet, certain bits are hardening, and all of it generally is gettin' warm and puffy."

Isabella quirked an eyebrow and asked, "Puffy?"

"Uh, well, swollen is such an unsexy word." Erin knew she must be blushing like mad.

"Does that mean you want me to stop buttoning up this shirt?"

"Yeah. In fact, I vote for unbuttoning it completely," Erin hastened to say.

Isabella scowled a little. "I'm afraid nursing bras are aren't exactly Victoria's Secret material."

Erin tried to catch Isabella's gaze. "If the ugliest bra in the world was filled with you, then it would be Victoria's Secret material to me. I'm not looking for a perfect underwear model. I'm looking for a real woman who takes my breath away, y'know? You breastfeeding and being a mother isn't going to turn me off. I get it if you're not feeling very sexy, but please trust me when I say you are sexy as hell to me. I'd love to see you undressed. If the nursing bra bothers you, just whip it off," Erin said, making sure to add a flirty smirk.

Isabella winked at Erin. That wink was just as sexy as the cleavage. With determined hands, Isabella Martinez undid her shirt and took it off. She made a point of not looking away or looking bashful as she looked into the camera, but Erin could see she was uncomfortable.

"Whoa. Look at you. God, I want to touch you so bad," Erin said in complete, awestruck honesty. Isabella was a total knockout, and Erin's panties were suffering for it. She was astonished that Isabella thought she couldn't be sexually attractive.

"Thank you, *preciosa*," Isabella replied quietly. She looked away from the screen, her eyes glazed over. There was a moment before she continued speaking. "You know, it's strange. My mother taught me to use my body as a weapon and a distraction to get my way. It was only when I was in my late twenties that I realized how sad that idea was. I started to use my sexuality only for what I wanted and my mind for the rest. But pregnancy brought on a lot of changes. All of a sudden, my body felt like it was for creating life and feeding Alberto and no longer for…my own pleasure."

"Is that one of the reasons why you haven't touched yourself in all this time?"

Isabella looked away from the screen, contemplating the wall next to her. She turned back to reply. "I suppose so, yes. I haven't seen myself as a sexual being."

"And how do you feel now that I'm looking at you and wanting you so much? Does that make a difference?"

"It feels...strange. In a good way, of course. I still feel unattractive, but there's a part of me that recognizes the power and thrill of arousing someone. And that part wants to take this further," Isabella said in oddly dark tones.

"Well, I'm happy either way. If this is as far as you are comfortable going, that's fine. If you want to go further, then I'm certainly not going to complain. Just know that I have no expectations here. I just want to be with you in any way I can," Erin said earnestly.

Isabella stared right at the screen, making eye contact over the camera connection, and suddenly, Erin realized the huge responsibility she was taking on. If she said or did the wrong thing, she could make Isabella's sexuality retreat again, which obviously wouldn't be a negative thing if Isabella had been happy that way. However, looking into Isabella's eyes now, Erin doubted that was the case. She forced herself not to shrink under the responsibility. She made herself maintain the intense eye contact, putting every ounce of her reassurance and affection into her gaze.

After what felt like an age, Isabella stood up and slowly began to unbutton her black slacks. Erin found it hard to breathe as the button was undone and the zip pulled down. This was so much bigger than Isabella undressing. It was scary, incredible, and almost painfully sexy.

Erin focused completely on Isabella, who slowly pulled her trousers down and bent to take them off completely. Her panties matched her bra, and Erin marveled at her elegance. Isabella was so much of an adult that she apparently matched her underwear and shaved her legs, even if no one was going to see either. Erin could probably count on one hand the number of times she'd done that.

Isabella took her socks off and backed away so that Erin could see her full figure.

Erin groaned. "Christ, woman. Could you stop being so perfect? You're making me feel bad about myself."

Isabella laughed, and some of the tension drained from her body. "You're just lucky it's dimly lit in here. Otherwise you'd see every wrinkle, blemish, and stretch mark.

At the sight of the slender but curvaceous body on her screen, clad in only panties and bra, Erin sighed happily. "I hope to do just that one day. I want to see it all up close. Preferably with the aid of my tongue."

Isabella hummed. "Have eyes on your tongue do you, *preciosa*?"

"Play your cards right, and you'll know everything about my tongue one day."

That sexy eyebrow quirked. "I'm almost naked on camera for you. Does that constitute playing my cards right?"

"Fuck yes," Erin mumbled, as her eyes trailed down Isabella's body once more. "Not to be rude, but I'm impressed you kept your hands off that body of yours for all these months. It's irresistible. *You* are irresistible."

"Not to me." Isabella put her hands on her hips.

"Are you sure? Maybe you just forgot how good that skin of yours feels."

"This skin?" Isabella let her hands travel over her hips onto her lower stomach. Her fingers brushed over the edge of her panties, and Erin forgot to breathe for a second.

"Hell, yeah," Erin said with a moan. Her heart was racing, and she kept licking her lips—her usual nervous tick.

While she seemed to thrive on the appreciation, Isabella still appeared a little unsure. It didn't stop her, though. Her hands moved over the length of her stomach and up to her breasts. When her fingers moved over that clasp at the front of her bra, Erin gasped, certain Isabella was going to undo it and let her breasts spill out. She was wrong. Instead, Isabella slowly caressed them and moved on to her collarbones and shoulders.

Erin admired those slim, long fingers in motion, and imagined them on her own flesh. They looked warm, although Erin had no idea why her brain assumed that. She resolved to stick to what she could actually see; the web of slightly protruding veins on the back of Isabella's elegant hands snagged her attention. She wanted to trace them with her tongue.

"I love your hands," she said in a breathy voice.

"To be quite honest, at the moment, I'm enjoying them too," Isabella admitted, equally breathy. They roamed back over her breasts and stomach until they reached the edge of the panties.

"Are you watching?" Isabella asked quietly.

"You know I am," Erin replied in the same muted voice.

There was a beauty to the moment. They both spoke softly, as though afraid that the moment was fleeting and fragile and could be plucked away from them in a heartbeat. They both seemed to ache for it to continue.

Isabella's right hand moved down over the panties until it rested between her thighs, cupping her sex in a careful hold. Erin shivered. She felt fevered and strange, like there was too much emotion mixed into her arousal. It was like nothing she had ever felt before. There was an intimacy that went so very deep and a connection she couldn't understand or explain.

She saw Isabella's grip tighten, squeezing her sex through the panties.

"Is it warm? I-I mean, I'm sure it is, but is it warmer than the rest of you?" Erin stuttered, aware of how inadequate the words were to express what she felt. They were clumsy and simplistic, and everything sounded wrong.

"I know what you mean, *preciosa*. Don't worry, I know. And, yes, it's warm, and I can feel dampness through my underwear. I'm not surprised. I knew I was wet."

"Does it feel good?"

"Yes," Isabella replied in a quiet but strangled voice.

Erin licked her lips nervously and cleared her throat before daring to speak. "Wanna move your hand a little? Massage it a bit?"

"Is that what you would do if you were here?"

"If I was there, I would've asked to take your underwear off quite a while ago," Erin answered honestly.

Isabella gave a soft little moan as she breathed in, and the sound made Erin's body respond instantly. "This…feels so good," Isabella whispered.

"What feels so good?" Erin asked. "What you have in your hand or what we are doing?"

"Both. What are we doing, Erin?"

"Whatever we want. Whatever you want. I want to make you feel good. I want you to feel as beautiful as you are. And I want to touch you. God, I want to touch you so bad. Even if it's just a hug, I want to feel you."

"Right now, I'd let you do a lot more than hug me," Isabella said throatily.

Without even touching herself, Erin felt her wetness seep into her panties and hoped the fabric under Isabella's hand was drenched.

There was some sort of padding in Isabella's bra, so she couldn't tell if her nipples were hard, but her own were. That was rare for her. Usually only cold affected her nipples.

Isabella's left hand was just resting on her lower stomach, as if nervously guarding one of her softest bits. Erin watched that hand, the innocent hand. She wanted it to be naughty too. She wanted all of Isabella to be engaged in this, nothing holding back or feeling unsafe. But that could only be achieved if Isabella was comfortable.

"Are you okay, babe? Is this all right?" Erin asked softly.

Isabella nodded slowly.

Erin let go of her last mental filters and said exactly what was on her mind; it was a way to be as vulnerable as Isabella. "Good. You're so beautiful, so exquisite. I feel like I'm looking at a piece of art or some genius piece of machinery. Does that sound weird?"

Isabella gave a quiet chuckle. "The last part sounded a bit…unorthodox. Machinery?"

"Well, not like in a factory. More like an expensive engine or one of those old clocks. You know, one of those that when you open it up, there are all these little perfect and intricate gears doing something you don't understand but all playing a necessary part. All working together to control and explain something as big as time. There's a kinda beauty in that, a beauty I could never wrap my brain around. You feel like that to me: something so perfect and advanced and so, so beautiful. I'm humbled by you. I'll never understand it, but I'll appreciate it anyway. I don't know, I can't explain what I feel."

"I think you just did, *preciosa*. I'm very flattered. In fact, it might be one of the most beautiful compliments I've ever been given," Isabella said with a smile.

Erin wanted to offer to take her clothes off too, to make Isabella feel less exposed and alone in this. But somehow, that felt like the wrong thing to do. It would make this about her and her sexuality when it needed to be about Isabella and how she felt about her body.

Her thoughts were soon abandoned, as she saw Isabella's left hand move from her stomach. It wasn't going to her breast, as Erin had expected. It was heading down to join her right hand but slid under the panties and down underneath the right hand.

Isabella's chest expanded in a big intake of breath, as her hand touched her naked sex. Erin checked her expression, as much to make sure she was okay with this as to see what effect her touch had on her. Isabella's eyes were glazed and wide in the shadows of the badly lit room. She bit her lower lip. and Erin desperately wished she was the one biting it.

"How does it feel without the panties?" Erin managed to ask.

"Hotter, wetter, needier," Isabella replied in a low, hoarse voice.

Erin couldn't help but groan. "If we don't stop this soon, I'm going to have to touch myself. You are so fucking sexy, Isabella. I can't stand it."

"Take your clothes off, and do it. I want you to do this with me. Just go slowly, okay? I'm still not quite..."

"Comfortable?" Erin suggested

Isabella shook her head. "No, I'm comfortable. You make me feel very safe. No, I'm just not sure if this is the right thing to do. We haven't even known each other for two months yet, we're not dating, and my son is sleeping in the next room. Should I be doing this?"

"Does it feel good?"

"Of course," Isabella replied. She proved it by moving the hands between her legs, caressing herself almost clumsily both from the inside and outside of her panties.

Erin swallowed hard and undid her shirt for the second time that night. As she undressed, she asked, "And does it feel right?"

"Yes."

"Then I think it's right. You deserve this, and if you want it, you should have it. It's your body, enjoy it."

"I think I am enjoying you watching me more than the actual touching," Isabella admitted.

Erin smiled. "Well, tonight, my arousal belongs to you, so go ahead and enjoy that as well, babe."

Isabella smiled back, and then her gaze traveled down to Erin's chest as Erin removed her bra. The chilly air of her apartment hit her naked skin, but that wasn't the reason why her nipples were hard enough to cut glass.

"Mmm, look at you," Isabella whispered reverently. Then she chuckled and looked down at the floor.

Erin, who was taking off her jeans, frowned at her screen. "What's so funny?"

"Oh, nothing you did, *preciosa*. Looking at your breasts, I remembered a line I read once in an awful book I borrowed from Marie. A woman's breast was described as 'rose-tinted tips on pale, cream skin.' That overly flowery line just popped into my head when I saw your breasts. Which are very pretty, by the way."

This little reprieve from the tense, reverent feel of the moment was nice. To be able to relax and laugh a little was important. "Ha! Well, I'm glad you think they are pretty and yeah, my skin's pale all right," Erin said. "I don't know about the cream or the rose, though. It's just my skin and my boobs. I've never really thought about the color scheme."

Isabella snickered, and Erin felt proud that she could make Isabella so comfortable again. The sense of reverence, of intimacy, was still there, but they were both easing into it now, getting more comfortable. At least, that's how it seemed to Erin.

She took her socks and panties off and then stood entirely naked in front of her laptop. It wasn't the first time she'd been naked in front of a web cam, but it was the first time it felt so significant. Isabella's gaze roamed shamelessly over her body, taking it all in. Erin felt as if that gaze was touching her, caressing and exploring. Almost.

Isabella gasped softly. "How can you be real? You're so slim and yet so sculpted. It's like someone made you out of clay and shaped every curve and muscle perfectly."

Erin looked down at her body. Yeah, she took care of it, but that was almost a side effect of doing exercise which kept her healthy and made her feel good. It was also part of the job, and she'd forgotten just how much it could impress women, especially a woman who was into muscles. Looking up at her screen and seeing Isabella's ravenous looks, she felt proud of her body. She also felt like screaming in frustration.

"Jesus, Isabella! This is not fair. I want to fuck you so much I can barely breathe. Why are you not here?"

Isabella smiled at her again. "I could ask you the same thing."

"I could be there, you know, I'm sure there's a train sometime soon. It can't take more than a few hours, right? I could be touching you tonight."

The smile faltered. "I, um, I don't think that would be a good idea."

Erin froze. "Shit. Was that too much? It was. I went too far too fast."

"No, it's nothing you did. I was thinking the exact same thing. And that's what made me pause. I just... I'm not sure about this. I've never been with a woman, I just came out of a relationship, and I'm not sure what I'm doing. This just got a little too real, too fast," Isabella said apologetically.

She took her hands away from her crotch and crossed them over her chest like a shield, her eyes flitting back and forth from the screen almost in fear and shame.

"I'm sorry. I shouldn't have broken the spell by talking about meeting up. We don't have to. We can just keep talking like this," Erin assured her.

"No. I really do want to meet up, just...not to have sex right away. I think I might have pushed myself a little too quickly here."

Internally cursing herself, Erin ran her hand over her face. "Nah, I was racing along, because I wanted you to feel good and to know how much I want you. Then my libido kicked in, and I just wanted more of you. I should have realized this was too much."

"Would you stop being so wonderfully considerate?" Isabella said with a smile. "You've been nothing but thoughtful, supportive, and kind. I can't thank you enough for helping me ease back into seeing myself as a sexual creature. Tonight's been sweet and sexy. But I think I need us to try being more platonic for a little while, take it in small steps like you suggested."

"Of course. Whatever you need."

"Thank you for being so understanding, and I'm sorry I teased you. By the way, this means I'm going to need you to put that sexy body back in some clothes."

Erin started to put her jeans on and noticed that she hadn't shaved her legs nor trimmed her pubic hair for a few days. She was mortified.

"Crap, I'd forgotten that I hadn't shaved. I hope that didn't freak you out."

"Don't apologize. I wasn't measuring your amount of body hair; I was too busy enjoying your body."

Isabella paused to reach down and put her socks on and then continued, unfazed. "I'm always neatly shaved, because I don't like the way hair on my body feels under my clothes. I never expected my boyfriends to shave, so why should I expect you to?"

Two things hit Erin, one was that Isabella was nicely enlightened. The second was a much sexier implication. She put her bra on and watched Isabella button her shirt. "So, um, does that mean that you shave *everywhere*?"

Isabella was bent over, stepping into her trousers, and looked up at the screen with a suggestive glance and a smirk. She said nothing, and somehow that was so damn sexy to Erin. She didn't know if that silence meant "I'm too much of a lady to tell you, you'll have to find out for yourself," or if it was Isabella's way of saying yes. Either way, Erin's clit throbbed a little to remind her that her body still needed release—and that it really, really liked Isabella.

Buttoning up her slacks, Isabella said, "So, you're still okay with meeting up soon? Even though nothing sexual would happen?"

"Of course, I am! I was desperate to meet up with you long before you took your clothes off. You know that. I just want to get to know you better and be a part of your life. Everything else can happen in its own time."

Isabella's eyes twinkled happily. "I'm so glad to hear it. How about we meet up earlier than planned? I can't wait, and I'm guessing you don't want to either. How about this weekend?"

Erin thought about it. Tomorrow was Friday, so that would give her some time to figure out the cheapest way to get to Philly and to figure out what the hell to wear.

"Yeah, that sounds good. Can we make it Saturday? I don't want to wait until Sunday."

Isabella made an amused sound in the back of her throat. "Neither do I. Lunch on Saturday? Or perhaps dinner, if you want to come a little later?"

"Hmm," Erin said. "It kind of depends on what mode of transportation I can get. I might not have much choice with times. Can I get back to you about that?"

When Isabella smoothed her thick, sable-colored hair and let it fall over her collar again, Erin thought she might swallow her own tongue.

"Of course," Isabella continued. "We'll discuss the arrangements tomorrow." Isabella paused. "Well, I think I might go have a shower now, preferably a cold one."

Erin hesitated. It was perhaps a bit forward to say what was on her mind right now, but it was important too that Isabella hear it, loud and clear. "You know, if you decide against having a cold shower and choose to have a hot one that includes some touching, that's okay. You know that, right?"

Isabella smiled enigmatically. "Yes. I'll let you know what kind of shower it turns out to be tomorrow."

"That doesn't sound very platonic." Erin smirked at her. "But it does sound great. I'd like to know."

"Then you will. What about you? Are you going to…?"

Erin grinned, unable to keep from pushing it. "Let's just say I'm glad I dusted off my sex toys."

"My, you really don't mind being honest, do you? You're incorrigible," Isabella said. "Well, enjoy your toys, and I hope you get to sleep tonight when you are done."

"Oh, I've got a feeling I'll pretty much keep going until I pass out."

"Erin!"

"What? It's true. Anyway, good night, beautiful. Thank you for trusting me and letting me see you."

"Thank you for being so sweet. I appreciate it more than you will ever know. Speak to you tomorrow, *preciosa*. Good night." With that, Isabella clicked her mouse and hung up their call.

Erin took a deep breath and exhaled, "god*damn*."

She looked over at the bedside table and knew exactly which drawer she was going to open. Striding over, she was already undoing her shirt for the third time that evening. Erin smiled. *I bet I'm getting a deep sleep tonight.*

Chapter 11

Talking it through

ISABELLA STARTED THE DAY WITH a crushing headache. The situation with Erin had all become so real, and her anxiety wasn't helped by the fact that they would meet tomorrow.

She kept picking up her phone without knowing why, checking her empty inbox, and looking at old texts. She wasn't looking for a message from Erin. She knew Erin had started work an hour ago. She was just restless.

They'd exchanged their usual morning texts, where Isabella had briefly explained that she'd not touched herself last night.

Touching myself was basically all I did last night, was Erin's reply. Isabella just shook her head at the phone with muted delight. They wished each other a wonderful day, and Erin told her she would call when she finished work.

Isabella had planned her day fully. Grocery shopping to fill the new fridge and freezer went to plan. But between the headache and her incessant phone checking, writing before lunch wasn't getting done.

Alberto lay in the baby gym her parents had given him. He seemed mesmerized by a bright-yellow and red butterfly to his left. Isabella sat down on the floor next to the gym and tapped the butterfly, making it sway above him. He tried to follow its movements and waved his hands and arms at great speed.

"That's it, *cariño*. Now try to reach for it," she encouraged.

They played for a while, but Isabella was very aware of the open document and her abandoned manuscript. After a while, she found herself reaching for her phone again. She cursed herself and fought the urge to throw the phone at the wall in frustration. Instead, she took a deep breath and dialed a number. She heard three rings before there was a reply.

"Isabella!" Marie exclaimed.

The familiar enthusiasm and the adoration in Marie's voice was enough to dampen some of Isabella's frustration. Familiarity—even an annoying one—was such a comfort.

"Hello. I hope I'm not disturbing you?"

"No, no, no. I've been wanting to talk to you forever. I'm supposed to be rehearsing my speech for tomorrow, but I know most of it by heart already," Marie replied.

Isabella rolled her eyes. Marie was a corporate motivational speaker who went to workplaces and held seminars on how optimism and positive energy could increase your energy and work output.

Once, Isabella had hosted a forum for her office staff. She'd almost thrown up when Marie bellowed, "Self-confidence will perk you up more than coffee ever could." She'd never asked Marie to come back.

"Okay. Well, if you are sure."

"Of course I'm sure, Isabella. How is it being back in Philadelphia?"

"Good, so far. I'm enjoying my own space, tiny as it may be."

"Glad to hear it. So, are you going to tell me why you called? I know you weren't just wanting to check in with me, because you never do. What's up, buttercup?"

With a deep sigh, Isabella wondered if this was a good idea. "I think I might be in love," she muttered.

"Yay!"

Isabella sighed and added, "But I don't think I'm ready for it."

"Less yay."

"The person in question has agreed to take it slow and just be friends until I'm ready."

"Yay!"

"But I think I'm very likely going to sleep with them soon, and that might ruin it."

"Ah, a little less yay."

"Marie?"

"Yes?"

"Don't use the word yay for the remainder of this conversation."

Marie laughed. "Okay, I won't. Well, I'm sure you won't ruin the opportunity by having sex. Nor by waiting. Nor by rushing into a relationship. If it's meant to be, it'll work out. And if not, well, you can just break up again. Don't overthink. Just go forward with a positive mindset, and everything will work out one way or another."

There was an annoyed crease on Isabella's forehead now; she was sure of it. "Did you just suggest I enter into a sexual relationship with someone using a positive mindset?"

"Certainly. Even sex can be improved if you just have the right mindset."

Isabella lost patience. "Oh, screw your mindset. I've got a headache, and my brain feels like it's stuffed with so many worries and possible scenarios that I can't think straight. I'm supposed to be writing this morning and then spending the afternoon moving the furniture around and picking out where I want some of my paintings. But I seem to be utterly incapable of focusing."

"Okay, this is serious. Tell me what's going on."

Isabella did. Without mentioning Erin's name or using female pronouns, she told Marie everything. About the role Erin had played in opening her eyes to how unhappy she was back in Florida. About Erin's patience and support. Finally, Isabella explained about them meeting up soon.

"Oh, that's so good to hear. I am thrilled you're turning over a new leaf. I always worried about you being with Richard—he never made you happy. Love should make you glow, and you never glowed."

"Well, I'm sorry if I didn't *sparkle* enough for you to have faith in my relationship."

"Oh, shush. You know what I meant. Anyway, I'm glad you're moving on. And I'm glad you found someone who helped wake you up and who supports you, someone whose energy aligns with yours."

Isabella tried to not roll her eyes, since that would make the ache behind her temples worse. "Thank you."

"So, are you buzzing with excitement over meeting this knight in shining armor face-to-face?" Marie asked.

In her head, Isabella could see the romantic twinkle in Marie's eyes. That wasn't helping her headache either.

"I'm looking forward to it, yes. I'm also..." She stopped, hating to admit weakness. "I'm also terrified of what might happen."

"What might happen? Do you mean being late?"

"No, you imbecile."

"Isabella, what have we said about name-calling?" Marie asked in a singsong voice.

"What have we said about speaking to me as if I were a misbehaving child?"

"Fine, let's just move on. Explain what you mean."

Isabella took a deep breath. "What if we don't know what to say when we are face-to-face? What if it's uncomfortable and quiet? You know I'm horrible at small talk. I'll just say something controversial to get the conversation started, and then we'll end up fighting."

"It won't come to that. You clearly have a lot to talk about. Just don't let nerves stop you from continuing that trend. And if against all odds it does end up being dreadful, text me. I'll call you and pretend I need you for an emergency."

"That's...actually a good idea."

"I know. I have them all the time. It comes with the job. But that wasn't your only worry about the date, was it?"

"Don't call it a date, please. That sounds so official and...puts too much pressure on me. I don't know if that is exactly what it is," Isabella muttered.

"It is."

Isabella's headache took the leap from thrumming to outright throbbing. "Oh, stop being such an intolerable know-it-all."

Marie just laughed. "Fine. Answer the question, honey pie."

"*Honey pie?* Really?"

Marie sighed. "Answer the question, and stop stalling."

"All right, fine. Don't hurry me along. You know this isn't easy for me."

"I know. At your own speed," Marie replied.

Isabella took a moment, choosing her words. "I'm afraid that it will go too well, and we'll end up...sleeping together."

"Right, you mentioned that before. And that's bad?"

"Yes. It would be bad," Isabella answered slowly. She heard her voice start to sound as if she were talking to someone dumber than a snowplow in summer.

"Why?"

"Because I told you that I'm not ready for the relationship to pick up speed like that, you moron!"

She heard Marie sigh. "*Moron?* Oh my, that's stress talking. I'm going to ignore that."

A vein pulsated in the middle of Isabella's forehead. She rubbed at it and took a few calming breaths. This was why she avoided long conversations with Marie. She avoided long conversations with anyone, really. *Why doesn't Erin annoy me? How does she calm this horrible, impatient part of me?*

"That was out of order," Isabella said. "I'm sorry."

"I know. Getting back to the subject at hand: if you're not ready, then don't have sex. Are you worried that your knight in shining armor will lose control and try to get into your pants?"

She fidgeted with the sleeve of her shirt nervously. "No. The person in question would never do that. In all honesty, I am more worried that *I* will lose control and push things." She stopped her uneasy fingers and looked up at the ceiling, trying to decide how much to say. She'd always hated talking about sex, especially with her little sister. She cringed, there was no other way.

Isabella closed her eyes and blurted out, "You see, last night, I nearly lost control and let my crotch make my decisions instead of my brain. This person does that to me. I just…"

Marie interrupted. "Isabella. Can you please stop doing that?"

Isabella frowned. "Stop doing what?"

"Stop using gender neutral pronouns and saying 'the person in question' instead of this mystery woman's name. Because I assume it's a woman."

"W-why would you say that?"

"Because I've heard you talk about lovers all your life, and you have always said he and used their names. The only reason for you to avoid it now is if the person happens to be a woman," Marie replied casually.

Was she that obvious? "Well…yes…that's very perceptive of you. Okay, fine. It's a woman, and her name is Erin. You can't tell our parents, though. I haven't told them yet."

"Haven't told them about Erin or about being attracted to women?"

"Either."

"Please don't worry about that. Your parents are intelligent and open people. They'll be fine."

Isabella bit her lip pensively and looked down at her feet. "Are you?"

"What? Fine with it? Of course I am. I actually think you'd work well with a woman. You always get annoyed with your boyfriends' colognes and mansplaining," Marie pointed out.

Relief washed over Isabella. "That's true. I'm still attracted to men, though. I think I'm bisexual."

"Be attracted to anyone you want. I don't care, as long as they treat you well and don't dislike me."

Isabella scoffed. "I dislike you."

"No, you don't. You just try, very hard, to convince yourself you do. It's part of your prickly exterior that hides the sweetness inside."

Isabella muttered something incoherent as a reply and turned to check that Alberto was all right.

"Everything's going to be fine, Isabella. I'm sure of it. And if it isn't, I and your parents will be here to help you clean up the mess. Just please hurry up and tell them about Erin. You know how bad I am at keeping secrets, especially when your mother starts."

Isabella grimaced. "Oh, I'm well aware. I'll tell them. I just want to wait until Erin and I decide that we're officially dating."

"Hmm. It's a bit of a weird situation, isn't it? Deciding that you will date but waiting for this magical point in time when you are ready for it."

"Are you saying I should just start dating her now?" Isabella asked tersely.

"No, no." Marie's voice turned gentler. "Wait until you're ready. Just don't wait for the perfect time, because there is no such thing. Circumstances are never perfect. You just pick a time and roll the dice."

"I know. If I could have controlled the circumstances, I would have waited until Alberto was older to start dating again. But my stupid heart rushed ahead, and now I can only hold off the inevitable for a short while before I let go and fall completely for a damned, blonde personal trainer with a caffeine addiction."

"Count your blessings. I've been dating for ages, and despite my incredibly positive mindset, I just can't seem to find a guy to feel that special spark with. They're all okay, but no one makes my heart race and my brain melt," Marie grumbled.

Isabella looked up at the ceiling and sighed, thinking about how she unraveled and turned into a lovesick mess every time Erin smiled. "Yeah. Well, that can happen at the most unexpected time and with the most unexpected person," she said.

She heard Marie give a surprised squeak. "Oh, I'm afraid I have a call on the other line. I should probably get that since I'm supposed to be working."

"Yes, go ahead. I think we are done here," Isabella said.

"Okay. Good luck tomorrow, sweetie pie. I'm sure it'll be great."

Isabella scoffed. "I'm not. But thank you, Marie. Talking has helped."

"I'm glad to hear it. I have to get that call. Bye."

Only when she had put the phone down and gone back to play with Alberto in his baby gym did Isabella realize that her headache was abating.

It was a little after six, and Isabella had finally managed to get her bookcase where she wanted and find the boxes of books to fill the shelves. She was currently contemplating whether to sort the books randomly or alphabetize them.

The phone rang, and to her great shame, Isabella dropped the scissors on the box and excitedly threw herself at her BlackBerry. She tried to sound calm and unaffected when she answered.

"Hello, *preciosa*."

"Hey you!" Erin said gleefully.

Isabella grinned.

"Okay, so I did some research about tomorrow, during my lunch break. There's three ways I can get to Philly. Fly, take the train, or get a friend with a car to drive me. I ruled out hitchhiking, because I don't want to be killed in the back of a Ford. I think it's too late to get a cheap plane ticket, and I feel bad about asking my friend, Erika, to drive me. So, I think it'll have to be the train. It's not cheap, but it's manageable."

Blood rushed in Isabella's ears. She tried to ignore it. "All right, are the trains cheaper at any point of the day? Alberto and I can be flexible."

"Yeah, obviously the times outside of rush hour are cheaper. Are there any particular times when Alberto needs to eat or sleep or something?"

"No, he's refused every attempt at a steady routine, I'm afraid. How long does the train ride take? I don't want you to have to get up at the crack of dawn."

"It's about two hours, so not too bad. What about meeting for afternoon coffee? That way you don't have to worry about making lunch, and I can sleep late. Unless you want to meet up in the evening?"

Isabella thought about Erin there, in her home, as the evening got dark and chilly and bedtime loomed closer. No, there was no way she'd resist pulling Erin into bed under those circumstances. Her heart was racing already. Why was she so panicked? The answer hit her square in the chest— because it mattered so much. Because Erin mattered so much to her. She needed to get everything just right with Erin. And, she had to admit, she was frightened by the strength of her emotions.

"No, afternoon sounds fine," Isabella finally replied.

Looking around, she wondered if they should really meet in the mess created by opening boxes. Isabella hated her home being in any sort of disarray, and God forbid, it wasn't immaculately clean. It didn't matter if Erin wouldn't mind, Isabella would. Besides, even in the middle of the day, having a bed and Erin so close to each other could be too much of a temptation.

"Perhaps you, me, and Alberto should meet out somewhere? There's a small coffee shop down the road that I saw this morning when I went out to get some groceries. It looked nice and boasted several different coffee roasts. I could, perhaps, get my father to be on standby to come pick up Alberto and babysit if he starts screaming the place down."

"Yeah, sure. They say that the first time you meet with someone you met online, you should meet them in a public place. Not just because they might be a serial killer, but also in case you don't get along, you can just ditch 'em and go home," Erin said.

"Ah. Well, that wasn't the reason for suggesting the coffee shop, but I suppose it makes sense. When did you become so sensible?"

Erin chuckled. "Just something you hear from peeps who regularly date people they meet online."

"I see. Anyway, I suppose I'll text you the name and address of the coffee shop, and you can just let me know when your train arrives."

"It's a deal. But Isabella?"

"Yes?"

"We're still talking on Skype tonight, aren't we? Midnight-coffee date?"

"Certainly. You'll be in trouble if I don't see you on Skype in a few hours," Isabella replied, hearing the joy in her own voice.

"Awesome. Talk soon. Bye, babe."

Isabella hung up and leaned her forehead against her phone, glad that no one saw her acting like a lovesick fool.

If someone had told her, six months ago, that she would enjoy someone addressing her as babe, she'd have given them a level-ten death glare. Erin had changed everything.

Chapter 12

The First Time She Truly Saw Her

ERIN GOT OFF THE TRAIN and entered the main terminal of 30th Street Station. The grandure almost distracted her from her sweaty palms and racing pulse. She was here. In Isabella's city. Unbelievable.

Isabella, with the beauty and elegance of a goddess, would be in her arms. Erin would hold her close within the hour.

She had showered that morning and spritzed on some Adidas, but no preparation could make this day less nerve racking. She swallowed hard and hurried out to hail a taxi.

After she'd paid the driver, Erin stared at the café sign across the street, trying to force her shoulders to relax and her stomach to stop its nervous churning.

Weeks and weeks of waiting to finally meet Isabella in the flesh had all led to this moment of the big reveal. Time for her only chance to make a good first impression. Erin almost forgot to breathe, as she made her feet walk forward.

Through the window, she spotted Isabella sitting at a booth in the chic, yet cozy, café. Erin's first reaction was the same in person as on camera. The woman she had fallen for was incredibly beautiful…and a bit scary. That starkly dark hair, those passionate eyes, those perfect lips with the small scar and dark-red lipstick, and that almost haughty scowl made Isabella look stunning and imposing, like a Greek goddess about to punish her.

Isabella looked down at Alberto, sitting comfortably in his car seat next to her. She smiled at him, and her face lit up as if someone had turned on a light, warming her from within. Everything that had been unattainable and intimidating about her features became warm and inviting. Erin had an overwhelming need to rush in and kiss her. She stopped herself. Just. She took a deep breath and walked slowly toward the table, her heart beating so hard it felt like it was trying to fight its way out of her ribcage. *Am I blushing already? God, I hope not.*

When Isabella spotted her, her face froze in an anxious look. Erin smiled, hoping it would calm them both. The smile she got back from Isabella eased Erin's panic, leaving only minor nerves and great excitement in its wake.

She put her bag on the floor next to the booth, then tucked her hands into her back pockets to keep them from shaking. Her smile felt like it would never go away, as she looked into those warm, intense eyes and simply said, "Hi."

"Hello," Isabella replied in a low, almost shocked-sounding voice. She moved Alberto's portable car seat to the side and got out of the booth. She stood right in front of Erin and seemed unsure what to do next.

Erin noticed that they were almost the same height, due to Isabella's high heels and her own flat sneakers. Her need to break the tension and feel Isabella in her arms kicked in. She lunged forward and pulled Isabella in.

The woman was clearly caught off guard, and Erin heard a little puff of breath as the impact of their bodies knocked the air out of Isabella's lungs.

"Oh God, sorry," Erin said and gave her room to breathe.

But she didn't get far before Isabella caught her by the arms and pulled her back. The hug started over, and Erin allowed herself to lean in and sniff Isabella's hair. In her nervous state, her brain didn't register the smell. But she didn't dare to repeat the gesture and make Isabella think she was some sort of sniffing freak. Still, she did notice that Isabella's body fit perfectly against her own. Erin had a feeling that they'd fit together even better when they weren't so tense. She was acutely aware of Isabella's hands on her. She wanted them to move, to caress her, to make her feel safe. Her heart was racing, and she wondered if Isabella could feel it.

The embrace lasted a little too long, and after a while, it started to feel awkward. Erin backed off. "So, um, it's really great to finally see you."

She felt like an idiot. She'd seen Isabella plenty of times on Skype. She was about to amend the statement when Isabella spoke.

"Yes, it is. And slightly surreal, I must say."

"I know, right? I suddenly feel like we're strangers, but at the same time, I know you really well. Mostly…I'm just so damn happy to be close to you. God, I'm so impressed with other couples who do long distance for like a year or something before meeting up. I think I'd explode."

Isabella smirked and looked less tense for a moment. "Did you just say 'other couples,' *preciosa*?"

Erin's heart skipped a beat, and she felt blood rushing to her cheeks. *What the hell is wrong with me? I can't blow this right off the bat.*

"Shit! I didn't mean we're a couple. I mean, other people who, um, happen to be couples."

"I know what you meant, Erin. It's okay. Sit down. Unless you want to go order us some coffee while I stay here with Alberto? I saved up my morning coffee ration to have some now, and I'm starting to feel the withdrawal symptoms."

Erin dried off her clammy palms on the back of her jeans. "Sure. What do you want?"

"Regular, black coffee. Dark roast, if they ask."

"Sure. Mind if I have cake or something? I'm feeling kinda peckish."

Isabella moved Alberto and sat down. "Of course not."

Erin stood in the line to order their drinks and decided on a flapjack to have with her coffee. It was impossible not to fidget as she waited, and she soon found herself touching her hair to check that the train ride hadn't flattened the curls she had worked so hard on that morning.

When she reached the barista, she was regaled with the full menu of origins and roasts, but Erin was too frazzled with nerves to remember more than scattered words like Arabica, low acidity, and something about nuts. She simply ordered two black, dark roast coffees. It was only when the barista turned that she remembered to ask for a flapjack too. She had to get her head in the game.

Balancing their order on a tray, she had a terrible vision of getting to the booth and dropping everything and burning Isabella and Alberto with steaming coffee. Erin bit her lip and made herself focus.

"Ah, there we go. Coffee at last." Isabella stared at the mug Erin placed before her.

Erin sat down and tucked into her flapjack, while Isabella blew on her steaming hot coffee. After a while, Erin asked, "So, how did the move go?"

"Surprisingly well. In fact, this might be my first move without any minor disasters."

Isabella took a sip, her lips leaving dark-red marks on the white mug. Erin was mesmerized. Nerves made her lick her own lips, and she tasted the chemical flavor of her Chapstick.

Stop staring at her mouth, Black! Chill.

"That's good. You guys settling in okay?"

Isabella nodded as she put the mug down. "So far, so good, yes. The neighbors seem quiet, which is always a relief."

"Yeah, I know what you mean."

There was a long, uncomfortable moment of silence, while Isabella sat rigidly with an unreadable look on her face. "How was your train ride?" she finally asked.

"Uh, fine. The worn seats were surprisingly comfy and I had great views out of a dirty window. I love seeing cities rush past and trying to guess who lives in all those houses."

Erin's nerves were growing. Something was wrong. She could feel it. She'd worried that Isabella would find her boring, but boredom wasn't the vibe she was getting, neither was normal nervousness. Was she imagining the weird mood?

The minutes ticked along, and Erin focused on eating her snack. As she ate, Erin furtively glanced at Isabella, who was definitely uncomfortable. Stress was clearly evident in her body language. Chewing and swallowing a bite of the flapjack, Erin considered how she could make Isabella relax.

"Hey, Martinez. Are you okay? Is this a bit too much too soon, or something?"

Isabella looked up, almost startled. "What? No, I'm fine."

"Come on, I can tell you're uncomfortable. Talk to me. Tell me how I can help."

"Seeing right through me, huh? Does this mean that dating a woman is going to make it impossible for me to hide my emotions?" Isabella said with a forced smile.

"No, not necessarily. I don't know if women are always better at emotions, but I'm not too bad, if I say so myself. And with you, well, I can tell when you're putting up a front. Oh—and right now, I know you're trying to change the subject."

Isabella shifted in her seat, and her brows knitted. "I...well, I suppose I'm just not sure how to behave. I've been very different with you compared to the way I am normally. Talking to you online, I've been more open and honest. More *vulnerable*, I suppose. Less prickly and sarcastic than normal too. Now we're meeting in real life, and I feel very self-conscious."

Erin put her fork down and shrugged. "Well...that right there was pretty honest and open. Listen, don't worry about it. I like you, even when you *are* sarcastic. I know it's the dumbest cliché ever, but please, just be yourself."

Isabella's smile still looked forced. "Clichés become clichés because there's a lot of truth to them. I'm just not sure how to 'be myself' right now. That's the issue."

At the sound of Alberto's coo, Isabella reached over to play with his foot, adjusting her son's little sock, which was sliding down a bit.

Is she avoiding my gaze on purpose? Erin took a sip of her coffee. She wanted Isabella as calm and happy with her up close and personal as she was online. Erin put the cup down and looked at the salt and pepper shakers next to her.

"I just thought of something. I never told you about how I used to think New Yorkers were crazy, did I?"

Isabella furrowed her brow. "No, I think I would have remembered that."

Erin chuckled. "Okay, long story time. You ready?"

Isabella rolled her hand for Erin to continue.

"I was twenty-two, and I'd moved around a lot, not really feeling at home anywhere. I guess it's hard to put down roots when you don't learn how to as a kid. My friend, Julian, who I met at a group home when I was about fourteen, told me I'd like New York. So I went. In this diner, in Queens, he introduced me to his roommate, Susan. Then he just took off, saying he had to go get something. That's typical Julian behavior, so I didn't worry about it."

Erin took another sip of her coffee. "Anyway, Susan was a bottle blonde in her late twenties and seemed pretty normal at first. She was looking for a new roomie, because Julian was moving out. Without my knowledge, this had become an interview for roommate candidates. Anyway, at one point, this woman poured a bunch of salt on the table and drew a heart with her finger. She pointed at it and asked me what I thought it was. I answered that it looked like a heart, and she—get this—she reached over and slapped my forehead. Hard. She said I was brainwashed by rom-coms."

Isabella had a puzzled look and laughed with the air of someone barely believing what she was hearing. She also seemed more at ease, so Erin forged on.

"I sorta rubbed at my forehead and decided I was not living with this woman, but I stayed polite. I asked her what it was actually meant to be, if not a heart. She said it was a symbol of how love—in the symbol of that heart—looks sweet and sugary, but if you get a real taste, it's salty and really bad for you."

Holding up her hand to stop Isabella from saying what they were both thinking, Erin said, "I know, sort of true, but mainly crazypants. Anyway, she kept talking about how her roommate couldn't burn incense, wake up earlier than eight thirty, or have any stuffed toys. I just nodded along and got the hell outta there as soon as I could. I actually had a bruise the next day. Can you believe that?"

With an amazed chuckle, Isabella's gaze focused on Erin. Her hand rested on Alberto's, who was focusing hard on the task of trying to grab at her fingers. Erin took another sip of her coffee and carried on.

"Despite this kinda scary start, I moved to New York and lived with this awesome guy called Rashan that my friend Luke was dating at the time. After a little while, Luke and Rashan convinced me to go out on a date with a woman they'd met at a club. So we went out for drinks. A little into the date, this chick asks the bartender for salt. When she gets handed the shaker, she pours salt on the bar, makes a heart in it, then asks what I think it is."

Isabella's eyebrows shot up her forehead. "You're kidding?"

"Nope. I was freaking out, thinking that either all New Yorkers are crazy, or this is some kind of cultural reference from a TV show."

"Well, what did you say?"

Erin shrugged. "Hoping for the best, I very hesitantly answered that it looked like a heart. She shouted 'Wrong,' then leaned over and slapped my forehead. She hit a lot gentler than Susan did, but still! Then she looked at my horrified face and started laughing. It turned out that Julian had told Luke what happened with Susan, and he'd asked my date to recreate that scene to mess with me."

Chuckling again, Isabella took a sip of her coffee before answering. "What did you do? On your date, I mean?"

Erin gave another shrug. "I laughed, and then we continued chatting and having drinks. I think she took me back to her place afterward, but I can't really remember. The heart thing was kinda the most memorable event of the evening."

"Well, I suppose the sex couldn't have been that great then," Isabella said with a wink.

Erin's face burned, and she smiled slightly. "No. Guess not."

Isabella smiled back. "I'm glad the joke didn't scare you off your beloved New York, nor dating."

"Oh, I don't know. If it had scared me off dating, I might not have ended up with Katie." Erin stopped and was quiet for a second before adding, "Actually, that's not fair. I have lots of great memories from that relationship, and I learned a lot. I wouldn't want to wish that away."

"But there *are* things you would want to wish away? How she left you, perhaps?" Isabella asked.

"Yeah." Erin sighed. "That. And what it did to me."

"Do you mean the fact that it made you reluctant to get into a relationship again?"

"Mm, that and you know…" Erin paused, unsure if she was ready to talk about this. Especially on their first, in-person date.

Isabella leaned forward and took her hand away from Alberto's torso to rest it on top of Erin's hand. Erin looked up and saw warmth and understanding in Isabella's eyes. She pushed herself to keep talking.

"…and that it messed with my sleep," Erin finally admitted.

Isabella's frown quickly turned to understanding. "Oh. That's when your insomnia started up again?"

Keep it together. Erin swallowed thickly. She focused on her hands, one warm because it was holding the coffee mug, the other warm because it was safely tucked under Isabella's. Erin took a sip of her coffee to give herself time to calm down. "Yeah."

Pensively, Isabella looked down at the table. They were both quiet for a while. Isabella didn't move her hand; it lay on top of Erin's, warm and somehow steadying.

"I wonder if your insomnia might not simply be about abandonment. I'm not a psychiatrist, but if it started when you were a child in foster care, unable to make roots, as you say, and came back when Katie left you… Could it be that you hate sleeping because you worry that when you wake up…" Isabella seemed to be looking for the right words. "…you'll be alone and feel unwanted?"

Tears crowded in Erin's eyes, and her vision went blurry.

Isabella gasped. "Oh, Erin, I'm sorry. Look at me just going on about this, even though we said we'd take that slowly and talk about it gradually. I just…came up with what I thought could be the solution and had to blurt it out. I'm so terribly sorry."

Clearing her throat, Erin answered, "No, don't apologize. Yeah, it's probably about abandonment. That and feeling that I'm not good enough. That's why people leave. Sometimes when I sleep, I wake up with this really strong dislike for myself. Like every thought and feeling I have is wrong and annoying."

Isabella looked at her searchingly. "You know that other people don't think that about you, right?"

Erin gave a reluctant nod. "Sometimes, yeah. At the same time, I know I'm not great at making friends or keeping them. Sometimes, I think the few friends I have just stick around because they pity me." The last words almost stuck in her throat, and broke her voice when they came out. She blinked rapidly, trying not to let the tears fall. She could only hope that her mascara wasn't smudging. "I'm sorry, this self-pity and whining can't be very appealing. We shouldn't be going into this emotional shit right now," she croaked.

"Erin, I just came out of a relationship with a man who wouldn't communicate with me. The fact that we can talk like this and that you just…let me look right into your soul is a miracle to me."

Erin sniffed and cleared her throat again, trying to get a hold of herself. "You're not calling me Miss Black anymore."

"No, it didn't seem appropriate right now. That moniker is more a jokey thing, not as intimate as your first name."

"I think I'd like to go back to jokey and take a break from intimate right now. I really don't want to start crying in public," Erin mumbled.

Isabella nodded. "Of course. I have to say, though, you're unfairly cute when upset, Miss Black. May I give you a hug?"

Erin didn't answer. She just jumped up from her seat and held her arms out. Isabella laughed and stood up to embrace her.

The hug was a lot less tense than their first one but lasted even longer. This time, Erin took her time and savored the complex scent of Isabella— spicy and sensual. Erin took deep, delicious breaths, filling her nose and lungs with the mix of Isabella's natural fragrance and whatever designer perfume she was wearing. Isabella's arms circled her, and she ended their hug by moving her hands forward to grip Erin's waist. Isabella's long fingers clasped around her midsection and squeezed gently.

"You feel so good," Isabella whispered before pulling away. When they were facing each other, Isabella looked deep into her eyes and said, "Well, you certainly broke the ice today."

Erin felt herself smile, despite the turmoil of emotions. "Yeah, I kinda have a knack for that. I just don't do normal small talk."

"Good. Neither do I. Although, I'm...not used to this instant connection we have, and it scares me. As I said before, I don't know how to act with you, which is a good thing but also very unnerving. I suppose I need you to show me the way here." Isabella swallowed thickly and fidgeted with her hair.

Whoa. I never knew someone so composed could look so nervous.

"Well, the first thing we should do is stop standing here staring lovingly and holding on to each other because the barista and that guy with the espresso are staring."

Isabella snorted at that. They sat down, and the spell was broken. They were back to their normal conversation, nervous but flowing easily. Alberto slept soundly next to Isabella, while they talked about any trivial thing from places they'd been served good coffee to dates that had gone wrong.

Erin took every opportunity to reach over and touch Isabella's arm or shoulder, and Isabella kept her hand on Erin's as long as she could. Finally, Alberto woke up and began to squirm and whine. Erin looked at him, terrified because he seemed so upset. He began to cry, and Erin found herself feeling guilty that she'd kept his mother away from him. It wasn't logical, but she felt it just the same. He was so small and helpless, and her heart ached as he cried on Isabella's lap, while his mother made those little rubbing circles on his belly.

After a while, Isabella looked up with a distraught look on her face. "I'm sorry, Erin. He isn't calming down. I think I should take him home and see if I can feed him or maybe even give him his medicine."

"Yeah, sure." Erin looked at her FitWatch. "Actually, it's later than I thought. It's almost five. My train leaves in about forty minutes. I'll walk you guys home and then try to find a cab to the station."

"It's that late? Wow, we really got to talking. All right, let's go." Isabella almost shouted over Alberto's increased wails.

Isabella cradled her crying son close to her chest as she stood. Erin grabbed the car seat for her and followed her out.

Alberto was still whimpering and sobbing occasionally, but getting out in the air seemed to calm him a little. Erin looked at the car seat she was carrying. Curious, she asked, "Why do you have a car seat if you don't have a car anymore?"

"Oh, it's one of the easiest ways to carry Alberto if I don't want to put him in the baby carrier—the harness that you strap onto your chest—or bring a bulky stroller. And he sleeps very well in it. Usually. I'm sorry he woke up. It's hard to date with a baby. Perhaps I *should* have had Daddy look after him. I just wasn't sure either of them was ready for that."

"Hey, please don't worry about it. We should be happy he was calm and quiet for that long. Plus, he stopped me from missing my train."

"That's true." Isabella stopped abruptly. "Well, this is where we live."

She opened the door to the tall, ornate building and stepped into what looked like a hallway leading to an elevator with a door opposite it. Erin knew that Isabella lived on the first floor, and she couldn't help but wonder if that was her door.

Smiling despite the crying Alberto, Isabella reached out a hand for the car seat. Erin handed it over, then backed away and stood there on the doorstep, staring at Isabella and trying to figure out how to say good-bye.

Luckily, she didn't have to worry about it. Isabella leaned over and kissed her on the cheek. The warm lips lingered on Erin's cheek long enough for her to wonder if there would be lipstick marks and to realize that she didn't care.

"Call me when you get home," Isabella said softly. "And thank you for traveling all this way to spend time with me. It was a wonderful date."

"No, thank *you* for coming out with the lil' man. It was great. And of course I'll call. I might even text you from the train."

Alberto gave out an ear-piercing wail, and Isabella looked down at him anxiously. Erin waved them off, and Isabella closed the door with an apologetic smile.

Walking back to a busier part of the street to look for a taxi, Erin was happy that she'd bought a return ticket for just three hours after the date started. She hadn't been sure about that at the time, but between the adrenaline, all the excited talking, and the emotionally draining chat about her insomnia, she was utterly exhausted. And it seemed like Alberto felt the date was at an end too.

Erin bit her lip. How did one get on the good side of a baby?

Chapter 13

Talking to Isabella

IT WAS AFTER BREAKFAST, AND Isabella had just gotten herself and Alberto washed and dressed. He was in her arms, cooing happily and laughing, a skill he'd learned in the past week.

She started swaying with him in her arms, and he grabbed onto little fistfuls of her blouse. She hummed a little and turned the swaying into dancing. She had a new home, a son who was clearly the best baby that ever existed, and yesterday she'd had an incredible date. With Erin.

The whole afternoon had been spent face-to-face with the most beautiful woman she'd ever met, and the whole evening Skyping with the same amazing woman, long into the night.

Isabella hadn't gotten to bed until 1:30 a.m, but she and Alberto had all the time in the world to sleep in this morning. She was still wary of how things were going with Erin, still half tempted to put the brakes on and take it slow. The other half of her wanted to ask Erin out for another date. Tomorrow. She wanted—needed—to see Erin again so much it felt like a craving.

"What do you think, Alberto? When would be appropriate to ask her to come see us again? She has to work in the week and can't just leave New York. That means we won't see her for a whole week." She thought a moment. "Unless we visit her. Do you think you could behave for the trip up there?"

Alberto gurgled and reached out his pudgy little hand to grip at her hair. With well-honed reflexes, she moved her head so he couldn't grab hold properly. It was nice that he was so fond of her hair, but not when he tugged it surprisingly hard.

She sighed. "No, you probably couldn't. It wouldn't be fair on you either. You've had enough upheaval with the move, *cariño*. We'll ask her to come over next weekend. That's probably good. Your mother shouldn't appear too eager, should she?"

He looked at her moving lips and suddenly, without apparent reason, laughed.

Isabella laughed too and tickled his side. "Stop laughing at me. I can't help wanting to see her again."

She resumed swaying and slowly dancing with him, while thinking about Erin. Last night had been different than their other Skype sessions. There was a relief in having met up and liking each other in the flesh, so to speak, but a new urgency to meet again. If she'd been desperate to touch Erin before, it was so much worse now.

Smiling, she thought back to the things Erin had said on Skype. She'd seemed almost starstruck and had spent a lot of the call blushing or making silly jokes and then apologizing for them. Isabella's heart melted even more, defying her when she chastised Erin for being an idiot after a particularly bad joke. She was desperate to kiss Erin's pretty pink lips to shut her up.

Kissing Erin. She'd been thinking about that a lot. In their rushed good-bye yesterday, she'd instinctively kissed Erin on the cheek, but as soon as she closed the door, she'd wondered if she should've been bold and gone for her lips. She grinned blissfully to herself. Next time. Definitely next time.

Recognition dawned on her. It was a Sunday, and Erin would be home. She picked up her phone to text Erin and saw a message from someone else. Richard. He wanted to know if she and Alberto were free to Skype; he wanted to see his son. Eager to help their relationship, Isabella texted back that they'd be online soon.

Five minutes later, Isabella was waving Alberto's little hand at the screen. Richard and Joshua, Alberto's half brother, waved excitedly while shouting, "Good morning," before the young boy ran off and left Alberto and the grownups to chat.

After telling Richard about the growth developments that Alberto had gone through—he was coming up to five months and learning things at an alarming rate—she said, "It's hard to believe, but with pillows propping him up, he can actually sit by himself."

Richard beamed. "Oh, wow. And if you remove the pillows?"

Isabella gave a quick laugh. "Then down comes baby. He's doing well for his age. We can't expect more than that."

Richard chuckled along with her. "No, of course not."

Alberto coughed, and they both looked at him until the coughing fit passed.

"So, how has he been coping with the move?"

"Fine, it seems. Other than not being a huge fan of the flight up here, he has been a happy little boy. As long as he gets food, sleep, and love, he's satisfied."

"The joy of babies, huh?"

Isabella realized that Richard wasn't looking at her. He was looking at his son's face as if he was trying to memorize Alberto's features.

She was happy to see his love for Alberto, though a small and self-absorbed part of her was curious; had Richard even missed her? Probably not. Still, she wanted him to be happy, and with Shay and Joshua, he clearly was. She couldn't ask for more than that.

"Yes, that's the joy of babies," Isabella repeated.

"How is the new place coming along?" Richard met her eyes before looking back to Alberto.

"Pretty well, I'd say. Between the pieces of furniture that I had shipped here and what I've ordered to be delivered, we should soon have a fully furnished home. Not a hard task with such a small space."

"That's great. Are you doing okay? Getting everything in place? I know you hurt your back sleeping in that armchair all those months. Don't overdo the heavy lifting."

Isabella smiled warmly at his concern. "I won't."

"Good. You have to be careful and stay safe. Speaking of which—is it a safe area you're in?"

"Yes. It's fine." She was losing patience with his Mother Hen routine.

"You sure? I mean, Philadelphia is a lot rougher than Naples. And neither you nor Alberto have taken any self-defense classes."

She gave him a scathing look. "Richard, remember when those two thugs tried to mug me when we were visiting your family in Miami?"

He sighed in defeat. "Yeah."

"Remember what I did to those little maggots?" Her eyebrow quirked.

"You stabbed one of them in the foot with your stiletto heel and threw hot coffee in the eyes of the other one. All while dialing 911," he intoned dutifully. "Look, Isabella, I'm not doubting you can look after yourself. I'm just asking you to be careful out there."

She relented. "Of course I will. I won't take any risks. I'm neither stupid nor reckless."

"I know. Anyway, how are you and...uh...what's her name again?"

"Erin." Isabella smiled at the mere mention of her name. She pulled herself together and hid her smile, hoping that Richard hadn't seen her be so sentimental. "We're doing well. We're...somewhere in the strange land between dating and not dating. I'm trying not to rush into a relationship. We both know how that worked out for you and me."

With a furrowed brow, Richard hummed before saying, "Well, yeah, but our circumstances were different. I don't think you should use us as a yardstick. If things feel right between you and Erin, then go for it. Life's too short not to take chances."

Isabella scowled and looked away while brushing invisible lint off her skirt. "Yes, well, I think I know best when it comes to my love life. Let's change the topic."

Richard seemed about to argue, before he glanced up and saw the look on Isabella's face and clearly thought better of it. They both knew Isabella wasn't much for talking about her feelings. And she certainly didn't enjoy defending her stance or her actions.

Scratching his head, Richard seemed to search for something to say. "So...um...how is the writing going?"

Isabella's shoulders relaxed. "At the moment, I have the bare bones of all the chapters, but I'm far from finished. There's a lot of work left and quite a bit of research I have to do before I can complete it."

"Well, you've never been afraid of hard work."

She gave him a scathing look, which he missed as he was looking at Alberto.

"No. It's just that conditions right now aren't particularly conducive to writing. I've just moved, and I have to make the house habitable. I've spent time with my parents and struggled with matters of the heart. Oh, and I left a long-term relationship, remember? One could say that there's been quite a lot going on."

He grinned. "Aha. There's the Isabella snark I remember so well."

This time, he actually looked up at her and acknowledged her existence with a smile. The teasing felt good and surprisingly natural.

They finished up discussing the details of the house sale before they signed off. She was relieved the call had gone well. Clearly, they could make these Skype calls a frequent habit without it being a chore.

She didn't know how much Alberto would get out of them now, but as he grew, the calls would probably mean a lot to him.

Finally, Isabella thought as she looked at Erin's face on her screen later that morning. It almost felt like she had been holding her breath since she last saw Erin and only properly exhaled now. Erin. There she was—right there and always so happy to see her. Wearing only shorts and an oversized T-shirt, she was sitting with her legs drawn up on her chair, her hair uncombed, a big coffee mug in hand, and that radiant smile on her elfin features.

"Hey, babe," Erin said.

Her voice was a little croaky from sleepiness and had lost its usual clarity. Isabella found it endearing. She laughed at herself, as she noted how far gone she was already. She had to force herself to keep strong and take this slow. If she didn't, she just might ruin the second-best thing to ever happen to her—Alberto obviously being number one.

She saw Erin knit her brows in confusion. "What's so funny?"

Isabella sighed. "You, *preciosa*. You are far too wonderful and beautiful to be real. It's almost criminal, you know."

She made a point of keeping it light, to bury her deeper feelings—for now, at least. She was sure Erin knew, but neither of them were ready yet. Well, Isabella wasn't.

"I doubt that." Erin tucked some of her tousled hair behind her ear in a self-conscious gesture. "I couldn't sleep last night, so I made up for it by sleeping late this morning. I just got up and probably look like crap."

"No, you don't. I like you all dressed up and in makeup, but I like you au naturel too. You're adorable." Realizing how sappy she was getting,

Isabella straightened up. "Anyway, I'm sorry you didn't get any sleep. Perhaps I shouldn't have asked for another midnight coffee date yesterday?"

"Nah, don't worry about it. I wouldn't have slept anyway. Insomnia mixed with being overexcited from our date isn't a good recipe for sleep. I don't care, though. I feel like I don't even need sleep anymore. Or food. Or exercise. I just need you."

Isabella blew out a breath. There it was, the proof that Erin was in as deep as she was. She wasn't sure if she felt relief or anxiety or a weird mix of the two, and that was…worrying. What was more worrisome was that it didn't seem to matter. She had a burning need to ask about seeing Erin again.

"So, do you still feel as positive about our first date as you did when we discussed it on Skype last night?"

A shy smile spread on Erin's face. "Hell, yeah."

Isabella took a deep breath, then took the metaphoric leap. "Then perhaps you would like to do it again? I know it is a long way for you to travel. I'd offer to come to New York, but it is rather difficult with Alberto."

"Sure, sure, I totally get that. No, I'll come to you. The train ride gives me a chance to read some new comics and play on my phone."

"Wonderful. I can lend you some good books, if you want. I assume you can't come during the week because of work. But if you come next weekend, that gives you more time to book a ticket anyway. Oh, and I'd like to pay for the ticket. You paid to travel here last time, and for our coffee too. This time, I want it to be my treat."

She saw Erin scratch her head as she considered the suggestion. "Yeah, all right. I pay half of my money in rent for this place, so I'm not gonna say no to being treated. As long as you can afford it?"

"Certainly. Just tell me how much it cost when you get here, and I'll have money for you. Thank you for letting me pay. It makes me feel more at ease with making you travel all this way to see me. Well…us." Isabella clarified with a nod in Alberto's direction.

Erin swallowed a sip of coffee. "Okay. I'll look into train tickets, and we can talk about it later."

Why didn't Erin want to decide it all right away? Isabella realized how fretting and impatient she was being and forced herself to relax.

"Good." She fished for a smooth way to change the topic. "Oh, by the way, Alberto and I listened to some more of your music while I had breakfast. Alberto didn't do much dancing. I think he was a little tired after his Skype chat with his father."

Erin laughed. "Did you?"

"Pardon?"

"Dance. Did you dance?"

Hoping that Erin wouldn't notice her discomfort, Isabella looked to the side, pretending to check on Alberto in his baby gym. "Well, no. I don't really dance, unless I have a partner."

"Then we'll just have to dance to some of the best tunes together." Erin's smile faded a little into a more bashful one. "I think I know just the one, actually."

Isabella looked back to the screen. "Really? Which one?"

Erin's gaze flitted away, and she scratched the back of her neck. "Have you gotten to the folder with the Siouxsie and the Banshees songs yet?"

"Hmm, no," Isabella answered.

She saw Erin bite her lip and look away for a second, as if in embarrassment. "There's, uh, a song there called *The Last Beat Of My Heart*. There was a moment…" Erin paused and licked her lips nervously. "When you were still with Richard, when I thought about you and about that song. It's, uh—well, let's just say I think it would be a nice song for us to dance to."

There was something there, Isabella was sure of it. Something Erin wasn't saying about that song made Isabella intensely curious. Were the lyrics sexy? What sort of things had Erin thought about that night? Was her current discomfort due to her dirty thoughts about someone who had been in a relationship? Or were the lyrics romantic?

She sensed that Erin had said all she wanted to. Isabella smiled noncommittally. "I'll make sure to give it my full attention."

"Good. Yeah, do that," Erin said in a relieved tone.

Still smiling as reassuringly as she could, Isabella asked Erin about the clients she had in the upcoming week and led the conversation back to its normal, relaxed nature. And the hours fell away.

Isabella thought she'd spoken to everyone she was going to that day. But shortly after dinner, her phone rang. She put down the picture she'd been about to hang and answered.

"¡*Hola*!" her father said.

Isabella rubbed her left temple with her free hand. She was too tired for Spanish tonight. Unlike her father, it was her second language and she had to concentrate on it.

"Hi, Daddy. Do you mind if we speak English today? I'm finding it hard to focus with…everything that's going on."

There was a beat of silence. "Of course. Whatever you want, sweetheart."

"Thank you."

Switching languages wasn't a big deal for him. But speaking in Spanish when they were alone together had become a sort of pact between them. It was the language Alberto Sr.'s father had brought with him from Puerto Rico and the language he taught his son at home. It was a way of acknowledging their heritage and maintaining something they shared that her mother couldn't control. It wasn't to exclude Judith. They always spoke English when she was a part of the conversation. Well, almost always.

Alberto had tried to teach Judith Spanish, but Judith had struggled. She said her brain was wired for logic, not for frivolous things like languages. Even after all these years, she barely knew enough Spanish to follow a conversation.

"How is little 'Beto?"

"He's fine. Sleeping soundly at the moment, despite the noise I'm making with moving furniture and hanging pictures."

"Good. He needs his sleep. I'm sorry to bother you, *mi vida*. But I wanted to speak with you. Regarding your mother."

"You never bother me," she lied, trying to spare his feelings. "What about her?"

He sighed. "I don't know if I should tell you this. It's nothing, really. She is only curious about your life and wants the best for you. But I know we lost you for some time after your mother disapproved of you moving to Florida with Richard. Now that we have you back…I just want to keep our relationship intact and drama free."

"I understand, Daddy. Tell me what she's done." Isabella hoped she'd managed to make her voice sound neutral. The muscles in her jaw tightened so hard, she wondered if he could hear it over the phone.

"Judith has been trying to press me for information about you and your, well, your love life. I've told her that I know nothing about it, but she doesn't believe me. She's sure you have confided in me."

Isabella swallowed hard. "About my love life?"

"Yes. She is convinced you're dating someone and hiding it from her. And she has jumped to the conclusion that it must be someone we—or, rather, *she*—will disapprove of."

"I see." Isabella closed her eyes. It was a good thing that she had put the hammer down before taking the call. Otherwise, there was a strong chance that she would have smashed it into the wall by now. *I knew this would happen. I knew she couldn't just leave me alone.*

"I don't want to cause any problems between you two by telling you this. She loves you very much and just wants to be a part of your life," Alberto said.

"She wants to be the controller of my life."

"Isabella, *por favor—*"

She cut him off. "You know it's true. Anyway, thank you for telling me. Don't worry. Some snooping and wild assumptions aren't going to make me stop talking to her. Or you. Just…next time she asks, remind her that I am a grown woman and that she doesn't get to decide what I do with my life. I do."

"I will try." He sighed again. "But we both know she won't listen."

He sounded apologetic, and for a moment, Isabella let herself hope he was starting to understand that his rosy image of his wife wasn't based on reality. But that was probably just wishful thinking on her part.

"I know, Daddy. I should get back to hanging my painting. Thank you for the heads-up."

"I love you, Isabella," he said quietly.

"I love you too. Try not to worry about all of this. Have a good night."

She hung up and took a deep breath. *What do I do if she decides to put her foot down again and "forbid" me from seeing Erin?*

Although it made her stomach ache, she knew the answer to the question. She'd have to do what she did when her mother forbade her to move in with Richard and have his child—cut her out of her life. The tragic part was that it meant cutting her father out of her life too, as he refused to stand up to her.

She'd hoped her father would be a part of her and Alberto's life now. She looked forward to introducing him to Erin, eventually, and seeing how well they got on. She could only hope that her mother wouldn't ruin it all.

Chapter 14

Don't Mess This Up

ERIN STOOD UP FROM THE leg press machine and wiped the sweat off her forehead. Her quads throbbed, and she grimaced at the pain. She might have overdone it a bit.

She had been punishing herself for being so stupid yesterday. How in the world could she have told Isabella about *The Last Beat of My Heart* and when she'd listened to it? Isabella would hear the song now and probably realize that, while she and her boyfriend were trying to make their relationship work and make a family for their baby, Erin was lying in bed weeping…and wishing.

Why the hell had she told her? Perhaps because the song stayed with her as she thought about being with Isabella. Still, it was probably going to scare Isabella away, or at least make her think Erin was way too sappy and selfish for worrying about the possibility of her own broken heart when she should have been thinking about Isabella's difficult situation.

"Good mornin', Er."

Erin jolted back to the present and the voice at her side.

"Want some breakfast? It's banana flavor." Chris Nash extended his protein shake to her.

She looked at the creamy, light-yellow drink that normally would have enticed her and grimaced. "No, I ate when I got up. Like normal people."

He looked at her like she had just slapped him. "Whoa. I know it's Monday morning, but that's a little *too* crabby. Especially for you. You're usually the nicest person in here."

"Crap. I'm sorry, Chris," she said to his hurt-puppy face. She put her hand on his shoulder to show her sincerity and make him smile.

"It's fine. Let me guess. Relationship trouble?"

"Yeah. Or no. I don't know. I think I'm just on the verge of getting into a relationship, but with my track record...I'm kinda waiting for the other shoe to drop."

"Sorry to hear that," he said softly. "I get that you're scared. Change is always scary, because it can lead to everything going to hell. But you still have to try." He carried on, despite her skeptical look. "Try looking at it this way. You're really lucky that you've found something new and interesting, something that wakes you up and makes you willing to risk everything. The rest of us, well, we're just trudging on the same old tracks."

Smiling at the annoyed frown on his chiseled face, Erin asked, "Feeling a bit bored with things, Chris?"

He blew out a breath. "You could say that. Between the gym and living next door to my sweet but clingy mom, I'm going stir crazy. I just want to get away from the responsibility some days. Just take off and see what else is out there. Maybe start dating or just be by myself for a while. Just..."

"Something new?"

He rubbed at his square jaw and shrugged. "Yeah. Just some change. See? You have that. Scary as it may be, you have something new and exciting on your horizon. Make the most of it, Er."

She squeezed his shoulder. "You know, you're not as dumb as you look, pretty boy."

He grinned. "Oooh, you think I'm pretty?"

She rolled her eyes at him. "I'm gay, not blind. You're like an ocean view. I can appreciate the beauty, even if I don't want to sleep with it." Erin put her hand up to stop his reply. "I just meant that you have a point. I mean, it's not going to stop me from freaking out, but it's something to keep in mind."

"Of course I have a point. And you have a client in five minutes, if I'm not mistaken. Stop working out, and start working." He chuckled, then took a big gulp from his protein shake.

Erin stuck her tongue out at him but dutifully walked over to reception to wait for her next client.

By late afternoon, Erin had said good-bye to her last client of the day. She'd managed to focus fully on work and keep her mind off her personal life. A rare luxury these days.

She was about to shower and head home, when she stopped and thought about seeing Isabella again. When they'd spoken about meeting up again, she'd wanted to book a ticket right away and plan every second they'd have together in miniscule detail.

That's when it had grabbed her, like a cold hand on her shoulder. Her head filled with anxious little demons that just wouldn't shut up. She'd worried so much about coming on too strong, because Isabella might get hurt that until that point, she hadn't stopped to seriously think about her own part in this relationship.

It was her MO—her modus operandi—to mess up human interactions—badly. What if she ruined this and Isabella stopped talking to her? What if getting all sentimental and talking about that song freaked Isabella out? Or what if trying to help Isabella get in touch with her sexual side was the wrong thing to do? What if, in the long run, Isabella would've been better off with Richard instead of alone with a kid or dating a sad loner who can't even sleep like a normal person? What if she was terrible with Alberto?

There were so many ways this could go wrong. And if Erin's history had taught her anything, it was that things never turned out well. People shouldn't love her, because it always ended badly…and then they left. She never figured out how, but she always managed to screw it up, and everyone—every single one—had to get away from her. The parents who hadn't wanted her. The friends who'd come and gone. Foster parents who had mostly just gone. Social workers who drifted her case file from one desk to another like a snowflake on the wind. Katie…who shattered everything inside her.

Could she risk that again? Her feelings for Isabella were already so strong, how would she make it through if it all went up in smoke? She'd barely survived Katie's betrayal, and she hadn't felt for Katie a tenth of what she already felt for Isabella. She couldn't—wouldn't—survive another broken heart.

Blood rushed through her veins and pounded in her ears, until all she could hear was the thunderous drum roll of her heart approaching its peak. She wasn't sure how much more it could take before it would explode. Her palms were sweaty, and it felt like her skin was crawling with…something.

She needed to quiet her anxiety. She needed to regain some semblance of control, and Erin knew only one way that worked for her. She needed to stay and work off her demons, not go home. Home would be too quiet, would give her too much time to think. She'd be climbing the walls, having a goddamn panic attack in seconds. Home would be a disaster. Right now, she needed to not feel, to not think. She needed to keep moving.

She sent a text to Isabella saying that she'd be home and ready to Skype after eight and headed over to a rowing machine. After three strokes, she wondered if she'd made a mistake. Maybe she should've gone home to talk to Isabella? Or to one of her friends? No, she decided, that wasn't her thing.

She hunkered down and rowed harder. She needed to clear the cobwebs and quiet the voices in her head. This was the only way to make everything simple, manageable. No matter what was happening in her life, working out was therapy. Temporary therapy, maybe. But *it* had never let her down.

When Erin got home, hair still damp after the bracing, cold shower at the gym, she fished her phone out of her bag and saw the text from Isabella. She was apparently trying to get Alberto to sleep and might be a little while.

Erin combed some leave-in conditioner through her hair, made coffee, and stood to watch the evening paint the sky in pinks and blues. The brooding dusk suited her melancholy mood perfectly.

It was almost nine when her laptop beeped and Isabella came online. She straightened up and adjusted her shirt collar, trying to shake her pensiveness and just enjoy seeing Isabella again.

The call window popped up, and Erin answered it with video. She saw Isabella open her mouth to greet her, then close it and frown. "What's wrong?"

Erin forced a smile. "What do you mean?"

"Erin, don't. You look like someone told you dogs were going extinct. What's happened?"

Cursing her bad poker face, Erin blew out a long breath, a stalling technique. She tried to weigh just how much she should confess. "I, um, I've been worrying a bit."

Isabella crossed her arms over her chest. "About?"

The question made Erin squirm in discomfort. "Jesus, Isabella. Chill!"

"Fine. Have it your way. We don't have to talk about it. But I am starting to feel like you are avoiding me, or at least, avoiding talking to me."

"No, no. I'm not avoiding you. Just kinda need to figure a few things out."

Isabella's stern look softened. "*Preciosa*, what's wrong? Let me help you if I can."

The time had come, the moment when Erin had to decide if she was ready for this. There were a thousand voices in her head telling her about everything that could go wrong and how everything had gone wrong her whole life. Every fear and feeling of inadequacy vied for her attention, and her heart began to race again. She had to trust Isabella. It was the only way this could work. She had to trust her not only with her heart but her mental wellbeing.

She'd made her life so simple, so manageable, and that had kept her safe. Opening up to Isabella now, letting her in, meant changing all that.

Opening up now meant there was no turning back.

Her breath was coming quickly, and she was getting light-headed. She tried to put her thoughts aside and focus on her breathing.

How long is a breath meant to be? Shit. Am I hyperventilating? Should I take longer breaths or would that be getting too much oxygen? What the hell should I do?

She looked up into Isabella's warm, brown eyes. She saw sympathy there, sympathy and that particular brand of Isabella Martinez confidence. Erin envied that confidence, that strength, and wished she had some of it right now. Even just for a little while.

Isabella's head cocked to the side slightly, and a worry line appeared between her eyes. Erin didn't want to distress Isabella, and she didn't want to lose this chance to be happy, to make them both happy, just because she was afraid. She looked deep into those mesmerizing eyes and tried to draw from that strength and warmth.

It was time to make her change. Time to leap.

Choking on the words, Erin blurted out, "I'm worried I'll mess this up." Then she cursed herself. Talking about her fears and panic seemed wrong. Talking to Isabella was meant to be fun and wonderful for both of them. She wanted Isabella to look forward to their chats, wanted them be a safe, happy thing in her new and potentially stressful life.

Isabella gave a soft chuckle and tucked a lock of hair behind her ear. "That's funny. I've worried about that myself."

Feeling surprised and a little offended, Erin asked, "That I'll mess this up?"

Isabella rolled her eyes, but with a kind smile to soften the gesture. "No, featherbrain. I worry that *I* might, to use your expression, 'mess it up.'"

"Really?"

"Yes, really. Look, I think we are both two very complicated women who haven't had the best luck in relationships. I also think that maybe we don't…have the highest opinions of ourselves. Perhaps that's one of the things that drew us to each other and let us connect so quickly and intensely."

Erin's breathing was gradually returning to normal. She tried for a grin and a jokey tone. "Ah, has my Ms. Writer been doing some sorta character profiles of us?"

Isabella scowled at her. "No. I'm just thinking out loud."

Shrugging, Erin agreed. "Well, you probably have a point. And I have to admit it makes me feel a little less of a screw-up to think that someone I admire as much as you can be kinda anxious and insecure and that you don't like yourself either."

"Self-loathing," Isabella said.

"Huh?"

"That's what an ex-boyfriend used to call it when I disparaged myself. He probably had a point. But, Erin, you should never feel that way about yourself. I've treated people I worked with badly, and I have to admit that even in relationships, I've mistreated some of the men I dated. I have to live with that and try to figure out why I did it. You, on the other hand, what have you ever done wrong? What could possibly make someone as lovely as you dislike yourself?"

Erin looked down at her hands. "It's not what I *do* to people that makes me dislike myself. It's just me. Things about me that make people leave." She swallowed hard, feeling as if there were something jagged in her throat, something that wanted her to stop talking. "That's what I can't stand about myself."

When she looked back up at the screen, she saw Isabella's full lips pressed together tightly.

"Erin. People don't leave you because of something about you. They leave because of external circumstances or because they're idiots or because they're...well, assholes."

There was an impressive fierceness to Isabella's voice and demeanor that Erin had to admit she liked, especially in her defense. And it was fun to hear Isabella say assholes too. Totally unexpected, but fun.

"We really need to talk about your abandonment issues," Isabella continued. "They're doing real damage to you, and I hate to see that. You deserve the moon and the stars. Yet all you give yourself is scorn."

Erin swallowed and looked away. She fidgeted with the top button of her shirt. She would've given anything to not have mentioned this at all. It was too hard. "Yeah," she whispered.

"*Preciosa*," Isabella said. Her normally smooth and low voice deepened even more, making it softer and more tender than Erin could grasp. "I'm not shouting at you here. It just breaks my heart that you treat yourself like this. I wish you could see yourself the way I see you—strong, warm, independent, beautiful, funny, passionate, smart, interesting, and so much more. Who in their right mind would ever abandon that? Abandon you? Please, don't be frightened of scaring me off. The only way I could ever stay away from you would be if you shut me out. So don't. Let me in. Be open with me and, *mi corazón*...I won't leave you. I could never leave you."

On the screen, Isabella reached out a hand as if to touch her and then put it back in her lap. She looked more sad and sympathetic than anyone Erin had ever seen. She was pretty sure that all the social workers and foster parents put together had never looked at her with such love and concern.

Overwhelmed and unsure of what to answer, Erin sniffed. "Shit," she croaked. "You're making me cry. Why do I cry so much around you?"

Isabella moved closer to the screen and smiled gently. "Because you're vulnerable around me. Like I am around you. And I think that's the main reason we're both so afraid of this, of us."

"Yeah, that's probably true," Erin said with a slow nod.

"Well, then. We can be afraid together." Isabella smiled encouragingly.

Erin smiled back, trying to lighten the mood a little. "Great. If that's what we're aiming for, can't we just watch a slasher movie or something?"

Isabella quirked an eyebrow at her. "All jokes aside, I mean it. Let's share our fears like we share all our other thoughts and feelings. How about... we just talk? Just let it all spill out? We won't interrupt each other or start coming up with solutions right away. We'll just listen."

Erin blinked to clear her wet eyes. "Okay. I like that. Yeah, I think it would be easier for me to share if you didn't reply right away. Which sounds kinda weird, but you know what I mean." She stopped and scratched the back of her neck. "Um, I've never tried this before. Could you start?"

Isabella frowned and looked down for a while. When she looked back up, she very slowly and quietly started her confession.

"I suppose one of my biggest concerns is jumping into a relationship too soon, like I did with Richard. We both know how that ended, although I am aware that the circumstances are different. Another worry is that my cruel and sarcastic side will start rearing its ugly head. And that it will make you hate me." She looked down, and when she spoke again, her voice was hoarse and quiet. "I also worry about my mother somehow getting between us. Not that I would ever let her keep me away from you, but the drama and heartbreak she would cause while trying...panics me."

It was hard for Erin to not reply to all those concerns and try to put them to rest, but she'd agreed to just spilling all the worries and talking them through later. But what about Alberto? If she told Isabella about her fears, how could Isabella not feel that she was hesitant about their relationship? No, that had to wait.

She opened her mouth and let some of her other fears come tumbling out.

"I worry about coming on too strong and scaring you off. Oh, and that I'm pushing you about the sex stuff, even though you're not ready, and new to being with another woman. Most of all, I worry that I'll make you abandon me because something inside me makes people leave."

They were both silent for a moment, and then they opened their mouths simultaneously to begin explaining why the other one should stop worrying about things. They stopped and laughed. Clearly, Isabella was as embarrassed and shy, yet also relieved, as she was.

"You start," Isabella said with a gentle smile.

"Okay, but you can't come up with arguments why I'm wrong until I've finished. I don't have your way with words, and if you make me lose my train of thought, I'll never get it back."

Isabella dipped her head in acknowledgment. "All right. Go ahead,"

Erin scratched her head, trying to remember Isabella's concerns, wanting to tick them all off. "First of all, we aren't jumping into a relationship that quickly. It's been a lot longer than most of my friends' dating phases, and don't forget that we have talked so damn much, I sometimes feel I know you better than anyone. And you know me better than anyone I've ever met. Oh, and about your mom, there's nothing she can do to drive me away from you. Any damage or drama she stirs up, we'll fix together." She paused. "Okay. What else was it you worried about?"

Isabella sighed. "My bad sides. My sarcastic comments, my annoyance with people, and my temper."

"Oh, that? That's actually, weirdly, one of the things I like about you. When you grow up alone and try so damn hard to make people love you, you sorta never say the mean things that pop into your head. You're always struggling to be nice and liked. The fact that you can be a bit...well, bitchy...I kinda find freeing and attractive. But, hey, if you get really mean or snap at someone who didn't deserve it, well, you know, I'll shut that down."

Isabella gave an amused little hum. "You make some good points. It's so hard not to voice my counterarguments. But I'm sure we'll revisit these discussions at some point. Right now, I need to explain to you why *you* shouldn't worry."

Erin steeled herself. "Okay. Shoot."

"All right. Firstly, you aren't coming on too strong. You've been very patient, and most of the pushing has actually been from me. Then I take a step back, only to revert to pushing again. The same goes for the sexual side of our relationship, I might add. And I won't abandon you. I learn more about you every time we speak, and the more I learn, the more I want to be with you." A smile tugged at Isabella's lips. "You fascinate me, Erin—fascinate and amaze me. I'm not someone who suffers fools, or generally people I don't like. The fact that I am this crazy about you after months of talking, well, it means you are very unlikely to make me want to leave—ever"

Erin chewed the inside of her cheek. "Man, you're right. It's hard not to answer back and come up with reasons why you're wrong. Although, you do make a good case on the last point, I suppose." Erin grinned at the camera and found she actually meant it. It was a comfort to remember that Isabella very easily got pissed off with people. So, if she was still putting up with her, it meant she'd probably gotten through the trial period.

Alberto started crying, and Isabella said, "Right back," and disappeared from view. Erin looked at her watch and realized in shock that it was 11:23 p.m.

Isabella came back with Alberto in her arms, his face was all flushed from crying. Erin realized that his little tufts of hair had grown since the first time she'd seen him, mainly because, right now, it was all standing on end. Isabella was smoothing it down and hushing his little angry babbling.

Soon, he was quiet and laid still in her arms, looking up at her. Erin recognized the adoring look in his eyes. The little Skype window revealed the same look in her own eyes. Isabella hummed gently at him and softly tapped his chin, making him smile a little.

Then she looked back up. "Sorry about that. Where were we?"

Erin felt like someone had hit her on the head with a pillow. She was so in awe of how beautiful and loving they were together. Their intimate connection should've calmed her fears about the baby, but it didn't. It made them worse. She could never be that natural and perfect around Alberto.

She cleared her throat. "Um, I think we were wrapping up our little therapy session. Can you believe it's almost half past eleven?"

Isabella looked up, startled. "What? Really? Oh, wow, that went by fast. Well, looks like we are getting closer to our midnight coffee, then. Want to celebrate our successful sharing of worries with a cup?"

"Yeah. Why not? I'll go put some fresh Azúcar Negra on."

"Great. Bring me a cup, will you?" Isabella joked. She adjusted Alberto in her grip and smiled at the screen.

"God, I wish I could. I so want to…help you and look after you and, well, spoil you."

Isabella beamed. "I feel the same way about you."

With a shy smile, Erin stood up and almost tripped over her chair. She heard Isabella chuckle and turned to poke her tongue out at the screen. Isabella got up, presumably on her way to the coffeemaker too.

By the time they returned with their coffee, the atmosphere was more relaxed. Alberto lay quietly in Isabella's arms, examining a multicolored plastic octopus.

Isabella sipped at her evening ration, and Erin drank deeply from her mug. The alluring scent of the coffee filled Erin's apartment, as lovely as normal coffee but far sweeter. Erin realized that the same aroma would be in Isabella's apartment and, as always, felt happy when they shared something.

Isabella looked down at Alberto who was gumming a yellow tentacle of his octopus. "So, now that we all have something comforting to occupy our mouths with," she joked, "we should get on with what is really important here. The second time we'll meet up."

Feeling lighthearted, Erin put down her mug and adopted a serious face. "Of course. What does the octopus-eating chairman suggest? Does he have a time and place in mind?"

Isabella, playing along, held Alberto up so that he was facing the camera. His little legs kicked out as soon as they were free in the air. His hands and mouth were still struggling with the octopus he was slobbering over.

Erin laughed at how intently he examined the toy with both mouth and hands, completely ignoring everything else. He looked quite perturbed at the plastic toy, and it was impossible not to feel affection and amusement.

"It would seem that our lil' chairman here is more interested in getting to the bottom of the octopus issue than the date issue," Erin said between giggles.

"Yes. He's a 'one task at a time' kind of person." Isabella put him back in his comfy position in her arms and smiled at the camera.

"Why don't you decide, *preciosa*? You're the one who has to travel all the way down here."

Erin looked at the little smile creases by Isabella's eyes and whispered, "Can I come over tonight? You're so beautiful."

Looking down bashfully but still smirking, Isabella replied, "I thought we decided it would have to be the weekend?"

Erin sighed. "Yeah. It will, I suppose. So, should we aim for me arriving after lunch on the Saturday again? That seemed to work pretty well for both of us and the lil' man too."

"Yes, that sounds good. Perhaps one instead of two? Oh, and I should have the apartment looking better and more furnished by then, so we could meet here if you'd like?"

Erin swallowed down a gulp of coffee. "Awesome. I'm looking forward to seeing the place. And one sounds perfect."

"Erin?"

"Yeah?"

"Do you perhaps want to get an open ticket? That way we don't have a time restriction. I'm paying, and I don't mind if there is an extra cost."

Erin's mind was racing. Isabella looked so wary. Was she just worried that Erin didn't want to be stuck with Isabella and Alberto if the date was uncomfortable? Was she afraid that Erin wouldn't want to stay for too long? Or was she intimating that Erin could stay the night?

"Um, yeah. I'll get an open-return ticket. Good idea. Just, you know, let me know if you need to get rid of me, and I'll get the next available train. On, um, one condition."

Isabella's brows knitted. "What's that?"

"This time, my good-bye kiss is a bit longer and, um…maybe even on the lips, if I'm a good girl," Erin said with a cheeky grin.

"Ha! Why don't you show some initiative and go for the sort of good-night kiss you want, Miss Black? Don't make me do all the work."

Exhilaration coursed through her veins. Biting her lip around a smile, Erin replied, "Deal."

Isabella sipped at her coffee and looked at the screen over the rim of the cup. Her soulful, brown eyes offered promises, and goose bumps erupted across Erin's body. Suddenly, all her fears and worries seemed unimportant.

Outside, the wind howled down New York's streets, but Erin didn't care. All she cared about were those warm eyes—the color so like the coffee that they both loved—gazing right into hers. Piercing through every defense.

Chapter 15

Visits

TIME PASSED THE WAY BOOKS had told her time always passes in a long-distance relationship—slow and bittersweet.

But Saturday finally arrived. Isabella's whole body was tense and rushing with adrenaline. She was filled with the kind of anticipation she could only remember from childhood Christmases and birthdays. She kept changing her clothes, and worse, changing Alberto's clothes. After Erin's little joke about them matching at her parent's house, Isabella wanted to make sure they didn't look the same.

Alberto was dressed in white, red, and blue, and she was in a plum-colored dress. Different enough, she decided. Especially as he was wearing dungarees with Cookie Monster peeking out of the cuff, and she was wearing a Ted Baker dress with a slit up her thigh.

They'd eaten an early lunch and were just waiting for one o' clock. At least she had Alberto to distract her. She'd be climbing up the walls otherwise.

She kissed his head and was just wiping away the lipstick smudge when the doorbell chimed. Isabella jumped, and her shocked reaction made Alberto's lower lip wobble. She smiled at him and nuzzled his neck to calm him, while she picked him up and went to open the door to Erin. She had to remind herself to breathe, as she walked the short corridor to the building entrance.

There was Erin, with a rucksack slung over her shoulder and hoodie under her arm. Isabella had that strange feeling of the world slowing, its rushed spinning settling to something more peaceful, more comfortable, the moment she saw Erin's smiling face. Her white tank top was criminally tight above a pair of gray, skinny jeans. Subtle makeup and carefully styled curls added to Erin's beauty, but Isabella was dazzled by that huge smile.

"Hey Martinez and Martinez Jr." Erin reached out a hand and softly prodded Alberto's tummy, right on Cookie Monster's face.

Alberto watched her finger intently. Erin retracted the finger as soon as she made contact, almost as if she were afraid he would explode.

"Well, Miss Black? Are you going to prod my stomach too?"

Erin looked down and smiled, before placing a finger just below Isabella's solar plexus. Slowly, Erin let it slide down, stopping to gently prod just before her belly button. Isabella felt very happy with her choice of such a tight dress, which allowed Erin to see exactly where her finger was going. Had Erin's finger gone any farther south, Isabella might not have been able to stop herself from pulling Erin by that tight tank top into her bed.

She swallowed thickly. "Right. Now that we have your strange greeting ritual over and done with, would you like to come in?"

"Well, yeah! I didn't come all this way just to poke your bellies."

Only the fact that Isabella was standing outside on the sidewalk in the middle of the day, and holding her son, stopped Isabella from asking what body parts Erin *had* come for. Controlling her reawakened sexual appetite around Erin was becoming…difficult.

She walked back into her apartment with Erin in tow. She put Alberto down in the safety of his baby gym and moved back to give Erin a hug. She hadn't expected Erin to pull her in for a bear hug, but laughed happily at its sudden appearance.

Erin smelled of something fresh and fruity, and Isabella breathed it in greedily. She could only hope that Erin might appreciate her own signature Guerlain as much. *Did I put on too much this morning?*

It felt so right to have Erin in her arms, and Isabella made a point to enjoy it fully. She even snaked her hands into the space between Erin's rucksack and the sculpted back underneath it. The tank top was thin, and she could feel the warmth of Erin's body as if she were naked. With a smile, she realized that Erin had burrowed her face into her hair and was nuzzling her ear. It made her heart flutter and her body temperature rise. *Time to end this delicious hug before it becomes something else.*

"That's enough of that. There's a young gentleman present."

"True. How are you doing, lil' man? I like your...um...soft cage thingy, there."

"It's a baby gym," Isabella explained.

Erin took her rucksack off and put it on the small dining room table next to her. "Oh, cool. Let's have a look."

Seeming hesitant, Erin crouched down next to Alberto. The two of them looked at each other for a while, before Erin said, "I, um, I like gyms too, kid. Mine tend to be smellier and less soft, though. I like yours."

Alberto waved his arms and legs quickly. Then he cooed and reached for the yellow and red butterfly above him, ignoring the bee, the bird, and the dragonfly.

"I think that butterfly is his favorite. He's been trying to grab for it for ages now."

Erin nodded intently, as if she was making a mental note. She seemed tense.

Isabella looked over at the discarded rucksack. There had to be a way to relax Erin. "What's in that?" she asked. "Let me guess, protein bars?"

"Yep. Well just one, I ate the other one. There's also some comics and a water bottle, and this." Erin reached into the rucksack and held up something colorful for Isabella to inspect. It turned out to be a rattle in the shape of an octopus. "I thought your octopus inspector might want a new test subject." Her head ducked slightly. "I hope it's okay. The woman in the store said it was safe for his age and stuff."

Isabella rewarded Erin's uncertain expression with a beaming smile. "It's adorable. I'm sure he'll love it. Do you want to give it to him now?"

She looked down at Alberto and then back up at Isabella. "Nah, you give it to him when it's the right time."

"Oh, I see. Perhaps when he needs a distraction because his stomach hurts, but his mother doesn't have time to walk around with him for ages, since she's busy flirting with her sexy date?"

Erin blushed a little, as she put her hands into her tight back pockets. "Well, you'll know better than me when he needs a new toy."

"I'm sure he'd want it right now, *preciosa*. Patience isn't his strong suit, and I think he might have spotted it already."

Bending down carefully in her tight dress, Isabella gave Alberto the rattle. She wanted Erin to see, right away, how much he would like it. In truth, he wouldn't care that it was an octopus, but he'd love how chewable it was and the noise he could make with it.

Alberto grabbed the toy and immediately stuck it in his mouth. As it moved, he noticed it rattling and took it out, then moved it again, mesmerized by the sound. He put it back into his mouth and gummed a tentacle until it rattled once more. When he took it out again, he managed to hit himself square in the face with it. He looked up at the two adults, incrimination in his little eyes. Then the bawling began.

Isabella wasn't surprised by any of it. He did this a lot and would be all right in a second, when he forget all about it. What did surprise her was Erin's look of abject horror.

"Shit! I'm so sorry."

"Why? He hits himself quite a bit like that. It happens when you have undeveloped hand-eye coordination and can't understand consequences of your actions yet. It has nothing to do with the toy or you. Don't worry about it."

"Um, okay." Nevertheless, Erin had gone quite ashen faced.

Isabella lifted Alberto up, grabbed a pacifier off the table, and put it in his mouth. She rocked him until he forgot the pain on the bridge of his nose where the rattle had landed. When he was calm, Isabella put him back down in the gym, took back the pacifier, and handed him the rattle again. He started gumming it as if nothing had ever happened.

"There you go. He's fine, and he loves his new octopus." Isabella squeezed Erin's arm and gave her a reassuring smile.

Despite her nod and smile back, Erin looked unconvinced.

Isabella rubbed her upper arm and spoke in soft tones, "Come on, let's go sit down so you can relax after your journey. Do you want anything to eat or drink?"

"No, I'm fine. Sitting down sounds nice, though."

They went to the sofa, and Isabella and chose the seat where she could best see Alberto, who was still investigating the new toy with his mouth. She looked over at Erin, who was leaning back in the navy blue couch.

"So, how was your trip?"

Sliding across the sofa in one suave move until she was right next to Isabella, Erin replied, "Worth it."

"Smooth, Miss Black."

Erin bowed. "Why, thank you. The trip was fine. It went by pretty quick, despite it raining like hell almost all the way. It magically stopped when I got to Philly, though. Clearly, the sun likes you."

Isabella crossed her legs slowly and enjoyed Erin staring at them. "Yes. I brought it with me from Florida."

"I'm impressed you got the whole damn sun into your bags. Remind me to come to you for packing advice."

Just like that, they were back to their normal, relaxed banter, and time seemed to speed up. With only one break to pick Alberto up and one for Erin using the bathroom, they kept talking and flirting nonstop. Right up until the point where Isabella heard herself say, "So, as this is our second date, I guess we are now officially dating?"

Erin's expression changed into something she couldn't interpret. But it didn't look good.

Isabella felt icy fear in the pit of her stomach. *Damn. Why did I say that?*

Chapter 16

Officially Dating

At first, Erin wasn't sure if she had misheard. She just sat there, disbelieving and confused. Had Isabella really said that they were officially dating? Erin decided she had, and before she could stop herself, celebrated by leaning forward and pulling Isabella into a hug. She heard Isabella sigh in what sounded like relief.

Speaking into Isabella's thick, soft hair, she murmured, "So I'm kinda guaranteed a good-bye kiss tonight, then?"

Isabella moved away and smirked. "You're guaranteed this."

She moved toward Erin and, with her senses all muddled, Erin realized that Isabella was pressing soft lips against hers. The kiss was so unexpected and felt so good that Erin actually heard herself groan with pleasure.

Isabella laughed enough that she had to break away from the kiss.

"Oh, no you don't," Erin muttered and leaned in to resume the kiss.

Isabella didn't fight her. Instead, she grasped Erin's face with both her hands and slid her tongue slowly between Erin's lips. Nothing else existed for Erin—not the past, not the future, not even anything else in that moment. Everything was just the sensation of her mouth melding with Isabella's, how their lips and tongues moved against each other. The softness shifted and turned more forceful, as the kisses became more fevered. Still, everything was warm, velvety, and thrilling. It was bliss—pure bliss.

Isabella's hands began to wander. Erin was impressed at how confident they seemed, considering they had never mapped another woman's body before. When she felt one hand slide along her shoulder and under the tank top and bra strap, Erin moved away as if she had been burned.

"No. God, no. If you put your hands under my clothes, I won't be able to control myself. Alberto's in the room, and we're supposed to be taking it slow." She held up her hands as a barrier between them. "This is your last and final warning, Isabella. Any further, and I might just explode."

Isabella smiled wolfishly and blinked her eyes slowly. She looked like lust personified. Her dulcet tones were even lower than usual and quite breathy as she said, "Fine. But at least try to be less tempting. You feel... incredible. God, your mouth, I'll be wanting more of that—much more— very soon."

At the mention of mouths, Erin stared at Isabella's. Her lips were kiss bruised and had lost all their lipstick. The scar seemed to stand out a little more, as if the light bruising of her lips had made it seem more severe. Erin swore to herself that she would spend a long time mapping that scar with her tongue. Just as soon as the timing was better.

Isabella turned to look at Alberto. He'd rolled over onto his tummy and was holding on to one of the bars of the baby gym. He seemed completely uninterested in them, but Erin still felt guilty. She'd almost pounced on his mother right there in the same room with him.

Isabella, who was smiling at the pudgy boy and calling his name to get his attention. Erin felt sure that Isabella would've stopped the kissing before it got too far. No matter what else Isabella Martinez might be, she was Alberto's mom first and foremost. Erin watched her happily wave at Alberto when she had gotten his attention. *I can live with that. In fact, I wouldn't want it any other way.*

Isabella sat forward on the sofa. "Right. Well, to keep from starting all that up again, I suggest we keep busy. As Alberto seems entertained and pain free at the moment, why don't we watch a movie or perhaps take him for a walk?"

It was quite late in the afternoon, but not late enough to be as dark as it was. "I think that rain I saw on the way over has reached Philly. It looks really dark out there," Erin concluded.

Isabella sat still and seemed to be listening to the outside weather conditions. "Yes, I think you're right. Want to watch a movie, then? Or perhaps we should start up a serious conversation that will keep us from getting…entangled."

Erin did her best to suppress a grin. "Sure, let's talk, and if that doesn't work, we'll watch a movie. Do you have a serious conversation in mind?"

"I do. But I think you might want some coffee before we begin, right?"

"Well, yeah. But I don't want to tempt you." Erin shrugged. "I'm guessing you don't want to have your little evening cup until later?"

"Oh, don't worry about that. I'll make you coffee. Just stay here, and let me know if the little prince does something dangerous."

"Okay," Erin mumbled and trained her eyes on Alberto.

She wondered what exactly he could do. She sat down on the floor to be able to see Alberto better. He was still on his stomach, and she wondered if that was by choice or if he only knew how to roll one way.

He was chewing on the handle of the octopus rattle she'd given him. The handle was one of the tentacles, longer than the others, and he sucked on the end of that. After a while, he got it too far into his mouth and made a retching sound.

Erin was right next to him in a second, ready to pull the octopus out and shout for Isabella. But he spat the rattle out himself and then busied himself trying to get his pudgy, tiny fingers around one of the smaller tentacles. Erin realized she'd been holding her breath and started breathing again.

"Careful there, kid. You scared me half to death," she muttered at him.

He looked up at her with slightly unfocused blue-green eyes and yawned.

"Well, I'm glad one of us is relaxed," she grumbled.

"What are you two talking about?" Isabella asked, as she returned with a mug of coffee for Erin.

"Global warming," Erin said, relieved that Isabella was back.

"I see. I'm sorry that he seems to be yawning. He is usually more interested in discussions about global emergencies and the effect we humans have had on Mother Nature."

"That's all right. It was a long chat with lots to think about. I get why he's tired."

They both smiled at each other until a sound broke their moonstruck looks. The sound came from Alberto.

"*Cariño*, please tell me that was just air and not substance." Isabella got up and walked over to him, undid his dungarees and lifted his T-shirt to check his diaper. She looked up at Erin with an apologetic grimace.

"Sorry. I'll be right back. Drink your coffee, then we can discuss the subject I had in mind."

Erin nodded, grateful that she was not the one changing Alberto. As the two of them left the room, Erin sipped her drink. It was just the right strength, and Erin congratulated herself on finding a woman who made such good coffee. Another plus in Isabella's column.

When Isabella returned, Alberto was almost asleep in her arms, and she placed him into his little baby bouncer. His eyes closed the second he was in.

Isabella walked quietly and gracefully back to her, and Erin couldn't help but stare, wishing she could make a movie of Isabella's smooth movements to play in her head when she needed distraction. Isabella sat down next to her and brushed her fingers across Erin's cheek.

"The subject I had in mind was your insomnia."

"Oh brother," Erin said with theatrical exasperation.

With a look of concern, Isabella reached out and ran her fingers through Erin's hair. "Don't be like that. I think it's important."

"Look, it's just a part of me, like being an introvert. I enjoy working out, and I'm into women. That's just me."

"*Preciosa*, we both know it's not that simple. Those other things are not hurting you. Your lack of sleep is. If you had always suffered from insomnia and there was no obvious cause, I could believe it was a personality trait. But we know that's not true. Your feelings of abandonment and fear of being unwanted cause it. That's not a personality trait, that's an issue which needs to be addressed."

Erin sighed but couldn't argue. "Fine. How do we address it?"

"You need to talk about it. Obviously, I volunteer for that but if I'm honest, I would suggest a professional too. I know you're wary of therapists and what they might uncover in that pretty head of yours. However, I firmly believe they can help you more efficiently than just talking to me can."

Biting her lip, Erin thought it over. Every part of her screamed that it was an awful idea and demanded she run from the scary plan. But she also remembered how much easier life was when she got at least six hours sleep every night. Besides, she wanted to be the best possible version of herself for Isabella, and that meant facing her biggest demon.

"If I," she hesitated, "if I do decide to talk to someone about this, will you help me? I mean, like, find a therapist or psychiatrist or ventriloquist or whatever it is I need?"

Isabella laughed and reached out to caress Erin's cheek again. "Of course, my sweet. I'll help you with anything I can. After all, I want to make sure you get some sleep on the first occasion you stay over. I can't have you keeping me up tossing and turning all night," she joked.

Erin turned to gently kiss the fingers resting against her cheek and smiled. "Okay. Someday soon, when we run out of things to do, we'll find me a headshrinker."

"It's a deal, *preciosa*."

Isabella placed a soft kiss on Erin's lips. A brief whisper of a kiss, lips brushing against each other lightly, yet it meant the world to Erin.

A while later, Isabella began making supper. It didn't take long for Erin to beg for a job so that she would feel that she was helping. Isabella prepared some sirloin steaks and *Dauphinoise potatoes*, while leaving Erin in charge of vegetables.

Erin regaled Isabella with the nutrition contents of the string beans and carrots she was slicing up, commending Isabella on choosing two vegetables that were different colors.

Isabella looked at her as if she had lost her mind. "The color scheme of the vegetables is important?"

"Well, not so much the colors in themselves as what they signify, y'know? It means there are different vitamins and minerals in them. To achieve a varied diet and make sure your body gets everything it needs, you want to fill your plate with food that's all the colors of the rainbow." Erin paused to put a piece of carrot in her mouth before quickly adding, "Natural color, not added food coloring."

Isabella cut into one of the steaks to check how cooked it was. "I'm glad you approve of the colors of the food. Let's hope it is as tasty as it is colorful. Speaking of colors, how pink do you want your meat?"

A dirty comment about liking to eat pink things almost burst out of her mouth, but Erin decided that it was too vulgar. "As long as it's not still alive and kicking, I don't really have a preference."

"I'll cook it medium, like I do my own, then. I need to check on the potatoes. Hand me that oven glove, *preciosa*."

Another comment popped out of Erin's mouth. This one wasn't vulgar, but it might still get her in trouble. "Hey, if you are going to keep calling me precious, could you do it in English and in a Gollum voice? That would be freakin' hilarious."

Isabella looked at her coolly, then walked over to the sink and turned the tap on, stuck her long fingers under the tap, and proceeded to flick the cold water onto Erin's face. "Stop being an annoyance, or I will call you something a lot less flattering, Miss Black."

Erin sniggered at the cold water running down her cheek and her neck. When she looked up, she saw a scowl on Isabella's face, belied by the twinkle in the sultry, brown eyes.

Down on the floor, Alberto was awake and watching them from his baby bouncer while pensively gumming three of his fingers.

Erin smiled at him and startled when his little face crumpled, and he immediately looked away. She knew intellectually that his reaction had nothing to do with her. Maybe he had gas or he didn't like the smell of the steaks or something.

Still, she felt strangely rejected. Still, she wasn't convinced this wasn't going to be a problem.

After dinner, Isabella showed Erin a bunch of DVDs which were, according to Isabella, "in a terrible state of disorganization," as they'd just been picked up from the box and shoved onto the shelf. Erin replied that she wasn't one to judge the collection since she didn't even have more than three DVDs, due to the convenience of streaming movies.

After rifling through artsy Italian and French movies, some classic black-and-whites, and a few she'd never heard of, Erin found something she hadn't expected to see in Isabella's collection. She turned to look at Isabella, holding the boxed-set trilogy. "I didn't peg you as someone who would watch *X-Men*."

Isabella lifted Alberto to the sofa. "It's not my usual style, no. I bought that set because it was on sale, and I...sort of have a thing for Hugh Jackman."

Erin's brows flew up her forehead. "Hugh Jackman and Angela Bassett, you have a varied palate, lady."

With a noncommittal shrug, Isabella looked down at Alberto in her arms a little too fast. Erin's brain whirred. So, Isabella wasn't agreeing with the varied palate idea. Then what did those two actors have in common? Erin's grin grew huge, as she figured it out.

"Ah. I see. Nice muscle tone."

Isabella looked up from the baby. "Pardon?"

"Hugh Jackman and Angela Bassett do have something in common. Well, I mean, they are obviously good-looking, talented actors who are older than you, but more importantly, they are also really fit and cut."

Isabella pursed her lips in annoyance. "Erin, just choose a movie and put it in the DVD player. I need to put Alberto to bed at some point, so we can't be here all night waiting for you to pick a film."

Certain that she had hit a nerve, it was impossible for Erin to resist a little more teasing. "You know, this boxed set is pretty heavy." She lifted it up and down, flexing every muscle she could in the most obvious way.

"Just get on with it," Isabella snapped.

"Really? You don't want a ticket to the gun show?"

"What I want is to smack your blonde head. Pick. A. Movie. Now."

Erin laughed. "Fine, we'll watch Hugh Jackman's muscles instead."

She put the first disc into the player and sat down next to Isabella and Alberto, who was drowsily looking at his fingers. Erin thought it looked like he was trying to count them. He started to fidget, and Isabella stood up, mumbling, "All right, into your little gym you go then, *cariño*," before placing him on his back in the gym. He immediately started to reach for the butterfly again, and Isabella gently dragged the gym so it was between the sofa and the TV. Now they could see him whirling about on his back while watching the TV.

Isabella sat down unnecessarily close to her, Erin realized. So close that she could feel their hips and thighs pressed against each other. She didn't dare to make a sound or a move, frightened that Isabella might move away. It was strange to imagine they'd been passionately kissing and groping each other earlier, and now she felt like they were two thirteen-year-olds sitting next to each other at the movies and wondering if they dared to hold hands.

Erin felt the heat of Isabella's body and remembered what it was like to touch it and to press her own against it. She clenched and unclenched her hands and forced herself to breathe, to keep herself from wrestling Isabella down on the sofa and tearing her dress off to get close to that tempting body of hers.

Erin realized, with surprise, that Isabella had started the TV and DVD player while she was daydreaming.

Get a grip, Black, she thought to herself, pushing away the thoughts of a perfectly shaped ass and soft, olive-toned skin. *Not yet. It's only the second date, and her kid is right there.*

Luckily, Isabella chased away the lecherous thoughts, as she languidly reached over and took Erin's hand in hers.

Erin couldn't remember the last time holding hands had felt so intimate and overwhelming. Isabella's hand was warmer than her own and very soft. The long fingers snaked between hers until they were perfectly threaded. Just when Erin thought the moment couldn't get any better, Isabella lifted their clasped hands and placed a tender kiss on the back of Erin's.

Erin sighed happily and braved resting her head on Isabella's shoulder, as the movie went into an action scene. Isabella smelled lovely, and Erin had the added bonus of a view down her cleavage, something she tried not to abuse. She failed miserably.

On the floor, Alberto managed to kick the butterfly with his little foot and immediately tried to do it again with great excitement.

They'd taken a break, halfway into the movie, for Isabella to put Alberto down in his crib while Erin fetched some chips and dip. Isabella poured them more of the red wine they'd had with dinner. It worked surprisingly well with the snacks.

After the movie, Erin wasn't sure what to do. It didn't seem like the right time to try and get Isabella into bed. Things between them were still too delicate, and Erin was far too scared to rush and ruin it all. She knew she was going to go for that good-night kiss, but she didn't want to push it any further.

So she sat there, wondering how to know when the evening was over. She didn't want to leave too soon or overstay her welcome. How long could she stay before Isabella was too tired? When was the last train back to NYC?

She needn't have worried. Isabella stood up as the credits of the movie finished, seeming restless and stiff from having sat there. "Right, should we check when your next train leaves?"

Erin nodded, grateful. Isabella went to get her iPad and checked train times, and discovered there was one leaving in a little less than an hour.

"Sounds good. I'll get that one."

"Let me call you a taxi, and then we get a little while to say our good-byes while we wait for it."

Erin smiled, as she leaned back and put her hands behind her head. "Cool. I'm, uh, glad that we both agree that I should go tonight."

Isabella gave her an inscrutable look and a smile that looked rather practiced. *What's that about? Does she want me to stay? But she was the one who checked train times.*

Feeling useless and confused, Erin sat there watching Isabella call for a taxi.

"It should be here shortly," she informed Erin upon returning to the sofa.

"Brilliant. Thanks for that. Oh, and thanks for paying for the train fare earlier."

"It was the least I could do." Isabella stiffly placed her hands on her knees. Her whole body language spoke of distance and discomfort. Erin wondered if she'd done something wrong, or if Isabella was nervous for some reason.

Erin tucked a lock of hair behind her ear. "I think I'll text Chris from the train, ask him if he could help me get cover one day next week. That way we don't have to wait another week to see each other again. I mean, if that is okay with you?"

Some of Isabella's stiffness mellowed. "Of course. That sounds like a marvelous idea. Just let me know when."

"Well, if he can help get some of the other personal trainers to take some of my pickier clients, then I suppose I should give him some time to arrange stuff. So probably not Monday or Tuesday. I'll ask him about Wednesday?"

"Sure, we'll be home."

"Awesome."

"So, Chris... That's the owner of the gym you work in, right?"

"Yeah, it's a small gym, so the personal trainers who work there are technically freelance, just working out of his gym. It's more like a collaboration than him really being our boss, I guess. But, yeah, he owns it. Not that it does him any good. He was telling me that he wants to change his life. He's sweet, because he's a teddy bear, but he seems pretty jealous that I've met someone amazing in exotic Philly."

Isabella laughed, and more of that stiffness drained. "Poor man. Is he single?"

Erin raised her eyebrows. "What? You wanna date him too?"

"No, featherbrain. I was more thinking that I could set him up with someone who is also bored and thoroughly loathes the Philadelphia dating scene. If he is worthy of my little sister, that is. She's a pain, but I love her dearly. Don't ever tell her I said that, though. And I would only set her up with a really great guy."

"Oh, Chris is an awesome guy. He's sweet, funny, kind. Not overly bright, but clever enough to run a gym and keep it in the black. I doubt he makes much profit off it, though. Shame, really."

"Sweet, funny, and kind is all she needs. She'll tell him what to think anyway, so he doesn't have to be the sharpest tool in the shed. I have to ask and risk making Marie sound shallow, but I know what she falls for. Is he handsome?"

Erin shrugged. "Yeah, sure. He's got a chiseled chin, kind-lookin' face, and plenty of muscles, of course."

Isabella whistled low. "Perhaps I *should* date him."

Erin scowled, and Isabella leaned in for a brief kiss on top of Erin's ear. "But, then, how could he ever compete with your mind-blowing smile, alluring sea-green eyes, and sexy, feminine muscle tone? I think I'll stick with you, *preciosa*."

"You better," Erin muttered and grabbed Isabella's face for a kiss. It took Erin's breath away. There was so much longing and desire in it. If their hand-holding throughout the movie had been tentative and juvenile, this kiss was mature and *all* adult. Erin felt it from her toes and all the way up to the crown of her head. The hairs at the back of her neck stood on end.

It was crazy sexy, but more than that, it was meaningful. This kiss spoke of patience and importance; it held a promise of something long lasting.

The honk of a horn startled them both.

"I suppose that is your taxi," Isabella said in a low, half-strangled voice.

"Fuck," Erin muttered. Her whole body seemed to hum and tingle.

Isabella smirked and ran her finger along Erin's jaw. "You're so wonderful. You haven't even left yet, and I can't wait to see you again," she whispered, as her finger brushed over Erin's lips.

The taxi honked again, and Erin began to stand reluctantly. "That's it. If I can't get cover for Wednesday, I'll fake illness. Screw the clients if they leave."

Isabella beamed at her and purred, "Good girl."

Erin felt her body screaming to stay and do things that would make Isabella call her a bad girl, but she stood and went to pick up her jacket and backpack.

She smiled at Isabella before opening the door. "Good night, beautiful. Next time we should have midnight coffee, you know. Sweet dreams, and we'll talk tomorrow."

"Safe travels and sweet dreams," Isabella replied and blew a kiss.

Erin pretended to catch it and then left with surprisingly little regret. After all, they were in no hurry. Erin was going to get this right. They might just have the rest of their lives to take turns being both good girls and bad.

Chapter 17

Things We Do for Our Mothers

WITH BREAKFAST POLISHED OFF AND her morning coffee downed, Isabella's writing was going well. The words were finally ready for the page, and Isabella made the most of it.

Granted, it wasn't the chapter on "Beauty and the Beast" that she was meant to be writing, but the "Rumpelstiltskin" chapter would do just as well. She breathed deeply, relieved at how easily the words arranged themselves into a neat, flowing order as she wrote.

She paused a moment to think of a synonym, and her eyes fell on Alberto. He was on his stomach and doing a strange wriggle, not quite crawling and not quite shimmying but something in the middle. He looked very focused on his movements and didn't seem to notice his mother staring at him with proud eyes.

"*Ay, cariño*, you're almost crawling. Come here. Aim for *Mamá*."

She sat on the floor in front of him, arms outstretched. He looked up at her, a little frown creasing his face, seemingly confused at her sudden appearance. His hold on the floor slipped, and he was flat on his belly again. With an adorable grunt, he tried to get back into his little shimmy, but he seemed to have forgotten how it worked.

"Sorry, Alberto. Did I make you lose your concentration? Never mind. It will come back to you next time you want to break out of your gym."

She picked him up and kissed his forehead. He blinked at her and tried to put her nose in his mouth. Laughing, she moved away when she heard a beep. She went to fetch her phone, assuming it would be another annoying inspirational message. Marie had begun sending them since Isabella told her about Erin. Messages like *seize the day* and *give love a chance* had been coming in almost daily, and Isabella promptly ignored them. She could never tell if Marie sent them to cheer her on or to mess with her.

"That woman needs a hobby. Or a boyfriend," she muttered, as she picked up the phone. She was happily surprised to see a text from Erin.

Good morning, beautiful. How's your Sunday going? Miss me yet? ;-)

Isabella beamed. Every day, she thought about Erin and felt the craving for her as if it were a physical thing. Yes, she was missing Erin. A big part of her wished Erin had never left the apartment after their date yesterday. She'd never felt so comfortable around anyone, well, except for Alberto. The feeling was very addictive. As were Erin's kisses.

Hello, preciosa. It's going well. I've managed some writing, and Alberto is making progress on the crawling front, which is good for his age. How are you?

A text came back in a flash.

You didn't answer if you missed me.

Isabella felt the corners of her lips pull into an evil smile.

No, I didn't.

:-P Tease! Well, I miss you anyway.

Isabella went to answer but then changed her mind and pushed the *dial* button instead. Erin picked up right away.

"Hey, Ms. Writer."

"Hello again. I thought this was easier than texting back and forth."

"Yeah, probably cheaper too," Erin admitted.

"Yes. Besides, telling you that I miss you and can't wait to see you again sounds better vocally, I think."

Erin gave a victory yell, and Isabella smiled to herself. Only her upbringing kept her from making the same kind of sound.

Instead, Isabella settled for sighing happily and adding, "I missed you the second you left, to be honest. Sad, isn't it? I missed you so much that I went online and researched some of your interests."

"Ooooh, what might they be? Dalmatians? Pastries? Sexy baby mamas?"

"No. And I'm not answering any more questions if you are going to keep clowning around like that. Speaking of questions, did you ask Chris about time off?"

"Yep. I did, and he said he'd see what he could do. I think we have a good chance of meeting up again on Wednesday."

Isabella felt herself breathe a sigh of relief. "That's great news. We're looking forward to seeing you again."

"Well, either that or Alberto's learning to crawl so he can get away from me when I visit."

"Don't be silly, Erin. He likes you."

There was a long pause on the line before Erin replied, "Okay. So, um, what are we doing for our next date?"

"I don't know. Activities can be a bit tricky with babies."

"Ah, the lil' man's no good at bowling?"

Isabella scoffed. "He's probably better at it than I am. Sports aren't really my forte." Erin sniggered, and Isabella felt a buzz at having made Erin laugh.

"Well, there are activities we can do at your place. I mean, third date is when a lot of couples do the deed, y'know," Erin teased.

"Ah, the third date and not the second? I suppose that explains why you left last night and didn't come to bed with me," Isabella countered without missing a beat. She was glad they were discussing the topic that bothered her even before Erin had left.

Erin was quiet for a while and then almost whispered, "You wanted me to stay?"

"Honestly? I didn't want to push you or seem too eager, but, yes, I thought that was where the evening was headed. You were so considerate, though, so I assumed you wanted us to wait."

Erin sighed, then laughed a little. "Well damn. I feel like such a dumbass. That explains your behavior at the end of the night. Um, yeah, I did want to wait, because I wanted to make sure you were ready and be certain I wasn't pushing you. Other than that, I was frickin' starving for you."

Isabella felt a jolt as adrenaline began to pump through her veins. She tried to sound calm as she replied, "Then we should feed that voracious appetite of yours on the next date."

"Are you sure?"

"Erin, I couldn't be more certain. I'm ready. I…I need you."

Isabella heard Erin blow out a long breath before saying, "Yay! Not only are you taking me to bed, but I now know what to expect. You are saving my nerves a lot of anguish here, doll."

Isabella smiled and tried to calm her thundering heart. "Likewise. And I can't believe you just called me doll. Who says that these days?"

Erin groaned. "Sorry. I picked that up from playing poker with old New Yorker guys when I first moved to the city. I'll try to stick to babe—if you're okay with that one?"

"It's not my preferred term of endearment. But I really like it when you say it."

"Cool." Erin cleared her throat. "So, um, what else are we doing on Wednesday? I mean, before the kid gets sleepy?"

Isabella laughed and looked over at Alberto, who had just managed to roll himself onto his back and was now trying to go back onto his stomach.

"Same as yesterday, perhaps? Dinner and a movie. Is that dull?"

"Babe. We have loads of X-Men movies to get through. I say we should do *at least* one per date."

Isabella closed her eyes as she laughed. "That's settled, then."

A few hours later, Isabella wished she was still enjoying the flirty banter with Erin over the phone and not stuck sitting at a long and expensive teak table. It didn't matter how elegant the dining room was or how lovely the soft sound of Brahms playing in the background, or how tasty the salmon coulibiac on her plate. Dinner at her parents' house was a long and somber affair. Uncomfortable silences were broken by long lectures from her mother. Isabella decided that moving back to Philadelphia had been a very bad idea.

She was almost relieved when Alberto cried and she had to take him out of the room to soothe his stomach. But once he'd settled, Isabella had to resume her place at the dreaded table. She focused on her food and the occasional, hushed small talk with her father.

Whenever Judith looked away, Alberto Sr. took the opportunity to tickle his grandson or let the baby grab one of his big fingers and gum it.

Suddenly, Judith put her cutlery down with her usual poise. "So, Isabella. How have you settled in to your new home? It's obviously rather bijou, but it seemed adequate."

"Yes. It's been fine. Plenty of room for me and Alberto." Isabella returned her focus to her food, reluctant to give Judith information, simply out of habit.

Judith took a sip of her wine. "I see. Have you had any help with getting the place in order?"

Isabella knew that tone of voice—*polite interrogation.* "Yes, little Alberto has been great help picking out curtains and blankets. He decided on a navy blue theme to match the sofa, and I have to agree with his decision. It looks lovely against the light-gray walls."

Alberto Sr. coughed quietly, probably to hide a snigger. Her mother caught her gaze and held it.

"Isabella Martinez," she said. "Are you being facetious?"

Isabella looked her straight in the eye, not wavering an inch. "No, Mother. I was merely making a joke."

Judith looked displeased, but as usual, she kept her cards close to her chest. She took another sip of wine before casually asking, "So, no visitors?"

Before she could pick up her water glass, Isabella stopped her mother's hand. *Oh well, now is as good a time as any.* She sat up straighter and ignored her quickening pulse.

"Yes, actually. One. Which reminds me," Isabella turned to her father. "Daddy, do you think you could babysit Alberto for a few hours one evening? In case I want to go out for dinner with someone?"

Alberto Sr. was just about to open his mouth to reply, but Judith spoke first. "You're asking him and not the both of us?"

Why would I want someone around my son who thinks denying a child dinner or locking them in the basement are acceptable child-rearing techniques? Isabella knew it wouldn't do any good to say that. They'd simply spend the rest of the evening arguing. Besides, if she caused a fight over this, it would be harder for her father to get away and babysit without her mother coercing him into bringing her along. Subtlety was the better plan right now.

"I didn't ask you, because I know how busy you are with work. Daddy's retired and likes being around children. That makes him the obvious candidate for babysitting. Besides, we all know that your grandson and your Chanel suits don't mix well." Her mother dipped her head as if to concede the point, and Isabella felt her breathing slow down a little. She'd pulled it off. "That is, if you are willing to babysit, Daddy?"

Once more, her mother cut in before her father could reply. "So, there is a romantic partner on the horizon? Someone you are dating?"

"I didn't say that, Mother. I might just as well be dining with a friend, an old acquaintance from work, or even Marie," Isabella replied without looking over at her mother.

She kept her gaze on her father, and he seemed to appreciate it. He gave her a nod which looked almost conspiratorial. *Oh, I bet Mother will make him pay for that later.*

"Of course, *mija*. I'll babysit the little tiger anytime. Oh, and speaking of Marie, have you heard about the new affirmation classes she plans to start running?"

Normally, Isabella hated talking about Marie's questionable doctrines, but her father had hit on the one subject guaranteed to drive Judith away from criticizing Isabella's life, criticizing Marie's.

"No. What does that entail?" Isabella asked innocently.

Judith glared at her, and Isabella knew that the subject of her love life was not over, merely put aside for the moment. Judith put her glass down and gave a heartfelt scoff before launching into a diatribe about how Marie's new classes would never take off and how she should get herself a "real job."

Well aware that her mother believed that writing was also on the list of jobs that were not "real," Isabella just nodded and finished her food. Her father did the same, both of them happy to be out of the firing line for a while.

Alberto Jr. blinked at his ranting grandmother as though he was trying to understand her point of view. Isabella smiled sadly at him. *If you can achieve that, you'll be the only one in the room who can.*

In the taxi home, Isabella texted Erin.

Hey, preciosa. Quick question: I know you said you had spoken to Chris about getting cover for Wednesday, but did you mention Marie to him? Xx

The reply took a while. Erin was apparently busy—maybe with working out or playing online poker? Just as the taxi neared her apartment and she was about to put her phone away, it beeped.

Hi, babe! So glad to hear from you. Does that mean you're freed from the dungeon now? ;-) Yep, I mentioned that you had a sister who was smart, sweet, and on the market. He seemed interested, esp. when I said what she did for a living. He said he likes positive women. He wants to see a pic. Lol. Xxx

Isabella smiled as she typed.

Yes, I'm free and almost home now. When I get in, I'll switch on the computer and call you, then send over a picture of Marie. I feel like I owe her a favor after letting Mother spend 40 minutes insulting her tonight. Besides, if she's not single, she won't text me so many "inspirational quotes for the day," and that would be a huge relief. Speak soon. xx

Chapter 18

Wednesday

MENTALLY THANKING THE TWO PERSONAL trainers who'd covered for her, Erin stepped off the train, stretched her legs, and ran for the nearest taxi. She was going to see Isabella, and every second waiting was torturous.

All throughout their Skype chat last night, Erin had looked at the woman that she was now officially dating and wished she could be in the same room as her. Breathe in her scent, touch her skin, and ask for another kiss. Or seven.

She sent a text from the taxi.

> *Hey babe! On my way to you now, should be there in a few minutes. I'm excited like a goddamn kid. Can't even pretend to play it cool. What the hell have you done to me? Xxx*

The reply came in right away, and Erin got an image of Isabella and Alberto pacing the apartment with one eye on the phone and another at the door, waiting for her. She was well aware that the image might be mere wishful thinking.

> *Good afternoon, preciosa. I'm excited too and nervous as well. Like a virgin on her wedding night, if I'm completely honest. It's pathetic, and I blame you entirely. Hurry up and get here (safely). Xx*

Erin stared at the text, a strange feeling growing in her stomach. Was Isabella alluding to the fact that they had talked about going to bed together tonight? Was that what the virgin comment meant? Or was she just using that as a metaphor for being nervous about seeing Erin in person again? *Is there any other reason for her to be anxious?*

She vowed to test the waters to make sure Isabella was still comfortable, that she wanted to sleep together as much as Erin did. She would point out that there was no pressure, and if something happened, she would be really frickin' gentle. And considerate…and passionate…and tender…and loving…and Erin felt nervous too. Just as the taxi pulled up at Isabella's apartment.

She paid the driver and, at the door, buzzed the intercom. Isabella opened the door with Alberto resting against her shoulder.

"Hello. I was at the window and saw you arrive. Come on in." Isabella stood aside, and Erin walked past her and Alberto into the corridor.

"What? I don't get to poke your stomach this time?" Erin joked.

Isabella gave her a scowl that quickly morphed into a tentative smile. Her uncertainty was endearing, but Erin got a feeling it was an alien and uncomfortable feeling for Isabella. She tried her best to think of ways to make Isabella comfortable.

Just before they went into the apartment, Erin leaned over and cheekily stole a kiss, softly, quickly pressing her lips to Isabella's before pulling back. It was Isabella who leaned in and returned the kiss, demanding more. The kiss was intense, deep, and passionate. It was so easy to get lost in the whispered promises of that kiss, that Erin forgot who and where they were, until Alberto made a noise that sounded like he was trying to imitate an owl.

Erin moved away, panting, and worried that she'd somehow upset him. Isabella interpreted Erin's actions differently and seemed to think Erin had reacted to the sound he had made.

"I know. I don't why he keeps saying that. He's been doing it all morning. I suppose he is just trying it out, but it's still peculiar."

She nodded and forced herself to smile. *Chill, Black. Everything's fine. He's not gonna throw a fit just 'cos you kissed his mother.* She shook her head to clear the fuzziness left over from the kiss…and the worry.

When they were inside, Erin dropped her rucksack onto the table. Isabella glanced over, and Erin wondered at what point she'd start asking

Erin to hang it up on the coat stand or something. She guessed she had another date or two before the romance wore off enough.

"So, protein bars, comics, and a water bottle as usual? It seems to be quite a big bag for so few items, if you don't mind me saying." Isabella placed Alberto in the baby gym.

Erin scratched her neck. "Actually, there are a few other things in there today."

"Oh, did you buy Alberto another toy? You don't need to buy his affection, you know."

"Um, no. It's not that. It's, um, some overnight stuff. You know, toothbrush, face wash, deodorant. That kind of stuff. Not to make any assumptions or to pressure you or anything."

Isabella fiddled with her watch, a slim thing in silver and black. "That's fine, Erin. I don't find it presumptuous." Isabella cleared her throat and tucked her hair behind her ear. Her gaze just to the side of Erin.

Cursing herself for doing the opposite of relaxing Isabella, Erin stepped forward and took Isabella's hand. "Seriously, though. There's no pressure, Isabella. I only want to take this further if you do too. I don't want you to be uncomfortable or, you know, afraid."

Isabella looked annoyed. "I'm not afraid. Jesus, Erin. What the hell is in those jeans of yours that could make me scared, a grizzly bear?"

The joke was nearly irresistible. "Nope. I trimmed when I showered this morning."

It seemed to take Isabella a short while before she got it. When she did, she clearly aimed for a disapproving look but broke into a grin instead.

Working on the good vibe she'd started, Erin brought Isabella's hand up to her mouth as if to kiss it. She turned it palm up and then blew a raspberry onto it; the farting sound made Isabella jump and Erin laugh.

"Erin! What are you—eleven?"

"No, if I was, I wouldn't need to trim," Erin said with a tired sigh.

Isabella gave a confused frown. "You make it sound like you spent hours cutting your pubic hair. When I saw it on camera, it seemed perfectly normal..." Isabella stopped herself midsentence. "Why are we even having this conversation? I'm turning into you. I'll have to beat some decorum into you, Miss Black."

Erin snorted. "You could try, lady."

149

"I hasten to add that I'm obviously not referring to actual violence. It's just a figure of speech."

Pulling Isabella into a hug, Erin mumbled, "I know. Relax..." into her neck. She breathed in Isabella's perfume and the smell of her skin, and calmed down; they both seemed to. Finally, she had Isabella in her arms, and everything was perfect.

From the floor, Alberto softly cried, "Hoo." Isabella laughed, and Erin smiled as she nuzzled the warm skin.

A couple of hours and many kisses later, Erin found Isabella staring at her while she kneeled next to Alberto in his baby gym. "What?"

"Nothing. Just watching you with him. You seem a little unsure. I've been assuming it's just because you aren't used to babies but..." Isabella trailed off.

Erin sat up. "But what?"

"Looking at you now, I wondered if there might be more to it than that. You look as if you are terrified of him. Have I...somehow scared you away from interacting with him? I know I can give the impression that he only responds to me, because I'm very tightly bonded to him, but he really is fine with other people."

Erin went to run her hand through her hair and remembered that she was wearing it in a long braid down her back. She settled for running her hand over the braid, stalling for time.

"No, no. It's nothing you've done." She looked down at Alberto, as he smiled up at his mother. She considered how much to tell Isabella and settled for a light version of her thoughts and feelings about Alberto.

"Like you say, I'm not used to babies. And, you know, it's a lot of responsibility. I guess I'm just worried about getting stuff wrong."

Isabella looked down at Alberto while she pondered Erin's statement. "I see what you mean. Yes, there is a lot of responsibility with babies and, yes, it's possible to get things wrong. But as long as you're sensible and care about his wellbeing, you shouldn't get it too hideously wrong." She looked back up at Erin and smiled at her before continuing. "Babies are a whole new world when you've never been around one. It was for me. During Alberto's first weeks, I'd ask Richard questions, as he had experience with

Joshua. But even then, Richard wasn't very present. He was always working or too tired for baby talk. So, I learned things by trial and error, reading baby books, and a surprising amount of Googling strange questions."

Licking her lips nervously, Erin nodded and looked down at Alberto, who was still trying to catch his butterfly. Isabella was still watching her. It made her uneasy.

"The only way we can get you comfortable with him, I think, is to let you handle him." Isabella bit her lower lip, clearly deep in thought. "It's about time to change his diaper. By the smell, I'd say there is nothing too horrible in there, but it is probably wet. Come with me to change him." Isabella reached out a hand to stroke her cheek. "Don't look so horrified, *preciosa*, it won't be that bad. And if it is, you can always leave again. I'll do everything. You just have to watch and have a chat with him, keep him entertained. I promise it'll be all right."

Unable to argue, Erin followed Isabella, who picked up her son and carried him off to the bathroom. The changing table held an assortment of diapers and creams. Erin looked at them carefully, trying to figure out what they all were, in case Isabella asked for one of them.

Isabella caught her staring at the label of one and smiled. "You look like you are trying to read the print off it."

"Just trying to figure out what does what, in case you need one of 'em fast."

"I appreciate that, but they're not surgical tools, and this isn't an operating theatre. I can reach all the creams, so there's no need for you to worry. Just stand here with me, and make silly faces at him if he grumbles."

Erin stood slightly behind Isabella so that she could hold onto her. With her arms around Isabella's waist and her head on Isabella's shoulder, the whole ordeal seemed a lot cozier and less worrisome.

Alberto seemed fine too, as Isabella took off his onesie and Erin took the time to smile at the fact that it was made to look like a little three-piece suit. She hadn't noticed that earlier. Out of his clothes, Alberto seemed even happier and reached up his chubby little legs trying to grab his feet. Isabella mumbled something in Spanish to him, and he cooed back, seemingly glad for her attention.

Erin nestled her head into the crook of Isabella's neck and was jostled a little when Isabella moved to take Alberto's diaper off.

"Oh, sorry. Should I move?"

"No, *preciosa*. Not if it helps you. I certainly don't mind having you close."

Erin chuckled, comfort seeping in as soon as they were flirting. "Good. I love being close to you. And I can still make funny faces at lil' man if you need me too."

"Glad to hear it. Although he doesn't seem to need any distraction right now. He seems to think it's funny watching you hide behind me."

Erin gasped. "I'm not hiding, I'm cuddling. It's not the same thing." She looked at Alberto, who was grinning toothlessly at her. The smile looked friendly and happy, and her heart soared as she looked at his adorable face. "He's damn cute like this, all happy to be in his birthday suit."

"Yes. The fact that he's getting all the attention and hasn't had any stomach trouble all day helps a lot too," Isabella said and tickled Alberto's round little belly.

He wriggled, and Erin laughed. "You're right, babe. This isn't bad at all."

Isabella turned her head and gave Erin a quick kiss on the lips. "I'm glad you feel that way. Trust me when I say that everything would be worse if there was something more unfortunate in that diaper."

"Ew." Erin playfully slapped Isabella's side. "Don't be silly. Look at him. He's all clean and cute. He doesn't do gross poos."

Isabella gave a mirthless laugh. "Oh, you'd be surprised. Although, they say it will get worse when he starts eating solids."

"Hey, I'm warming to the kid here. Don't put me off."

"Fine. I'm sorry," Isabella said with a laugh. She reached for a clean diaper just as her phone rang. She looked out into the room behind them to where the phone was but then shook her head. "We'll let it ring. They can call back." Isabella started to unwrap the diaper. The phone kept ringing, and Erin saw Isabella look out into the room again.

Erin looked at the happy baby and felt quite brave suddenly. "Why don't you go get it?"

"You sure that's okay?"

"Yeah. Why not? He can't fall off of this table because of the raised edges, and he seems to be in a great mood. Go answer it. I'll scream to high heavens if he turns green or tries to stab me with a tube of cream."

Isabella gave her another peck on the lips and smoothly wriggled out of her arms. "Okay. I'll answer it and get rid of them quickly. I'm putting the diaper over him here, I'd leave it there if I was you. I'll be right back, *preciosa*."

"Yeah, sure. Hurry, before they hang up!"

With Isabella out of the room and on her way to the phone, Erin moved closer to Alberto. "Hey, lil' man. You okay? Mommy will be back soon."

He cooed happily at her and grabbed the diaper that his mother had laid over his lower regions. He started to pull the diaper up so he could look at it. Seeing no harm in him investigating it a little, Erin let him. After all, it was keeping him entertained.

She stopped him from gumming it to make sure none of it came off in his mouth but otherwise, they were both happy with the way things were. Until the moment he was babbling nonsense at her, waving the diaper around, and Erin felt a stream of warm pee hit her torso.

"Oh, crap," she screamed and backed away quickly.

Isabella said something on the phone, then hung up, and came running over. "What happened? Are you both okay?"

"He frickin' peed on me, Isabella!"

Isabella put her hand over her mouth. "Oh, Erin," she whispered. "That's why I told you to keep the diaper on him."

"Well, you should've explained more!"

It was clear that Isabella was trying to be sympathetic and not to break into laughter. It was also clear that she was losing the battle.

A piteous whine escaped Erin at the sight of her own wet shirt. "You promised me this would be all right. This is totally not all right."

Isabella's laughter greeted her, along with an apology that was barely audible through the giggling. But it didn't take long before Erin was laughing with her.

On the table, Alberto simply said, "Hoo," and waved the diaper triumphantly.

Fifteen minutes later, Alberto was changed and dressed, Isabella had called her father back to explain what had happened, and Erin was still in the shower, soaping and resoaping her chest with lavender-scented soap.

She heard Isabella knock on the bathroom door. "Erin? Do you want to borrow a clean shirt from me? That way you can keep whatever change of clothes you brought for tomorrow?"

Thinking about it, Erin slowly turned the shower off to answer.

"Uh, yeah, please. Can I borrow a bra too? To wear tonight and tomorrow. Mine got soaked, and I didn't bring a spare."

There was a moment of silence before Isabella carefully said, "Are you sure you need one? I mean, I understand why you need one tomorrow, but I'm washing your clothes now. They should be dry by tomorrow, so you can wear your own for the travel home."

Erin smirked. "So you think I should be braless tonight, huh?"

"Well, I don't see why you would need a bra for these few hours."

Her grin grew bigger. It was only five. There was plenty of evening left to require a bra.

"Well, if you're cleaning my clothes, then I don't need to borrow a shirt either. I can just wear my second outfit tonight and my newly cleaned shirt tomorrow?"

Silence. Then Isabella grumbled, "I'm not going to stand here talking through the door like some jailer in a prison. We will discuss it when you come out."

You mean when I come out and I'm topless and in your bedroom? Yeah, I think that is why you wanted me to borrow your clothes. Erin grinned, happy at the thought.

Suddenly, she wished she hadn't teased Isabella. She should've just played along and stood topless in front of Isabella's clothes, slowly picking out a garment and enjoying Isabella's glances. Then she realized how nice it'd be to wear Isabella's clothes. They'd smell like her. Or, at least, like her pricey fabric softener. Most importantly, the shirt would be Isabella's.

"Actually, Isabella…I'd like to borrow a shirt," Erin called toward the door.

There was no reply, and Erin wondered if Isabella had left or if she was ignoring her. She hurried up and dried herself off with a thick, mauve towel that matched the bath mat and the shower curtain. She smiled and mused that Isabella was the most adult person that she'd ever met.

She considered stealing some lotion to soften up for tonight's romantic action, but realized that Isabella's soap was so moisturizing that she didn't need it. She put on her panties, socks, and red jeans and then stepped out of the plush little bathroom.

Isabella had been sitting on the sofa, playing with Alberto, lifting him up in the air and making him squeal. She stopped, baby in midair, and stared at Erin's naked chest.

Erin smiled shyly and resisted the urge to shimmy and show off her assets...and make herself feel a little less self-conscious.

"Could I borrow a shirt after all? You know, um, just in case my shirt doesn't dry for tomorrow?"

"O-of course," Isabella stuttered. She averted her eyes, cradled Alberto in her arms, and walked into the bedroom to fetch a top, leaving Erin alone in the room, cold after her hot shower.

She crossed her arms over her naked chest and considered asking for a bra as well before deciding against it, pretty sure that Isabella wore at least one size bigger than she did. She let her mind wander and was surprised to realize that she didn't feel too worked up about what had happened. Yes, something had gone wrong. Yes, it might have been avoided if she'd listened to Isabella's advice about keeping the diaper in place. However, Alberto was fine. Sure, Erin had gotten sprayed, but she was clean now, and what really mattered was that Alberto was okay. In fact, he'd come out of their little adventure smiling and cheerful. He hadn't even complained when Isabella put his diaper and clothes on.

Had he been older, Erin would've wondered if Alberto had done it on purpose to mess with her, but he was just a baby. He'd been lovely and sweet while she was getting ready for her shower, oblivious to anything wrong. Erin took comfort in that.

Isabella returned with a black, long-sleeved T-shirt, and Erin realized that she had missed her chance to play the bare-breasted temptress and make Isabella watch as she chose a top from her wardrobe. She rolled her eyes at her lack of suaveness before accepting the shirt. She stopped herself just as she was about to put it on.

"Damn, I forgot to get my deodorant from my bag."

"Use mine, it's closer. It's on the top shelf there," Isabella pointed to the bathroom cabinet visible through the open door, still averting her gaze from Erin's bare chest.

The deodorant was right next to a small glass bottle with foreign text beneath a black dress. Erin opened it and sniffed the pink contents.

Isabella's perfume. A pleasant shiver went down her spine. She put the bottle back and focused on why she was in there. It felt strangely intimate using Isabella's deodorant. She could get used to this, being so close to Isabella and covering herself in Isabella's things. She gave the deodorant a moment to sink in, then pulled on the shirt.

When she returned, Isabella had put Alberto in his baby bouncer and was busy taste-testing the food she'd obviously started cooking while Erin was in the shower.

"I hope you like chicken enchiladas. I prepared them this morning and just finished them in the oven. I think we spoke about enchiladas once, and you said you liked them?"

"I don't like them. I frickin' love them," Erin said with a huge grin.

Isabella gave her a pleased smile and gestured toward the table. "Excellent. Would you set the table?"

"Sure. Does lil' man need a plate?" Erin asked jokingly.

"Not unless you'll be changing his diapers and staying up with him when his stomach turns into a war zone," Isabella deadpanned.

"Fine, let him stick to milk, and I'll eat all the enchiladas."

Erin got two plates out of the cabinet Isabella had opened for her, while smiling like a fool. *I could get used to this.*

The wine looked dark in the candlelit room. Erin swirled it around her glass, watching it turn from dark-red to black, depending on where the light from the candles hit it.

She was sitting on the sofa, still digesting the large quantity of food she'd eaten, an hour after dinner. The enchiladas had been amazing, and while she didn't know what was in Isabella's salad dressing, she did know that it turned a humble salad into a little bowl of heaven.

Isabella was in the tiny room that served as Alberto's nursery, putting him down for the night. And Erin missed her. Ten feet away and she actually missed her. *She's only been gone ten minutes. What's wrong with you?*

She swirled her wine one last time, then swallowed it all in a dangerously big gulp. After that, she needed a steadying breath. With dinner over and Alberto asleep…well, the next step was pretty obvious.

She was looking forward to touching Isabella more than she could say, but she was scared too, frightened that she'd make Isabella feel unsafe or uncomfortable. She knew that if it hadn't been for that worry, she'd have probably made a move earlier. God knew, she wanted Isabella enough. She burned so damn hot for her, she could power a nuclear reactor.

If only Isabella would make the first move. Erin rested her head back on the sofa and looked up at the ceiling. Just thinking about making love to her made her heart race. In the good way. But the thought of getting it wrong and ruining Isabella's first time with a woman—her first sexual interaction in months—made Erin's heart race in a very, very bad way.

When Isabella came out and quietly closed the door behind her, she padded silently across the room, graceful and beautiful as ever. She sat next to Erin. They were perfectly still for a long moment; neither of them spoke, nor moved a muscle.

"I think all that wine has gone to my head. I feel kinda warm," Erin said to break the silence.

Isabella looked at her strangely. "It was nonalcoholic wine. That's why I had some too. Remember?"

Erin scratched her forehead, avoiding eye contact. "Oh right, yeah. Sorry. It must be something else, then."

Isabella edged a little closer. "Yes. I think I'm feeling that *something else* too."

She put two fingers under Erin's chin and tilted her face toward her. She leaned in and slowly let their lips connect.

Erin's breath stopped. She tried not to panic. It was happening. Right now. They were kissing, and surely there was only one place this could lead. Erin gently broke off the kiss. "Isabella. Won't we wake Alberto if we..." The master bedroom was right next to his little room.

"Make love?" Isabella shook her head gently, barely moving away from Erin's lips. "As long as his stomach doesn't bother him, he sleeps quite soundly these days. Besides, I can think of a number of ways to muffle that wonderful mouth of yours."

She kissed her again. This time, Erin didn't stop to worry about anything. After all, if Isabella's mouth could feel this heavenly, what was the point to thinking about anything else?

Chapter 19

Connecting

Isabella stood on trembling legs. Everything felt slightly surreal, and she worried about sensory overload. She'd never been as aware of the combination of lust and love as she was right now. It was a strange sensation, feeling like an insecure teenager overcome with affection and a grown woman who knew what her body wanted at the same time.

When Erin stood up and took her hand, it felt comforting, steadying. She knew that, any second, Erin would ask if she was okay and if she was sure. Erin would reiterate—for the fifteenth time—that they didn't have to do this. Isabella clasped her hand tightly, and before Erin could open her mouth to speak, walked them toward her bedroom. Erin followed silently and closed the door behind them.

They stood facing each other in the darkness. Only the moonlight pouring in the window allowed them to see one another.

Erin still looked worried, and Isabella wished she could put on her usual mask of confidence to convince Erin that she was fine. She was perfectly fine, and she wanted this more than anything. But that didn't mean she wasn't nervous.

She could handle hostile corporate takeovers, heated political debates, and even Judith Martinez. This, however, was something new. She'd never felt like this about anything or anyone. Overwhelming passion, laced with such worry about getting it wrong. And the fear that she would shake her head and realize it had all been a dream.

To keep Erin from talking—Isabella couldn't talk any more now, she needed action—she began to undress. Soon her cashmere cardigan and her dress lay in a pool around her expensive heels. She stepped out of the shoes, as well, and stood in front of Erin in only a black bra, panties, and stockings.

It worked like a charm. Erin sucked in a loud breath and moved forward. She reached out a hand and almost touched Isabella, who closed her eyes, nearly begging for that touch. The heat of Erin's hand was amazing, as it trailed just above the skin from her neck, down over her shoulder, and rested over her right breast. When she felt the hand hover over her breast, Isabella worried about milk leakage but pushed the thought out of her mind. Whatever was going to happen would happen. All she could do was relax and focus on being in the moment. She'd never get this night back, and she was determined to enjoy and memorize every second.

When, finally, Erin's hand gently touched her bra-clad breast, Isabella actually gasped in pleasure. But almost immediately, the horrible thought hit her. What if the rapid intake of breath had caused her nipple to leak? She had to stop panicking, but she didn't know how.

"Don't worry, sweetheart. Everything will be all right. I promise," Erin whispered.

Her voice was so sweet and tender, that Isabella couldn't help but smile. She reminded herself once more to enjoy, not overthink.

"Kiss me, and I'll believe you," Isabella whispered back.

Erin bridged the gap between them and softly connected their mouths. Lips locked, and hands found places to hold onto. Quickly, Erin's hands began to move, gliding over her arms and her sides, and settling on her hips. She licked at Isabella's lower lip and then kissed where she'd licked, before returning her tongue back into Isabella's mouth.

Dazed, Isabella's hands ran over Erin's neck and shoulders. When she felt Erin's long braid, she gently took hold, letting it anchor her as the room began to spin.

A small, lucid part of Isabella's brain realized that Erin was undoing her jeans, and without breaking the kiss, was pushing them down her legs. The naked skin of Erin's thighs pressed against the bared bit of thigh above Isabella's stockings, sensitive bits of skin that had never before touched each other—a teasing taste of what was to come.

Isabella needed more. Erin's mouth was wonderful, but there was so much more to explore, and her lust was impatient. Her lips had to conquer; they had to know that Erin was truly hers. She brushed them over Erin's neck in their feverish exploration and happened upon her pulse point. The beat was hard and fast, like a creature trapped under Erin's beautiful jawline. Isabella kissed there, deliberately this time, and felt the beat quicken against the delicate skin of her lips. She pressed tighter, no longer able to separate Erin's pulse from her own as it thrummed in her lips.

With a soft groan, Erin broke away and pulled off the borrowed shirt. Isabella was eternally grateful that Erin hadn't borrowed a bra, as her breasts caught her eye in the light of the full, pale moon.

Erin's skin looked almost translucent in the white light, and the pink areolas stood out clearly, calling to her. Isabella held her breath and bent down to kiss them, one and then the other, without hurry. Erin quietly moaned Isabella's name and threaded strong fingers through her hair. Still, Isabella needed more. With her mouth busy, Isabella tugged Erin's panties down and reluctantly let go of Erin's nipple to follow them down Erin's legs. Crouched at her feet, she helped Erin step out of the jeans, her panties, and finally her socks.

Erin stood before her, naked with her chin thrust out, wearing a smile that was equal parts encouragement and tenderness. It made Isabella's heart ache to know that in a moment like this—when Erin should be absorbed by her own desire and needs—her focus was to look after and reassure her.

Isabella took Erin's outstretched hands, feeling her fingers interlocking with her own. Isabella raked her gaze over Erin's nakedness. She was breathing far too fast. She'd have to calm down, or she was going to hyperventilate.

Indeed, everything seemed to slow. Things that normally mattered became unimportant. She became a creature of sensation; thoughts, plans, and the notion of decorum didn't matter. All that mattered was Erin's body and how she could connect with it, how she could get close to it—to Erin—the person who somehow made her feel both more vulnerable and more invincible than she had ever felt before.

She was stunning—her breathing shallow, her eyes glazed, and her cheeks flushed. They kissed, and there seemed to be no instigator, it merely happened, as if it was unstoppable. As if a kiss could be a force of nature.

With hands that trembled ever so slightly, Isabella undid her bra and took it off. Erin helped her remove the panties and garters, dropping it all in a messy pile on the floor. Then she placed hot, reverent kisses over the front of Isabella's thighs before getting back up.

When they both stood facing each other once more, Isabella bridged the gap between weeks of fantasies to what could now be real. She let her hands trail over every bit of Erin she could reach, then Erin pulled her into another kiss.

There'd been so much longing, so much distance, and now...now it all fell away. Just like their clothes. They were both here and blessedly alone. She'd never felt more free or more captivated by another person. She felt as if her heart was going to beat out of her chest.

The kisses grew wild, and she felt teeth against her lips. She'd always hated being bitten during kisses, but now it seemed like the only reasonable way of doing things. She would bite and be bitten. Taste and be tasted. Devour and be devoured. There was no stopping what they'd started.

Hands cupped her ass, and she groaned into the kiss, desperate for this abundance of romance and emotion to grow dirty. She wanted it all, and she could feel that Erin did too. Her own hands roamed the arch of Erin's lower back and up to clearly defined shoulder blades. She caressed them worshipfully, then reached up to grab at the shoulders, pulling Erin even closer to her, so close that it was hard to draw breath properly. What did that matter? Why would she need to breathe when she could just melt into Erin instead?

Erin sucked gently but hungrily on Isabella's tongue. Isabella let it happen. Her hands ran down Erin's arms and caught her hands. Their fingers intertwined, and somehow that innocent touch led her so much deeper into her need. Her body buzzed with it, and she knew she'd be soaked by the time they actually got into bed. *Good. Let her see how much I want her. Let her feel what she does to me.*

She broke off the kiss, knowing she was running out of patience with this foreplay. "Bed. Now," she ordered.

"Great idea," came Erin's reply.

They fell against the tightly tucked bedding of Isabella's queen-sized bed, Erin on top. Isabella closed her eyes and moaned at how eager Erin's touch had become. Before long, those needy hands trailed over Isabella's inner thigh and up to her core. Neither of them could stay quiet when Erin's fingers touched where they were most needed. Isabella slid her body down on the bed, clumsily forcing Erin's fingers into her body. Erin gasped with surprise and broke off their kiss.

"I—oh God—I couldn't wait any more," Isabella said breathlessly. "I need you."

She tugged Erin's head back to hers and kissed her again, as she began to move on Erin's fingers in a slow, steady rhythm. It felt so sweet and strangely familiar. Erin accommodated her and moved to meet her on every dip. She placed her wrist against Isabella so that it brushed against her clit every time the fingers slid inside.

Perhaps it was clichéd, but Isabella felt time stop. They'd be here forever, she was certain of it, and it would be heaven. Her body, however, had other ideas. It was certain this pleasure wouldn't—couldn't—go on forever. Very soon it would be uncontrollable.

They both moved faster, the friction growing rougher, needier. Erin's fingers curled to find the spot inside that would undo Isabella, who marveled at how easily Erin found it. Soon, she couldn't marvel at anything. Her vision filled with light, and her body tingled with pulsing energy from deep inside.

She grabbed onto Erin, one arm around her shoulders and a hand clutching her braid, as she let go and let the orgasm take her over. It'd been so long since she last came that, for a moment, she wasn't sure if it had always been this intense, or if this time was extra forceful.

In her pleasured confusion, it took a few moments to realize that the orgasm wasn't ending. It rolled through her body, both energizing and draining her in the same instant. On and on, it claimed her—Erin claimed her.

When she finally relaxed, the pleasure slowly became manageable and eventually ebbed away. That hadn't been just any old orgasm. That had been the best one of her life.

"You feel amazing," Erin said with a low groan. Her fingers moved inside Isabella, and Isabella tried to give them a little squeeze, letting her sex show the appreciation her speech center was too exhausted to manage.

She closed her eyes, trying to regain her equilibrium. Her body was exhausted, but she was still aroused. She wondered if this was it, if from now on she would want Erin every minute of every day for the rest of their life. The thought made her smile.

Erin kissed the smile away, and soon Isabella's world centered around their mouths as they connected again. Tasting Erin's mouth made her curious for more. She wanted a more concentrated flavor of Erin.

Between kisses, Isabella mumbled, "Roll us over."

Erin obeyed without question until Isabella was on top. She left Erin's mouth, kissing her way down her neck and her clavicles. She explored Erin's breasts once more, then moved down her stomach, smiling into her kisses when she hit a ticklish spot and felt Erin giggle. Erin caressed her tousled hair and her neck, while Isabella kissed her way down.

Soon, Isabella's lips were tickled by little wisps of hair, and the warm scent of arousal grew stronger. She'd thought about going down on a woman so many times, wondered what it would be like. Excitement, happiness, and pride filled her mind. Erin would be her first. She'd waited until she found the very best of women to experience this new pleasure with.

Gently, she let her lips and the tip of her tongue try out everything they found. The taste was nicer than male lovers had made her think, but maybe that was just Erin. There was a slight tang, a hint of spices, but mostly it tasted warm and inviting. A complex taste that grew stronger the more aroused Erin got. Soon, Erin was writhing and muffling needy whimpers.

Every action and reaction told Isabella that Erin had needed this for as long as she had. She didn't expect Erin to last very long. She sucked softly on the protruding bundle of nerves, and Erin gasped.

From the corner of her eye, she could see Erin's hands grab fistfuls of the bedding. Isabella could just make out her muscles moving as she gripped the fabric. She wished the light was better. She wanted to see Erin's body succumb to pleasure, and she needed to see the look on her beautiful face.

She let her tongue move over the clit hiding in its little hood and sucked softly, until Erin could no longer muffle her moans. She cried out, her back arching off the bed.

Isabella felt a rush of pride; she'd made a woman come. She'd made *Erin* come. Her Erin. She felt her lover's body grow taut and tremble before slowly softening and landing limply back on the bed.

She kissed her way back up to Erin's mouth. Erin's breathing was ragged and hot. The quick, warm breaths hit Isabella's lips before they kissed. If

Erin minded tasting herself on Isabella's tongue, she certainly couldn't tell. Erin kissed her as passionately as if her life depended on it, until Isabella rolled over to the side, thinking they'd kiss a little more and then fall asleep. Erin moved with her so that they lay on their sides facing each other, kissing tenderly. The worst of the urgency had abated.

Isabella had been right about the kissing, but not about what would follow. Erin's hands grabbed her hips and brought her forward, pushing her thigh between Isabella's. Erin was pressed against her hot core. Sleep would have to wait, and Isabella was okay with that.

In fact, she was ecstatic.

Chapter 20

The Day After the Night Before

ERIN WOKE UP FEELING A myriad of things. She was confused at where she was; the room looked nothing like her apartment. She was blissed out and physically tired—even a little sore in a few intimate places.

As her consciousness switched to full power, she remembered where she was and why. She also realized that, somewhere in this bed, Isabella must be sleeping next to her. Another bit of her brain woke up, and she heard something—a whispered conversation and what sounded like an owl hoot.

Erin opened her eyes and saw Isabella sitting with Alberto at the foot of the bed. She was wearing a black silk robe, and Alberto was playing with the belt. They were facing away from her.

"Good morning," she said quietly to get Isabella's attention.

Isabella smiled over her shoulder. "Good morning, *preciosa*. Alberto didn't want to be alone in his crib, and there really isn't anywhere to sit in his nursery, so I brought him in here. Sorry if we woke you."

"No, I think I woke up naturally." Erin felt strangely nervous. Last night, she'd been worried about Isabella, but Isabella's eagerness had allowed her own confidence to grow. Now that that world of passionate sex and whispered terms of endearments was gone, the strange realm of responsibility for a child and "the morning after" was upon her. She felt a lot less confident now.

Isabella turned to look at her again. "If you're hungry, you can go prepare some breakfast. Alberto seems to be quite hungry, so I was going to feed him just now."

Erin felt groggy and unsteady, and her sudden shyness made the idea of rummaging through Isabella's kitchen for food—or using her fancy coffeemaker for that matter—uncomfortable.

"Actually, I'm not really awake yet. I'll just chill for a bit and then get up, if that's okay."

"Oh. Right. Of course. I…do need to feed Alberto, though. Do you want me to go in another room?"

Erin forced herself to wake up and clear her head. *What's going on here?* "No. I mean, um, I can go if the two of you want privacy?"

"I'm fine with feeding him in front of you. I believe that mothers should be able to breastfeed wherever they please. I only decided not to do it on camera with you that one time because…well, I suppose it was really for the same reason that I'm hesitating now," Isabella said with a self-deprecating laugh.

Erin sat up, pulling the covers with her to shield her nakedness since Alberto was in the room. "What's that?"

Isabella let out a long breath. "I suppose I want you to connect the sight of my breasts with erotic feelings, not with feeding people."

She got a reassuring smile from Erin in return. "Babe, nothing in the world could stop me from admiring and being turned by your tit…hrm…I mean breasts."

Isabella's scolding look quickly turned into a smile, and Erin took a deep breath, glad that she'd said the right thing. She'd meant it, though. The female body had many uses; that didn't stop it being the sexiest thing Erin knew.

Isabella opened her robe and lifted Alberto. To make sure she didn't make either of them feel self-conscious in any way, Erin lay back down and stretched lazily. She snuggled into a pillow to breathe in Isabella's scent.

It calmed her nerves, but she still felt unsettled and unsure what she was meant to do this morning. *Should I just eat breakfast and then go? Or stay the whole day?* This was why Erin preferred her life as a loner sometimes; social rules and expectations could be such a pain in the butt. Her stomach growled.

Isabella laughed. "Oh dear. Seems like Alberto isn't the only hungry one."

Sitting up and trying to locate her clothes on the floor, Erin agreed, shame coloring her voice, "Yeah. Sorry 'bout that. It just kinda hit me." She spied her clothes and wrapped one of the blankets around herself to retrieve the scattered garments.

"Ah, going for the Roman toga look, I see. Very fetching," Isabella teased.

Erin stuck her tongue out in response. Isabella shrugged it off with a laugh and looked down at Alberto, nursing peacefully. Erin felt her heart tug in that almost maternal way. He was eating happily and trying to reach her hair to play with it. It was just a little too short for him to reach, but he kept trying.

"Man, you look so cute together. Is he trying to play with your hair or something?" Erin asked while she wriggled into her panties and jeans under the cover of the blanket.

"You can drop the blanket, *preciosa*. He can't see you or understand the concept of you being naked, although I appreciate the gesture. And, yes, I used to have longer hair, before you and I started chatting, and he used to play with it as he ate. Since I cut it, it's just out of his grasp."

Erin *tsk-tsked* while throwing the blanket back on the bed and yanking up her jeans. "Sorry about that, lil' man. Life's tough."

She left the room, went to the dryer, and took out the shirt and bra that Isabella had washed for her after Alberto's little accident. She pulled them on and hesitated while she overcame her discomfort. Hunger drove her to the fridge to pour a glass of orange juice. Bringing the tall glass back into the bedroom, she picked up her conversation with the eating baby again.

"Yeah, life's tough. As soon as you get used to something, it can be taken away from you, kid. Tell you what, though, my hair is long enough to reach all the way over if I sit next to you guys." She looked questioningly at Isabella while she sipped her juice.

"Are you asking if you can sit next to us and let Alberto play with your hair?"

She wondered if that had that been a dumb, or maybe even weird, thing to suggest. Erin shrugged, suddenly embarrassed.

But Isabella just gave her a beaming smile. "That's so sweet of you. I'm sure he'd like that. And I always want your company."

Erin put her juice down on the windowsill and undid her slowly unraveling braid. Her hair was tangled and crimped when she shook it out, but it'd do as a baby toy. She picked up her juice again, sat down next to Isabella on the side where Alberto's face was, then bundled some tresses and placed them in Alberto's little hand.

He looked confused at first and seemed to stop sucking. Then his little hand closed around the fistful of blonde hair, moving his fingers around it to feel the texture, and returned to eating with a soft suckling noise.

Isabella caressed his head, smoothing down the tufts of dark hair. Erin felt the warmth in her cheeks at the adoring smile Isabella then gave her, and she realized just how proud she felt to be able to help, even if it was just with this little thing.

She kept sipping at her juice, Alberto kept eating his breakfast, and Isabella switched between sending Erin loving glances and stroking Alberto's head. Occasionally, Alberto would tug a little on the hair, but Erin didn't mind. She'd made both him and Isabella happy, and that was an amazing feeling. Well worth any discomfort.

When Alberto had eaten, it was time for Erin and Isabella to have their breakfast. Alberto snoozed in his baby bouncer, as they sat at the table, handing each other plates of breakfast foods that Isabella had rustled up, and sneaking glances at each other.

"Is everything all right? I mean, are *we* all right?"

Erin swallowed a mouthful of her yogurt and granola. She put the spoon back in the bowl as she thought about how to answer that. "Yeah. I mean, um, I think so. I mean, last night was…"

"Incredible?" Isabella said and looked down coquettishly.

Erin burst out laughing. "I'm glad you thought so. And yeah, that was kinda what I was thinking too. I'm really happy. I just don't know what we do now, today, I mean."

"Whatever we want." Isabella looked back up and made eye contact. "The day is ours. If you want to stay, that is? You have to be back at work for tomorrow, but that still gives us all day before your train home. If we were in different cities, we'd probably end up talking on Skype. So let's talk, but we'll do it right here where we can reach out and touch each other if we like. Does that sound okay to you?"

Erin's heart felt like it was too big to fit in her ribcage. She knew she was grinning like an idiot, but she couldn't help it. She imagined doing everyday things while holding Isabella's hand or reaching over to kiss her.

"I'd really like that. Maybe we could take a walk in the park with lil' man? Or just a long walk around town so I can see some of Philadelphia?"

"That's a terrific idea. It will have to wait, though."

"Because we haven't finished breakfast?" Erin asked and ate another spoonful.

"Well, yes, but also because he's busy," Isabella said and pointed to Alberto, who was napping soundly in his bouncer.

Erin smiled at him. It was so less scary when he slept. The worst thing she could do then was wake him up.

"Yeah. We'll wait until the kid has gotten his post-breakfast nap in."

Nodding her agreement, Isabella swallowed the last bite of her sandwich. When she finished, she looked deep into Erin's eyes and teasingly asked, "Whatever shall we do until he wakes up?"

Erin pushed her bowl of granola away and stood, grabbing Isabella's hand and pulling her toward the bedroom. Isabella laughed, scrambled out of her chair, and followed.

The sun was setting, and their day had been lovely. From the morning lovemaking to the long walk, to hours of looking at pictures of Alberto. There had also been old pictures from Isabella's childhood that her mother had scanned into the computer. The day was perfect.

Evening loomed, and Erin had to take the 8:35 p.m. train back to New York. She would have plenty of time to shower and hopefully catch up on some sleep before Thursday morning and work.

They decided against cooking and ordered sushi instead, eating it while cuddled on the sofa. Food wrappers and boxes finally trashed, Erin lay across the couch with her head in Isabella's lap. There was still time before she had to leave, and Erin was struggling to decide how to spend the precious moments.

Isabella combed her fingers through Erin's hair and mumbled, "I missed a bit here."

Erin grimaced and got slapped on the arm for it. Before they went for their walk, Isabella had decided that Erin was going nowhere with her hair so tangled. Armed with Erin's leave-in conditioner from her overnight kit and a fancy hairbrush, Isabella fought valiantly with her long, unruly locks until they were smooth and sleek. Erin tried to be brave about the rough brushing at first, but soon realized it was more fun to whine when it hurt and either be consoled with a kiss or get that adorable quirked eyebrow and an eye roll. Messing with Isabella was one of her favorite things; Isabella allowing it was another.

Satisfied that she'd gotten the last tangle, Isabella surprised her by asking, "So, you want to talk about that song?"

Erin's brow furrowed. "What song?"

"That Siouxsie and the Banshees song that you mentioned listening to and thinking about us. Back when I was still with Richard?"

For the first time that day, Erin felt a distinct feeling of fear taking root deep in her chest. "*The Last Beat Of My Heart*?" She wished, once again, that she'd never told Isabella about that. "Uh, yeah, I suppose we can talk about it."

"I listened to it. It's melancholy, but hauntingly beautiful. I haven't been able to get it out of my head."

Unsure of what to say, Erin nodded.

Isabella, as usual, picked up the slack. "I think I understand why it was important to you at that particular juncture, but I could have misinterpreted it."

"Shoot, and I'll let you know," Erin muttered, her eyes closed against the uncomfortable conversation that was marring their otherwise perfect day.

"Well, listening to the lyrics, it seemed to me to be about someone who had been hurt in the past and had some…bad experiences. But now that person had found someone, or something, that was precious, but they weren't certain they deserved it, or that they could have it."

Worrying the wristband of her FitWatch, Erin almost whispered, "Yeah. That's pretty much how I interpret it too. It stuck in my head when I realized I was falling for you and that you weren't mine to fall for. You were so incredible, and every bit of me wanted to be with you, but you were with Richard, and the two of you were trying to make your relationship work for Alberto's sake. I felt selfish and horrible for wanting you to be with me instead."

Isabella put her hand on Erin's to stop them from toying with the wristband and to get her full attention. "Leaving Richard was the right thing to do, and afterward, taking a break to get back on my feet was the right thing too. But now, I think the right thing is to do what the lyrics of that song say. To stay close to you until the last beat of my heart." Isabella winked at her. "Or until you get tired of dating a daydreaming writer and her spoiled little baby."

Erin smiled, trying to hide her insecurity. Every part of her hoped that Isabella's words were true. But there was still that tug of fear in her chest. No one ever stayed. No one ever let her stay. Well, if this relationship ended, it sure as hell wouldn't be her who was going. She was going to fight for this. "Never gonna happen, babe," she said. "I'm sticking around."

Isabella brought her hand up to her mouth and gently kissed it. "Good. Because you can ask for this, Erin. You deserve to be happy and in love. And I think I do too. We've both done our time feeling lonely and thinking we didn't deserve any better."

The assurance made Erin jump up, suddenly feeling lighter. "Enough talking. Great music shouldn't just be talked about, it should be listened to, even if it's played on a crappy cell phone."

She got her phone out and located *The Last Beat of My Heart*. Isabella accepted the proffered phone without pause. "I told you about this song, because I wanted to dance to it with you, and I guess there's no time like the present. May I have this dance, Ms. Martinez?"

As she got up, Isabella nodded, then stopped to tug her trouser legs down. Those slacks of hers were way too tight and had been riding up her legs all day, but Erin wasn't going to complain. Isabella looked so much more casual than usual. Gone were the suits and designer dresses. Instead, she wore tight, black slacks, and a taupe turtleneck sweater. Erin cuddled her face into the amazing softness of that sweater, when she pulled Isabella into her embrace. Isabella's left hand slid under Erin's hair and along her neck. The other snaked around her back, as the lyrics started. Erin closed her eyes and held Isabella tighter, beginning to dance.

They moved slowly, hesitant at first, as they both seemed inclined to lead. It took only a few missteps and fits of embarrassed laughter before they were in sync, until it felt natural. Erin grinned triumphantly into Isabella's shoulder.

The song was set on repeat. As it started over, Erin hoped Isabella wouldn't pull away. She didn't. In fact, she nuzzled into Erin's hair, her mouth brushing Erin's ear. Erin shivered with pleasure.

They danced to it three times before Erin had to leave, and the song stayed with her long after. On the train back to New York, she found herself humming, feeling her heart switch between pulsing joy at Isabella loving her back and aching pain at not being able to sleep in Isabella's arms that night.

She vowed she'd do whatever it took to get them in the same city and under the same roof just as soon as was humanly possible. To do that, she'd need a nest egg.

Chapter 21

Much Loved Nuisance

ISABELLA SAT AT HER TABLE, sipping her morning coffee. She'd saved it for after breakfast, a breakfast dessert of sorts. As soon as she stopped breastfeeding, she'd drink gallons, but for now, each cup was savored.

She smiled. Her coffee rationing was a bit like getting to see Erin in the flesh. All she wanted now was more of each of her addictions and to race to the day when she could have her fill of them both—but in the future, when they were used to each other. Would she miss the bittersweet torment of her current intense, crazy need for Erin? Or would she be relieved that the emotional roller coaster was in the past and that she could have as much coffee and Erin as she could possibly want?

Erin. She missed Erin far more than coffee, more than she'd ever missed anything or anyone. It was as if life only made sense now when Erin was there with her. Erin's calm presence and joie de vivre had become part of Isabella, and her world already felt dull without it.

Her landline phone rang. Isabella picked up the cordless phone and heard Marie's chirpy "Hello."

"Good morning, nuisance."

"Did you just call me nuisance?" Marie shot back. "Why do I talk to you again?"

"Because my witty rudeness is delightful?"

Marie laughed. "That's up for debate. You do sound like you are in a good mood, though, sugar pie. Could that have anything to do with a certain visit from a certain personal trainer?"

Isabella smirked. "I'm not going to deny that."

Marie's voice sounded unimpressed. "Well, that isn't the most flowery, romantic thing I have ever heard. Oh, come on, Isabella. Let me hear how thrilled you are, sweetie pie. Are you over the moon? Are you walking on sunshine?"

"I'm not going to buy into your clichés. Nor do I appreciate you calling me various nicknames ending with *pie*. I am, however, happy and very much in love."

Marie gave an ear-piercing squeal of joy.

"Calm down," Isabella complained through the beaming smile she couldn't shake.

"I'm just glad to hear you sounding so cheerful. You haven't sounded like this since the day Alberto was born."

Isabella furrowed her brow. "I seem to recall that the day Alberto was born, I threatened to pull your ears off and stuff them in your handbag."

"During labor, yes, because you needed someone to scream at. But when he was born and the worst of the pain was gone, you had this tone in your voice. A tone I had never heard before. It was sort of…unguarded and unapologetically happy. I can't remember that tone from when we were kids or ever since, actually. Until now. And it's so great to hear."

Isabella didn't know what to say. For a moment, she was surprised to know that this "tone" had broken through her usual controlled front. But then again, Erin could probably break through the Great Wall of China with her charm and sweetness.

"She's…something else, Marie. I think you'll like her," Isabella said softly.

"Oh honey pie—I mean, honey, I'm sure I will. Anyone who can get you to relax and be happy is A-plus in my book. I'm going be her best friend."

Alberto began to grizzle in his baby gym, and Isabella went to pick him up, causing a pause in the conversation. "Sorry, I had to go get Alberto. He likes her too, actually. Well, as much as a baby can like someone who isn't their primary caregiver. She lets him play with her hair, pokes his tummy, and buys him toys."

"Sounds like she likes him too," Marie chirped.

Isabella hesitated. "I hope so. I think she's a little frightened of him."

"Frightened of him, or of babies in general?"

"I don't know. She doesn't want to talk about it. I don't think she dislikes babies, though. She's crazy about animals and a very warm, nurturing person. I'll get to the bottom of it. Now, I just want to arrange our next date," Isabella said a little wistfully.

"So, do you feel different about her now that you have met her in person?"

Isabella thought about that. "No, not really. I knew I was in love with her before. Talking for hours and hours, especially in the safety and anonymity of online chats, meant I got to know her well before I even saw her pretty face on the screen, never mind seeing her in person. If I'm more cheerful now than other times after talking to her, it's because we, um, crossed a significant barrier."

Marie gasped. "You slept with her!"

Rocking Alberto and sighing, Isabella replied, "Yes. Please don't make a big deal of that or ask for details or anything else inappropriate. I only mentioned it because it was sort of this unspoken question between us—if I'd be comfortable having sex with another woman. It…went well, though. We've dealt with that now, and we're very compatible in bed. Now we can focus again on the emotional and practical stuff."

"But you are still going to sleep with her every time she comes over, right? I mean you have to make the most of it, for heaven's sake."

"Marie Bowman, that's none of your business."

"I'm just saying that you can't see her that often, so you should take it when you can get it, if you catch my drift."

"Yes, I catch it a little too well. Change the subject, please," Isabella muttered while putting Alberto back in his baby gym.

For some reason, Marie had been impervious to Isabella's parents' particular brand of modesty when it came to talking about anything private. Her biological parents must have been more open—much more open—but Isabella couldn't remember.

For Marie, very little was off the table when it came to girl talk. It never ceased to amaze Isabella how the saccharine-sweet and innocent-looking Marie could go on and on about sex, simply claiming, "Oh honey, it's all natural. It's only a big deal if you make it one." According to Marie, "that's the power of managing your thought patterns." She claimed it helped you banish your shame and just be open. It had never worked on Isabella. She sometimes wanted to scream until her sister developed more decorum. This conversation was no exception.

Clueless—or at least pretending to be—to Isabella's discomfort, Marie replied, "Okay. Hmm. So, I mean, you said 'no details,' but is it true that lesbians just keep climaxing until someone falls asleep?"

"Marie!"

"Sorry, sorry. Fine. All right, we'll talk about my amorous adventures instead. How are we on the handsome-gym-owner front?"

"Erin's told him all about you, and I e-mailed her a great picture of you to send to him. So I assume you'll hear from him any time now."

"Yeah, right. Like I'm just going to sit here and wait for him to call me. This isn't 1917. Give me his number, I'll text him. He sounds wonderful, and it's not like I'm afraid of rejection, it's a natural part of life."

"Apparently, he likes positive, overachieving women, so I'd say you are unlikely to get any form of rejection."

"Naturally. I'm one hell of a catch."

Isabella rolled her eyes. "Is that the positive thinking talking or just your inflated ego?"

"Isabella!"

"Fine, fine. You're a catch. At least for lobotomized people with exceedingly low standards."

"Oh, ha ha," Marie grumbled.

"I'm asking Erin for his number right now," Isabella said while texting Erin.

"Okay, just hurry up. I'm not having you coupling up and leaving me the sad spinster. Judith would never let me forget it. Not that there is anything wrong with being single. Being single is only a problem if you don't want to be. That's my issue. You were always the one happy with focusing on your career, while I wanted a family. Look at us now. You've got a brilliant kid and a cool girlfriend, while I'm crying into my solo cup of ginseng tea."

Isabella sighed at her sister's whining. "Calm down. I'm doing it now."

"Good. Hearing you so blissful makes me want to be in love and, you know…getting some."

"I swear to God that if you don't stop with the sex references, I am hanging up right now," Isabella growled.

"Now who needs to calm down? Fine. No more sex talk."

Isabella momentarily ignored Marie and smiled at her BlackBerry when she saw a message beginning with the words *hi there, beautiful.*

"Erin just replied and sent his number. She's at the gym and talking to him right now. She says he loved the picture of you but has been too shy to send you a message. He thinks you're out of his league."

"Aw, poor puppy. Give me his number right now!"

"I'm doing it. Let me finish copying and pasting it into a text for you before you badger me to death."

"Paste faster," Marie whined again.

"There. I sent it. Now, text Romeo and leave me alone, you nuisance."

"Will do. Give my love to Alberto and tell him that his auntie will be over to kiss him soon."

"I'll pass the message on. Good luck with Chris. Be careful. Don't... you know...let him treat you badly in any way. I'd hate to have to kill him."

"Pft. He wouldn't dare hurt me. I'm pretty dangerous in my own right, and I'm sure Erin has told him what a vicious bitch my sister can be."

"I'm hanging up now," Isabella growled.

Marie laughed. "Okay, honey. Take care. We'll talk soon. Love you loads and loads, Sis."

In a slightly embarrassed mutter, Isabella replied, "*Te quiero.*"

She hung up the landline but kept staring at her BlackBerry and Erin's message. It was mainly about Chris, but she kept staring at the ending.

I can't wait to see you again. You're all I can think of. I've never been this happy before. Thank you for being in my life, Isabella.

Isabella turned to Alberto, who was watching her from his baby bouncer. She sighed and smiled at him.

"Is this what love is supposed to be like? This...pure and natural?"

He answered with a single, "Hoo."

Chapter 22

The Idea

I<small>T WAS</small> F<small>RIDAY MORNING</small>. E<small>RIN</small> was at the gym, offering pointers and encouragement to a regular client, Corrie, who was trying out the chest press machine. While Erin's mouth was saying, "That's it. One more, you can do it," her brain kept pulling her off track, thinking about Isabella.

How long had they known each other? Three months? It was strange. Somehow it felt like they had known each other a lifetime and as if they'd just met.

"Are you listening to me?" Corrie asked.

"Oh, sorry. I was miles away. What did you say?" The heat of a blush crept into Erin's cheeks.

"I was asking if you had a stroke. That smile did not look normal, young lady."

Erin laughed but put real sincerity into her apology. "No, just thinking about someone. I'm really sorry. I'll get a grip."

"Well, he or she is very lucky. If you like the buff type, that is. I prefer a little more cushion for the pushin'. Now, am I doing this right?"

Erin blinked a few times. "Um, yes. You might want to up the resistance, though."

"All right. You're good at what you do. I hope you get to stay when the place changes management," Corrie said.

It felt like someone had slapped her. "Huh? Changes management?"

"Yes. Haven't you heard? Chris is selling up."

"What? I mean I knew he wanted a change but not that he was actually going to get rid of this place," Erin replied.

"Yep. He's looking for buyers, but he's being picky. Says he doesn't want some big chain to take over. There's enough of them around here. He wants to keep this place for everyone who isn't a gym bunny."

Erin thought about the large group of retired boxers who met up at the gym every afternoon to chat and occasionally spar a bit. "Yeah. I see his point. This place should be kept the way it is, nice and laid-back, a little rough around the edges."

"That's what he was saying. I'm sure they'll keep all of you personal trainers on," Corrie said. She started asking questions about the machine she was using, and Erin answered her. But her thoughts were whirring like tightly wound clockwork.

Erin finished her lunch and decided to use her remaining time to look for Chris. She found him in the dingy little cupboard he called an office.

"Hey, Er. How are you today?"

"Doing good, thanks. What about you? I hear you've been talking to a certain Ms. Bowman since Isabella gave her your number?"

He smiled, almost shyly. "Yeah. We've been on the phone to each other pretty much nonstop. Man, I've never met anyone like her. She's like a force of nature."

He had this dreamy, sappy look on his face. She needed to snap him out of it. If she didn't, they'd never get around to what she needed to talk about. "Glad to hear it, big fella. Yeah, it must be a big change for you." She exhaled deeply. "I hear you're looking to make another big change. With the gym?"

He frowned. "Damn. Let me guess. Corrie told you? I was going to brief everyone tonight. I only told her this morning, because she caught me grinning and wouldn't quit. Sorry you had to hear it from someone else first."

"It's fine. Besides, her telling me about it might benefit us both."

"Really? How so?"

Erin leaned against the wall, using its cool, firm texture to make herself feel less shaky about what she was about to say. "I have a proposal. Please don't say no right away. Just give it some thought."

Chris looked increasingly perplexed. "Um, okay. Shoot."

"Is it true that you aren't just taking the easy way out and selling to one of the big chains? You want someone who'll love this place and keep it the way it is?"

"Preferably. My uncle built this place from scratch, and I'd like it to stay like this in his honor. Besides, the people who use Nash's Gym don't want it to change, and I feel like I owe them something for being so loyal all these years."

"Chris, I really care about this gym and the people who use it. I *am* one of the people who use it. If you'd be willing to make a little less money and at a slower pace…maybe you could think about…maybe selling it to me? I could only pay a little at first, and then the rest in installments. And I couldn't pay top dollar or anything, but I can guarantee the place would be loved and kept as it is."

He sat back in his creaking office chair and stared at Erin. Then he smiled. It looked like a smile of relief to Erin. "You know what? That sounds pretty good. That way, if my new life goes to hell, you'd probably let me come back and help out at the gym or start in your current line of business?"

"Absolutely. I mean, I'm sure that you'd do great in whatever you decide to do, but if you change your mind, just come back. We could run this place together or something. I just want to get a chance to put down some roots, maybe save up a bit of money. I mean, I'm dating someone pretty seriously now, and, as you know, she's got a kid." Erin found herself licking her lips in her normal nervous tick and swallowing repeatedly. She forced herself to stop, relax, and continue talking. "I need to think about being responsible now. Get a nest egg and all that."

"Sure, that makes sense. If the two of you end up living together, you'll have to make some changes." He paused, chewing the inside of his cheek for a moment. "You know what? Selling to a friend I can trust is a lot more appealing than selling for a bigger wad of cash. Especially, as I've already got a decent job lined up in Philadelphia."

A warmth rose in her chest. Chris considered her a friend? She'd always just seen them as work acquaintances. Then she caught up with what he had just said. "You've already got a job? In Philly?"

Chris blushed beetroot red. "Uh, yeah. I've been talking a lot to Marie the last couple of days. Turns out that she's desperate for a security guy. She does all these gigs and classes, and sometimes people get a little too close and creepy when they want to talk to her afterward. She says she doesn't have the budget or the desire to get a real security company in to help, so she just wants to hire someone strong and dependable to stay around her and make sure she's safe and comfortable."

Erin tried to hide her smile. From what she had heard about Marie from Isabella, she wondered how much was true and how much was clever invention. She didn't think that Marie was straight-up lying, maybe just exaggerating her need for security to get Chris to come to Philadelphia and spend lots of time with her, especially since Marie knew Chris was desperate for change.

Nevertheless, it was a solution that would make everyone happy, so she wasn't about to question it or, more importantly, make Chris question it.

"That sounds like a great idea. You're not, you know, gonna live with her too, are you? 'Cause that seems a bit premature."

Chris looked startled. "No, of course not! There's a place that rents cheap but clean rooms just a block from where Marie lives. I don't really have any stuff I want to keep, except for some clothes, dad's old punching bag, and my collection of baseball cards, so I don't mind renting a room until I know if I'm staying and more money's coming in."

Erin bit her lip. "So you'd be okay with me slowly paying off the cost of this place? It might take years. You gotta think this through, big guy."

"Sure, I will. We aren't drawing up the contract today, are we?"

"No, no. I'm not even sure this is a serious offer. It just sorta came to me when I heard you were selling and wanted a buyer who'd love the place. I still need to think about it, see what money I can scrape together, and talk to Isabella. I mean, this would tie me to New York, so she needs to know."

"Yeah. I bet she'll tell you if it's a dumb idea. Marie says that Isabella's very honest and direct." His grin told Erin that Marie might have elaborated on just how direct Isabella could be. Erin grinned back at him.

"Hey, I hear *your* Philly chick can be pretty up front as well. So, we'll think about this and run it past our clever brunettes before making any decisions?"

Chris laughed, smiling at her conspiratorially. "Yep, we'll discuss it with our new better halves."

She was about to go back out into the gym when Chris called her back.

"Hey, how's it going with the kid, by the way? You two getting along?"

She leaned on the wall again and sucked her teeth before replying. "I think we made some progress. He played with my hair while he ate. It felt like a bit of a breakthrough to me. I felt…needed, you know? Like I was helping out with him and not just potentially screwing him up."

"That's good. Look, I'm sorry if I scared you about dating moms when we first talked about it. Don't let my concerns get in your way. You're much more, well, *maternal* than I am. I don't mean because you're a woman, but just because you're you. You'll be great with him, I'm sure."

"I don't think I'm very maternal at all. I'm still not ready to be part of raising a kid. I mean, I can't even keep a cactus alive. How am I supposed to help care for a baby?"

"You're caring, responsible, and considerate. Sounds pretty maternal to me. Anyway, have you talked to Isabella about this?"

"No, not really. I told her I was worried, but I kinda downplayed it, y'know? She's being great, though. Trying to help and to make me feel comfortable around him. And I've gotta say, he's an adorable kid. I just… don't want to screw him up the way my childhood screwed me up."

Chris looked away and scratched his head. Erin had once told him she was an orphan, but nothing more.

"Erin, I'm really not the person to talk to about difficult stuff like this, but it seems to me that you turned out pretty good, despite a shitty start. You being in his life doesn't mean he'll have a shitty start. In fact, I think it means the opposite. You had no parents, but if you build this relationship with Isabella, you'll be giving him two parents instead of one."

"While we're together, yeah. But what if we break up? I mean, Isabella is amazing. One day she's gonna wake up and realize that I'm just…well, me. Then I'll have to leave him. Leave them both. I don't want him to feel left behind or unwanted. I'm not doing that to a kid. I can't."

"So, stick around." Chris supplied simply. "If you break up with Isabella—and I'm not saying you will, because you're awesome too—but if you do, stay in Alberto's life anyway. I'm sure Isabella wouldn't cut you out if the two of you have a bond."

Erin took a breath. No, Isabella probably wouldn't do that. Sure, she could be hotheaded and hard if she had to be, but never in a way that would have negative consequences for Alberto. If Alberto wanted Erin around, if it was in his best interests, Isabella would bend over backward to make it work, just like she was doing with Richard and their Skype chats and future visits.

That could work.

"I hadn't thought about that. No, I don't think she would."

Chris shrugged. "As I said, I don't know much about this stuff. The person you need to have this discussion with is Isabella."

"Yeah. I just need to be ready for that discussion," Erin said with a somber sigh. "Anyway, I better get back out there before my next client arrives. Thanks for the chat, Chris. Think about my offer, and we'll talk it over with our...prettier halves."

She grinned at him, and he laughed.

"Anytime. Let's talk more tomorrow."

Erin nodded and walked away. Focusing on work would be even harder now. It had been difficult when she'd been daydreaming about Isabella. Now she was worrying about Alberto again and pondering the biggest financial decision of her life. She could only hope to keep it all at bay throughout the workday. She'd have no chance once she finished work. *Well, what's one more sleepless night?*

Chapter 23

Date Night

"RASPBERRY WINE OR POWER RED?" Isabella waved two tubes of lipstick in front of Alberto as he sat in his bouncer, trying to get his opinion on which would go best with her deep-red dress. She liked talking to him, even if he didn't answer back. Yet. And she happily used the excuse of bettering his language skills. He cooed and waved his arms excitedly.

"Raspberry wine, it is. Good choice, *cariño*."

It was Saturday, and getting her look just right was important. Erin was due any second for their two o' clock date. This day—or rather this night—was even more important than usual. It would be their first real date outside of the house.

It was Isabella's idea. After Erin dropped the bomb last night on Skype, about buying Chris's gym, Isabella had decided that this life-changing decision was not something to be settled over a distant Internet connection. No, this needed to be discussed and celebrated over a proper meal in a nice restaurant.

They would spend the afternoon at the house, playing with Alberto, letting him be the focus of attention. At six thirty, her father would come over to babysit for a couple of hours, while she and Erin went out for a meal and undisturbed conversation.

The doorbell rang, as Isabella finished applying her lipstick. "Good timing," she mumbled to Alberto and picked him up. She was practically running to the door and shaking poor Alberto, but her eagerness made it hard to slow down.

When she opened the door, her heart did its usual somersault at seeing Erin, but something else hit her too. Erin wasn't looking like she usually did.

"A dress?"

Erin rolled her eyes while smoothing down the front of her modest, black dress. "Yeah. You said we were going to some fancy restaurant, so I thought I'd look the part. I don't have a suit, but I found two dresses in my closet. This one didn't smell of mothballs. Not that I can keep up with your designer dresses and perfect hair, but…well, never mind."

"Please don't put yourself down, *preciosa*. You look amazing. I mean, you always look amazing, and I love your usual attire. But it's interesting to see a new style on you. However, I do think we should buy you a suit or tux at some point. You'd look amazing in one."

"Cool. Does that mean you and lil' man are gonna stop blocking the door?" Erin joked.

"Oh, right. Sorry, of course, come in."

As Erin walked passed her into the apartment, putting her backpack down on the table, Isabella sneaked in another appreciative look. Erin's hair had been curled, and it hung loose. Isabella could smell whatever eau de toilette Erin always wore, and she felt giddy with the desire to strip Erin of everything but the perfume and take her to bed.

A grin flew across Erin's face. "You keep staring at me like that, and we might not make it to the restaurant tonight."

Isabella swallowed hard and tore her gaze away from the perfectly sculpted shoulders holding up thin dress straps. "Right. So, how was your journey?"

She was treated to a fresh, beaming grin. "I'll tell you after I steal my hello kiss. Hold on to the baby, I'm coming in."

Erin walked over and carefully put her arms around them both. The kiss was gentle but soulful, and Isabella fought hard not to sigh with pleasure. She was starting to feel particularly girly and ridiculous, and she needed to get a grip.

"Ow," Erin yelped and pulled away. Alberto held a handful of blonde curls, pulling them to his mouth.

"Alberto! Let go of Erin's hair," Isabella chided.

"No, no. It's okay. I'm the one who let him play with my hair. I'll stand by that decision."

"Fine, but he needs to learn to be gentle at some point."

Erin waved the concern away. "Yeah, he will. For now, I'm just glad he found something about me he likes."

What was she thinking? Erin was struggling with Alberto, that much was clear. But why? "Do you really think that?"

"I don't know. I mean, he's a baby, so there is only so much he can feel, right? I don't think he hates me or anything." Erin laughed, but it sounded forced to Isabella.

She kept looking at her, searching for clues. Her arms were crossed over her chest as she cast wary glances at Alberto, as though frightened she'd offended him.

Isabella waited until she caught Erin's eye. "Babies respond to those who take care of their needs. You've only been around Alberto a few times, but on all those occasions you've brought him things he liked, helped with anything you could, and paid attention to what he might need or want. Neither he nor I could possibly ask for more." Isabella caressed her cheek. When she spoke again, she made her voice as gentle as she could. "You're doing a great job with him, and you'll be even better with more experience. He likes you just fine, Erin. All of you, not just your hair. You'd know if he didn't, trust me. You'd hear it."

Erin stared down at Alberto. He was playing with his fingers but looked up at her when he noticed her looking at him. Erin swallowed hard, blinked a few times, then smiled at him.

"I just want to do right by him." Erin looked from Alberto back up at her. "And you."

Isabella gave her a warm smile. "You're doing just fine. We're both happy, safe, and feel quite appreciated. I'd say gold star for you, Miss Black."

Chuckling and visibly trying to relax her posture, Erin leaned in to kiss her lips. after a second's hesitation, she placed a gentle kiss on Alberto's head.

He blinked rapidly and giggled when her hair tickled his face. The reaction seemed to reassure Erin. So, Isabella grabbed a lock of blonde hair and tickled him under the chin with it. He squealed with mirth and squirmed to get away from it.

When Isabella looked up, there was a look of awe and what might have been pride on Erin's face.

As the summer evening descended on Philadelphia, Isabella put on some more lipstick and checked her hair before she walked back into the room. Erin was kneeling over Alberto in his gym, watching him play.

"Right. Daddy should be here in about fifteen minutes. I decided against pumping milk for Alberto. Instead I'll feed him now, and he should be fine until we come back. I wasn't sure how Daddy would cope with the feeding process. Alberto isn't very fond of the bottle. We're only having dinner, so we'll be back soon." Even Isabella could hear the stress in her own voice and grimaced.

Erin offered a reassuring smile. It helped. Just a bit. So did the calm tone in Erin's voice when she said, "We won't even have dessert, babe. We'll be back in no time. They'll be fine."

Still, Isabella gave a curt nod. She wasn't convinced she shouldn't leave some milk. Or perhaps not leave at all.

She picked up Alberto and sat down to feed him. Erin gave them some space and when they were all set, sat down next to them and offered Alberto a bunch of blonde locks to toy with. He grabbed on right away this time, with his chubby little fingers moving over the strands of hair as if he was trying to ascertain the texture.

Suddenly Erin's eyes widened. "Is this okay? Sorry, I should've asked first."

Isabella felt her heart melt once more and wondered just how much it could take. "Of course it is. In fact, I was just thinking how sweet you are. You live up to your nickname, my precious darling."

Erin smiled shyly, but it soon turned into a cheeky grin. "Whoa there, Ms. Gushy."

Isabella made sure her full mask of disdain was in place. "Tell anyone, and I'll poison your coffee."

"Oh, I'd know about that right away. I know when someone's reheated my coffee, I'll sure as hell know if you put something in it, lady."

With a scoff, she decided to ignore Erin and looked down at Alberto instead. Alberto was still playing with the hair, but his fingers were moving slowly now, as if it was hard work. His eyes fluttered shut and then opened again. Isabella heard Erin give a little whimper.

"Aw, look," she said quietly. "He's so tired, but he's still fighting to keep awake. He's so frickin' cute."

Isabella hummed her agreement, pride swelling in her chest.

"He must have gotten that cuteness from his dad, because his mom's an ogre."

Isabella gave her another glare, this one laced with extra contempt. But she was loving the banter, and the desire to kiss that cheeky grin off Erin's face was almost overwhelming. Instead, she simply drawled, "I see you're not hoping to get lucky tonight."

"Babe, I saw the way you looked at how much shoulder I'm showin' tonight. I think my odds for getting laid are pretty high."

The corners of Isabella's mouth twitched, and she had to force them not to break into a smile. "Not if you keep being so cocky, they're not."

"You're right. That was a bit much," Erin admitted with an adorable lip bite. "But hey, as long as I'm in your company, I'm pretty damn lucky. So I guess I win either way."

Isabella laughed. "Now who's being gushy?"

Instead of answering, Erin leaned in and gave Isabella's ear a soft kiss. It felt strangely familiar and gloriously intimate. And Isabella instantly wanted more.

Chapter 24

Talking, Deciding, Kissing.

ISABELLA SMILED WHEN ERIN INTERLACED their fingers, as if it were a normal gesture they did every night when they were out walking.

"I think your dad liked me," Erin said.

"I think so too." Isabella's smile widened. Not only was she walking hand in hand with her lover on their way to a restaurant, but Erin had picked up on her father's approval. Joy rushed through her veins.

"Thank you for not spelling out that we're dating. I'm sure he'll just assume we are two friends going out for a meal. I will explain how much you mean to me soon. In fact, I want this to be when I sow the seed for that conversation. When Daddy comes home, Mother will question him about who I was with and she...well, she'll ask what we wore and how we behaved. She'll probably suspect that you're more than a friend."

"It's okay. Handle it however you're comfortable. You're not the first woman I've dated while she was coming out. Granted, the other two were younger and a lot higher on the Kinsey scale...but I've been through this before. I can be discreet. And patient."

"What's the Kinsey scale?"

"Uh, well, simplified, it's a scale where one end means you're one hundred percent straight and the other ends means you're one hundred percent homo. The theory is that we all land somewhere on the scale."

"I see. Well, thank you for being patient and understanding about my parents. If everything goes to plan, I'll tell them about you next week. If

I'm feeling particularly cowardly, I'll rope Marie in to come and help talk Mother down when she hits the roof."

"Still think she'll be angrier about me being a lowly personal trainer than me being a woman?"

Isabella gave a mirthless laugh. "Positive."

"Then maybe she'll like me better if I own a gym?"

Squeezing Erin's hand, Isabella replied, "Perhaps. But I don't want you to choose your path in life to impress my mother. Trust me, I've tried. It only leads to misery. She's never satisfied and will find fault with everything. It's her greatest talent."

"Don't worry, babe. I won't let her decide anything. It's up to you and me. At least, I want it to be."

Isabella looked at the sign above them to check that they were in the right place. "We'll discuss it over dinner. We're here now."

With a hand resting gently on Erin's lower back, she led them in to the best table in the house.

The sea bass was perfectly cooked, and the nonalcoholic chardonnay she chose complemented the fish well. She watched Erin carve into her steak with gusto and smiled.

"So, are you going to talk to me at any point, or should I leave you and that T-bone alone?"

Erin stopped the fork that was halfway to her mouth. "Oh, sorry. Let's talk. So, me blowing my itty-bitty savings on buying a gym and thereby anchoring myself in New York—for or against?"

Isabella laughed. "Well, that was succinct. I've given it a little thought, and I think it might be a good idea, if you feel that owning a gym is the right thing for you. It'll mean a lot more work. It would also mean a lot of research and learning how to run your own business, which isn't easy."

Erin took a sip of her beer. "I think I'm ready for that. I'm outgrowing my old life. I'm tired of drifting around like everything's temporary. The way I lived before I met you was simple but not very fulfilling, you know? I was just…getting by, not really living." She paused, holding up her beer and looking at it as if the right words might be floating in the foamed liquid.

"I didn't see any reason to challenge myself and try new stuff. I didn't believe I could, even if I wanted to. Meeting you changed that," Erin continued, cautiously. "I feel like it's time to grow up and take responsibility. I feel like I might be able to pull it off. I want to own something, put effort into it, and watch it thrive. I want something that's mine. Plus, it means not having to deal with clients every damn minute, which will make my introvert brain happy." They shared an amused look before Erin continued. "The whole thing still freaks me out, but I feel like I might be able to do it. If you're with me."

Isabella took a breath before diving in. "That brings us to the next point. Me being with you. You haven't said it, but underlying this whole discussion is the theme of you doing this to have more money and stability for a life with me and Alberto. Correct?"

Seemingly close to choking on her beer, Erin hurried to reply. "I'm not assuming anything, babe! It's just that what we have seems to be serious. At least, I hope it's serious. I'm not sure if we can be a lifelong thing, because I'm such a mess, and you're…"

"A mother?" Isabella filled in.

"Well, yeah, that too. But I was going to say 'a real adult.' Unlike me, you know how to settle down and start a family."

Isabella smoothed out her napkin. "Hardly. I failed at that, remember? That's why Alberto and I are here."

"Aw, c'mon now. You didn't fail. You just…picked the wrong players for the game."

Isabella smirked at her. "Sports metaphors are lost on me, *preciosa*."

"Fine, fine. You had the wrong pieces for your chess game, then. You had one of those tower thingies when you needed…"

"A queen?" Isabella flirted and took Erin's hand across the table.

Erin's smile lit up the dim restaurant. "Yeah, why not? I'm the queen you need to win the game."

Isabella resisted the urge to inform Erin that a game of chess was better played with all the pieces in play, but she understood the point Erin was trying to make and had to agree. Richard, Alberto, and she looked like a perfect family on paper, but it was all wrong. Now, she, Alberto, and Erin, well, that was much more promising.

"I'm going to be completely frank with you here, Erin."

She scrunched up her nose. "Why? Don't be Frank, I like you as Isabella."

Isabella closed her eyes in defense against the silly joke and let go of Erin's hand. "Don't start."

That earned her a snigger. Erin held her hands up. "Sorry, sorry. I'm back into old habits. Go on."

"I don't have any doubts about our future, Erin. I've waited, experimented, and evaluated things enough. I'm ready to commit. So don't worry about anchoring yourself in New York. If you buy the gym, Alberto and I will move to New York one day, either to my own place if you're not ready for further commitment, or if you are, then somewhere nice and big with you."

Erin stared at her openmouthed. "Moving in together? Whoa! We haven't even known each other for six months yet."

Isabella shrugged and sipped her wine. "I'm used to analyzing the options, deciding what I want, and then going for it. *You* are what I want. In fact, I think *you* are what I need."

She paused to put her glass down, wanting to make sure she had Erin's full attention for what she was about to say. "Now I repeat, we don't have to move in together right away, and I'd like to add that me and Alberto moving to New York wouldn't happen for a while yet. But the apartment we're in now will be too small as Alberto grows older and needs a room that can fit more than a crib." She took Erin's hand again, and Erin immediately interlaced their fingers. Isabella smiled and continued. "You've been hinting about us building a future, even if you aren't consciously aware of it. That's why you keep talking about getting a nest egg and learning to take responsibility. Sounds to me like you're gearing up for a life with me and Alberto."

Erin puffed out a breath. "I-I...um, yeah, but not so soon! I mean, one day, yes. But what's wrong with long distance for a while?"

With a patient smile, Isabella tilted her head to the side. "Erin. Look at our hands. We can't stop touching each other. We miss each other like love-stricken teenagers when we're apart. There's only so long we can stay in a long-distance relationship. As I said, there's no hurry, I'm just letting you know that I'm ready whenever you are. Your talk of putting down roots helped me see that."

Erin swallowed visibly, and the hand in hers felt warm and damp.

"Calm down. I'm not asking you to marry me here," Isabella joked.

"You're not?" Erin looked relieved.

"No, *mi amor*. Not yet." Isabella laughed and got a beaming smile in return. She watched that smile dissipate, as Erin ran her free hand over her neck and stared down at the table. They were quiet for a while, holding hands.

"Yeah. I guess you're right," Erin said, finally breaking the silence. "A life together was what I was thinking about when I came up with this plan. In the long run, I'd be making a lot more owning the gym than as a self-employed trainer. And I think I'd be good at it. I really care about the place. I've watched Chris run it, and I've seen where he's gone wrong. I don't know about timelines for our future, and I don't think I'm quite ready to talk about that yet. But if you're okay with the idea of moving to New York one day…I think I'll tell Chris I'm serious about my offer."

With a smile, Isabella retracted her hand and picked up her fork to continue eating. "Good. Then it's settled. Tomorrow we'll discuss finances. I might even invest some money from the house sale if it's a sound business proposal."

Erin fidgeted with her dress strap, still looking shell-shocked. "Really? Um, I don't know if I can let you do that. I'd be happy for the financial advice, though."

"Great. Now, tuck into that steak. You'll need your energy tonight," Isabella purred and winked.

A tentative smile began on Erin's pink lips. She was clearly happy their conversation was back on familiar ground.

They walked back, hand in hand, and were almost back at the apartment when Isabella turned her head, only to find Erin looking at her.

"Hey, beautiful," Erin said.

Isabella smiled so big it made her cheeks hurt. "Hey, yourself."

Erin looked down at the pavement where her kitten-heeled shoes clicked in time with Isabella's higher heels. "You know, I'm kinda sorry we're almost back at your place," Erin said quietly.

"Why's that?"

"Your dad will be there, so I'll have to stop touching and kissing you."

"Well, we'll just have to kiss right now then, to have something to tide us over until he leaves," Isabella replied.

She pulled Erin toward her and caught her by the waist. The kiss was tender but promised a night of less gentle activities. Soon Erin's arms embraced her, both hands gripping her behind.

Isabella's opened her eyes a little in shock at Erin's firm, sexy grasp of her rear. Before she closed them again and settled into the kiss fully, she saw a car make a dangerous U-turn and speed off, then thought nothing more of it, too occupied with how wonderful Erin felt and how overwhelmingly happy she was.

Chapter 25

Everything Out In the Open

ISABELLA WOKE TO THE SOUND of her phone vibrating on the nightstand. She tried to sit up to reach it, but Erin's arm and leg were draped over her heavily. Awkwardly, she shimmied to the side. The screen said *Mother* and showed Isabella she'd already missed two calls. She swore under her breath.

"Hello? Mother? You're calling early. Is everything okay?" she asked drowsily.

"I don't know, Isabella. You tell me. Has the woman you allowed to grope you in public left you intact, or should I worry that she is an axe murderer too? Hmm? Is that why you have kept her a secret?"

Shit, shit, shit. She knows. Shit. Well. There's no going back now.

Isabella forced the sleep from her voice. She needed to sound stern and confident for this conversation.

"Grope me in public? What do you mean? And how do you know about her?"

"I arrived early to pick up your father. I saw you with my own eyes, Isabella. And I could scarcely believe it. But that is neither here nor there, I asked my questions first, young lady. And I expect answers."

Isabella rubbed at her forehead, remembering the car and its dangerous U-turn as Erin had squeezed her ass the night before. She decided, for the time being, to ignore the fact that her father had driven himself and that the only other logical reason for Judith's drive-by was spying. She addressed the issue at hand. "Mother, I was going to tell you about her. I was going to come over next week for dinner and tell you both that I'm dating someone and that it is serious."

"I see. Why don't we push that forward to right now? I shall get your father and we will come see you in around fifteen minutes."

Despite knowing her mother couldn't see her, Isabella pulled the covers over her naked body. "What? No, not right now."

"She's there, isn't she? That is why you haven't been answering your phone. You have been busy doing God knows what with *some woman*. Well, you will tell me everything about her, starting with where she is from and what she does."

"Mother! You can't talk to me like that and make those sorts of demands. I'm an adult, and even if I wasn't, I'd still deserve better than being spoken to like this."

"You will answer me. Right now."

"You want answers? Fine. Her name is Erin Black. She's a personal trainer on a modest wage, she doesn't come from money, and is unlikely to inherit half of Pennsylvania when some distant uncle dies."

"Don't take that tone with me, Isabella Martinez. You did that when you ran off with your conservationist hippie, and look how that turned out. When will you learn that a race horse cannot mate with donkeys? You need someone who deserves you and can keep up with you."

Pulling the covers over her head, a barely awake Erin mumbled a reply, and Isabella couldn't help but laugh. Erin's comment, and how adorable she looked, momentarily trumped any anger or worry she had about her mother. Besides, it was amusing to hear her mother grind her teeth at the interruption.

"Isabella? What was that?" Judith snapped.

"That, Mother, was Erin. She was asleep until you so rudely woke us. She said she can keep up with me, as long as she hydrates. And that you should stop yelling, because you are giving her a headache."

"What? How dare she speak to me like that?"

"Honestly, Mother? I cannot tell you how happy I am that she did. She's usually much sweeter and more patient, so the fact that she reacted like that should tell you all you need to know about your behavior. It certainly tells me all I need to know. You are being vile and rude. And I agree with her.

You should stop yelling. Especially as I'm not listening anymore." Isabella hung up and squeezed her eyes shut, trying to ignore the menacing echo of her mother's voice in her head.

She looked over at the incredible woman next to her. Erin had clearly fallen back asleep. Her wheat-blonde hair was all over the pillow and tangled beyond belief. Isabella's own fingers had done quite a lot of that tangling, and she vowed to help Erin with it later.

Erin's pink lips pouted a little in relaxation, and her breaths came slow and deep. It was calming to watch her. More than just calming, Isabella decided. It was heavenly.

She reached out to touch Erin, careful not to wake her. She removed a few strands of hair from her beautiful face and traced her jawline to her chin. Her skin was so smooth. She caressed her cheek and watched a smile form. She wondered if her lover was aware of her touch or if she was dreaming.

Part of her wanted to wake Erin, to see those clear, blue-green eyes looking back at her. But she wouldn't be so selfish. Erin needed to sleep whenever her insomnia would allow.

She snuck out of bed, picked up her robe, and went to Alberto's room. He was still sleeping too, his own lovely blue-green eyes hidden from Isabella's gaze, just as Erin's were. She closed the door behind her and went to the kitchen, poured a glass of apple juice, and picked up the phone. She needed to talk to someone about her mother. And there was only one person who could relate—and who was always up and ready to chat in the morning. She dialed Marie's number from memory and waited while sipping her juice.

"Hello, beautiful sister. Isn't it a gorgeous day? Sure, it's a bit cloudy, but that can have its special beauty too. Look at that mesmerizing gray light!"

Isabella rolled her eyes. "Hello, Marie. Yes, the cloudy, gray day is stunning," she muttered.

Marie ignored her comment, as she usually did when Isabella was sarcastic or rude. "It's so nice to hear from you. How was your date last night? Tell me all the gossip."

"Last night was wonderful. Daddy babysat and said that everything went well. When Erin and I came back from the restaurant, we saw them playing airplane on the sofa, both giggling like mad. You should see them together, Marie. Daddy was made to be a grandfather."

Isabella felt downright blissful at the memory. Not only did that make her happy, but it would be wonderful for Alberto too. His grandfather would be a friend, a babysitter, and a male role model. And playing with his grandson would keep Daddy from sitting in his office, drinking scotch and re-reading Mark Twain. She drank some juice and remembered how happy they'd both looked last night.

"Aww. That's really great. I'm glad for the positive energy their bond brought to your home and the meaningful relationship they'll have. But it's not gossip. Get to the juicy bits. What happened between you and Erin?"

Her glass went down on the table with a sharp thud. "Marie?"

"Yes, honey pie?

"Please tell me this isn't going to get sexual again?"

"Well." Marie drew out the word like it had twelve syllables in it.

Isabella frowned. "If it does, I am hanging up."

"Spoilsport. Fine. No sex. Just the lovey-dovey stuff. How did the talk about Erin taking over the gym go?"

Isabella gave her a quick rundown of what had been said.

"That all sounds really good. So, clearly, that's not why you sound so negative."

Isabella sighed. "No. That is courtesy of Judith Martinez."

"What? Did she come to babysit last night too?"

"No. But she came to pick him up. Which makes no sense. Daddy didn't know when me and Erin would be back, so he drove over in the Jag. He left Mother the Mercedes, in case she wanted to go visit one of her horrible friends while he was away. Clearly, she decided to skip any visits and stalk me instead. And that was when she saw us kissing on the way back from the restaurant. She called me a little while ago to interrogate me."

Marie made a hissing sound, as if she was in pain.

"Precisely." Isabella ran a hand through her hair, resisting the urge to tug.

"Well, I hate to tell you the positives, because I know you hate it when I see things from the bright side."

"But?" Isabella prompted.

"At least it's out now, and you don't have to worry about how to tell her. And me and Alberto are off the hook."

Isabella felt her forehead furrow in confusion. She wished Marie had gotten into the habit of calling their parents something other than their first names. "I assume you mean Daddy, and not my Alberto?"

"Yes, Alberto Sr," Marie clarified. "Judith's been convinced that you were hiding something, and a new partner was on the horizon. She also assumed you were hiding him because the man in question was somehow inappropriate. Neither of us said anything, Alberto because he didn't know, and me because I'm the best sister in the world and would never do something like that."

Knowing how bad Marie was at keeping secrets, Isabella just rolled her eyes and finished her apple juice.

"Apparently, she's even discussed the matter with Rupert," Marie added.

Isabella's attention came back in full force. "Rupert Claremont?"

"Yes, silly. She doesn't know any other Ruperts, does she? She told me that she talked it over with him in the office. I don't know what she thought that would achieve. You know what he's like, hard as nails and even more controlling than Judith. I mean, the man has a hole in his soul he just can't fill, so he attacks others to keep them from seeing his emptiness. He really needs to do some work with his inner child and see why it lashes out like that. I could probably recommend…"

"Can we stop psychoanalyzing Rupert and go back to why our mother is discussing my love life at work? And with that beast of a man, of all people?"

"She was really upset that you were keeping secrets from her and that neither I nor Alberto seemed to care. She told me that she discussed it with him, because she needed advice on how to force you to tell her and stop you from dating someone else who's 'beneath you.' Her words, not mine. Although I might have made a naughty joke about the choice of words when I spoke to Judith," Marie admitted.

"I'm sure she loved that."

"She threatened to cut me out of the will. Again. She really needs to let go and allow herself to be a sexual creature. Or embrace being asexual and thrive in that. We only get one life. It's far too short not to have fun when you can. Besides, it can't be good for her to be so uptight. I mean, just her colon alone is…"

"Marie. Stop right there."

"Okay, fine. You get my point. Either way, she's become obsessed—I'm talking level-twenty obsession here—with you dating someone. And how to stop you. I think she worries equally about you dating someone who doesn't deserve you, and the Martinez fortune. She knows that you'll cut ties like you did after she tried to break you and Richard up."

Isabella ran a hand over her face. "Do you think she ever considered talking to me. About trying to find a solution that works for everyone?"

Marie snorted.

The corners of Isabella's lips tugged into a sardonic smile. She was just so tired of this. "Exactly."

"Look, unless you marry someone she thinks is right for you, like a doctor or a lawyer—preferably with a trust fund and a mansion to inherit—she's always going to disapprove and meddle. If you're serious about Erin, you're just going to have to face Judith and deal with her."

"Or cut ties again."

"Yes. That's always an option. But I thought you wanted to keep your father in your life? They're a package deal, sweetie pie."

Isabella sighed. "I know. That's the biggest problem."

"You need to talk to him."

"What's the use? He worships the ground she walks on. He's not going to fight her just to see me and Alberto behind her back."

"Isabella, he worships the ground you walk on too."

Isabella hummed noncommittally.

"Look, just think about it. Anyway, I have to go. I have boogie-burst aerobics in fifteen minutes. It's my first time. I'm so excited," Marie said with an shrill squeal to prove her point.

Isabella considered asking what the hell boogie-burst aerobics was, but decided she was happier not knowing. "Okay, *hermanita*. Thank you. I really needed to talk this over with you. Oh, and enjoy flailing about to boogie music."

"Thanks! And you go enjoy your girlfriend. Wait. Is, ahem…morning glory…a thing with lesbians?" Marie giggled like a schoolgirl, and Isabella shook her head at the sound.

"Good-bye, Marie," Isabella said before hanging up.

She leaned back and listened. There was no sound from either of the bedrooms. She was still the only one awake. Marie's suggestion to speak to their father tumbled through her mind. What would she say? Was there even a point in trying?

Calling was a bad idea. Mother would probably take the phone or start yelling at him for speaking Spanish so she couldn't understand.

That eavesdropping witch.

Isabella closed her eyes, letting memories wash over her of the years when she would get grounded for weeks on end for some minor offense perceived by her mother.

She'd often spent those long hours in her room writing an entry in her diary or a letter to her father. When she left for school the next morning, she would slip it under the door to his office, and when she came home again, there would be a reply waiting for her on her bed. She could still see the beautiful, personalized stationary that he used, the embossed envelope, with the words *mi vida* in his sloppy handwriting. She'd felt so special. He took time out of his busy work day to reply to her on his best stationary. It had been their secret, and it had made her feel less alone. It had probably made him feel less alone, too.

She would write him a letter.

With her much-cheaper stationery, Isabella sat down at the kitchen table. Things became so much clearer when they were written down. Whether it was a note explaining her past to Erin or a letter explaining her future to her father, putting pen to paper helped her think clearly.

She wrote more than a page before she stared at it in disgust. She was rambling and explaining things to him as if he were a child. This wouldn't do.

She started over and simply wrote:

Dearest Daddy,

I know Mother has been bothering you with questions about my love life. And I know she is probably running around the house throwing things and cursing my name right now. I'm sorry you have to be in the same house with her today.

I would like to ask you to ignore that for a minute. To ignore her for a minute. Focus on yourself. Focus on how much fun you had with Alberto last night. Focus on the fact that with you retired and me working from home, we can finally spend as much time together as we want. The woman you love is threatening to take that away. For no other reason than her pathologic need for control.

Daddy, I won't let her meddle in my love life again. You remember what it was like last time. The screaming, the frosty stares, the guilt trips, trying to keep you away from me as a punishment. Cruel remarks, even trying to set me up with other men in front of Richard. Do you remember that?

I can't go through that again. I won't subject Erin to that. If Mother doesn't let me be with Erin without making us both miserable, then I'll simply break all contact between her and me.

Oh, and I'm sorry that I didn't tell you what Erin means to me last night. I sort of left you to assume. I know that because she's a woman you probably thought that we were just friends. But I also know that you read me like an open book and could probably see that we're in love.

I adore her, Daddy. With all my heart. No one has ever made me feel like she does, and I want to give her the world. I think you liked her last night, didn't you? She made that joke about you and Alberto having the same haircut, and you wouldn't stop laughing. She has great comic timing, doesn't she?

So what if she doesn't have a fortune, or she isn't a social climber with a huge paycheck? She is hardworking, funny, smart, loving, strong, and so very kind. Just like you. Get to know her, and I am sure you'll love her.

I don't know what exactly I am asking you to do here. I don't know if there is any way you can get Mother to calm down. Or if you would ever consider seeing me and Alberto even if I cut all ties with Mother. But I'm asking you to try and do something. I want you in my life, Daddy, but I need Erin. Please, don't make me choose between you. Please.

Te quiero,

Isabella

She addressed the envelope and slipped the letter inside. Her father usually picked up the post, so it should be safe from her mother's clutches. She found a stamp and put the letter by the door to mail later.

Chapter 26

We Need to Talk About Alberto

It was just after dinner, and Erin felt exhausted. She'd spent the day trying hard to be light and cheerful for Isabella, who'd played along dutifully. Ever since that call, Erin wanted to shake Isabella's mother for the sadness she was causing her daughter.

She finished her glass of water and listened to Isabella changing Alberto's diaper. He cooed at her, and she answered in Spanish. Erin stretched to wake her tired muscles after their frenzied lovemaking the night before and grinned proudly. *We must have invented some of those positions.*

Bored and missing Isabella's presence, Erin walked into the bathroom as Isabella buttoned up Alberto's onesie. She put her arms around Isabella's waist and kissed her hair.

Isabella leaned into her while tickling Alberto's belly. He writhed and squealed. He was looking in her direction, as if he was looking for eye contact; so she looked into those green-blue eyes, so different than his mother's, but strangely like her own.

Suddenly her stomach flipped. He was looking at her. Right at her. As if he was waiting to see what she would do and say. As if he was hanging on her every word and action, ready to soak up her behavior like a sponge. *Chill, Black, you're imagining things.* But her pulse quickened.

She had a woman in her arms who was fighting with her mother because of her, and a baby looking to her to be his second parent. On top of that, she was about to own a gym she would have to learn how to run. If she failed at any one of those tasks, she'd let down Isabella, Alberto, and Chris. Three wonderful people who, for some reason, were depending on her. Her heart raced and her vision blurred.

"*Preciosa*? Are you all right? I can feel your heart pounding like a jackhammer."

Her body gave up too many of her secrets. Erin moved away from Isabella.

"What's the matter?" Isabella asked with a worried frown. "You're deathly pale."

"I'm okay. Just, dealing with stuff," Erin kept looking at Alberto, who kept staring right into her eyes.

Isabella looked from Erin to Alberto and then softly said, "I see. Would that 'stuff' happen to be my son?"

"Huh? Why would you say that?"

"You're staring at him like he's an object from outer space. I know you have concerns. Please, talk to me about them? Properly?"

Unsure of how to say *no, thank you* to that, Erin just shrugged.

She heard Isabella take a deep breath. "Remember how talking about your insomnia helped a little? Well, this is even more important for you to talk about. This concerns a human being who will always be part of your life when you're with me. We're going to end up having lots of talks about Alberto. Why not start with what's worrying you?"

Closing her eyes, Erin thought long and hard. Isabella was taking so much grief from her mother, and was worried about losing her father. The last thing she needed was to worry about what her girlfriend wasn't telling her. Especially since she already knew it was about her son. There should be no secrets, no more holding back. If Isabella was prepared to deal with this whole nightmare with her parents over their relationship—she could probably deal with another Erin-has-baggage-and-freaks-out issue. She had to trust Isabella. Trust their relationship. She took a breath and tried to figure where to start.

"I…never had parents. There were adults in my life, though. Some were a good influence and some weren't. Sometimes they'd say things that stuck with me. Changed me. I watched and learned from them, good stuff…and bad." She licked her lips, trying to find enough moisture to get the next words passed them. "If I'm part of Alberto's life as he grows up, I'll do that to him. I'll…shape him. All my weirdness and dumb behavior, he'll see that and pick it up."

Isabella looked like she was about to argue, but she closed her mouth again. She tilted her head and said, "Give me an example of something you might say or do and how you think it might influence him?"

"Jesus, if I could tell you everything I could do wrong, I could just make sure I never did that. I don't know, that's kinda the point."

In a soft voice, Isabella answered, "I see. And you believe that this is a unique situation for you?"

Erin looked at her, puzzled. "What do you mean?"

It was the saddest smile Erin had seen in a long while. "I'm trying to be respectful and let you figure out something for yourself, but as it isn't working, I'll spell it out for you, *preciosa*. All adults can be bad role models or say the wrong thing and influence a child. I had two parents who loved me when I grew up. But one of them was always toxic and the other tended to fade into the background. My mother said and did many things that shaped me for the worse, and I doubt she ever gave it a thought."

Erin frowned, unsure of where this was going. "Okay?"

"The fact that you are aware of how much everyday things can influence a child and that you worry about it, makes you a better candidate to be around children than most. There are no guarantees as to what will stick in a child's mind. You might make a joke about their nose, and they laugh and forget all about it, *or* they start worrying their nose is too big and develop an issue with their appearance." Isabella rubbed Erin's upper arm and smiled a little. "You can't let that hold you back, because if we all did that, no one would ever dare talk to kids. All you can do is act like a decent human being and try to keep communication open with them. That way, if something you've said or done bothered them, they'll come to you and talk about it. If they're even aware of it, that is. If not, there isn't really anything you can do until the problem surfaces."

"Your presence *will* influence Alberto. That's what happens when you're around a child. However, have I ever given you the impression that I wouldn't do whatever it took to give Alberto everything he could ever want or need?"

"No." Erin shook her head vigorously. "Definitely not. I mean you were even trying to stay in a loveless relationship just to give him a dad."

"There you go. Now, I've found a person who is unique; so genuine, so interesting, passionate, funny, and so caring. I found you. And I wouldn't have let you be part of my son's life unless I thought you would improve it. Unless I thought you'd be a good, stable role model for him."

A lump was forming in Erin's throat. "What if I screw him up?"

Isabella sighed and looked at her son. "Well, something screws everyone up at some point. If the most dangerous thing in his formative years is you...then he will truly have had a blessed childhood. Anyone would be lucky to have you in their life."

They were silent for a while, both looking at Alberto. Isabella's hand was still on Erin's upper arm, rubbing gently. Erin's mind filled with thoughts and the lump in her throat felt like it might suffocate her soon.

"Do you really mean that?" Erin asked quietly, not able to meet Isabella's gaze.

"With all my heart, *preciosa*."

Erin swallowed. She wanted—needed—to be everything Isabella and Alberto could ever want. But was the desire to do well enough? Was it that simple? "Do you...do you think that this is something I should talk to a therapist about?" Erin asked.

Isabella looked over at her, sympathetic brown eyes meeting Erin's unsure glance. "It's more important what you think, *preciosa*. But, yes, if you are going to see someone about your insomnia then you can certainly talk to them about your worries about Alberto as well. I don't think worrying about raising a child correctly is something you need therapy for, but if it helps you, then why not? Is that what you want?"

Erin looked at the boy on the changing table. He had a grip on his feet and was looking at his fat little toes. He looked so perfect and so vulnerable.

The urge to protect him surged within her. She had to make sure he got the best upbringing anyone could possibly get. She couldn't give him that now. She was sure of that. But maybe if she learned more about herself and what she could improve, then...maybe...she could give him everything she never got.

She wanted to try. She had to. She wanted to help raise Alberto. No matter how terrified and unprepared she felt. *Was this how Isabella felt when she found out she was pregnant?*

"Do you really think I can do it?" Erin asked in a small voice.

"I'm certain. You've got so much love to give, so much experience to impart. Alberto is lucky to have you in his life. We'll both make mistakes, Erin, but if we're both in his life, then we can counteract each other's mistakes and talk to him about any slipups. We'll be a team. I'm sorry to ask you to be part of that team, even though you don't feel ready, but I'm afraid me and Alberto come as a package deal."

Erin's head snapped back to Isabella. "Oh God, don't think for a second that I wish you didn't have him. Seeing you as a mother made me fall for you all the harder, and he's amazing. I want Alberto in my life, even if he pees on me. I just want to be something positive in his life, not negative."

"As long as you want to care for him and protect him, it will be."

Isabella's reassurances made the idea a lot for Erin to take in. "I think I want to talk to a shrink about this," she said. "I want to be the best I can be, for all of us. I want to be ready to help him along at every stage of his life."

Isabella chuckled with eyes that glittered. "There you go again. Planning for a lifetime with us. And you still believe you haven't made a long-term commitment."

The teasing had its desired effect, Erin's shoulders relaxed a bit, and she stuck her tongue out at Isabella, who laughed. And her low, melodic laugh set Alberto off laughing as well.

Erin tried for her most charming smile. "All right, so maybe I'm rushing ahead in this relationship too. Are you complaining, doll?"

"Not about you unconsciously making commitments, but perhaps about being called doll." Isabella smacked Erin's arm playfully.

Erin grimaced at her slipup. "Ah, sorry. Does it help if I say that you're as beautiful as a doll?"

Isabella quirked an eyebrow at her, picked Alberto up, and left the room while muttering, "I hope you're referring to children's dolls and not the adult kind."

Erin stood locked in place, trying to figure out what Isabella had meant. When she got it, she gasped loudly.

"Wow. That took an embarrassingly long time to sink in, featherbrain," Isabella called back from the other room.

"Featherbrain? Oh, I'm gonna get you for that, Martinez."

And she knew just how. She went out to find Isabella and tickle that sensitive spot just under her ribs.

By the time it was Alberto's last feeding of the day and his bedtime, it was time for Erin to look for a train home. She wished she didn't have to go, but she had work in the morning. And considering how long it took for her to get to sleep, she needed to be back in New York at a decent hour.

Isabella sat on the sofa with Alberto and unbuttoned her shirt. Without a word, Erin sat next to her. Alberto reached out, and Erin guided a handful of hair into his little fist.

"He lies still more when you let him play with your hair," Isabella said with what sounded like gratitude.

Erin looked at the chubby baby hand squeezing and toying with her hair. She noticed the little dimples where knuckles should be and smiled. She was helping. She was actually helping.

Gently touching the small hand, that strange feeling of pride and belonging filled her, as it had when she first offered to let him play with her hair. She was serving a purpose in their little unit.

How could something as innocuous as her hair grant her this lovely feeling? So many times, she'd cursed her own vanity in keeping it so long. It would be so much easier to cut it short, just put in some gel and go. But her long hair was part of who she was, and it had always been her pride and joy. Now, entertaining a baby with that hair was her new pride and joy.

She looked up at Isabella and quietly said, "Tonight, before I go, could we look for a shrink together? I want to deal with my issues. I can't hide from them forever."

Isabella smiled at her, a smile so warm and clearly smitten that Erin's heart leapt in her chest.

"Whatever you need, my love. Who knows? If you find someone who can help you, perhaps I'll talk to them about my defense mechanisms."

"What? You mean the moodiness and all the insults are defense mechanisms? I never would've guessed!" Erin said, faking shock.

Isabella glared at her. "Careful, I could always put the baby down and get you."

Erin smirked. "Yeah. You know, that doesn't sound like such a threat, my fierce lioness."

Isabella made a growling noise, sounding just like a lion, and Erin tried to keep from laughing too loud and spooking Alberto.

Chapter 27

Galvanizing

IT WAS LATE AFTERNOON, AND Isabella was writing. With the exception of a short walk to the mailbox to post the letter to her father, she'd written like a machine all day. She was surprisingly happy with it and felt a little twinkle of belief in what she'd created.

Blowing out a long-held breath, she put a period after the final paragraph of the epilogue and sat back in her chair. She briefly considered starting the second draft, rewriting and editing her finished material right away. But decided she was too mentally exhausted and giddy to start on the next batch of hard graft right away.

Instead, she opened the top drawer in her desk and got out a thick folder marked *writing*. Inside was a business card, thumbed to the point where the print was almost worn off. It didn't matter. Isabella knew the name. And she knew how to contact him.

Santiago Gomez. One of her father's best friends. She hadn't thought about him since that first morning in Philadelphia when she berated her father for eating too many churros at his house every Sunday.

She'd once asked for his business card and had kept it in the folder for many years, only taking it out to hold and think about using it when her writing had been going particularly well. Santiago was a publishing agent. He worked with writers, represented them, and made sure their books got published.

Having had the backing of her parents' well-known name and the family fortune to fall back on, Isabella had built a career in the catering business with confidence. However, the talk of nepotism had always been a burr in her side.

Contacting Santiago, letting him know that she had finished the book she'd been talking about for years, would that end up the same way? Would she ever feel like she'd achieved what she had without the help of the Martinez name? She'd worried about that since he'd given her his card.

She sighed, as she stared at the damn thing and accepted she'd just have to live with it. Finding an agent who believed in your book was extraordinarily hard, and if this was a chance to get some help with that, she'd be a fool to say no. Isabella Martinez was many things, but a fool was not one of them. She placed the battered card by her phone and was just about to put the folder away when the doorbell chimed.

Isabella quickly looked over at the sleeping Alberto in his baby bouncer. She breathed a sigh of relief that he hadn't woken up. She hurried to the door, assuming the person ringing was a neighbor, as the outside intercom hadn't buzzed.

She wasn't that lucky.

"Mother?"

"Hello, Isabella. May I come in?"

Isabella scowled. "Preferably not. But as you have somehow gotten this far, I can't say no, can I?"

She stepped aside, and Judith walked in. "One of your neighbors let me in as he was leaving."

"Ah, that explains it. I just assumed you used some form of black magic."

Judith glared at her. "I know you are upset, dear. Nevertheless, there is no reason to call me a witch."

"If the pointy shoe fits," Isabella muttered.

Judith sighed, as if Isabella was merely a petulant child who disappointed her. "I admit I might have been a bit...hasty...in our last conversation. I was furious because you have, once again, shut me out of your life when you needed me the most."

"I did not shut you out." Isabella scoffed at the idea. "I didn't tell you about my private life, because you have shown, time and time again, that you do nothing but judge and try to meddle. I always planned to tell you. Frankly, I would have done so sooner, if I hadn't known it would end in disaster."

"This is hardly a disaster. A disaster would be you entering into another relationship like the one you had with the scruffy nature buff."

"Richard. His name is Richard, and he does important work helping to conserve our nature reserves. You just never liked his profession because you don't understand it. Oh, and because it didn't give him the prestige and salary you feel is so goddamn important."

"Calm down, dear. I'm certain it is an important job, but hardly one for a real man. Just like that…" Judith pointed to the folder marked *writing* which lay on the table, "is a nice pastime while you are at home with your child but not full-time employment for a family of logical, strategic minds like the Martinezes."

Isabella felt an icy chill of humiliation and refused to look at the folder. "There's nothing wrong with writing. You've made it very clear that you think it's nothing more than a silly little hobby, but I disagree."

Judith waved her hand dismissively. "Never mind all that. I came here to discuss this new turn in your disastrous love life."

This strategy was all too familiar. Isabella refused to rise to the bait and lose her temper. "Mother, we've talked about this so many times. You can't stop me from dating people I am attracted to. You can't actually stop me from doing anything. I'm an adult."

"That is beside the point. That woman is the point. As your mother, I want to know more about her."

Despite her resolve, Isabella could already feel her tenuous control faltering. She barely resisted the urge to throw something at her mother. "It's not beside the point! You need to learn boundaries. I've already told you all you need to know about Erin. You'll find out more *if* you can learn to behave like a decent human being. If you do, I might bring her over for dinner. Considering the way you're acting now, you deserve nothing more than the door. Slamming in your face." Isabella's voice was shrill. She'd tried to stay calm, but Alberto woke and Isabella hurried to pick him up before he started crying. Cuddling him close to her chest, as much to comfort herself as him, she stared at her mother.

Judith sat down at the table. "You are exaggerating, Isabella dear. However, if it will calm you, I will explain further. My worry is twofold. Firstly, I feel upset to know that you embarked on something as important as choosing a new partner, and someone to bring into Alberto's life, without telling me and your father." She paused as if to let that sink in. It drove Isabella mad that her mother was so calm. Her demeanor no different than if they were discussing the weather. "Secondly, I had to watch you make a mess of your life once. No matter what I said or did, you just rushed headlong into that disastrous situation. I mean, quitting your job and moving to Florida to be with a man who was so unsuitable for you? I couldn't bear to watch. To have you make that mistake again—I simply cannot stand it, my dear."

Isabella's blood thundered in her ears. There was only so much longer she could stand this conversation before she screamed at her mother. She didn't want Alberto subjected to that. She breathed deeply to calm herself. "Mother, my relationship with Richard was a failure, yes. But not because of where he lived or what he did for a living. Nor because I quit my job to be a mother and a writer. It failed because I didn't love him. I love Erin. I love being with her, and I love the life I could have with her, writing and raising Alberto."

Judith pointed to the folder marked *writing* with a sneer. "As we are back on the topic of writing, I see you are proceeding with that little hobby. Dearest darling, you are many splendid things, but we both know you are not a new Virginia Woolf. Authors are creative but damaged people living on the edge of society. You are a Martinez. We run society."

Isabella gritted her teeth and tried to ignore her heart pounding against her ribcage. "We are not a superhuman race, Mother. We're individuals sharing genetics and a last name. Oh, and I find it interesting that you speak about damaged people as if you and I weren't severely damaged."

For the first time, Judith's mask of superiority and righteous anger slipped. She looked unsure for a moment, and then it was back in place.

"I'm sure I have no idea what you are talking about."

"Really? You think undamaged people lock their children in a cold, damp basement overnight because they refused to wear the dress you chose for them for their birthday party? Without food. Or water. You think something like that wouldn't damage a child? That it wouldn't damage the relationship between the two people involved? Really?"

Judith shook her head, frowning. "That was never about the dress. It was about you learning to obey me without question and to respect those who know better than you."

Isabella stomped her foot, shaking Alberto, who grabbed onto her shirt. "That's the problem. You think you know better than everyone else and that you have to set the rules to keep the world from sliding into chaos. But it's not true. You are not God, and I'm not some frail, idiotic sliver of a human being who needs your divine guidance."

Judith scoffed. "Melodramatic as always, Isabella."

"I'm still right. Besides, I can't believe you are lecturing me about what it is to be a Martinez. You married into this family. Who made you the expert?"

"That is *exactly my point*, dear. Your father didn't choose an heiress like he was supposed to. He chose someone with ambition. Someone working their way up in the world. I was getting my law degree and educating myself on culture and etiquette. All while working painfully hard to pay for my own education. Your father chose someone who knew the value of money and status. Someone who could safeguard his family's legacy."

Judith paused to look at her, and Isabella recognized the "pay attention because this is important" look her mother was wearing.

"So, you see, it is not snobbery that makes me want to ensure you marry the right sort of person, it is simply having grown up in a harsher world than you did. I have seen the good that successful people can achieve and the bad that people who are less…industrious have to live with."

"That sounds absolutely fascist," Isabella spat out. Her tone of voice upset Alberto, and he mewled a little in her arms. She held him tighter, hushed him, and kissed his forehead. She looked back at her mother. "Daddy didn't choose to marry you because you were 'industrious.' Or likely to make a lot of money. Or somehow uphold the family name. He married you because he fell in love with you. Though I can't see why. I'm assuming he was dazzled by your confidence. Or perhaps he hit his head. Either way, he didn't sit down and pick your name out of some goddamned breeder's catalogue. He fell in love. Like I have."

"Calm down, Isabella. I am not saying that you cannot fall in love. I am just trying to ensure that you don't fall for some useless hippie again, or as the case seems to be now, some pretty little gold digger."

"Erin is not a gold digger," Isabella said through clenched teeth.

Judith held up her hands. "Fine. Then you will have no qualms in letting me meet her and make up my own mind about that. Nor about apologizing."

Seriously? Isabella stared at her and her haughty look of satisfaction. She wondered if Judith could hear herself and had any clue how absurd she sounded. "Me? Apologize to you? What for?"

"For keeping this woman secret from me, and for not telling me that you were…not heterosexual. How am I supposed to help you with the mess you make of your life and guide you if you do not share all the facts with me?"

"I never asked you to guide me! Firstly, I just found out that I'm attracted to women myself. Secondly, when it comes to Erin, I would've told you about her and I would've let you meet her. But now…" Isabella shook her head before continuing. "Erin's a precious, sweet soul. I don't want your callousness and twisted worldview anywhere near her. Nor me and Alberto, come to think of it."

This time, Judith's composed veneer cracked. She stood up so fast she knocked over the chair she had been sitting on. Her face set itself into deep rage as she venomously spat out her words. "Excuse me? I am your mother. And in the absence of your father properly running this family, I am the head of the Martinez clan. I will not have you speaking to me like that."

"Fine. I won't. I won't speak to you at all. Get out."

"You can't throw me out. I will not let you shut me out of your life again. If you do, not only will I make sure Alberto doesn't make the mistake of seeing you. I'll disown you. You'll be forcing my hand, Isabella."

Isabella gave a mirthless laugh; it rang hollow and angry in the small apartment. "Disown me? What century are you living in, Mother? Get out of my home. Now!"

Judith opened her mouth to speak, then shut it again with a snap. Her face contorted in disgust. She turned on her heel and marched out of the apartment.

Unsuccessfully, Isabella tried to take deep breaths to calm her raging fury. Flashes of white light swarmed in her vision. If she hadn't had Alberto in her arms, she would've been screaming and throwing things.

Instead, she leaned her hot face against his head and breathed in his sweet scent to calm herself down.

Her mother had made her feel trapped, frightened, furious, and worthless too many times. Without even realizing it, Isabella had just let her do it. Because she was her mother. Because everyone said she did it out of love. Because sometimes Isabella just wanted not to have to fight for herself all the time.

She could do that again now. She could let her mother keep pushing her around to keep the peace, to keep her parents in her life. And maybe someday, her mother would come around and behave like a normal human being. Was it such a bad thing to wish for that? Was it such a bad thing to wish her mother could love her, just the way she was?

Perhaps I should just let her meet Erin and make the decision she undoubtedly will—that Erin isn't appropriate. Then she can shout herself tired and leave.

Would that be the end of the world? She could spend her time rolling her eyes while her mother mistreated her and Erin. It's not like they'd have to meet that often.

Then she could keep both Erin and her father without a war with her mother.

Little cogs clicked into place in her mind, changing her perspective. There would be no war. No, instead she'd fight hundreds of battles every time she spoke to her mother. Or when Erin and her mother were in the same room.

No. She'd spent her life putting up with her mother, obeying her, making excuses for her. Feeling ashamed of her and for her. Pitying a woman so broken she had to break everyone around her. She wouldn't subject Erin to that, no matter what the cost. Erin was too sweet and pure a soul to withstand that kind of torment. She had so many demons of her own, Isabella wouldn't force her into the arena with hers too.

Someone had to teach Judith Martinez that she couldn't control everything. And who better to do it than the person she wanted to control the most?

Resolve and rebellion took root in her stomach and spread their strong tendrils up into her chest, enclosing her heart in the warm glow of their protection. The doubts she'd felt about sending her father that letter had gone, crushed by the ever-growing desire to protect and nurture and love, to care for Erin and her son. But shockingly, she wanted to care for herself too.

Discovering Erin's love for her had shown her that she was worthy of the purest kind of love, that unflinching, unrepentant, unapologetic love she'd never allowed herself to hope for, never believed she deserved. A lifetime of indoctrination and esteem-stealing degradation by her mother had all but convinced her that not only did it not exist, but she would never have found it even if it did.

I don't have to believe that anymore. I don't have to listen to her or worry about what she thinks. She doesn't know what's best for me. She doesn't know what writing means to me or what Erin means to me. Or what I mean to her. To hell with her and her pathological need for control.

She blinked until her vision cleared, kissed Alberto's head, then squared her shoulders. She walked over to the phone and dialed the number on the business card.

"Hello," the man's voice said.

Isabella cleared her throat to try to make her voice sound normal. Deep down she knew that she should've waited until she was calmer, but she couldn't. She had to do something.

"Santiago? It's Isabella Martinez."

The line went silent for a moment. "Oh, hello, Isabella. I haven't spoken to you in quite a while. Is everything all right with you and your father?"

Isabella tried to relax her tense frame. "Daddy's fine. Although I wish you and the rest of your group of silver foxes would help him keep an eye on his eating habits."

Santiago laughed. "No luck there. We're all as bad as each other. You didn't answer about how you were doing."

She wasn't in the mood to hide the truth. Isabella closed her eyes with a sigh. "No. That's because I'm furious with my mother. I apologize for my frankness, but I've just been told by her that my life choices are all wrong, including my choice to pursue a writing career. However, my mother is an idiot. I've a finished manuscript that I have faith in, so, I'm going to be very bold here. I'm calling to ask if there is any chance that you would consider representing me?"

Santiago hummed. "I'm surprised to hear that. About your manuscript I mean, not about your mother. It's been so long since I heard mention of you writing that I assumed you had given up your writing plans."

"No, it's just been a slow process due to all the changes in my life lately. I want to learn to be a writer," Isabella said, nervousness creeping into her tone.

"I see. And you've finished a manuscript?"

"Yes," she said, this time with confidence. That was one thing she could be sure of. All those pages, all those words…they were hers, and the story they painted was completed.

"Great. Then read it as if you were your worst critic, imagine being your mother. That should do the trick. Revise your first draft. Then revise and edit your second draft. Polish it until it's clean, sleek, and sharp. Maybe get someone else to read it and give their views. Then send it to me, and I'll tell you if I'll represent you or not." He paused, seemingly for effect. "Now, Isabella, I don't represent people because of who they are related to or what relationship they have to me. *If* your finished manuscript shows promise, I'll help you start a career as a writer and happily prove your mother wrong. On one condition."

Isabella swallowed. "Name it."

"If your manuscript is good, and if I manage to sell it to a publisher for you, you'll let me be there when you tell your mother you have a publishing deal."

A smile parted her lips. "Deal. I'll start the rewrites and send it to you when I can't improve it anymore."

"Good. Oh, and Isabella, just for the record, I've known your mother a lot longer than you have, and she's frequently wrong. Well done on letting her disapproval drive you instead of stopping you."

"Thank you," Isabella said, surprised by the compliment.

They said their good-byes, and Isabella hung up. She still felt upset. Emotion gnawed at her, and she suspected her mother would always have this effect on her to some extent. But Santiago was right. She wouldn't let Judith's disapproval stop her. She couldn't. She couldn't let her win like that.

Instead, that voice in her head would galvanize her. It would drive her to achieve her dreams. She knew what she wanted. She wanted to write, to raise Alberto, to see that happiness is being honest with yourself. She wanted to do it all with Erin by her side.

Chapter 28

Travel, or the Lack Thereof

ERIN WAS EXHAUSTED WHEN SHE left the gym after a long workday, a hard workout, and a brisk shower, but, as always, she was in dire need of a talk with her girlfriend. She smiled at that. *Her girlfriend.*

She waited impatiently for Isabella to pick up.

"Hey, *preciosa*."

"Hey, babe. Everything okay?"

Isabella sighed. "Well, no, not really. There've been some developments here."

Erin furrowed her brow and stopped walking. "Developments? That doesn't sound good."

"Some of it is good, and some of it is…," she huffed out a breath before continuing. "infuriating. And by 'some of it,' I mean my mother."

"Ah. You've spoken to Judith again?"

"She showed up here and told me how disappointed she was in me. Then she explained that writing's not for me and that the woman I…that *you* are most likely a gold digger. She demanded to see you and wants me to stop writing."

That furrow grew deeper. No one had ever called her a gold digger before. "Okay. So, what did you say?"

"I threw her out. Then I called an agent I know and asked him to represent me. And I decided that I can't wait to spend my life with you. And, no, not because I am rebelling against my mother's control, but because having to defend and explain what I want made me realize just how much I want it."

Erin laughed. "Whoa. Slow down there. First of all, congrats on the book and on contacting an agent. I don't know anything about publishing books, but that sounds like a good start. Secondly, are you sure you should've thrown her out? I mean, she's important to you. She's also Alberto's grandmother and the woman who could stand between you and your dad, if she wanted to."

"Of course I worry about cutting her out of my life. Despite everything she's done, I still love her. She's a huge part of my life and should be a huge part of Alberto's life. Yes, she can, and will, keep me from seeing Daddy. Less importantly, she can remove any financial support that she might've offered if I was ever in dire straits. Nevertheless, I can look after myself. Who knows, maybe Daddy will stand up to her one day, then I could keep him in our lives. When it comes to Mother being a part of our lives, she can certainly be let back in. Just as soon as she shows a shred of respect and faith in me," Isabella said at great speed.

Erin frowned. What to say to that huge information dump? How was she supposed to feel about it, even? She was proud of Isabella for standing up for herself and for their relationship. And she was thrilled that Isabella was seriously pursuing her dream of being a writer.

But there was a ball of worry in the pit of her stomach. Would Isabella end up regretting cutting ties with her parents? Erin had never had a family. Not a real one. The plethora of foster families and social workers didn't count. They'd never lasted for more than a few years anyway. They weren't the deep ties of a parental bond. She had nothing to compare Isabella's feelings toward her parents with, but it had always been her greatest wish to have a family. To belong. There had been many painful situations growing up that family would've helped with, had there been anyone there who had genuinely cared for her. That part of her hated the idea that Isabella would go through such pain because she wanted to be with Erin.

It's not really the same. I was a kid and wanted to be with the people I missed. Isabella is a grown-up who just wants her mother to stop hurting her. Different circumstances, different needs. I can't put myself in her shoes. I've just gotta trust she knows what she needs now.

"Okay," she started quietly. "You've clearly thought this through. Good. Well, um, you know what you want to do and how best to do it. Is there anything I can do to make things easier for you?"

"Just talk to me. About anything. Hearing your voice helps."

Relief at being able to help flooded Erin. "That I can do. I've gotta say this one thing, though. I just signed with Chris and his lawyer to start buying the gym. The lawyer thought it was a weird way of doing things but said that as long as we were both happy, everything else could be sorted out. I'm gonna start shadowing Chris to see how he runs the place." She stopped, realized that she was digressing, and gathered her thoughts to get her point across. "What I'm getting at is what I asked you about the other night. Would your mom be okay about us being together if she knew I was buying a gym? Would it fix things between you if you told her that?"

"Honestly? I don't know. You'd probably rise in her esteem, yes. But I don't want her to accept you merely because of a job title. I want her to accept you because *you* are the partner I chose. Neither you nor I need to 'fix this,' she does. So no, I'm not giving her any more chances or information until she apologizes."

"Okay. What about your dad?"

"I don't know. I suppose we'll see what Daddy does when he reads my letter."

Erin started walking again. "Sure. I just wanted to float the idea."

"Thank you. It was sweet of you to consider it. I'm glad you made it official with Chris and the lawyer. I have to admit that I'm being a bit selfish and worrying how your shadowing him will cut into our time together."

Anxiously running her fingers through her wet hair, Erin grimaced. "Yeah, we need to talk about that. Most nights, I'll be coming home later in the evening. I'm sorry, babe. It's just for a little while, though. I'll work on convincing my clients to transfer to other trainers connected to the gym. But until I get rid of all of them, I'll pretty much be working two jobs."

"I thought so. Don't worry. It'll be painful to get less time with you, but it's an investment in our future. To be honest, after my fallout with Mother, the idea of moving to New York is even more appealing."

Erin smiled but then noticed a man on the sidewalk staring at her. She resisted the urge to tell him to stop and focused on Isabella instead.

"I'm still sorry. And I'm also sorry you've had to go through all of this with your mom. I don't know what her major malfunction is."

She heard Isabella sigh. "Basically, she has a lot of issues from her own childhood. But, unlike you, she hasn't identified them as a problem and decided to do something about them. She just makes her life, and everyone else's, a misery. It's sad, really."

Not sure of what to say, Erin just hummed sympathetically.

"Speaking of therapy," Isabella added as an afterthought, "did you book that appointment?"

"Yep, for tomorrow. I'm freaking out, but hoping it'll make me feel better and sleep properly almost makes up for it."

"Good. As I said before, if the therapist is any good, I might book an appointment too. God knows I could talk about my mother for a few hours."

"I think that could take ages and be super expensive," Erin replied.

"Mm, probably true. Speaking of which, are you going to be all right paying for your therapy while managing the payments on the gym?"

She was glad Isabella couldn't see her grimace. "It's gonna be tight. I'll manage, though. Who needs to eat anyway? I might have to wait a while with buying more train tickets to Philly, though. And that sucks worse than any of the other ways I have to tighten my belt."

"Yes, it does. But luckily for you, I can pay for tickets. And I'm still interested in investing in the gym."

Erin chewed the inside of her cheek. Isabella investing made her so damn uncomfortable. It didn't take much insight into her own baggage-filled brain to know that it wasn't just about the money. What if she failed? She'd be failing Isabella too. Add to that the fact that she just wasn't used to getting help, or money, from anyone. Ever. No matter what. She just didn't know how to explain it without hurting Isabella's feelings.

"I don't know about that, babe. You need to keep your savings for you and Alberto. At least until your writing brings in some money. Especially now that you might not have your parents for backup if anything goes wrong."

"I have plenty of money saved. There's also the money from the house sale, and Richard pays child support for Alberto, so there's money coming in."

Erin looked down at her feet. Her heart felt like it was being squeezed. "Still, we should probably be careful with travel costs. It's not like we can't see each other on Skype, right?"

For a moment, there was silence on the line.

"We'll work something out. I don't want you to feel guilty about this, Erin. You're pursuing a future for yourself, and I'm so proud of you for moving forward and being so brave. In fact, I'm proud of both of us for building a life we can grow into, one in which we can grow old together. You buying the gym, me going all-in with my writing, all to build a future for us in New York? It's worth a little sacrifice right now."

Erin chuckled. "Yeah, I suppose. You know what? I'm glad we're both old enough to know that. Putting a stable future ahead of my need to kiss you right now—yeah, that's not something I would have been able to do when I was twenty-five."

"I know. Anyway, let's talk about more cheerful things."

Stopping by a crossing, Erin nearly walked straight into an old man in the crowd. She smiled an apology, as she waited for the lights. "Sure," she told Isabella, "I just have to say…thank you for being so supportive and for understanding what I'm trying to achieve here. You're a gem."

"'A gem' might be overselling it. I'm just being the understanding girlfriend. I realized I had to step up my game if I was going to be the Maggie Sawyer to your Batwoman."

The light changed, and this time, Erin did walk into the old man ahead of her. "Sorry," she mouthed, then held her hand up and ducked her head in apology. He scowled at her and shook his head before ignoring her and carrying on. Erin turned back to more important matters. "You've read *Batwoman*?"

"Remember that phone call when I said I'd looked into some of your interests, but then you annoyed me with your stupid guesses?"

Erin knitted her brows. "Vaguely, yeah."

"Well, I ordered *Batwoman 1, 2,* and *3* of the *New 52* series and read them on my iPad. Not really my cup of tea. I prefer more words in my reading. But I see why you like the characters. I'm glad I got an insight into something important to you."

Erin bit her lip around her smile, not caring if anyone saw her looking all lovesick and goofy. "Thanks. I'm not used to people paying attention to my interests like that. That's, um, some serious girlfriend points there. Not to mention some serious woman-loving-woman points for reading about the coolest lesbian superhero ever."

"Why thank you. I love…" Isabella trailed off. "Alberto, where are you going?"

"What? Lil' man is leaving?"

"He's sort of wriggling away on the floor. Out of his baby gym and toward the kitchen."

"Maybe he's making a sandwich?"

"Very funny. He's really got some speed up. I wish you were here to see this."

Erin sighed. "Yeah. Me too."

"Don't be sad, *preciosa*. One day we'll all live together, and you'll be tired of the sight of him."

"Unlikely. The kid looks a lot like you. I could stare at him all day. Besides, he looks funny when he gawps at you and says hoo."

"The last bit did not sound like a compliment. Be careful or I'll have you change his diaper again."

"Fine. I'll wear a raincoat and gas mask."

"I'm sure that would suit you nicely. Hurry home to your Wi-Fi, and I'll see you on Skype. If he's still wiggling about then, you can see it on camera."

"Okay. I'll hang up and hurry home. Tell the kid not to stop."

Finally home, Erin made coffee while impatiently waiting for her laptop to power up. As soon as everything was ready, she called Isabella. Three signals and Erin's screen was graced with Isabella's face.

"Hey, beautiful," Erin said.

"Good evening, *preciosa*. I'm afraid you missed it."

"What? He stopped crawling?" Erin tried not to look at deflated as she felt.

"Yes. Well, crawling might be a generous term for what he was doing. But whatever it was, I'm afraid it exhausted him. He's asleep now," Isabella replied.

"Dammit!" Erin crossed her arms over her chest.

"I'm sure he'll do it again soon. We'll see when he wakes up."

"Yeah, you're right. Hang on, I'm gonna go get some coffee." When Erin came back, Isabella was sitting back in her chair and smiling at the screen. "Hey, what's that smile about, Mona Lisa?" Erin asked.

"I was just thinking. You're here, I'm here, and Alberto…is fast asleep," Isabella answered, her seductive smile and bedroom eyes making it very clear what she was thinking about suggesting next.

Erin felt the corners of her own mouth pulling up in a smirk. She loved it when Isabella looked this…naughty.

"Yeah? Maybe we should remind ourselves that we don't have to travel to get some action."

"Take off the tank top, and we'll see how lucky you can get, Miss Black."

"Oh, hell yeah," Erin said with a grin, stripping quickly.

Chapter 29

Next Steps

THREE WEEKS PASSED. THREE WEEKS with only one visit from Erin. What those weeks did have plenty of were seemingly endless days when Isabella sat and missed her.

Admittedly, Erin's busy schedule had turned out to be a blessing in disguise. It had given Isabella lots of time to fill and an abundance of restless energy. In short, she'd managed to finish editing and proofreading her manuscript.

Two weeks to the day after she'd called him, Isabella e-mailed Santiago the document. She worried that maybe she should've spent more time honing the manuscript, but she also knew she was a perfectionist at heart. She could easily spend the rest of her life moving commas around if she didn't send the thing off. Now, it needed to be seen by someone else to get feedback on what needed polishing.

Alberto could not only crawl perfectly but also shuffle himself around on his behind. Isabella was proud of that. Apparently, most babies seemed to do one or the other, not both. She wasn't sure if this was something other parents would be proud of, but she didn't care.

She watched him shuffle toward her foot. He liked to do that, to grab her socks and try to pull them off. She smiled at him and said, "Look at you go, *cariño*. You'll have to show your father." Just as Alberto reached her foot, the intercom buzzed. "Speak of the devil," Isabella crooned to him. She picked him up and went out into the hallway to open the front door.

As she maneuvered the door open despite the fidgeting Alberto, Isabella saw Richard, Shay, and little Joshua on the doorstep.

"Hello there. How was your trip?" Isabella asked.

"It was good, thanks," Richard replied.

He stretched and took a deep breath of the balmy afternoon air. After a moment of apparent indecision, he gave her and Alberto a hesitant hug. He quickly moved back as if he'd been burned.

It was such an uncomfortable moment that Isabella didn't know how to respond. Luckily, Shay stopped any awkwardness by coming over and hugging Isabella too and then lifting Joshua up so he could do the same.

Isabella didn't know Shay or Joshua very well, so the hugs weren't exactly normal fare, but she smiled as if it were a perfectly natural situation.

Wondering if the visit had been a bad idea, Isabella fell back on the best icebreaker in the world—a child.

"Alberto, can you wave to Daddy, Shay, and Joshua?"

The baby looked from Isabella to their guests and gurgled. Isabella grabbed his little hand and made him wave.

Richard beamed. "Can I hold him?"

She smiled encouragingly. "Of course. Go ahead."

Reverently, he lifted Alberto from Isabella's arms, leaving Isabella free to walk in with Shay and Joshua while the reunited father and son brought up the rear.

The scene was set for the rest of their visit. Shay and Isabella discussed moving and babies, while Joshua drew and played with some toys he'd brought along. All the while, Richard and Alberto stared at each other.

A little later, Isabella served homemade brownies and coffee and some apple juice for Joshua. Shay looked over at Richard, who'd missed the brownies altogether and was just holding his forgotten coffee, too busy grinning at his youngest son. Alberto reached out his little hand to feel the bristles on his chin.

Shay smiled at them before calling out, "Earth to Richard!"

He looked over at her. "What?"

"Just wondering if you were going to let Joshua take a closer look at his half brother, or if you were going to hog the baby all night."

"Of course." Richard looked apologetic. "Come here, champ. You can fist bump Alberto. Look, I'll hold out his hand, and you can bump it."

Shay turned back to Isabella, who was sipping her coffee and secretly counting down the minutes until they left and she could call Erin. As if she could read Isabella's mind, Shay asked, "So, Richard told me you were dating someone new. Emily, was it?"

"Erin," Isabella corrected her with a smile.

"Sorry. I'm so bad with names. Well, I'm glad you seem to have landed on your feet. It's nice to see that some breakups leave both parties happier than before."

"Yes, well, it's hard to be heartbroken if you weren't truly in love to begin with. What Richard and I had was an initial crush that led to a friendship, nothing like what he has with you, or I have with Erin."

Shay smiled. Isabella recognized that smile from Joshua, who was an exact copy of his mother, other than his lighter skin. It was a fetching smile, as beautiful as the rest of her. Combined with her quick wit and warmth, Isabella found it very easy to see why her ex-boyfriend had fallen for Shay. The second she thought that, she realized with a jolt that it hadn't been a purely platonic thought on her behalf. *I'm a lot gayer than I realized.*

"I see your point," Shay said. "So, she lives in New York, right? How are you getting on with the long-distance-relationship thing?"

After a moment's hesitation, Isabella replied, "Not great, to be honest."

"Ah, that's a shame. But not surprising. I've done long distance in the past. It's hard. If you feel like telling me what you are struggling with, I might be able to help."

Sharing wasn't really her thing, especially with a virtual stranger, and Isabella weighed how much she wanted to tell. But she knew she needed to vent. And there were only so many times she could listen to Marie tell her to keep her chin up and to "think of the shining bright future you're building together" before ordering a hit on the poor woman. Or saving the money and doing it herself.

She shrugged and put down her coffee. "Erin's saving all her money, as she's in the middle of buying a gym. Which means she can't afford to visit much. Sadly, she's far too proud to let me pay for all her train tickets. She's also basically working two jobs right now, while she takes over the gym and finds other trainers for her old clients. So she doesn't have much time to come visit anyway."

"I see. Yeah, that's gotta be tough. Well, if she won't let you pay for tickets for her, and she doesn't have time to come here, why don't you and Alberto go there?" Shay asked and sipped her coffee.

"You mean move to New York?"

"Erm, no, I meant for a visit."

Isabella grimaced at her mistake. "Oh, of course. I suppose we could go up there for a weekend, yes. Erin doesn't work such long hours on weekends. It's not so easy traveling with Alberto and all the baby paraphernalia, though."

Shay rolled her eyes. "Yeah, I remember that pain. It's crazy how much stuff they need, considering they're so small. I'm so relieved that Joshua's old enough not to need much for the journey up here. Still, you survived the flight from Florida with Alberto, I'm sure you'd be okay with the short trip to New York."

It did sound like a good idea, now that she thought about it. Isabella hummed thoughtfully. She'd have to look into it.

"I suppose that means you're planning to move there one day? If Erin's investing in a gym?" Shay took another sip.

"Yes. When the time's right. I'm quite prepared to move, but Erin…has a few things she wants to work through first."

"Okay. Well, I'd recommend not waiting too long. Long distance takes its toll on a relationship, especially if you can't talk very often. Sorry, this is none of my business. I'll butt out now."

"No, no. I asked for your advice." Isabella smiled. "More coffee?"

"Not right now, thanks. I thought I'd see if I can convince Richard to let me hold Alberto for a second. I'm really missing babies."

Isabella laughed. "Well, from the awestruck look on Richard's face when he looks at Alberto, I think he might be prepared to have another. So, if you want a sibling for Joshua, I'd start working on your campaign now."

Shay grinned conspiratorially at her. "I might just do that."

Chapter 30

Assets

IT WAS LATE IN THE morning when Erin walked into the gym. Most of her clients had gone to other trainers, so she easily fit a therapy session into the morning, as long as Chris didn't mind. Which, of course, he never did.

This morning's session with Dr. Ariadne Hopkins had gone well. Erin really liked her; she was kind, patient, and surprisingly funny. Maybe Erin's confidence in Dr. Hopkins was why she felt like she was making progress, because she was. Something which she had sworn to rub in Riley's face when she gave her all the details. Riley had been doubtful, actually downright skeptical, about how much good therapy could do for Erin. According to Riley, therapy was only for those with a clinical diagnosis. Now, Erin could cheerfully tell her she was wrong.

Progress aside, Erin wasn't sleeping much better. She was sure that was mainly due to the stress of all the changes in her life. Plus, they'd examined her sleep patterns and realized that the nights she slept the best and the longest were the ones when she'd spent a lot of time with Isabella.

Dr. Hopkins called Isabella Erin's "anti-abandonment medicine" but stressed that Erin needed to find that security within herself and not rely on other people for it. That way would lead back down the rabbit hole if things went wrong. Erin was well aware of that. It was the whole reason she was in this mess to begin with. Not that she begrudged a moment of lost sleep. Without the insomnia, she knew she never would have found Isabella.

The sense that the sessions were working made Erin feel much calmer and more confident. Thoughts of screwing up Alberto and his entire childhood didn't send her off into a wild-eyed panic anymore. Nope, now they just made her hyperventilate. A huge step forward.

She walked into the locker room to get ready for Riley's session with her head held high. Riley had so far been impossible to pawn off on another trainer. Erin couldn't be completely sad about that. She enjoyed Riley's company after all…and their chats about Isabella.

"So. Chris is leaving next week, right?" Riley was lacing up her sneakers.

"Yep. End of the week. He says I'm ready to take over." Erin sighed, trying not to sound as skeptical as she felt. "He seems to think I have picked up most things he does on a daily basis, and the books on managing your own company are…well, they're half freaking me out and half enlightening me. Still, Chris says they're teaching me more than he knew when he took over the place. His uncle passed away so suddenly, he didn't have time to ease into it. It was jump in and sink-or-swim time, you know?"

"I heard." Riley squeezed her shoulder. "You'll be fine. Most of the people who come here know you're new at managing. Besides, most of them have been here so long they'll probably tell you how the place is run."

Erin chuckled. "Fair point."

"Is that weekend manager guy sticking around? What do they call him? Doc?"

"Yeah, he's staying on with me. He'll continue to manage the place on weekends and when I need some time off."

"There you go, then. He'll be a big help. Oh, and you've got an accountant, right?"

"Yeah. I'm using the same accountant as Chris did. He's cheap and seems to know what he's doing. Always a bonus."

"Then you'll be just peachy. I don't know what the hell I'll do, though. I don't want another trainer, I only come to our sessions because you feel more like a friend than someone who's paid to tell me what to do."

Erin rolled her eyes. "Then we'll find someone else that you can be friends with. Maybe Tyler?"

"Nah, Tyler wants to date me, so he's out. I need to find the right person, or I won't get my ass down here. I want someone inspiringly buff and hot like you, but not someone who I need to worry about constantly hitting on me, ya know?"

"Riles, I could've hit on you."

"Nope. I hinted that I wasn't interested in our first session, and you're too good a person to try after that. People see my skimpy outfits and hear how freely I talk about sex and assume I'm up for anything, and I'm really not. You got that about me and never made a move. And you never, ever made me feel slutty or weird. That's rare, Er."

Erin picked up two kettlebells they'd be using and brought them over to the mat. "That's really sad, but I'll take your word for it. What about Elise? She's fit as hell and straight as a ruler."

Riley scrunched up her nose. "She seems so serious."

"Nah, she's just shy. When you get her to come out of her shell, she's got a really filthy sense of humor and loves to overshare about her boyfriend. You'd like her."

"Hm. Maybe I'll go with her, then. I don't want to switch, though. I want to hang out with you," Riley whined.

"Riles, I'm not going anywhere. I'll still be in the gym, doing paperwork, checking everyone is okay, and sneaking off to do crunches whenever I get the chance."

"Fine. But I won't see you as much, so we'll have to make other plans to make up for lost time. When you and Ms. Posh-in-Philadelphia move in together, you gotta let me arrange a housewarming party."

Erin rolled her eyes again. "Fine, yeah, sure. Keep in mind, though, that's not likely to happen soon."

More interested in the chat than the workout, Riley ignored the kettlebell Erin placed in front of her. "Why? Still got cold feet about settling down? I thought your therapy sessions were supposed to help with stuff like that?" She sniggered.

Erin saw her chance to tell Riley about her progress in therapy and had to remind herself not to forget that they were supposed to be working out.

"Actually, it's helping with a lot of stuff, and I'm so glad I went for it. I mean, to just sit and talk about myself and my problems was hard at first, but when I got into it, it was such a relief. The process has been a lot easier than I expected too. Dr. Hopkins seems to think that it's 'cause me and Isabella have done a lot of the work in advance. Like, we already figured out that I've got abandonment issues which caused my insomnia and probably led to me freaking out about caring for the kid. And most of my other hang-ups."

"Huh. No offense, but did you really need all that? You're a grown-up, Er. You've dealt with whatever shit happened, and you're like all adults. I mean, look at you. Business woman, considerate girlfriend, and now with an insta-family to boot. You're all responsible and sensible. Maybe this woman's only making you think she's helping you, because you don't really need help."

Erin frowned. Did Riley really see her like that? It was so contrary to how she saw herself. She shook her head. No, even if that was how Riley saw her, how other people saw her, therapy was about changing how she saw herself. Other people's opinions were good, but not what mattered. Dr. Hopkins had showed her that.

"It's not like that, Riles. She really is helping me to get mentally stronger and calmer." Erin stretched out her triceps.

"How?" Riley's forehead furrowed in a way which made her look uncharacteristically pensive. "You just sit there, and, like...tell her stuff?"

"Kinda. I spent a few sessions just spilling my guts, and Dr. Hopkins asked me follow-up questions. After that, she confirmed the diagnosis about abandonment issues and suggested that I keep coming to therapy to find what she calls behavioral patterns and try some healthy coping mechanisms for them. That's what we're doing now."

"And are you?"

"What?"

"Coping, dumbass."

Erin thought about the tiny steps forward she'd made in her own head. How she was learning to recognize the negative thought patterns when they started, and how instead of wallowing in those destructive ideas, she was seeking out more positive ones. They were words that didn't just sound good and pretty—that she was a strong person, a good person, one who deserved to be loved—but words she was starting to believe too, little by little.

"Yeah. I'm improving."

Riley scanned her face. "You know what? I think I can see that. I'm really glad she's helping you." Grinning mischievously, she added, "Shame a shrink can't make you brainier, though."

"Oh, shut up. Anyway, all you need to know is that therapy can help anyone." Erin sighed. "What it doesn't help with is my money situation. And that's the thing that's really holding me back when it comes to moving in with Isabella. The payments on the gym, the therapy sessions, and the New York sized rent on my rat hole of an apartment, are sucking me dry, Riles. I can't afford a big move or a bigger rent payment right now."

"Let Isabella pay a bigger chunk, then. I'm sure she wouldn't mind. From what you've said, she's desperate to get away from her mom and shack up with her buff lesbian lover."

"Riles, call me 'buff lesbian lover' again, and I'll make you do pull-ups until your arms turn to jelly." Erin glared at her challengingly.

But Riley looked unfazed. "Yeah, whatever. My point stands, though."

"I just don't want her to fritter away her savings, y'know? Her money is meant to be a safety buffer for her and Alberto." Erin moved the kettlebell closer to Riley on her mat as a hint to start, but to no avail. They were clearly going to finish this conversation.

Riley tilted her head to the side. "So there's no working-class pride getting in the way of you accepting her money?"

"Maybe a little, but not enough to make much difference. If I had more available money than her, I'd want to pay for things, so I get that. I just don't want to make her end up in the same shitty financial situation as me, just because she believed in me," Erin said with a shrug.

"No offense, honey, but that's her decision, not yours. And by the sounds of it, she's better with money than you and me put together."

"I know. Just like I know she was really supportive of me buying the gym, but sometimes I wonder if I should have just stayed a personal trainer," Erin admitted.

"Dude, what? And give up this golden opportunity? This was too perfect for you to miss. Besides, you *are* improving your financial situation in the long run and giving yourself a more stable job, right? Putting down roots is a good thing. Stop overthinking shit and just get on with it. Start running the gym, and start planning to move in with your lady love. Not like, eventually, but now. Right now. I'm tired of seeing your mug all lovesick and lonely."

"Well, I'm glad to hear I'd be doing all that just to make you more comfortable when you look at my face," Erin joked. "No, seriously, thanks. I'll work something out."

Riley smirked. "I suppose you mean that Isabella will do most of the work and sort something out for ya?"

"Yeah. Coz some of us are in a steady relationship and have the perk of being in a team. Not like your poor, single ass," Erin said with a grin.

"And there is my bratty, annoying Erin Black again."

"Enough chatter. We're supposed to be working out, not gossiping the day away. Pick up that kettlebell. We'll start with goblet squats."

Riley groaned. "Damn. I was hoping you'd forgotten about the exercise bit. Well, I suppose I better get this single ass of mine looking as good as possible, so I can pick up my own sexy writer someday."

Erin smiled as she adjusted her ponytail. "Funnily enough, you don't get those by having a great ass. You have to talk to them online and compliment them on how they told a misogynist actor where he could shove it."

Riley finally picked up her kettlebell. "Pretty sure your buff ass didn't put her off, though."

Chapter 31

New York

SHAY'S SUGGESTION HAD REALLY TAKEN root, and Isabella had spent a few short days planning a surprise visit to New York. She found a cheap, last-minute flight that took off Friday afternoon. As in, that afternoon. As in, a taxi was coming for her in an hour, and there was no backing out now.

Everything was arranged: taxi to the airport, a quick flight, and then a taxi to Erin's apartment. First, she'd searched out the address Erin had given her when she'd sent her that package, then she'd Googled the street name. It was in East Harlem, not far from the Upper East Side, she noticed.

Looking at the map, she realized she knew very little about New York. Her experiences of the city were two or three childhood sightseeing visits and a couple of quick work trips, when she'd seen little more than her hotel and the conference halls or offices. All had been restricted to Manhattan, and they'd all been brief.

She had no idea what it was like to actually live and work in New York. The snippets she'd picked up from Erin hadn't enlightened her much either.

Isabella remembered a song that her father used to listen to about New York. She seemed to think it was sung by Ella Fitzgerald. As she prepared for the trip, the start of the chorus echoed in her mind.

She felt an increasing thrill, the sort of thrill she used to feel when she traveled somewhere new for work. She never told anyone about that feeling. She needed everyone to assume she was a suave, jaded businesswoman at all times. But, yes, there had always been a buzz for her in getting to know a new place. It was always like the start of a new relationship.

Isabella had packed up everything she could foresee Alberto needing and was staring at her half of the suitcase. She only planned to stay two days, so she didn't need much. *Should I pack lingerie? No. If I know my Erin, there's no need. It'll be ripped off the second Alberto is asleep for the night.*

My Erin.

She couldn't help but grin, as she got out the baby carrier. If she was bringing the foldable travel crib and a big suitcase, there was no way she was taking a stroller too. Alberto would just have to be strapped to her chest. Hopefully the back pain wouldn't be too bad, though Alberto was quite heavy now. Part of her wished she still had a car and could have driven to New York.

She shook her head. All the planning and trouble would be worth it when she saw the astonished look on Erin's face. Erin had said she loved surprises. Well, she was certainly getting one tonight.

Isabella stopped fretting and packed the last bits. In a last-minute frenzy, she also packed her newly arrived packet of Azúcar Negra. Erin would surely be out of hers by now and unlikely to splurge on a new pack.

She went to check if Alberto was ready for the trip, quietly singing "We'll Have Manhattan" under her breath.

The first thing that hit Isabella when she got out of the taxi was the smell. The odor of the garbage bags lining the sidewalk and the smell of food being cooked in a nearby street cart competed bravely with the overpowering vetiver-scented cologne on the businessman next to her, shouting into his cell phone. She walked on, dragging the suitcase and travel crib behind her.

When they'd hit rush hour traffic, she'd asked the taxi driver to let them out. She'd rather walk and experience more of the city than be stuck inside the stuffy car. According to the Google Maps app on her phone, it was only a ten-minute walk to Erin's apartment building from where they'd been let out.

As soon as Isabella got away from food carts and over-cologned businessmen, she could smell rain in the air. The sky was darkening, and she hoped she'd get to Erin's before the downpour.

Despite the rain clouds and heavy feel of the damp air, New York was captivating in the gray early evening. Smoke bellowed from a grate on the sidewalk. She smiled as she remembered being a child and seeing the same thing. When she'd asked her father if there was a dragon underneath New York, he'd told her that there most definitely was a dragon, but that she never needed to worry. That he would protect her from all the monsters in the world. Her smile now felt bittersweet. If only that had been true.

God, she missed him. Not just her father, but the father she believed he was when she'd been a child. Her protector and defender, the man who would do anything just to see her smile. She couldn't remember how long it had been since she'd lost that man. It was a damn sight longer than the few days since her mother's last "intervention."

Alberto was asleep in his carrier, leaning his heavy head against her collarbone. It wasn't comfortable, but she'd suffer any discomfort when she'd dragged him all this way. She comforted herself with the fact that he seemed to like Erin, so he'd be glad to see her. Besides, he'd have to get used to New York if they were going to live there one day. They both would.

At a busy intersection, Isabella stopped with the crowd around her. They waited for the go ahead from the police officer standing in the middle of the street, directing traffic. When he signaled for them to walk, he glanced at Isabella and Alberto and smiled. When they walked right by him, he said, "*Lindo bebé*". The Spanish phrase gave Isabella a feel of belonging, a sense that this could be home—a good home—for them both. She thanked him with more exuberance than was her custom.

He was right, of course, Alberto was a cute baby. Isabella felt blessed to have such a beautiful child, and such a beautiful girlfriend too. She couldn't wait to see Erin. She hurried her steps, her arms complaining about the heavy case and the crib, and her back strained at the weight of the sleeping baby. It'd all be worth it. Just as soon as she kissed Erin again.

She'd asked what time Erin thought she'd be home, pretending to set up a Skype date to ensure Erin had finished work and was in her apartment when she and Alberto showed up. Still, the nagging fear badgered her that Erin wouldn't be home, and she'd be caught in the rain with a baby and heavy luggage without a place to go. She chased the fear away, reminding herself that East Harlem would have plenty of places for her to find shelter and something to eat while she waited.

She needn't have worried. When she approached the tall and rather shabby building that Erin lived in, she saw a blonde with a gym bag tossed over her shoulder. She was struggling, violently punching a code into the display by the door while sipping from a large takeaway cup of coffee. Oh yes, she was in the right place.

"Would you like some help with that, Miss Black? I don't have a free hand at the moment, but unlike you, I'm an adult and capable of putting something down to free up my hands."

Erin swiveled around at lightning speed and stared at her openmouthed. It was impossible for Isabella not to laugh lovingly at the adorable expression of surprise and utter incomprehension on Erin's face.

"I-Isabella? Y-you're here? What the hell?"

"Well now, is that any way to welcome your girlfriend after she traveled all this way? Carrying all this stuff, and a baby too," Isabella teased.

Erin dropped the gym bag on the ground and rushed over to hug her, careful not to tip her coffee over Isabella or the sleeping Alberto. Erin's kiss was so intense that Isabella forgot to breathe for a moment.

Erin broke away from the kiss. "You're here. How are you here?"

Deep affection hit Isabella like a wave and filled her heart. There was so much love and awe in Erin's voice. Suddenly, it seemed so utterly pointless and stupid to live far away from Erin.

"Because I missed you. And because there are things called airplanes, *preciosa*. They fly in the sky and transport people from A to B. It's really clever, actually."

Isabella's teasing words couldn't hide her joy at seeing Erin, as the blonde grinned and said, "Whoa. Look at that smile. You've got it bad."

Erin kissed her again and then gently nuzzled their noses in an Eskimo kiss. Without a word, she went to a trash can and threw her coffee away, then returned to the console and carefully tapped in a code to open the door. She held it open with her foot, her gym bag tossed back over her shoulder, and took the suitcase from Isabella.

"The elevator's over there. You lead the way. I've got your case."

"Thank you. Quite the gentleman there, Miss Black."

"Excuse me, gentlewoman, if you don't mind. And nope, I'm just helpful. And, y'know, looking for any opportunity to watch your ass in those jeans."

Isabella pouted, pretending to be shocked and held her free hand over Alberto's head. "Don't use that sort of language in front of the baby, you brute!"

Erin laughed. "Oh, so first I'm a gentleman, and now I'm a brute? Get in that elevator before I give you a hickey in front of the baby and all of New York."

Isabella breathed a sigh of relief. She was finally in Erin's apartment and had the baby carrier off her back. Alberto slept safe and sound in his travel crib. Isabella stretched her back, hearing it crack loudly.

"Here, let me help you," Erin murmured and stood behind her. She circled her thumbs on the muscles of Isabella's lower back, finding the sore parts without having to ask. Through Isabella's linen shirt, the pressure was firm enough to get into the muscle but not so hard that it was painful. Isabella sighed with pleasure and leaned into the impromptu massage.

Erin kissed her neck. "How's that? Not too hard?"

"No, it's perfect, *querida*. Thank you."

"My pleasure," Erin whispered into her neck.

Erin's words and her warm breath made the little hairs on Isabella's neck stand up, and a certain pull in her lower stomach made itself known. She moaned at the sensation and heard how sexual it sounded. Erin was murder on her normally impeccable poker face.

"God, I've missed the feel of you, the sound of you, the scent of you. Everything about you," Erin mumbled against the goose-pimpled skin of Isabella's neck.

"I feel the same. I had to see you," Isabella answered breathlessly.

"Thank you for coming. I'm so sorry you had to. I'm sorry I couldn't come to you."

Isabella hushed her by turning and leaning in for a kiss that made everything around her fade away. There was only Erin—her loving embrace, her little noises of affection, and her heart beating against Isabella's. There was only the safe, charming, bubbly presence of the woman Isabella loved.

Affection flooded Isabella's heart. She barely had time to register the rain coming down hard against the windows, before her whole world consisted only of Erin's soft mouth and wandering hands.

The loud sound of thunder caught their attention, and they both looked outside. Bright lightning cut through the gray-blue twilight.

Erin looked back at her with a frown. "Will lil' man be okay with this noise? Should we check on him?"

Isabella smiled tenderly. "He'll be fine. He's not very sensitive to loud noises, and he's not aware of what thunder and lightning is. But, yes, for our peace of mind, let's make sure it didn't wake him." They walked, hand in hand, to the travel crib set up next to Erin's bed.

While they walked, Erin cleared her throat and said, "Sorry, my place is so small and…crappy. I would've cleaned if I knew you were coming."

"Oh, don't worry, *preciosa*. I like it. It's nicely decorated, warm, and tastefully simple. Everything in here is very *Erin Black*, and that happens to be one of my favorite themes at the moment."

Erin chuckled and looked away, a slight pink tinge to her pale cheeks. Isabella wondered if Erin could possibly be any cuter or if this was the limit for how adorable a human being could be.

They both looked down into the crib. To Isabella's surprise, Alberto was awake and looking up at them. He didn't seem perturbed by the weather or his new location. He was smiling up at them and waving his arms and legs forcefully, happy for some attention and company.

"Hello there, little prince," Isabella said softly. She picked him up and kissed his cheeks and nose. "Now that you are awake, say hello to Erin."

"Hey lil' man." Erin beamed at him. "Welcome to New York."

She took a step close to Alberto but then stopped as if she wasn't sure what she would do when she got to him. Isabella waited a few heartbeats. Erin still stood frozen, looking at Alberto hesitantly.

Isabella took a deep breath. *Let's give this a try.* She closed the gap between Erin and herself and lifted Alberto over toward Erin.

"Would you mind holding him for a second? Don't worry, I'll be right here. I'll help you."

She went wide-eyed, but Isabella showed her how to hold him scooped comfortably in her arms. Erin stared down at him without blinking. "Do I need to hold his head somehow? They always talk about that in movies."

"Not anymore, no. His neck muscles are strong enough to support his own head now."

Alberto lay still in Erin's arms, staring up at her as if he were deciding whether he was comfortable or not.

Please don't cry, please don't cry. Isabella desperately needed this to go well, for Erin to know that Alberto was comfortable around her. Erin's therapy was helping her, but in the end, it would be Alberto who convinced Erin that they'd get along fine.

"Um, what do I do now?" Erin asked, her voice shaky.

"Nothing. He seems happy enough just being out of the crib."

Another loud crash of lightning split the darkness of the night sky. *Please don't cry. Oh, please don't cry, Alberto.*

Erin leaned her head forward to check her grip on him. As she moved, the long, blonde strands of her hair swiped themselves over Alberto's face.

He giggled and made a thrilled cooing noise. Erin pulled back, looking at him to see what had happened.

With a smile, Isabella explained. "Your hair tickled his face. I think he liked it."

For the first time since she had Alberto in her grip, she was beaming. "Did he? Really? Should I do it again?"

"I don't see why not."

Erin inclined her head, and her hair brushed over Alberto's stomach, neck, and face. He laughed this time, a genuine baby laugh that rang out in the apartment. They all smiled as Erin made the move a third time. Alberto laughed again, but then the sound was interrupted by a yawn.

"Aw, man. Even his yawning is freakin' adorable," Erin said.

A wave of relief crashed over Isabella. It was going well, and Erin was clearly smitten with Alberto.

Erin spoke quietly to him. "Hey, sleepyhead. Me and my hair are gonna be around for a long time, so if you wanna get some sleep, we'll be here when you wake up."

He wriggled a little, probably to get more comfortable, and yawned again.

Wanting to keep this development going, Isabella stood behind Erin. She put her arms around Erin's waist and rocked them all back and forth, just as she would've done had Alberto been in her arms and she'd been rocking him to sleep.

"Follow my lead," she whispered into Erin's hair.

Erin immediately began to rock with her, and Alberto slowly drifted into sleep as he swayed in Erin's arms. It felt comfortable, as though she and Erin were meant to do this. Together.

Relaxing into the rocking movement, Isabella breathed in Erin's scent with every calm breath. The thunder outside and a slightly creaky floorboard beneath their feet were the only sounds outside their gentle breathing.

It took Alberto a little while to drift off, but neither she nor Erin seemed to mind. They were all together, holding each other, safe and warm inside Erin's apartment, while the summer storm wreaked havoc over New York.

The next time Isabella peered over Erin's shoulder, Alberto was sleeping, his little mouth open in an O shape and his tiny hands clasped over his stomach.

"He's asleep. Well done," she whispered again into Erin's hair and felt Erin's body relax. She hadn't realized that Erin was so tense. "You can put him back into the crib now." She moved away from them.

Erin walked across the room, every step as careful as if she were carrying a bomb that could go off any second. Carefully, she put Alberto in the crib, and Isabella worked very hard not to admire Erin's muscles flexing as she kept her grip on him steady all the way down to the little mattress.

When Erin looked back at Isabella, she smiled tentatively, then whispered, "Isabella, I think maybe I can do this. I think I can look after him."

"I know you can, *preciosa*. And so does he. He wouldn't have been so comfortable with you otherwise. He certainly wouldn't have fallen asleep in your arms if he didn't feel safe and happy."

Erin looked at the sleeping baby and licked her lips a few times. In a voice that sounded very young, Erin murmured, "I want to spend more time with him. I want to learn to care for him."

"Good. Fewer diaper changes for me," Isabella teased.

Erin turned back to her and stuck her tongue out. The childish gesture made Isabella laugh.

"Why don't you come over here and put that thing where it belongs?" She pointed to her own mouth and watched Erin hurry over in an adorable attempt to pounce on her but still walk quietly, so as to not wake Alberto.

Having made love and cuddled for most of the evening, Isabella felt the fuzzy warmth of satisfaction and affection throughout her body.

It was late now, just after eleven thirty, and Alberto had just woken up. Isabella knew she should feel guilty and annoyed that they'd let him sleep the entire evening away and ruined his night's sleep, but she was too blissed out to worry about it right now.

Erin crouched down next to Alberto, who sat on the floor, investigating the plastic spatula she'd fished out of her cutlery drawer for him. He was gumming the handle pretty roughly, but Erin didn't seem to mind. She gazed at him as if he were some sort of miracle.

"He won't sleep tonight now, you know," Isabella said.

Erin shrugged. "Well, I probably can't sleep anyway, and if he and I aren't sleeping, I doubt you'll get any sleep either."

"Meaning I would want to stay awake with you two or that you two would keep me up?"

"I'm saying nothin'." Erin grinned. "I know when I'm about to get in trouble."

The thunder and lightning seemed to have stopped, but it was still raining outside. Isabella looked out at the night.

Erin had clearly followed her gaze and asked, "I guess you didn't get the chance to see much of New York on the way here, huh?"

"Not much, no."

"Well, if you and the kid don't mind getting wet, I know a café that's open 24/7. The coffee's always fresh, though pretty bad, and admittedly, the place gets filled after 2 a.m. with drunk partygoers wanting donuts. But right now it should be quiet. It's not the Empire State Building or Central Park, but I think the place has a New York vibe to it."

It was something Isabella would never have done. Drinking coffee at midnight was reckless and unhealthy enough on its own. Going out in the rain and traipsing around New York to do it—was ridiculous.

Ridiculous…and yet strangely appealing. This was a new chapter of her life. She might as well try some new behavior. "You know what?" she said, "I think I might like that. Maybe the fresh air will make Alberto sleepy again and give us a couple of hours when we get back."

Erin sniggered. "Yeah, or the coffee fumes will keep him up for days."

Isabella rolled her eyes, as she went to her suitcase to pick out warm clothes for Alberto. She made Erin jump when she swore under her breath and threw the lid of the suitcase shut. "I didn't bring any rain clothes. How could I be so stupid?"

"Hey, it's okay. Calm down. You can borrow my raincoat. It's pretty big, so it will probably cover you and Alberto if he's strapped to your chest."

Isabella looked at her for a second, unsure whether to ask or not. "Perhaps you want to carry him? My back could use the break, and it will be an extra workout for your muscles."

Looking over at Alberto, who was still trying to chew the spoon, Erin asked, "You think he'd be okay with that?"

"Of course. As long as we have him facing forward and he can see everything, including me, he'll be fine."

"Okay. Sure. He and I will wear the raincoat, then. But what about you? Won't you get soaked?"

Isabella looked over at the coats hanging by the door. "Maybe I can borrow your leather jacket? It's got a hood, right?"

"Yeah it does. Go ahead!"

Erin seemed unexpectedly happy at the idea, and Isabella thought she knew why. There was a certain intimacy in sharing each other's clothes, and if she was honest, she was looking forward to wearing Erin's beloved leather jacket. She only hoped it would smell of Erin.

They were finally drying off a little. After realizing just how heavy the rain was, Erin had decided to hail a cab halfway to the café.

Isabella was endlessly happy for it. The short ten-minute walk they'd managed before Erin got hold of the taxi had drenched her to the bone. She'd hidden her face under the hood as much as she could, but she was sure the little makeup left after an evening of making love must've been lost to the rain.

Erin was sitting with Alberto, still in his baby carrier on her chest. Isabella had offered to take him for a while, but Erin had wanted to keep him with her. Isabella wasn't about to argue. Right now, Alberto was happy and Erin was happy. She wouldn't do anything to endanger the nascent relationship.

The waitress had poured them both steaming hot coffee and had taken Erin's order for two portions of the staple New York cheesecake. Isabella guessed one of those portions was for her, but with Erin and her ferocious metabolism, she wasn't going to bet on it.

She blew on the coffee and sipped. Erin was right; it was bad coffee but fresh enough to drink. The warmth heated her from the inside, and she hoped that it was helping her soaked hair to dry.

She was about to ask Erin how long it would take for her long tresses to dry, when she caught her doing something unexpected. Erin was sniffing the top of Alberto's head, making the little dark hairs blow about. He clearly felt it and tried to look up at her, the angle defying him.

Erin smiled at him and quietly said, "Sorry, lil' man. Just me. You smell nice, you know that? I like your aftershave."

"Eau de baby," Isabella joked along.

Erin looked almost abashed as she met her gaze. "So, they all smell as good as him?"

Isabella felt a pulse of pride. "Well, not in my opinion. But, yes, babies naturally smell nice. As long as you don't wash them too rarely or too often, of course."

Erin knitted her brows. "You can wash them too often?"

"That's what most of my baby books said. It's bad for their skin to lose all the naturally occurring oil. If you stick around, Miss Black, I'll teach you everything I know about caring for Alberto, and maybe a few things about how to care for me."

Erin's blue-green eyes radiated devotion so fiercely it took Isabella's breath away. "Trust me. I'm not going anywhere." She paused, her eye contact unwavering. "I love you, Isabella."

Isabella swallowed, so overwhelmed she couldn't speak. She dropped Erin's intense gaze and glanced down at her coffee, just for a second, before she trusted her voice to hold.

She lifted her head and hoped Erin could see even half of what she felt. "I love you, too. So very much."

Outside, the rain spattered down in a furious drumbeat, but even the knowledge that they would have to go out in that at some point couldn't ruin the mood. Alberto giggled, at the sound of the rain hitting the windows.

It was now truly midnight, and Isabella was ready to bet that neither of them had ever been so happy not to be asleep.

Chapter 32

All Change

TWO DAYS LATER, THE BRIGHT morning sun spread over the cityscape of New York. Erin reluctantly woke up in her lonely bed and blinked at the bright sun. She'd managed almost eight hours of sleep.

Not that she felt like she'd gotten a good night's sleep, despite the number of hours. In fact, she felt sluggish. She was glad that she had the day off. After weeks of shadowing Chris, doing occasional sessions with straggling clients, and trying to fit in sleep, exercise, therapy, and as much time talking to Isabella as possible, Erin was exhausted.

She dragged herself out of bed, rubbing at the imprint of the pillow creases she could feel on her cheek. She made coffee and stumbled back to bed.

She lay there, watching the small apartment grow lighter in the July sun. She breathed in the scent of her coffee and wondered what it was about coffee that felt so sacred to her. It was clearly more than just a drink to her and many people in the world. It was almost a cultural phenomenon.

Obviously, caffeine made coffee special—that and modern pop culture's obsession with the bitter bean. But she still felt that the caffeine was the key. It kept you going, made you sharper. Of course, too much of it was bad for you. So many people used it to start the day or to ramp up in the afternoon.

Erin knew that she drank way too much of coffee and did so too late at night. She'd discussed it many times with her fellow health-conscious trainers. Stopping the habit had done nothing for her insomnia, but she knew the caffeine wasn't helping her sleep either.

There was a recklessness, a taste of the forbidden, to drinking coffee late at night. Like a disregard for prudence and wellbeing, Erin realized, while yawning loud enough to almost drown out the sound of the coffeemaker.

She had to stop being reckless if she was going to be a child's guardian, a stepmom, even. She had to be a better role model. But then, being reckless and up late at night messaging someone, daring to fall in love with them, had led to the best things in her life. Isabella and Alberto. *Maybe a little recklessness is good for you.*

Her phone pinged. She looked, bleary-eyed, at the screen. She had an e-mail. From Isabella. That woke Erin up more than a cup of coffee ever could. It was as much of an excited message as the sophisticated Isabella Martinez would ever send. It even had exclamation marks, for crying out loud.

Santiago—her agent—loved Isabella's book-to-be and had decided to represent her. He had found a publisher who was interested, and Isabella had been asked to send a finished draft to an editor.

The full story was attached to the e-mail, which said in its final words:

I know you haven't read the manuscript, and I'm not sure if it is something you are interested in reading. If not, don't feel bad. However, whether you read the whole thing or not, I highly recommend that you read the acknowledgments and the dedication at the start of the book.

Despite Isabella asking her not to, Erin felt bad that she hadn't read the book by now. She'd just been so busy that she just hadn't gotten around to it. And Isabella had been so cagey about the editing of the final draft. Now, Erin would read the story.

She got up and pulled on a robe. She poured some more coffee, buttered some wholegrain toast, and sat down at the table while she downloaded the Word file on her laptop. She blew on her hot coffee and took the first divine sip as the document opened. The pages loaded, and Erin searched out the dedication.

For Erin and Alberto.

Erin stopped drinking and just stared at the words. Someone had dedicated a book to her? No, not just someone. Isabella had dedicated a book to her. Dedicated her book to the mess of a loner who was abandoned by her parents without an explanation. The girl who grew up in the foster system and never thought she'd be remembered by anyone. Erin's name would live on in the beginning of a book, preserved on shelves in libraries and in people's homes.

She was gobsmacked. And overwhelmingly proud. That feeling only grew stronger as she read the acknowledgments.

First, Isabella thanked Richard who had given her space to start writing, then her father and Santiago for believing in her ability to write, then little Alberto for sleeping enough to give her time to complete the story.

Finally, thank you, Erin Black, for believing in me, inspiring me, setting me free, and for showing me what I want in life—my writing, and a family consisting of you and my son. Our son. I love you.

Erin read it again and again, before she realized she was crying. Fat tears rolled down her cheeks in silence, and then the sobs began. She found herself half laughing and half crying; she was so overwhelmed, her heart felt like it was about to burst.

Smiling, she shook her head before getting some tissues to wipe her face and blow her nose. She sent a text to Isabella, knowing that Isabella checked her phone more than she did her e-mails.

Just read your dedication. That was so unbelievably sweet of you. I don't have the words to tell you how much it means to me! I'm gonna start reading the book now, so you'll get a longer message later. I f***ing love you, Isabella Martinez. You know that, right? <3 xoxo

When the text was sent, she sat back down and started to read Isabella's retelling of fairy tales in the form of a fairy tale.

Erin fidgeted impatiently in her chair as she called Isabella a few hours later. She'd washed up and gotten dressed, but not bothered with makeup or doing her hair. She had to talk to Isabella as soon as possible.

After a single ring, Isabella's face appeared on her screen, her brown eyes glittering and a smile leaving beautiful lines at the corners of her mouth.

Erin groaned, stupidly overcome with affection at the sight. "Goddammit, you're so frickin' gorgeous. Are you smiling because you're happy to see me or because you know your dedication put fireworks in my brain?"

Isabella laughed. "Are fireworks in your brain a good thing? I'm smiling because the text you sent before you read my book had one 'I love you' with added profanity. And the text you sent asking for this call, had 'I love you' four times with even more profanity to express how deep your love is. That's a lot of love. Who wouldn't be smiling?"

Tucking some of her messy hair behind her ear, Erin felt herself blush a little. "Yeah, I might have been a little overexcited. Sorry."

"Don't ever apologize for your enthusiasm, Erin. You know that I love how passionate and unguarded you are. So, you liked my dedication and acknowledgment, then? I meant every word, *preciosa*. I can't imagine I would have actually finished the book if it hadn't been for you."

"You give yourself too little credit, babe. I'm sure you would have. But hey, if I did anything to help this book get written, I'm damn proud. It's an awesome read."

"Really? You liked it?"

There was uncertainty in Isabella's voice, something Erin knew her girlfriend would have hidden from other people. "I loved it!" she exclaimed. "I mean, I'm no expert. I don't read that much. The last few weeks, my only reading material has been a few Dummies guides to running your own business. But I couldn't stop reading your book. I actually read it in one day. That never happens."

She saw Isabella try to hide a proud smile. "Well, technically, it's not a book yet. It's not even been edited. It's just a manuscript."

"Fine, okay, manuscript. Whatever it is, it's really good."

"I'm so glad you think so. Your opinion is the one that matters the most to me," Isabella said.

Pride threatened to make a permanent home in Erin's chest. In fact, it had just ordered some curtains and a rug. She'd never thought an educated, highly accomplished businesswoman and brilliant writer would think her opinion was the one that mattered most.

"You make me so happy," Erin said on an exhale.

Isabella smiled as if they shared a secret. "Likewise."

"I wish I could show you how much I love you right now. I want to hug you so damn close and kiss every little inch of you."

"That sounds like heaven, *preciosa*. One day. One day, I'll be right there next to you."

"Yeah. You looking forward to moving to New York? I mean, you really like apples and this is *the Big Apple*. Get it?"

Isabella rolled her eyes. "Yes, Erin. I get it. Very funny. And, yes, I can't wait to move. I became quite enamored with New York when we visited. I can actually see it being my home. Our home."

Suddenly, Erin was very aware of every beat of her heart. She could hear it. The sounds of the noisy city outside her window faded away. She studied Isabella's face and felt that strange thrill of looking down from a tall building—the panic that you might fall mixed with the thrill of excitement at your own bravery.

With a dry mouth, Erin sucked in a deep breath and stepped—no, leapt—into her future.

"I know this is dumb, because we don't really have the finances in place, but...do you wanna start looking at places to live? I mean, we'd have to rent, because I can't get a mortgage until work stuff is settled and I'm not bleeding money all over the place. But, renting would be okay for a while, right?"

"Erin, I..." Isabella began.

But Erin couldn't stop. Her mind was whirring like a machine, and the words spilled out of her mouth at a dizzying speed. "I mean, I get that this would mean lots of moving for you and the kid. You only moved to Philly a few months ago, and if we find a place to rent you'd move there. And when we find a place to settle down and manage to get a mortgage, you'd have to move again. That's a lot. So I get it if you say no."

"No, that's fine. I think..." Isabella tried.

Erin knew she should let Isabella answer, but she wanted to show her, before Isabella politely declined, that she knew how ridiculous an idea it was to do this now. She would understand if Isabella said no. Because surely, that was what Isabella was about to do. Isabella was the sensible one. Far too sensible to uproot a newly moved baby to come live in some rented little hole in New York with a woman who was broke. *Especially if that woman is you*, the voice in Erin's head added.

So Erin kept talking. "And, um, yeah, I get why you wouldn't want to move in with me until my financial situation is less shitty. And maybe after I've had more therapy so that I can sleep at night and spend time with Alberto without freaking out. Oh and—"

Isabella put her fingers to her mouth and wolf-whistled.

Erin stopped talking and stared at Isabella, surprised not only at the sound but that Isabella knew how to do that. "I've always wanted to learn to do that," Erin whispered, deflated.

Isabella looked distinctly unimpressed. When the silence had lasted long enough to take root, and Erin still hadn't resumed babbling like a self-deprecating brook, Isabella spoke in a matter-of-fact tone.

"Fine. I'll teach you to whistle like that. We'll start our lessons as soon as we find an apartment we can all live in. I suggest we start looking for places that are not too tiny, in safe neighborhoods." Isabella looked to the side and tapped her fingers against her chin. "We won't be able to afford anything extravagant, of course. But we only need one bedroom as long as Alberto can share with us and be relegated to the living room when we want to make love at night. I'll start a spreadsheet to tot up our pooled incomes and expenses and see what we can afford to spend each month."

Erin merely stared. How had it been that easy? She'd suggested something ridiculous, hadn't she? Why had Isabella just gone along with it?

"You mean, um, you'll come live with me?"

The question almost seemed to annoy Isabella. "Of course. I told you that night in the restaurant, I'm ready to move in with you, to commit to our relationship. We were only waiting for you to be ready too. Now you are. So, we'll see what we can do with our financial situation and make it work."

Calmly, Isabella sat back on her chair and looked down. The sounds of Alberto cooing in the background bubbled up from underneath the screen. "Alberto's too young to care where he lives, as long as he has access to me and some toys. Oh, and your hair, apparently. I don't mind moving again if it gets me closer to you. And farther from my mother is always an added bonus."

"Yeah, I see why you'd want to get away from her. What about my therapy? Don't you want me to get further with that first?" Erin heard how pitiful her voice sounded. She hated herself for it, but she had to ask. She had to get it out there.

Isabella frowned and tilted her head. "*Preciosa*, I love you. All of you. You *are* perfect to me. I don't need you to have therapy for me to want to live with you. Nor for me to want you to help raise my son. *Our* son. Unless you mind me calling him that."

Erin blushed. She struggled to think of Alberto as her son. She felt more like an awkward aunt than a stepmom.

"Um, no. That's fine. I mean, if you are okay with that, then I am too," she said with a smile.

The truth was that it scared the hell out of her. But her therapy was teaching her that she had to fight through that fear, because it was only holding her back. She wanted Isabella and Alberto. They were her family. That meant she couldn't run off scared any time something freaked her out.

Her mind scurried back to the idea of moving in together. Now that they were talking about it, it seemed less ridiculous and more...inevitable. As if it had just been waiting around the corner for a long time like a fully finished painting just appearing on an empty canvas in one brush stroke.

They'd move in together, here in New York, and they'd do it as soon as they could. It felt so obvious now, and she realized that she wasn't actually afraid. Well, not as much as she'd expected to be.

Alberto cooed again, louder this time. Isabella smiled and bent over to pick him up. Erin's screen was filled with the woman she loved and the little boy she was growing to love.

Isabella pointed toward her iPad camera and murmured something in Spanish to him.

Erin made a mental note to learn some more of the language just as soon as she had the time. Alberto grinned toothlessly and reached for the iPad. To Erin, it looked as if he was reaching out to her, and she felt her heart tug with affection. She wanted him to be able to reach her, even if it wouldn't always end well. Even if it ended with him accidentally pulling her hair or slobbering all over her fingers as he gummed them.

She wanted to be right there with him, even when he scared her with the wobbly chin that signaled the start of a crying fit. Not that he was crying much these days, she suddenly realized.

"Isabella. Is it just me, or does his tummy seem to be improving? He goes long periods without having those stomach cramps now, doesn't he?"

Isabella kissed Alberto's nose and then looked back at the screen. "Yes, he does. He only seems to succumb to it a few times a week now. Such a relief. The doctors always said he'd grow out of it, but I never dared to believe them. Perhaps he can sense that I am more content these days? Perhaps that lowers his stress levels somehow."

"Sure. Or maybe he's just growing out of it as his body is developing."

"Perhaps. No matter what caused it, I'm glad he's doing better. For the first time, I actually wish Mother was here."

Erin wrinkled her brow. "Really? Why?"

"She always claimed it must be something I was doing wrong," Isabella said with some discomfort.

"What? Why?"

"Because she never had that issue with me when I was a baby. And if she hasn't experienced a problem, then it must be all those people suffering from that issue are doing something wrong. Simple Judith Martinez logic."

Erin rolled her eyes. "Ugh. Well, thank goodness she's an expert on everything."

Isabella's smile looked almost relieved. "I know. She even had the audacity to say that Alberto had gas because I didn't burp him properly."

"What the hell? I see you burp him all the time."

"Yes, but Mother said I must be doing it wrong. Otherwise, he wouldn't be ill."

"Well, holding him upside down, shaking him, and shouting 'burp, you little monster' might not be the best way. You should really stop doing that, ya' know."

Isabella tried to glare at her but couldn't help smiling. When Erin laughed at the mental image she'd just painted, Isabella laughed with her.

"No, seriously, babe. You're a great mom. Don't let her get to you. I mean, sure, that's easier said than done. But you know what I mean."

"Yes, I do. Thank you for the reassurance. And while I know you don't believe me—not yet, anyway—I have to tell you that you'll be a great parent to Alberto too. I've found that it mainly takes love, common sense, patience, and practice. You'll be great."

Erin hummed noncommittally. She swallowed her concern, rubbed the back of her neck, and asked, "So, we're really doing this now?"

"Yes, *preciosa*. Unless you get cold feet, we're doing this now. As I said, I'll make up a spreadsheet to see what price bracket we should be aiming for. You think about areas that are affordable but safe enough. Then we'll start looking for a place to live. All three of us. Preferably one with room for you to exercise a little at home. Just, you know…because it's important for your job."

Erin allowed herself a cocky smile. "Just to ensure I'm a good billboard for my gym, huh? That's the only reason?"

Isabella's voice was low and playful when she said, "Of course. I'd never ask you to do push-ups or squats just to watch your skin shimmer with sweat, your muscles ripple, and your cleavage move in a taunting rhythm as you breathe more and more rapidly."

Erin felt her smile grow. "Well that's a shame, because you're the only person in the whole wide world that I want to objectify the hell out of me."

"I'll hold you to that. Frequently." Isabella raked her gaze over Erin's chest and shoulders to make the point, and Erin had to laugh.

"I'll gladly work out at home, as long as you join me, Ms. Writer. And we need to get you back into running. I haven't forgotten that running gear you had on when I showed you those back stretches. We'll have the kid growing up in a home where exercise is just a part of life. Hopefully, that'll make him think of it as something natural and not a chore."

"Like I do, you mean?" Isabella asked with her eyebrow quirked.

"I didn't say that, babe."

"No. But it's true, nonetheless." Isabella shrugged and gave a half smile. "All right, let's get down to brass tacks. You go get those calculations we made when you decided to buy the gym, and I'll find my spreadsheets with my income and expenses. Let's see what sort of nest we can afford to rent."

Erin tried not to grimace at having to replace flirting with complicated finances. She tried very hard. She failed, of course, but Isabella kindly ignored it, and they moved on to the important calculations about their future together.

Chapter 33

Some Things Have to Be Painful

THE CHANGING LEAVES WERE PAINTING New York in reds, yellows, and browns instead of the greens it had sported when Isabella visited back in summer.

Fall had set down roots in New York, and so had Isabella and Alberto. They'd all moved in together a couple of days ago, and the place was slowly starting to feel like home to Isabella. The apartment wasn't perfect, but it was certainly better than being away from Erin.

Chris and Marie had beat them to the moving-in-together stage. The idea of Chris just working as her security had lasted about a week before they vowed eternal love. Isabella shook her head at the thought. In her opinion, those idiots had heads full of romantic notions rather than common sense. Nevertheless, it meant Erin now ran the gym without Chris's presence. It was thriving.

With Erin at the helm and a little help from Isabella, some new marketing techniques recruited quite a few new members. Together, they'd also found cheaper providers for electricity and maintenance, helping to produce a healthier balance sheet.

Isabella didn't have a lot of free time between caring for Alberto and the editing process for her book, but what time she did have she focused on helping Erin get settled in her new role. In return, Erin helped with Alberto as much as she could, something she seemed more than happy to do—now that she didn't believe her every action would scar him for life.

Standing at the window and watching the multicolored leaves, Isabella breathed a sigh of relief as she thought about how well Alberto and Erin were getting along now. They still had their wobbles when Alberto would start to cry or Erin would freak out because she didn't know how to handle a situation. But it was always sorted out.

Erin loved singing lullabies to him and turned out to be much better at carrying a tune than Isabella, something she tried not to be bitter about. Whether Erin realized it or not, Alberto took almost as much comfort from her as he did Isabella these days. He clearly saw Erin as a secondary guardian and one who was extremely fun to play peek-a-boo with. He still adored playing with her hair.

Isabella looked away from the leaves outside, quickly glancing past the unfinished edits on her computer screen to Alberto. He was sitting on the rug, playing with a set of stacking cups.

He'd almost gotten the hang of how they worked, but most of the time he just chewed them or threw them around. Apparently, making adults fetch them was a hilarious game.

He looked nice in his soft linen shirt and baby jeans, with his tufty, dark hair combed down to lay flat on his little head.

They were expecting visitors soon. The two romantic idiots were visiting New York and were going to stop by for coffee. She was looking forward to seeing Marie again; she still hadn't fully vetted Chris.

Tearing her gaze away from her adorable son, Isabella sighed to herself. There was no escaping it. She had to stop staring out the window or at Alberto, and go finish the edits of her twelfth chapter. Rolling her shoulders, she returned to her desktop and sat down with forced determination.

When Isabella opened the door to Marie and Chris, Alberto greeted them both with a long line of babbling. Chris played along, pretending he understood everything Alberto was saying, asking follow-up questions, and nodding along as Alberto made constant noises.

"You can hear the cadence of actual speech there," Marie said to Isabella.

"Yes, he's doing a good job at imitating speech patterns. He's gotten close to saying *mamá* a few times, but I don't know if he knows what it means. I've read that scientists think babies are trying to communicate something when they babble like this. It's just that we don't understand what they're saying."

Marie looked over at Chris who was crouched on the floor with the still-babbling Alberto. "Well, not all of us understand it. My Chris seems to be a natural."

Isabella scoffed, but it wasn't unkind. So far, Chris was living up to his reputation as a sweet, funny guy, and she could see how crazy her little sister was about him.

She remembered when a grief-stricken teenaged Marie had moved in, and they had to make the change from reluctant friends to foster sisters. Marie started stealing her clothes as soon as she arrived and threw tantrums if Isabella ever complained about it.

Back then, Isabella couldn't have fathomed feeling as warm and maternal toward Marie as she did now, watching her gaze at the man she loved. Isabella made a point of not showing her affection, knowing Marie would be insufferably sappy if she knew what Isabella was thinking.

"Should I pour us all some coffee?" Isabella asked.

"Sounds like an excellent idea. We brought Peanut Chews to give you a taste of Philadelphia," Marie said.

Chris held up a plastic bag with the treats for inspection.

Isabella gave an approving nod. "Ah, good choice."

"I knew they'd turn your frown upside down," Marie chirped.

"I wasn't frowning until you said that," Isabella muttered on her way to the coffeemaker.

They all froze at a knock on the door.

"Are you expecting anyone else?" Chris asked.

"Only Erin, but she'd use her key. And no one has buzzed from downstairs," Isabella replied. She walked over to the door and looked through the peephole. Her breath caught in her chest. Her stomach clenched, as she turned to Marie, staring at her with wide eyes. "Mother is here."

"Judith's here? But she doesn't know where you live! I refused to tell her. Just like you wanted," Marie whispered urgently.

"Clearly, she found me," Isabella muttered. She straightened up and took a deep breath before opening the door.

"Hello, Isabella." Judith looked past Isabella's shoulder. "Good afternoon, Marie and…I'm sorry, dear, what was your name?"

Chris stood up, stoic under Judith's piercing gaze. "Chris. Chris Nash."

"Oh yes, that's it. I knew it was a salt of the earth kind of name. Very charming. Isabella, dear, will you let me in? This stairwell reeks of disinfectant."

Isabella gritted her teeth. "Well, if you'd told me you were coming, I could've put scented candles out." Reluctantly, Isabella moved aside and felt the rush of wind as her mother stepped past her. "Or perhaps some sort of bitch repellent to keep you away," she muttered under her breath but still loud enough for Judith to hear.

"How did you know where to find her? I didn't give you this address," Marie asked.

"No, you didn't. But you did tell Alberto you were going to see Isabella today when you spoke to him on the phone. I overheard you." Judith wiped down the front of her suit jacket as if she'd said everything she needed to. When she looked up and clearly saw the angry and confused faces, she continued explaining. "So, I drove to your house, waited outside your apartment, and then followed you. I gave you a while to speak in peace, and then I came up."

She turned and directed her next words solely toward Isabella. "No matter how we left things, you should still give your mother your new address. It's only civil. Besides, what if there had been an emergency and I needed to reach you? Hmm?"

Instantly enraged, Isabella felt the vein in her forehead pulse. "What? What happened to me being 'disowned'? Now I'm expected to be civil and your emergency contact. You've got some nerve stalking Marie all the way here, then waltzing in and scolding me for not inviting you to a housewarming party. I should call the police!"

The sound of a key in the door interrupted her tirade. Erin was home. She'd asked the weekend manager to cover her for a couple of hours. Isabella had told her she didn't have to, but she wanted to see Chris and spend more time getting to know Marie.

Erin walked in, fiddling with her keys and throwing a gym bag on the floor. "Hey gang," she said. "Sorry I'm late."

Isabella looked from her mother to her girlfriend. Judith looked Erin up and down with a grimace.

Erin was wearing her Nash's Gym T-shirt. That, in itself, wouldn't have been a problem. Erin owned the gym, and it made sense that she'd wear its merchandise. This was a T-shirt Isabella and Erin had ordered especially to advertise the gym. Isabella had suggested getting T-shirts, gym bags, towels, and hoodies that all tied in with the gym's old New York boxers feel.

The T-shirt was designed to look vintage and distressed, and Isabella knew Judith's snobby, old-fashioned sense of style. To her, it would merely look tatty with a worn logo and unraveling seams. The fact that Erin wore a size that just barely fit her, making it tight over her sculpted arms and breasts, didn't help.

Customers loved the design, and Isabella loved watching Erin *in* one of those T-shirts, especially when Erin paired it with a pair of skinny jeans with more holes than fabric. But, unfortunately, she could see through her mother's judgmental eyes, which undoubtedly saw a shabbily dressed, soft-butch woman, with her hair in a crooked, messy braid.

Definitely not the sort of look Judith Martinez would approve of. Isabella closed her eyes and scolded herself for caring. Still, it was hard to shake the opinion of one's parent. No matter how wrong she was.

Judith cleared her throat. "Ah. Well, I suppose that sort of outfit would be more acceptable here in Brooklyn than Philadelphia. I see why you had to move, Isabella."

Erin looked up in shock. Isabella was about to furiously defend Erin's outfit and where they lived, but Erin surprised her. Erin looked the unwanted guest right in the eye.

"Hello there, Mrs. Martinez. I recognize your voice. Nice to meet you. No, actually, not very nice, considering how you've hurt Isabella, but at least I can be polite. One of us has to be, and clearly, it ain't gonna be you."

Erin squared her shoulders and stood to her full height. She was at least an inch taller than either Isabella or her mother. "Brooklyn's a very sought-after area these days. We chose it because my friend, Erika, recommended it. She's a top translator for a big-ass investment company that you'd recognize if I name dropped. She lives here and is willing to babysit, so there's that too. This neighborhood's affordable but out of the way enough to be safe and quiet. It makes a lot of sense for us right now, and we both love it, don't we, babe?" Erin directed the last sentence to Isabella.

Judith flinched and turned to Isabella with an air of incredulity. "Did she just refer to you as 'babe'?"

"Yes, Mother. I can't see why *that* was what you took away from that statement or how you dare be so rude to Erin in her own home. But, yes, she called me 'babe,'" Isabella replied defiantly.

"Like the little lamb or piglet or whatever it was from that children's movie?" Judith asked disdainfully.

"I'm certain that that's not the context she had in mind, but, yes, I suppose so."

Judith grimaced. "How undignified."

"Yes, love can be like that." Isabella glared at her. "What it lacks in dignity it makes up for in warmth. Anyway, why don't you ask her instead of me? She's right next to you, Mother."

Erin waved at Judith, surprisingly cheerful. In fact, she was smiling as if she'd just found the solution to all their problems. Everyone in the room focused on her as she pointed at Judith. "You know what? I think I've figured you out. You just need to feel like you're in control. Especially when it comes to your family. Fine, you wanted Isabella to be with a person who was ambitious and hardworking? I run my own gym. One day soon, I'll own it outright. I'm making sure that it not only does well, but does so well that one day, I'll open a second one. Maybe even set up a whole franchise—with Isabella's help and advice, of course. Isn't that what *you* wanted for her?"

Isabella couldn't help grinning, and neither could Marie. Chris looked confused, and Judith, well, Judith merely glared at Erin as if she were a cockroach darting across the floor.

"I'm glad to hear that you have such high-flying plans. However, I think it might be a little early in our acquaintance for you to assume to know me," Judith said acerbically.

"Likewise, Mrs. Martinez," Erin countered. "This is the first time we've met, but you decided I'm not good enough for your daughter before I even walked through that door. Talk about the pot calling the kettle black."

Isabella stared in shock. Part of her wanted to cheer Erin on, and the other part was waiting for her mother's backlash and vitriol to begin in earnest.

Marie, ever the peacemaker, stepped forward. "Surely, you came here to check that Isabella and Alberto are doing well, Judith? Look around you; they're happy and safe. That must put your mind at ease, right?"

Everyone was quiet while they waited for Judith's reply. Instead, the silence was broken by Alberto who had crawled over to the sofa and was trying to climb up. He was whining as he failed miserably.

Erin was closest, and she walked over to pick him up. He instantly busied himself with grabbing onto her braid and tugging at it. She laughed. "Not so rough, lil' man. We've talked about this."

Judith was staring at Erin and Alberto. Every part of Isabella ached to have Judith say something positive. Isabella was an adult. She didn't need her mother's approval, but she couldn't stand any more negative comments to taint her beautiful little family and their new home. She was happy and didn't want her mother to dampen that. Not again. Most of all, she didn't want her mother to hurt Erin. Ever. She vowed that if her mother said one vicious thing, she'd throw her out. Physically, if she had to.

Judith gave the deepest sigh Isabella had ever heard her utter. "I can't say I'm happy about all this, Isabella. But there seems to be very little I can do to change it. And my reason for coming here today does somewhat limit my actions here."

"Your reason for coming here? Was Marie right? Are you here to check up on me and Alberto?" Isabella asked.

"Well, yes. I had always planned to come talk to you when you had some time to calm down. However, in these past weeks…well, your father has been acting most peculiar. He has been grumpy, argumentative, and generally difficult to deal with. Apparently, losing contact with you has taken its toll on him. He is even refusing to sleep in our room until I repair our relationship and he can have you and little Alberto back in his…in our lives."

"Wow! Well done, Alberto." Marie gave an excited clap of her hands.

Judith glared at her. "He hasn't saved someone from a burning building, Marie. All he did was walk into the dining room and inform me he had received a letter from Isabella. Apparently, one that made him think. So he informed me that he'd decided he wasn't going to put up with the way I treated our daughters anymore." She stopped to scoff. "He claimed I was driving you both away. As though everything that has happened has all been my doing."

Her nostrils flared, and Isabella could see her visibly reigning in her temper. Was she angry at Alberto Sr. for finally standing up to her? At Isabella, for making him think in the first place? Or at the prospect of having to admit fault and take responsibility for her own actions? Isabella couldn't be sure, but she'd be willing to put money on options A and B... and leave C to its own devices.

"He went as far as to liken me to Rupert and his behavior, which is absurd. That man is a power-crazed tyrant with no redeeming qualities. Well, except for being an excellent lawyer. But he is still despicable. Anyway, we quarreled and..."

Marie broke in. "Alberto *fought*? With *you*?"

"No. With the refrigerator," Judith muttered.

Isabella almost smiled at the comeback until she felt uncomfortable. She loved and respected her little sister, so she was allowed to tease her. But no one else could, especially not the woman who had bullied them both for years.

Marie stepped a little closer to her foster mother. "I see no need to be so condescending, Judith. We all know that Alberto's not the fighting type. He is a creature of peace and kindness. For him to do such a thing, you must have been really out of order. It's clear to everyone here that you are. You *have* been turning into a female version of Rupert Claremont, and if you don't want to be as hated as he is, I suggest you start listening to those who love you."

Isabella couldn't decide who she was more proud of. Her father for standing up to his wife or her sister for answering back. *Hm. Daddy wins. Just. But only because he was more under her thumb.* Isabella walked over and put her arm around Marie, giving her a quick kiss on the temple. Marie leaned into her and smiled.

"Anyway," Judith continued, looking confused by Marie's comment. "Alberto has given me this ridiculous ultimatum. If I don't mend fences with you enough to ensure that you stay in touch, Isabella, we will keep having separate bedrooms and eating separately. He says he will not even sit at my table at functions and fundraisers. Can you imagine how inconvenient and embarrassing that would be? So, yes, I suppose I have no other choice but to allow you to make your own bed and lie in it."

Isabella didn't answer; she was still stunned by what her father had done. He had never stood up for her, not properly. He had muttered and grumbled at the worst injustices his wife had rained down on Isabella, but he'd never taken a firm stand. Isabella knew he must have been truly furious to turn assertive enough that her mother took him seriously. She was touched…and proud of him.

Not getting any response, Judith crossed her arms over her chest and adopted an almost bored look. "So, for the peace of my household, and since not one of you would give me the information I needed, I was forced to follow Marie and Dave all the way here just to speak with you."

"My name is Chris. Just like it was the other ten times you got it wrong," Chris muttered.

"Yes, yes, of course," Judith dismissed him without looking at him. She was staring intently at Erin and Alberto.

Alberto was gumming the tip of Erin's braid. Isabella grimaced. She was forever telling Erin she shouldn't let him do that, to no avail.

"Now that I am here, I wonder if there is a chance that I might have… underestimated you. I want it known that my problem was never the fact that you are a woman," Judith said tersely. She was almost wincing, as she looked at Erin. Every friendly word seemed to be causing her pain.

Erin looked away from Alberto's happy little face and back to his grandmother's less jovial one. "Well, I don't think you're over the moon about me not being a man, if we're honest. But I think your main problem with me is that you didn't pick me. Isabella did." Erin stopped to take a breath before carrying on. "I gotta say, Mrs. Martinez, I really hope this means that you'll trust Isabella to make her own decisions from now on. Because she's the smartest, most capable person I know. She knows what she's doing." Erin readjusted Alberto in her arms. "I'm not perfect, by any means, but I adore her. My main aim in life will always be to love and protect her and Alberto. I'll work my ass off to make sure we can move out of here and into a fancy neighborhood and a big house one day. Make sure that we have vacations together and send Alberto to the best schools and stuff. I might not be the man you chose for the job, but I am the woman who is up for the task."

Isabella scoffed, trying to hide a smile. "Did you just refer to me and Alberto as 'the task'?"

Erin shrugged and grinned mischievously. For a second, Isabella forgot about the people around her. She just wanted to kiss the smile off that pretty mouth. She suppressed the urge.

"Mother, Erin's right. She will look after us, and she is a worthy partner. That's what you've always said you wanted for me, right?" Isabella let go of Marie, put her hand on her mother's arm, and squeezed gently. They'd never been physically affectionate with each other, so the gesture did its job and got Judith's full attention. Isabella continued, her voice authoritative. "More importantly, Erin makes me the best person I can be, and that includes making me want to look after her. We're good for each other, and we'll stay together no matter what you think or say. So, you have a choice. If you're prepared to apologize and treat me and my family better, then you can stay. Or you can walk out, not see me or Alberto again, and deal with the ultimatum Daddy gave you. It's that simple."

Judith raised an eyebrow and looked as if she was about to argue. She closed her eyes and pulled in a deep breath through her nose. After a moment, she opened her eyes again and muttered, "I'm sorry if my attempts to guide you misfired. I suppose the feeling that you know better than everyone else can make you forget to listen and objectively evaluate your actions and words. I don't want to be Rupert Claremont and, more importantly, I don't want to push you away. I'm not going to change who I am, but I will try to take a step back and hold my tongue. And I am sorry if who I am…has hurt you."

There was no doubt that the confession had been difficult for Judith, and Isabella was as surprised as she was relieved that she'd managed it.

Isabella nodded. "You're right. You're not going to fundamentally change. Neither am I." She took a step closer to her mother, still unsure if she was doing the right thing. "However, if you're willing to work on letting me make my own decisions and not controlling me and if you're ready to accept Erin as the partner I've chosen, then I'll let you back into our lives. At least for a trial period.

"Maybe us living in the same city was pushing it. The distance between Brooklyn and Philadelphia might be good for us. Fewer visits might make it easier for us both to accept my independence." She turned to Erin. "Those visits obviously don't have to include you, *preciosa*. You only have to come if you feel like it."

Erin smiled at her. "Where my girlfriend and lil' man go, I go. Besides, I won't have you gossiping about me behind my back."

The small relief made everyone laugh. The mood in the room had been as thick and ominous as storm clouds since Judith arrived.

Marie cleared her throat. She'd been fidgeting for the last couple of minutes, as if she was keeping in a stream of words she had to unleash. "As someone who works with positive thinking, I really encourage the idea of mending your family relationships. There's so much love at the bottom of this, and while that's not always enough, it would be a waste to not try and tap into that great power. I'd recommend that you build the new foundations on honesty, respect, calm discussions, and less...stalking." Marie looked at Judith as she spoke, and her mother bristled.

"I would not have had to if you would have just told me the address when I asked you."

Marie snorted. "No way. I know what Isabella does to people who break her confidence." She turned to Erin, raising her eyebrows. "I hope you know your lady can be, well, *volatile*."

That made Erin laugh. "I'm too cute for her to be volatile with me."

Grinning, Chris pitched in with, "Ha. I bet the two of you are going to have loads of fights. I know how stubborn you are, Er."

Isabella's hand slid up and rested on Erin's shoulder. "Stubborn or not, she's perfect. Absolutely perfect for me."

As Isabella came closer, Alberto cooed. The tip of Erin's braid fell out of his mouth, and Isabella grimaced at how soggy it was. Baby drool spilled onto Erin's T-shirt under the braid.

"Look at the mess you two have made," Isabella chided. She grabbed Alberto and turned toward Marie to get her to hold him for a while.

But her mother held out her arms. "Let me take him while you go get something to clean...*Erin's* hair with," Judith said.

Isabella paused at the sign of burgeoning respect. *That's a good first step, at least. She'd better keep that up.* She gently handed Alberto over to his grandmother, trying not to grin at the way Judith looked at Alberto and his drool-covered chin. Yes, her mother was making an effort, but she was still very clearly Judith Martinez.

Isabella looked back at Erin, who was trying to investigate the damage to her soaked braid with a muttered "I think lil' man might have eaten some of it. Is that bad for his tummy?"

That was when Isabella realized that it didn't matter just how much *Judith Martinez* her mother was, as long as her partner kept being this much *Erin Black*.

Chapter 34

Alberto

Erin looked at Isabella, who crouched down to tie her sneakers.

"Babe, I think it's great that you're getting back into running, but are you sure you should leave me alone with Alberto? It's Sunday, and Erika isn't working. She could babysit, and we could go running together."

"And have you constantly checking out my running style and shouting instructions? No, thanks. You and your insane level of fitness can stay here. You'll be fine with Alberto. He's been fed and changed, and he's almost asleep already. You just have to rock him to sleep like you've done plenty of times before on your own. I'll be back in half an hour, and if you really need me, just call my cell. I'll come right back. Okay?"

Erin nodded hesitantly, and Isabella gave her a one-armed hug before turning away to grab her headphones.

Alberto was in Erin's arms, his head drooping toward her chest. He really did look very comfortable snuggling up to her. It was so overwhelming and big and wonderful that Erin struggled to process the scene.

Almost to herself, she said, "I can't believe I'm someone's stepmom."

Isabella hesitated before speaking. "You know, you're raising him, and you're his second parent. I don't think he'll see you as his stepmother; he'll see you as his second mother."

Erin's breathing grew rapid. She stared down at the drowsy baby with his pink cheeks and his slowly closing eyes. "I can't be his mom. You're his mom," she whispered urgently.

"Children with two female parents have two mothers. Alberto's no exception." Isabella gave her a calm smile. "It's up to you. If you feel more comfortable calling yourself his stepmother, then go ahead, but I think he'll see you as his second mother. I know I do."

Erin kept staring at the kid in her arms. Being a stepmom had already been a big step for her. Her pulse rate sped up. "Y-yeah. I suppose. Um, I'll have to digest that one."

With her headphones in her ears, Isabella leaned over to kiss Erin on the cheek. "Of course. You digest, while I see how long I can run before my calves hate me. Call me if you need me, *mi amor*."

And then she was gone.

Erin was left with Alberto growing heavier in her arms, as he gradually started to fall asleep. She put a pacifier in his mouth and gently rocked him. He grew heavier still, and his breathing slowed.

He's almost sleeping now. I'm doing pretty good.

Obviously, that was tempting fate. A loud noise from the demolition crew across the street jolted him awake, and then he was crying. Erin's blood froze. *Chill, Black. You've calmed him down loads of times before.*

Still, when she put his pacifier in his mouth, he just spat it out again. No matter how she rocked him, hummed to him, or let him play with her hair—he still squirmed. And screamed.

She knew he'd been fed just before Isabella left, so that couldn't be the issue. Erin wondered if his stomach acid problem was flaring up again. To make things worse, the house phone started to ring. Erin rolled her eyes. She'd told Isabella they didn't need a main line, that they'd be all right with just their cell phones, but Isabella had been adamant. And now the damn thing just kept ringing.

Erin looked from the ringing phone to the wailing boy and decided just to answer the damn thing and shut it the hell up. She picked up the handset, fully expecting some insurance guy or Isabella's agent. She had to get them off the phone quickly and figure out what to do with Alberto. But all thoughts of getting rid of the caller disappeared when he introduced himself as Alberto Martinez.

For a millisecond, Erin's stressed brain short-circuited. She was about to answer, "That's impossible. He's a baby and all he's saying right now is WAAAAH. I know. I can hear him very clearly."

Then the penny dropped. Alberto Martinez Sr. was obviously calling to speak to Isabella. That made sense, Isabella had told her that he wasn't fond of cell phones.

"Hello, sir. Sorry about the noise. Alberto's throwing a bit of a fit, and I'm on my own," Erin shouted, as she tried again to rock the squirming baby.

"Oh my! I'm sorry to hear that."

"Uh, yeah." Erin wondered how she could hang up without being impolite.

"Sounds like he's as stubborn as Isabella was. When she started up like that, she was almost impossible to soothe. She didn't want food, toys, or distraction until she'd calmed down. There was only one trick that could quiet her. Oh, listen to me going on when you clearly need me to hang up so you can focus on the little prince."

Alberto's tears spilled down his cheeks, and Erin felt like he'd hate her forever. On a practical level, she knew that a baby crying was a frequent occurrence. As soon as he was calm again, he'd forget all about it. But on an emotional level, she felt like she was failing him.

"No, that's all right. I'm, uh, I'm kinda in over my head here. Could you tell me what you did with Isabella when she was a baby?"

"Of course. Ice," Alberto Sr. said happily.

The world was suddenly much more overwhelming than it had any right to be. The noise was getting to her. "What? You put Isabella on ice?"

"No, no, no. I used to take an ice cube and let her hold it in her little hand. If she wouldn't hold it, I'd gently rub it on her lips. The cold surprised her out of her screaming fit. When she was distracted, I could offer her something, like looking out the window or playing with a favorite toy."

Erin struggled to make out his words over the screaming going on in her arms. Once she understood, she tried not to sound too skeptical. "You think that would work with Alberto?"

"I don't know. You could try it. I'll hold on the line. If it doesn't work, we can think of something else together. When babies are tired and cranky and start getting themselves worked up, they just can't seem to stop again. They scream, and the screaming hurts, and then that makes them scream more. You need to break the cycle by diverting their attention, you see?"

"Right. Um. Okay. I'll try the ice. You sure you don't mind waiting on the line?"

"No, of course not. Hurry up and try it before you both lose your hearing," he said calmly.

Erin put little Alberto in his baby bouncer and rocked it so that he was moving. She fetched an ice cube and tried to put it in his hand. His hands stayed balled into fists and he waved them away from her.

She gently slid the ice cube over his lips. He'd paused in his crying when she took the pacifier out and was just about to start into a new session, when he felt the ice. His eyes went wide, but he didn't move his head away.

Erin ran the dripping ice cube over his little mouth again. He still didn't scream. He just looked very confused and stared at the ice cube. Erin felt a momentary reprieve from the panic.

"Weird, isn't it? Do you want to hold it, lil' man? It's all cold and slippery. Want it?"

She held it close to his hand and pushed it against his fingers. He opened his hand slowly and took the ice cube. It looked so much bigger in his little fist. It was melting fast and slipped out of his hand. Erin was convinced he was going to start screaming again, but he just looked down.

On impulse, Erin nudged the ice cube across the floor with her foot. Alberto watched it, and she took advantage of the moment to fetch the portable phone and hurry over to the freezer for another ice cube. By the time she got back to Alberto, he was trying to push himself out of the baby bouncer, probably to go chasing after the ice.

She distracted him from his escape with the second cube, sitting with him as he explored and making sure he didn't hurt himself. She took a deep breath and pinned the phone between her ear and shoulder.

"Hey. You still there?"

"Yes, Miss Black. I'm here. Sounds like my grandson is happier now."

Erin smiled. "Yeah. Phew. He seems to really like the ice. Thanks for the tip. From now on, I'll do whatever baby tricks you suggest without asking questions. Oh, and call me Erin. I'll just call you my freakin' hero."

Alberto Sr. laughed. "No need for that. Being around a baby can be very frightening, especially when you are new to it. You feel like a fish out of water and so terrified of getting it wrong."

"Yeah, exactly! I'm just starting to get used to it. Man, I'm so grateful you helped me. Isabella went for a run, and I really wanted to give her a half hour to herself."

"She'll be proud to see how well you solved the problem, Erin."

Erin scratched the back of her neck. "I didn't. You solved it."

"No, no. I merely came up with a suggestion. You were the one who made it work. Don't underestimate how much of dealing with babies is down to instinct and body language. You staying coolheaded will calm the baby."

"Thanks. That's actually really reassuring to hear."

Erin took the ice cube away from Alberto when it had melted enough for him to fit it into his mouth. She might not be a baby expert, but she knew about the dangers of choking. She gave him back his pacifier, softly dried his tearstained cheeks, and leaned over so that he could play with her hair.

She heard Alberto Sr. clear his throat and say, "Oh, don't mention it. I want to help you and Isabella. And little Alberto, of course. I want us to be a family. I know you've met Judith and me." When he picked back up the thread of his sentence, his voice sounded unsteady, "I don't want you to assume I'm like her. She has her good sides and her bad ones, and…well… For all my faults, I'd like to think I don't share hers."

"I know you don't. Isabella has told me a lot about you. She really adores you, y'know?"

"And I adore her." His voice sounded thick, like it was too full of emotion. "I made mistakes while Isabella was growing up, and heaven knows so has Judith, but we both want to make amends and try to be the parents Isabella deserves.

"That reminds me: I was actually calling Isabella to ask if she wanted me to come over and babysit one evening. You know, in case the two of you want to go out and celebrate the publication of her book?"

"Wow. That's a really nice offer. You sure, though? It's a long drive." Erin winced. Alberto had just tugged a little too hard on her hair. She loosened his grip a little, and he started clumsily rolling the hair between his fingers.

"Not too long when it comes to seeing my little namesake. Besides, I can get a hotel room and drive back the next day or so. Have a little vacation away from…things."

Erin suppressed a chuckle. She had a feeling that she knew just *who* Alberto's "things" were. "Okay, sure. That would be awesome. I'll run it by the other half when she gets back."

"Splendid. Tell Isabella I said hello and that I miss and love her very much."

It warmed Erin's heart, how effortlessly he expressed his affection. "Will do. Thanks again for the help with Alberto. We're both very grateful."

"Don't mention it. Feel free to call me if you want to tap into my limited experience at any point. Good-bye, Miss Bla—I mean, Erin."

"Bye, Alberto. Have a good one."

She hung up and smiled at the phone. She was glad to have a partner in crime when it came to the mysteries of babies, but she was even happier to be talking to someone who clearly loved Isabella and her son as much as she did. Her son. Isabella's son and...

My son.

As she felt the grip on her hair loosen, she looked down at Alberto in his baby bouncer. He was falling asleep. The screaming fit had exhausted him.

She sat down more comfortably and quietly hummed a lullaby, as she rocked the bouncer. Soon he was fast asleep, and she could breathe easily again. She picked him up carefully and carried him to his crib.

He felt heavy in her arms and slept deeply against her shoulder. She'd never felt so important to someone before. It amazed her to realize that it wasn't just scary, it was also a privilege. A privilege that Alberto and Isabella had given her.

Pulling the blanket over him, Erin reveled in the sense of warmth and safety she got just from looking at him. She knew she was supposed to keep him safe, but somehow, just watching him made her feel more serene and safe. Her heartbeat slowed, and she smiled. Alberto made the house a home, without even trying. How could she not love him?

Sighing happily, she heard Isabella's key in the lock.

She couldn't wait to tell Isabella that she'd just overcome her first Alberto crisis without her there. She also couldn't wait to tell her that they were getting a babysitter, guaranteeing a date night to celebrate Isabella's book launch next week. But most of all, she couldn't wait to tell Isabella that her father loved her so damn much. And he wasn't the only one.

Chapter 35

Epilogue

ON A LATE FRIDAY EVENING, when winter was creeping into New York through chilly winds, three people were cuddled up on a sofa. Erin had spent the afternoon with her accountant, who told her the gym was doing better than ever. Isabella had been plotting out a book about her experiences in the catering industry. And Alberto had said his first word that morning and had known its meaning. This won him great popularity, since the word was *Mamá*. The feat was even more popular, because he had said it to Erin. Isabella was sitting in the corner of the sofa with Alberto half-asleep in her arms. Erin rested against her shoulder and draped her long legs across the rest of the sofa.

Isabella kissed her girlfriend's hair and thought about how far they'd both come. Yes, Erin still had long periods of being asocial, and yes, Isabella was still snarky and quick-tempered. But she was glad they were still themselves. What had changed was the loneliness, the hopelessness, and the feeling of going through the motions they'd once felt.

Nothing was perfect, but everything was so much better than it had been before the night she saw a message from a stranger on Twitter. Now their lives were filled with nice, normal days, interspersed with moments of excitement and joy that felt like a shot of brandy right in the heart. It was like nothing Isabella had ever experienced and much better than any fairy-tale ending she'd ever heard of.

The sound of branches tapping urgently against the window woke her from her reverie. The wind was picking up, and Isabella wondered if a storm was on its way. It didn't matter. They were safe and warm where they were.

Unsure if Erin was asleep, she whispered her name. "Erin?"

"Yeah?"

"Do you ever think about how lucky we are that we found each other?"

Erin's sigh sounded happy, and she nuzzled into Isabella's hair. "Yep. 'Disgustingly lucky,' Riley says. She's got a point. We couldn't possibly ask for more. Except..."

Isabella looked down at what she could see of Erin's face, worried that Erin was missing something in her life. "Except what?"

"Except a puppy. We need a puppy, Isabella. Or two. Maybe three if they're a small breed."

Isabella rolled her eyes. "Fine. We'll get one, just one, when Alberto's bigger."

"Score. Then I can't ask for more."

"Actually, there is one more thing you'll need." Isabella reached over the side of the sofa carefully, so as not to disturb Alberto. She picked up a packet and handed it to Erin to inspect.

There was a look of recognition in Erin's face at the brand, but the lighter color of the package and the extra word underneath, *Azucar Negra*, seemed to take her by surprise. Erin wasted no time in questioning that extra word.

"Um, Isabella? Does that say *decaf*?"

"Yes, it does. Let's finally get some proper sleep."

Erin stared at her openmouthed.

"You're a mother now, *preciosa*. Therapy and time to settle might have gotten you ninety percent there, but the next step is to cut down on the caffeine after 9 p.m. You're a parent. That means being responsible and a good role model."

"Hmm, I'll give it a go. But if it tastes weaker, I'm back to caffeine 24/7," Erin growled and lay back in Isabella's arms, her head resting on a cashmere-covered shoulder.

Isabella smiled and kissed her hair again. She had initially hated the smell of Erin's strawberry conditioner. From the second they moved in together, she had begged Erin to change to something that smelled more adult and less like candy. Now, she realized that the scent added to the safety of their little home, guarding against the winds outside.

On her chest, Alberto snored a snuffling sound, as his little hand squeezed a fistful of her sweater. Erin caressed the back of his head and snuggled in closer, as if to go to sleep.

Isabella was about to say that they needed to get ready for bed. Alberto needed his crib and his pacifier. Besides, the two of them couldn't stay here and sleep with their makeup on and in positions that would give them both aches and cramps. But she was tired, and everyone was sleeping so sweetly on her. She decided she could close her eyes and enjoy it for a few minutes. She rested her head back against the sofa and closed her eyes, too.

Calm descended on the little family, and they slept long beyond the stroke of midnight, unfazed by the storm outside. And untroubled by any insomnia.

About Emma Sterner-Radley

Having spent far too much time hopping from subject to subject at university back in her native country of Sweden, Emma finally emerged with a degree in Library and Information Science.

Now she lives with her wife and two cats in England, there is no point in saying which city as they move about once a year. She spends her free time writing, reading, daydreaming, working out, and watching whichever television show has the most lesbian subtext at the time.

Her tastes in most things usually leans towards the quirky and she loves genres like urban fantasy, magic realism, and steampunk.

Emma Sterner-Radley is also a hopeless sap for any small chubby creature with tiny legs and can often be found making heart-eyes at things like guinea pigs, Dachshunds, wombats, marmots, and human toddlers.

CONNECT WITH EMMA
Facebook: www.facebook.com/AuthorEmmaSternerRadley
Twitter: @EmmaSterner

Other Books from Ylva Publishing

www.ylva-publishing.com

Long-Distance Coffee

(The Midnight Coffee Series – Book 1)

Emma Sterner Radley

ISBN: 978-3-95533-910-4
Length: 200 pages (65,000 words)

New York personal trainer Erin lives a solitary life plagued by insomnia. One sleepless night on social media she is drawn to Isabella, a former CEO-turned-writer in Florida who has a sleepless baby and a broken relationship. Over midnight cups of coffee, they form an instant bond that will change everything.

A long-distance lesbian romance about closing the distance.

Popcorn Love

KL Hughes

ISBN: 978-3-95533-265-5
Length: 347 pages (113,000 words)

Her love life lacking, wealthy fashion exec Elena Vega agrees to a string of blind dates set up by her best friend Vivian in exchange for Vivian finding a suitable babysitter for her son, Lucas. Free-spirited college student Allison Sawyer fits the bill perfectly.

You're Fired
Shaya Crabtree

ISBN: 978-3-95533-754-4
Length: 193 pages (61,000 words)

When an inappropriate Secret Santa gift backfires, Rose needs her smarts to save her job, while Vivian, her sexy boss, needs her smarts to save the business. Can they stop bickering long enough to do a deal?

Shadow Haven
AJ Schippers

ISBN: 978-3-95533-845-9
Length: 322 pages (115,000 words)

A holiday on a private island comes with an erotic surprise when Julia meets the alluring Alexandra, a professional dominatrix. An explosive first meeting leads to friendship and something more sensual. Can Julia overcome her fears to explore a submissive relationship with Alexandra? What happens when power is not just left to the imagination?

Coming from Ylva Publishing

www.ylva-publishing.com

Survival Instincts

May Dawney

Civilization ended long before Lynn Tanner was born. Wild animals roam the streets, but mankind is still the biggest threat to a woman alone in the ruins of a world reclaimed by nature. Lynn survives by sleeping with one eye open at all times and trusting no one but her dog.

When she is forced to go on a dangerous journey through the concrete jungle of New York City, Lynn does all she can to scheme her way to safety. Her guard, Dani Wilson, won't be played that easily, however. As their lives become entwined, Lynn finds herself developing feelings for Dani and is forced to find the answer to the question that scares her most: is staying alone really the best way to survive?

Fast-paced and full of adventure, *Survival Instincts* introduces a post-war dystopian world where the only person you can rely on is yourself… unless you fall in love.

Coffee and Conclusions
© 2018 by Emma-Sterner-Radley

ISBN: 978-3-95533-930-2

Also available as e-book.

Published by Ylva Publishing, legal entity of Ylva Verlag, e.Kfr.

Ylva Verlag, e.Kfr.
Owner: Astrid Ohletz
Am Kirschgarten 2
65830 Kriftel
Germany

www.ylva-publishing.com

First edition: 2018

Credits
Edited by Andrea Bramhall, Michelle Aguilar, and CK King
Cover Design and Print Layout by Streetlight Graphics

www.ingramcontent.com/pod-product-compliance
Lightning Source LLC
Chambersburg PA
CBHW030351020726
47493CB00003B/771